Praise for *Death in a St* ✂ **P9-CFT-162**
the Commissario Brunetti mysteries

"Brunetti remains one of the most persuasively characterized protagonists in crime fiction."
—The Good Book Guide (U.K.)

"Commissario Guido Brunetti, most charismatic current
Euro-cop, uncovers a deadly ants' nest of corruption.
Highly accomplished, scary read."
—*The Guardian* (London)

"Smuggling, sexual betrayal, high-class fakery and, of
course, Mafia money make for a rich brew. . . . Exactly the
right cop for the right city. Long may he walk, or wade,
through it."   —Sarah Dunant, author of *The Birth of Venus*

"Leon's books shimmer in the grace of their setting and are
warmed by the charm of their characters."
—*The New York Times Book Review*

"Superb . . . An outstanding book, deserving of the widest
audience possible, a chance for American readers to again
experience a master practitioner's art."
—*Publishers Weekly* (starred review)

"Richly atmospheric, Leon introduces you to the Venice
insiders know."
—Ellen Hale, *USA Today*

"A new Donna Leon book about . . . Brunetti is ready for
our immediate pleasure. She uses the relatively small and
crime-free canvas of Venice for riffs about Italian life,
sexual styles, and—best of all—the kind of ingrown business and political corruption that seems to lurk just below
the surface."   —Dick Adler, *Chicago Tribune*

"*Uniform Justice* is a neat balancing act. Its silken prose and considerable charm almost conceal its underlying anger; it is an unlovely story set in the loveliest of cities. . . . Donna Leon is indeed sophisticated."
—Patrick Anderson, *The Washington Post*

"There's atmosphere aplenty in *Uniform Justice* . . . Brunetti is a compelling character, a good man trying to stay on the honest path in a devious and twisted world."
—*The Baltimore Sun*

"Venice provides a beautifully rendered backdrop for this operatic story of fathers and sons, and Leon's writing trembles with true feeling."
—*Star-Tribune* (Minneapolis)

"One of the best international crime writers is Donna Leon, and her Commissario Guido Brunetti tales set in Venice are at the apex of continental thrillers. . . . The author has written a pitch-perfect tale where all the characters are three-dimensional, breathing entities, and the lives they live, while by turns sweet and horrific, are always believable. Let Leon be your travel agent and tour guide to Venice. It's an unforgettable trip." —*Rocky Mountain News*

"Events are powered by Leon's compelling portraits."
—*The Oregonian* (Portland)

"The plot is silky and complex, and the main appeal is the protagonist, Brunetti."
—*The Cleveland Plain Dealer*

"Leon, a wonderfully literate writer, sets forth her plot clearly and succinctly. . . . The ending of *Uniform Justice* is not a neat wrap-up of the case with justice prevailing. It is rather the ending that one would expect in real life. Leon says that 'the murder mystery is a craft, not an art,' but I say that murder mystery in her hands is an art."
—*The Roanoke Times*

A PENGUIN / GROVE PRESS BOOK

DEATH IN A STRANGE COUNTRY

Donna Leon, who was born in New Jersey, has lived in
Venice for many years and previously lived in Switzerland,
Saudi Arabia, Iran, and China, where she worked as a
teacher. Her other novels featuring Commissario Brunetti
have all been highly acclaimed. Also available from Penguin
are *A Noble Radiance*, *Uniform Justice*, and *Acqua Alta*.

To request Penguin Readers Guides by mail
(while supplies last), please call (800) 778-6425
or e-mail reading@us.penguingroup.com.
To access Penguin Readers Guides online,
visit our Web site at www.penguin.com.

PENGUIN BOOKS

Published by the Penguin Group
Penguin Group (USA) Inc., 375 Hudson Street, New York, New York 10014, U.S.A.
Penguin Group (Canada), 10 Alcorn Avenue, Toronto,
Ontario, Canada M4V 3B2 (a division of Pearson Penguin Canada Inc.)
Penguin Books Ltd, 80 Strand, London WC2R 0RL, England
Penguin Ireland, 25 St Stephen's Green, Dublin 2,
Ireland (a division of Penguin Books Ltd)
Penguin Group (Australia), 250 Camberwell Road, Camberwell,
Victoria 3124, Australia (a division of Pearson Australia Group Pty Ltd)
Penguin Books India Pvt Ltd, 11 Community Centre,
Panchsheel Park, New Delhi - 110 017, India
Penguin Group (NZ), cnr Airborne and Rosedale Roads, Albany,
Auckland 1310, New Zealand (a division of Pearson New Zealand Ltd)
Penguin Books (South Africa) (Pty) Ltd, 24 Sturdee Avenue,
Rosebank, Johannesburg 2196, South Africa

Penguin Books Ltd, Registered Offices:
80 Strand, London WC2R 0RL, England

First published in the United Kingdom in 1993 by Chapmans Publishers Ltd
This edition first published in the United Kingdom in 2004 by Arrow Books
This edition published in Penguin Books 2005

3 5 7 9 10 8 6 4

Copyright © Donna Leon, 1993
All rights reserved

PUBLISHER'S NOTE
This is a work of fiction. Names, characters, places, and incidents either are
the product of the author's imagination or are used fictitiously, and any
resemblance to actual persons, living or dead, business establishments,
events, or locales is entirely coincidental.

LIBRARY OF CONGRESS CATALOGING IN PUBLICATION DATA
Leon, Donna.
Death in a strange country / Donna Leon.
p. cm.
ISBN 0 14 30.3482 0
1. Brunetti, Guido (Fictitious character)—Fiction. 2. Police—Italy—Venice—Fiction.
3. Americans—Italy—Fiction. 4. Venice (Italy)—Fiction. I. Title.
PS3562.E534D43 2005
813'.54—dc22   2004053481

Printed in the United States of America

for Peggy Flynn

Volgi intorno lo squardo, oh sire, e vedi qual strage orrenda nel tuo nobil regno, fa il crudo mostro. Ah mira allagate di sangue quelle pubbliche vie. Ad ogni passo vedrai chi geme, e l'alma gonfia d'atro velen dal corpo esala.

Gaze around you, oh sire, and see what terrible destruction the cruel monster has wrought in your noble kingdom. Look at the streets swamped in blood. At every step you see someone groaning, the spirit leaving a corpse swollen with horrible poison.

Idomeneo

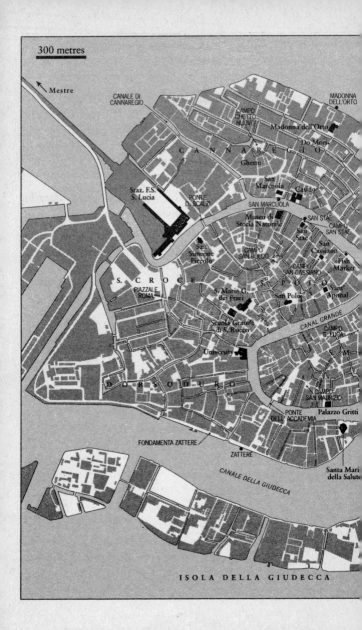

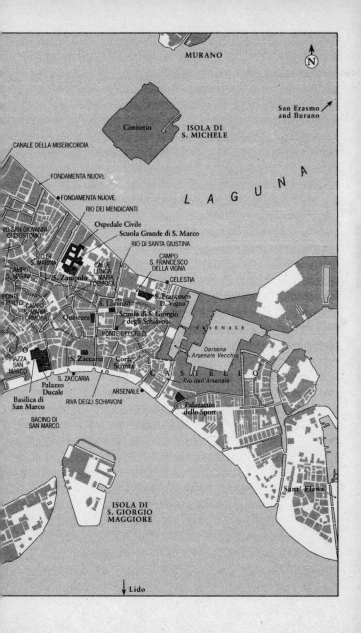

new tide to take over the day's work. Caught in the calm, the limp thing bobbed on the surface of the water, dark-clad and invisible. Time passed in silence and then was broken by two men who walked by, chatting in soft voices filled with the easy sibilance of the Venetian dialect. One of them pushed a low cart loaded with newspapers which he was taking back to his newsstand to begin the day; the other was on his way to work in the hospital that took up one entire side of the vast open *campo*.

Out in the *laguna*, a small boat puttered past, and the tiny waves it raised rippled up the canal and toyed with the body, shifting it back up against the embankment wall.

As the bells chimed five, a woman in one of the houses that overlooked the canal and faced onto the *campo* flung open the dark-green shutters of her kitchen and turned back to lower the flaming gas under her coffee pot. Still not fully awake, she spooned sugar into a small cup, flipped off the gas with a practised motion of her wrist, and poured a thick stream of coffee into her cup. Cradling it in her hands, she walked back to the open window and, as she had every morning for decades, looked across at the giant equestrian statue of Colleoni, once the most fearsome of all Venetian military leaders, now her nearest neighbour. For Bianca Pianaro, this was the most peaceful moment of the day, and Colleoni, cast into eternal bronze silence centuries ago, the perfect companion for this precious, secret quarter-hour of silence.

Glad of its sharp warmth, she sipped at her

coffee, watching the pigeons that had already begun to peck their way towards the base of the statue. Idly, she glanced directly below her, to where her husband's small boat bobbed in the dark-green water. It had rained in the night, and she looked to see if the canvas tarpaulin that covered the boat was still in place. If the tarpaulin had been pulled free by the wind, Nino would have to go down and bail the boat out before he went to work. She leaned out, providing herself a clear view of the bow. At first, she thought it was a bag of rubbish, swept from the embankment by the night's tide. But it was strangely symmetrical, elongated, with two branches sweeping out on either side of the central trunk, almost as if it were . . .

'Oh, *Dio*,' she gasped and let her coffee cup fall into the waters below, not far from the strange shape floating face down in the canal. 'Nino, Nino,' she screamed, turning back towards their bedroom. 'There's a body in the canal.'

It was this same message, 'There's a body in the canal', that woke Guido Brunetti twenty minutes later. He shifted up onto his left shoulder and pulled the phone onto the bed with him. 'Where?'

'Santi Giovanni e Paolo. In front of the hospital, sir,' answered the policeman who had called him as soon as the call came into the Questura.

'What happened? Who found him?' Brunetti asked, swinging his feet out from beneath the covers and sitting up on the edge of the bed.

'I don't know, sir. A man named Pianaro called to report it.'

3

'So why did you call me?' Brunetti asked, making no attempt to hide the irritation in his voice, the clear result of the time indicated on the glowing face of the clock beside the bed: five-thirty-one. 'What about the night shift? Isn't anyone there?'

'They've all gone home, sir. I called Bozzetti, but his wife said he wasn't home yet.' As he spoke, the young man's voice grew more and more uncertain. 'So I called you, sir, because I know you're working day shift.' Which, Brunetti reminded himself, began in two and a half hours. He said nothing.

'Are you there, sir?'

'Yes, I'm here. And it's five-thirty.'

'I know, sir,' the young man bleated. 'But I couldn't find anyone else.'

'All right. All right. I'll go down there and have a look. Send me a launch. Now.' Remembering the hour and the fact that the night shift had already gone off duty, he asked, 'Is there anyone who can bring it?'

'Yes, sir. Bonsuan just came in. Shall I send him?'

'Yes, right now. And call the rest of the day shift. Tell them to meet me there.'

'Yes, sir,' the young man responded, his relief audible at having someone take charge.

'And call Doctor Rizzardi. Ask him to meet me there as quickly as he can.'

'Yes, sir. Anything else, sir?'

'No, nothing. But send the launch. Right now. And tell the others, if they get there before I do, to

4

close things off. Don't let anyone get near the body.' Even as they spoke, how much evidence was being destroyed, cigarettes dropped on the ground, shoes scuffed across the pavement? Without saying anything further, he hung up.

Beside him in the bed, Paola moved and looked up at him with one eye, the other covered by a naked arm against the invasion of light. She made a noise that long experience told him was an inquisitive one.

'A body. In a canal. They're coming to get me. I'll call.' The noise with which she acknowledged this was an affirmative one. She rolled onto her stomach and was asleep immediately, certainly the only person in the entire city uninterested in the fact that a body had been found floating in one of the canals.

He dressed quickly, decided not to spend the time shaving, and went into the kitchen to see if there was time for coffee. He opened the lid of the Moka Express and saw about an inch of coffee left over from the night before. Though he hated reheated coffee, he poured it into a saucepan and put it on a high flame, standing over it and waiting for it to boil. When it did, he poured the almost-viscous liquid into a cup, spooned in three sugars, and downed it quickly.

The bell to the apartment sounded, announcing the arrival of the police launch. He glanced at his watch. Eight minutes before six. It must be Bonsuan; no one else was capable of getting a boat here that quickly. He grabbed a wool jacket from the cupboard by the front door. September

5

mornings could be cold, and there was always the chance of wind at Santi Giovanni e Paolo, so near to the open waters of the *laguna*.

At the bottom of the five flights of stairs, he pulled open the door to the building and found Puccetti, a recruit who had been with the police for fewer than five months.

'*Buon giorno, Signor Commissario,*' Puccetti said brightly and saluted, making far more noise and motion than Brunetti thought seemly at that hour.

Brunetti answered with a wave and headed down the narrow *calle* on which he lived. At the edge of the water, he saw the police launch moored to the landing, blue light flashing rhythmically. At the wheel, he recognized Bonsuan, a police pilot who had the blood of countless generations of Burano fishermen in his veins, blood that must certainly have been mixed with the waters of the *laguna*, carrying an instinctive knowledge of the tides and currents that would have allowed him to navigate the canals of the city with his eyes closed.

Bonsuan, stocky and heavy-bearded, acknowledged Brunetti's arrival with a nod, as much an acknowledgement of the hour as of his superior. Puccetti scrambled onto deck, joining a pair of uniformed policemen already there. One of them flicked the mooring cable free of the piling, and Bonsuan backed the boat quickly out into the Grand Canal, then swung it sharply around and back up towards the Rialto Bridge. They swept under the bridge and swung into a one-way canal on the right. Soon after that, they cut to the left, then again to the right. Brunetti stood on the deck, collar raised against the wind and the early-morning chill. Boats moored on either side of the canals bobbed in their wake, and others, coming in from San Erasmo with fresh fruit and vegetables, pulled to the side and hugged the buildings at the sight of their flashing blue light.

Finally, they turned into the Rio dei Mendicanti, the canal that flowed beside the hospital and out into the *laguna*, just opposite the cemetery. The proximity of the cemetery to the hospital was probably accidental; to most Venetians, however, particularly those who had survived treatment at the hospital, the location of the cemetery was a silent comment upon the proficiency of the hospital staff.

Halfway down the canal, clustered on the right, Brunetti saw a small group of people drawn up close to the edge of the embankment. Bonsuan stopped the boat fifty metres from the crowd in what Brunetti knew would be, by now, an entirely vain attempt to keep any evidence at the site free from the effects of their arrival.

One of the officers approached the boat and held out a hand to Brunetti to help him climb ashore. *'Buon giorno, Signor Commissario.* We got him out, but, as you can see, we've already got company.' He gestured to nine or ten people crowding around something on the pavement, their bodies obscuring it from Brunetti's sight.

The officer turned back towards the crowd, saying as he walked, 'All right. Move back. Police.' At the approach of the two men, not at the command, the crowd pulled back.

On the pavement, Brunetti saw the body of a young man lying on his back, eyes open to the morning light. Beside him stood two policemen, uniforms soaked to their shoulders. Both of them saluted when they saw Brunetti. When their hands returned to their sides, water trickled to the ground beneath them. He recognized them, Luciani and Rossi, both good men.

'Well?' Brunetti asked, looking down at the dead man.

Luciani, the senior of the two, answered. 'He was floating in the canal when we got here, Dottore. A man in that house,' he said, pointing to an ochre building on the other side of the canal, 'called us. His wife saw him.'

Brunetti turned and looked across at the house. 'Fourth floor,' Luciani explained. Brunetti cast his eyes up, just in time to see a form pull back from the window. As he stared at the building and at those beside it, he noticed a number of dark shadows at the windows. Some retreated when he looked at them, others did not.

Brunetti turned back to Luciani and nodded to him to continue. 'He was near the steps, but we had to go in and pull him out. I put him on his back. To try to revive him. But there was no hope, sir. It looks like he's been dead a long time.' He sounded apologetic, almost as if his failure to breathe life back into the young man had somehow added to the finality of his death.

'Did you check the body?' Brunetti asked.

'No, sir. When we saw that there was nothing

we could do, we thought it would be best to leave him for the doctor.'

'Good, good,' Brunetti muttered. Luciani shivered, either with cold or the awareness of his failure, and small drops of water fell to the pavement below him.

'You two get yourselves off home. Have a bath, get something to eat. And drink something against the chill.' Both men smiled at this, grateful for the suggestion. 'And take the launch. Bonsuan will take you home, both of you.'

The men thanked him and pushed their way through the crowd, which had grown larger in the few minutes Brunetti had been there. He gestured to one of the uniformed men who had come with him on the launch and told him, 'Move these people back, then get their names and addresses, all of them. Ask them when they got here, if they heard or saw anything strange this morning. Then send them home.' He hated the ghouls who always gathered at the scenes of death and could never understand the fascination so many of them had with it, especially in its more violent manifestations.

He looked again at the face of the young man on the pavement, now the object of so many pitiless stares. He was a handsome man, with short blond hair made darker by the water that still puddled around him. His eyes were a clear, limpid blue, his face symmetrical, nose narrow and fine.

Behind him, Brunetti heard the voices of the police as they began to move the crowd back. He called Puccetti over to him, ignoring the new salute the young man gave him. 'Puccetti, go over to that row of houses on the other side of the canal and see if anyone heard or saw anything.'

'For what time, sir?'

Brunetti thought for a moment, considering the moon. It had been new two nights ago: the tides would not have been strong enough to carry the body very far at all. He would have to ask Bonsuan about last night's tides. The hands of the dead man were strangely shrivelled and white, a sure sign he had been in the water for a long time. Once he knew how long the young man had been dead, he'd leave it to Bonsuan to calculate how far he could have drifted. And from where. In the meantime, there was Puccetti. 'Ask them for any time last night. And get some barriers set up. Send those people home if you can.' Little chance of that, he knew. Venice had few events like this to offer its citizens; they would leave only reluctantly.

He heard the sound of another boat approaching. A second white police launch, blue light pulsing round, pulled into the canal and stopped at the same mooring Bonsuan had used. This one also carried three men in uniform and one in civilian clothing. Like sunflowers, the faces of the crowd turned from the sun of their attention, the dead man, and swirled around towards the men who jumped down from the boat and approached the crowd.

At their head walked Doctor Ettore Rizzardi, the Coroner for the city. Unperturbed by the stares he was receiving, Doctor Rizzardi approached and extended his hand in a friendly fashion to Brunetti. '*Buon di*, Guido. What is it?'

Brunetti stepped aside so that Rizzardi could see what lay at their feet. 'He was in the canal. Luciani and Rossi pulled him out, but there was nothing they could do. Luciani tried, but it was too late.'

Rizzardi nodded and grunted at this. The shrivelled skin of the hands told him how late it had been for any help.

'It looks like he's been in there for a long time, Ettore. But I'm sure you can tell me better.'

Taking this compliment as no more than his due, Rizzardi turned his full attention to the corpse. As he bent over the body, the whispers of the crowd grew even more sibilant. He ignored them, placed his bag carefully in a dry spot near the body, and stooped down over the corpse.

Brunetti wheeled around and walked towards the people who stood in what had now become the front rank of the crowd.

'If you've given your names and addresses, you can go. There's nothing more to see. So you can go, all of you.' An old man with a grizzled beard bent sharply to the left to look past Brunetti and see what the doctor was doing over the body. 'I said you can go.' Brunetti spoke directly to the old man. He straightened up, glanced at Brunetti with complete lack of interest, then bent back down, interested only in the doctor. An old woman yanked angrily at the leash of her terrier and went off, visibly outraged by yet more evidence of police brutality. The uniformed men moved slowly among the crowd, turning them gently with a word or a hand on the shoulder, gradually forcing them to move away, abandoning the area to the police. The last to leave was the old man with the beard, who moved only as far as the iron railing enclosing the base of the statue of Colleoni, against which he leaned, refusing to abandon the *campo* or his rights as a citizen.

'Guido, come here a moment,' Rizzardi called from behind him.

Brunetti turned and went to stand beside the kneeling doctor, who held back the dead man's shirt. About five inches above his waist, on the left side, Brunetti saw a horizontal line, jagged at the edges, flesh strangely greyish-blue. He knelt beside Rizzardi in a chill pool of water to get a closer look. The cut was about as long as his thumb and now, probably because of the body's long immersion, gaped open, curiously bloodless.

'This isn't some tourist who got drunk and fell into a canal, Guido.'

Brunetti nodded in silent agreement. 'What could do something like that?' he asked, nodding towards the wound.

'A knife. Wide-bladed. And whoever did it was either very good or very lucky.'

'Why do you say that?' Brunetti asked.

'I don't want to poke around in there too much, not until I can open him up and see it properly,' Rizzardi said. 'But if the angle is right, and that's indicated by what I can see from here, then he had a clear path right to the heart. No ribs in the way. Nothing. Just the least little push, the least little bit of pressure, and he's dead.' Rizzardi repeated, 'Either very good or very lucky.'

Brunetti could see only the width of the wound; he had no idea of the path it would have followed within the body. 'Could it have been anything else? I mean, other than a knife?'

'I can't be sure until I get a closer look at the tissue inside, but I doubt it.'

'What about drowning? If it didn't get his heart, could he still have drowned?'

Rizzardi sat back on his heels, careful to pull the folds of his raincoat under him to keep them from the water below. 'No, I doubt it. If it missed the heart, there wouldn't have been enough damage to keep him from pulling himself out of the water. Just look at how pale he is. I think that's what happened. One blow. The right angle. Death would have been almost immediate.' He pushed himself to his feet and delivered the closest thing the young man was to get to a prayer that morning. 'Poor devil. He's a handsome young man, and he's in excellent physical shape. I'd say he was an athlete or at least someone who took very good care of himself.' He bent back over the body and, with a gesture that seemed curiously paternal, he moved his hand down across his eyes, trying to force them closed. One refused to move. The other closed for a moment, then slowly slid open and stared again at the sky. Rizzardi muttered something to himself, took a handkerchief from his breast pocket, and placed it across the face of the young man.

'Cover his face. He died young,' muttered Brunetti.

'What?'

Brunetti shrugged. 'Nothing. Something Paola says.' He looked away from the face of the young man and studied, for the briefest of instants, the façade of the basilica and allowed himself to be calmed by its symmetry. 'When can you tell me something exact, Ettore?'

Rizzardi gave a quick look at his watch. 'If your boys can take him out to the cemetery now, I can get to him later this morning. Give me a call after lunch, and I'll be able to tell you exactly. But I don't think there's any doubt, Guido.' The doctor hesitated, not liking to have to tell Brunetti how to do his job. 'Aren't you going to check his pockets?'

Though he had done it many times in his career, Brunetti hated this first invasion of the privacy of the dead, this first awful imposition of the power of the State on the peace of the departed. He disliked having to go through their diaries and drawers, to page through their letters, finger their clothing.

But since the body had already been moved from where it had been found, there was no reason to leave it untouched until the photographer could record where it lay in the precise posture of death. He squatted beside the young man and reached a hand into his trouser pocket. At the bottom he found a few coins and placed them beside the body. In the other there was a plain metal ring with four keys attached. Unasked, Rizzardi bent down to help shift the body to its side so that Brunetti could reach into the back pockets. One held a sodden yellow rectangle, clearly a train ticket, and the other a paper napkin, equally sodden. He nodded to Rizzardi, and they lowered the body back to the ground.

He picked up one of the coins and held it out to the doctor.

'What is it?' asked Rizzardi.

'American. Twenty-five cents.' It seemed a strange thing to find in the pocket of a dead man in Venice.

'Ah, that could be it,' the doctor said. 'An American.'

'What?'

'Why he's in such good shape,' Rizzardi answered, entirely unconscious of the bitter incongruity of the tense. 'That might explain it. They're always so fit, so healthy.' Together, they looked at the body, at the narrow waist that showed under the still-open shirt.

'If he is,' Rizzardi said, 'the teeth will tell me.'

'Why?'

'Because of the dental work. They use different techniques, better materials. If he's had any dental work done, I'll be able to tell you this afternoon if he's American.'

Had Brunetti been a different man, he might have asked Rizzardi to take a look now, but he saw no need to hurry, nor did he want to disturb that young face again. 'Thanks, Ettore. I'll send a photographer out to take some pictures. Do you think you can get his eyes closed?'

'Of course. I'll have him looking as much like himself as I can. But you'll want his eyes open for the pictures, won't you?'

Just by a breath, Brunetti stopped himself from saying he never wanted those eyes open again and, instead, answered, 'Yes, yes, of course.'

'And send someone to take the fingerprints, Guido.'

'Yes.'

'All right. Then call me about three.' They shook hands briefly, and Doctor Rizzardi picked up his bag. Without saying goodbye, he walked across the open space towards the monumental open portal of the hospital, two hours early for work.

More officers had arrived while they were examining the body, and now there must have been eight of them, formed in an outward-facing arc about three metres from the body. 'Sergeant Vianello,' Brunetti called, and one of them stepped back from the line and came to join him beside the body.

'Get two of your men to take him to the launch, then take him out to the cemetery.'

While this was being done, Brunetti returned to his examination of the front of the basilica, letting his eyes flow up and around its soaring spires. His eyes shifted across the *campo* to the statue of Colleoni, perhaps a witness to the crime.

Vianello came up beside him. 'I've sent him out to the cemetery, sir. Anything else?'

'Yes. Is there a bar around here?'

'Over there, sir, behind the statue. It opens at six.'

'Good. I need a coffee.' As they walked towards the bar, Brunetti began to give orders. 'We'll need divers, a pair of them. Get them busy in the water where the body was found. I want them to bring up anything that could be a weapon: a knife, blade about three centimetres wide. But it might have been something else, even a piece of metal, so have them bring up anything that might have made a wound like that. Tools, anything.'

'Yes, sir,' Vianello said, trying to write this in his notebook while walking.

'Doctor Rizzardi will give us a time of death this afternoon. As soon as we have it, I want to see Bonsuan.'

'For the tides, sir?' Vianello asked, understanding immediately.

'Yes. And start calling the hotels. See if anyone is missing from his room, especially Americans.' He knew the men disliked this, the endless calls to the hotels, pages and pages of them on the police list. And after they'd called the hotels, there remained the pensions and hostels, more pages of names and numbers.

The steamy warmth of the bar was comforting and familiar, as were the smells of coffee and pastry. A man and woman standing at the counter glanced at the uniformed man, then went back to their conversation. Brunetti asked for espresso, Vianello for *caffè corretto*, black coffee with a substantial splash of grappa. When the barman put their coffees in front of them, both spooned in two sugars and cradled the warm cups in their hands for a moment.

Vianello downed his coffee in one gulp, set the cup back on the counter, and asked, 'Anything else, sir?'

'See about drug dealing in the neighbourhood. Who does it, and where? See if there's anyone in the neighbourhood with a record of drug arrests or street crimes: selling, using, stealing, anything. And find out where they go to shoot up, any of those *calle* that dead-end into the canal, if there's a place where syringes turn up in the morning.'

'You think it's a drug crime, sir?'

Brunetti finished his coffee and nodded to the barman for another. Without being asked, Vianello shook his head in a quick negative. 'I don't know. It's possible. So let's check that first.'

Vianello nodded and wrote in his notebook. Finished, he slipped it into his breast pocket and began to reach for his wallet.

'No, no,' Brunetti insisted. 'I'll get it. Go back to the boat and call about the divers. And have your men set up barricades. Get the entrances to the canal blocked off while the divers work.'

Vianello nodded his thanks for the coffee and left. Through the steamy windows of the bar, Brunetti saw the ebb and flow of people across the *campo*. He watched as they came down from the main bridge that led to the hospital, noticed the police at their right, and asked the people standing around what was going on. Usually, they paused, looking from the dark uniforms that still milled around to the police launch that bobbed at the side of the canal. Then, seeing nothing at all out of the ordinary beyond that, they continued about their business. The old man, he saw, still leaned against the iron railing. Even after all his years of police work, he could not understand how people could so willingly place themselves near the death of their own kind. It was a mystery he had never been able to penetrate, that awful fascination with the termination of life, especially when it was violent, as this had been.

He turned back to his second coffee and drank it quickly. 'How much?' he asked.

'Five thousand lire.'

He paid with a ten and waited for his change. When he handed it to Brunetti, the barman asked, 'Something bad, sir?'

'Yes, something bad,' Brunetti answered. 'Something very bad.'

2

Because the Questura was so near, it was easier for Brunetti to walk to his office than go back on the launch with the uniformed men. He went the back way, passing the Evangelical church and coming up on the Questura from the right side of the building. The uniformed man at the front entrance opened the heavy glass door as soon as he saw Brunetti, who headed for the stairway that would take him to his office on the fourth floor, passing beside the line of foreigners seeking residence and work permits, a line that extended halfway across the lobby.

His desk, when he reached his office, was just as he had left it the day before, covered with papers and files sprawled across it in no particular order. The ones nearest to hand contained personnel reports, all of which he had to read and comment upon as part of the Byzantine process of promotion through which all State employees had to go. The second pile dealt with the last murder in the city, the brutal, crazed beating to death of a young man that had taken place a month ago on the embankment of the Zattere. So savagely had he been beaten that the police were at first sure it was the work of a gang. Instead, after only a day, they had discovered that the killer was a frail wisp of a boy of sixteen. The victim was homosexual, and the killer's father a known Fascist who had instilled in his son the doctrines that Communists and gays were vermin who deserved only death. So, at five one bright summer morning, these two young men had come together in a deadly trajectory beside the waters of the Giudecca Canal. No one knew what had passed between them, but the victim had been reduced to such a state that the family had been denied the right to see his body, which had been consigned to them in a sealed coffin. The piece of wood which had been used to beat and stab him to death sat in a plastic box inside a filing cabinet on the second floor of the Questura. Little remained to be done, save to see that the psychiatric treatment of the killer continued and he was not allowed to leave the city. The State made no provision for psychiatric treatment for the family of the victim.

Instead of sitting at his desk, Brunetti reached into one of the side drawers and pulled out an electric razor. He stood at his window to shave, staring out at the façade of the church of San

Lorenzo, still covered, as it had been for the last five years, with the scaffolding behind which extensive restoration was said to be taking place. He had no proof that this was happening, for nothing had changed in all these years, and the front doors of the church remained forever closed.

His phone rang, the direct line from outside. He glanced at his watch. Nine-thirty. That would be the vultures. He switched off the razor and walked over to his desk to answer the phone.

'Brunetti.'

'*Buon giorno, Commissario*. This is Carlon,' a deep voice said and went on, quite unnecessarily, to identify himself as the Crime Reporter for the *Gazzettino*.

'*Buon giorno*, Signor Carlon.' Brunetti knew what Carlon wanted; let him ask.

'Tell me about that American you pulled out of the Rio dei Mendicanti this morning.'

'It was officer Luciani who pulled him out, and we have no evidence that he was American.'

'I stand corrected, Dottore,' Carlon said with a sarcasm that turned apology to insult. When Brunetti didn't respond, he asked, 'He was murdered, wasn't he?' making little attempt to disguise his pleasure at the possibility.

'It would appear so.'

'Stabbed?'

How did they learn so much, and so quickly? 'Yes.'

'Murdered?' Carlon repeated, voice heavy with feigned patience.

'We won't have any final word until we get the

results of the autopsy that Doctor Rizzardi is conducting this afternoon.'

'Was there a stab wound?'

'Yes, there was.'

'But you're not sure the stab wound was the cause of death?' Carlon's question ended with an incredulous snort.

'No, we're not,' Brunetti replied blandly. 'As I explained to you, nothing will be certain until we have the results of the autopsy.'

'Other signs of violence?' Carlon asked, displeased at how little information he was getting.

'Not until after the autopsy,' Brunetti repeated.

'Next, are you going to suggest he might have drowned, Commissario?'

'Signor Carlon,' Brunetti said, deciding that he had had enough, 'as you well know, if he was in the water of one of our canals for any length of time, then it is far more likely that disease would have killed him than that he would have drowned.' From the other end, only silence. 'If you'll be kind enough to call me this afternoon, about four, I'll be glad to give you more accurate information.' It was Carlon whose reporting had caused the story of the last murder to become an exposé of the private life of the victim, and Brunetti still felt enormous rancour because of it.

'Thank you, Commissario. I'll certainly do that. One thing – what was the name of that officer again?'

'Luciani, Mario Luciani, an exemplary officer.'

As all of them were when Brunetti mentioned them to the Press.

'Thank you, Commissario. I'll make a note of that. And I'll be sure to mention your cooperation in my article.' With no further ado, Carlon hung up.

In the past, Brunetti's dealings with the Press had been relatively friendly, at times more than that, and at times he had even used the Press to solicit information about a crime. But in recent years, the ever-strengthening wave of sensationalistic journalism had prevented any dealings with reporters that were more than purely formal; every speculation he might voice would be sure to appear the following day as an almost direct accusation of guilt. So Brunetti had become cautious, providing information that was severely limited, however accurate and true reporters might know it to be.

He realized that, until he heard from the lab about the ticket in the man's pocket or until he got the report on the autopsy, there was very little he could do. The men in the lower offices would be calling the hotels now, and they would inform him if they turned up something. Consequently, there was nothing for him to do but continue to read and sign the personnel reports.

An hour later, just before eleven, the buzzer on his intercom sounded. He picked up the receiver, knowing too well who it would be. 'Yes, Vice-Questore?'

Momentarily surprised at being directly addressed, having hoped, perhaps, to have found

Brunetti absent or asleep, his superior, Vice-Questore Patta, took a moment to respond. 'What's all this about the dead American, Brunetti? Why wasn't I called? Have you any idea of what this will do to tourism?' Brunetti suspected that the third question was the only one in which Patta took any real interest.

'What American, sir?' Brunetti asked, voice filled with feigned curiosity.

'The American you pulled out of the water this morning.'

'Oh,' Brunetti said, this time with polite surprise. 'Is the report back so soon? He *was* American, then?'

'Don't be cute with me, Brunetti,' Patta said angrily. 'The report isn't back yet, but he had American coins in his pocket, so he's got to be an American.'

'Or a numismatist,' Brunetti suggested amiably.

There followed a long pause which told Brunetti the Vice-Questore didn't know the meaning of the word.

'I told you not to be smart, Brunetti. We're going to work on the assumption that he's an American. We can't have Americans being murdered in this city, not with the state of tourism this year. Do you understand that?'

Brunetti fought back the impulse to ask if it would be all right to kill people of other nationalities – Albanians, perhaps? – but, instead, said only, 'Yes, sir.'

'Well?'

'Well what, sir?'

'What have you done?'

'Divers are searching the canal where he was found. When we find out when he died, we'll have them search the places from where he might have drifted, assuming he was killed somewhere else. Vianello is checking for drug use or dealing in the neighbourhood, and the lab is working on the things we found in his pockets.'

'Those coins?'

'I'm not sure we need the lab to tell us they're American, sir.'

After a long silence that said it would not be wise to bait Patta any further, his superior asked, 'What about Rizzardi?'

'He said he'd have the report to me this afternoon.'

'See that I'm sent a copy of it,' he ordered.

'Yes, sir. Will there be anything else?'

'No, that's all.' Patta replaced his phone without saying anything else, and Brunetti went back to reading the reports.

When he finished with them, it was after one. Because he didn't know when Rizzardi would call, and because he wanted to get the report as quickly as possible, he decided not to go home for lunch, nor spend the time going to a restaurant, though he was hungry after the long morning. He decided to go down to the bar at the foot of Ponte dei Greci and make do with a few *tramezzini*.

When he walked in, Arianna, the owner, greeted him by name and automatically placed a wine glass on the counter in front of him. Orso, her ancient German shepherd, who had developed a special fondness for Brunetti over the course of the years, hauled himself arthritically to his feet from his regular place beside the ice-cream cooler and tottered over to him. He waited long enough for Brunetti to pat him on the head and pull gently at his ears and then collapsed in a heap at his feet. The many regulars in the bar were accustomed to stepping over Orso and tossing him bits of crusts and sandwiches. He was especially fond of asparagus.

'What would you like, Guido?' Arianna asked, meaning *tramezzini* and automatically pouring him a glass of red wine.

'Give me a ham and artichoke, and one with shrimp.' Fan-like, Orso's tail began to beat softly against his ankle. 'And one asparagus.' When the sandwiches came, he asked for another glass of wine and drank it slowly, thinking of the way things would be complicated if the dead man did turn out to be American. He didn't know if there would be questions of jurisdiction, decided not to think about that.

As if to prevent him, Arianna said, 'Too bad about the American.'

'We're not sure that he is, not yet.'

'Well, if he is, then someone is going to start crying "terrorism", and that's not going to do anyone any good.' Though she was Yugoslavian by birth, her thinking was entirely Venetian: business first and above all.

'There are lots of drugs in that neighbourhood,' she added, as if talking about it could make drugs be the cause. He remembered that she also owned a hotel, so the very thought of the mere rumour of terrorism was bound to fill her with righteous panic.

'Yes, we're checking that, Arianna. Thanks.' As he spoke, a stalk of asparagus worked itself loose from his sandwich and fell to the floor at Orso's nose. And, when that one was gone, another. It was difficult for Orso to get to his feet, so why not let him eat takeaway?

He placed a ten-thousand-lire note on the counter and pocketed his change when she handed it to him. She hadn't bothered to ring it up on the cash register, so the sum would go unreported and, therefore, untaxed. He had, years ago, ceased caring about this perpetual fraud committed against the State. Let the boys from the Finance Police worry about that. The law said she had to ring it up and give him a receipt; if he left the bar without it, both of them were liable to fines of as much as hundreds of thousands of lire. The boys from Finance often waited outside bars, shops, and restaurants, watching through the windows as business took place, then stopped emerging clients and demanded to be shown their receipts. But Venice was a small town, and all the men from Finance knew him, so he'd never be stopped, not unless they brought in extra police from outside the city and had what the Press had taken to calling a 'blitz', staking out the entire commercial centre of the city and, in a day, taking in millions of lire in fines. And if they stopped him? He'd show them his warrant card and say he'd stopped to use the toilet. Those same taxes paid for his salary; this was true. But that no longer made any difference to him, nor, he suspected, to the majority of his fellow citizens. In a country where the Mafia was free to murder when and whom it pleased, the failure to produce a receipt for a cup of coffee was not a crime that interested Brunetti.

Back at his desk, he found a note telling him to call Doctor Rizzardi. When Brunetti did, he found the Coroner still at his office on the cemetery island.

'*Ciao*, Ettore. It's Guido. What have you got?'

'I took a look at his teeth. All the work is American. He has six fillings and one root canal. The work stretches back over years, and there's no doubt about the technique. It's all American.'

Brunetti knew better than to ask him if he was sure.

'What else?'

'The blade was four centimetres wide and at least fifteen long. The tip penetrated the heart, just as I thought. It slipped right between the ribs, didn't even scrape them, so whoever did it knew enough to hold the blade horizontally. And the angle was perfect.' He paused for a moment, then added, 'Since it was on the left side, I'd say that whoever did it was right-handed or at least used his right hand.'

'What about his height? Can you tell anything?'

'No, nothing definite. But he had to be close to the dead man, standing face to face.'

'Signs of a struggle? Anything under his nails?'

'No. Nothing. But he'd been in the water about

five or six hours, so if there was anything to begin with, it's likely it would have been washed away.'

'Five or six hours?'

'Yes. I'd say he died about midnight, one o'clock.'

'Anything else?'

'Nothing particular. He was in very good shape, very muscular.'

'What about food?'

'He ate something a few hours before he died. Probably a sandwich. Ham and tomato. But he didn't drink anything, at least not anything alcoholic. There was none in his blood, and from the look of his liver, I'd say he drank very little, if at all.'

'Scars? Operations?'

'He had a small scar,' Rizzardi began, then paused and Brunetti heard the rustle of papers. 'On his left wrist, half-moon shaped. Could have been anything. Never been operated on for anything. Had his tonsils, his appendix. Perfect health.' Brunetti could tell from his voice that this was all Rizzardi had to give him.

'Thanks, Ettore. Will you send a written report?'

'Does His Superiorship want to see it?'

Brunetti grinned at Rizzardi's title for Patta. 'He wants to have it. I'm not sure he's going to read it.'

'Well, if he does, it's going to be so filled with medical school jargon that he'll have to call me to interpret it for him.' Three years ago, Patta had opposed Rizzardi's appointment as Coroner because the nephew of a friend of his was just then finishing medical school and was in search of a government job. But Rizzardi, with fifteen years' experience as a pathologist, had been appointed instead, and ever since then he and Patta had conducted guerrilla warfare against one another.

'I'll look forward to reading it, then,' Brunetti said.

'Oh, you won't be able to understand a word of it. Don't even try, Guido. If you have any questions, call me and I'll explain it to you.'

'What about his clothing?' Brunetti asked, though he knew this was none of Rizzardi's responsibility.

'He was wearing jeans, Levi's. And he had one Reebok, size eleven.' Before Brunetti could say anything, Rizzardi continued, 'I know, I know. That doesn't mean he's American. You can buy Levi's and Reeboks anywhere today. But his underwear was. I've sent it over to the lab boys, and they can tell you more, but the labels were in English and said "Made in USA".' The doctor's voice changed, and he displayed a curiosity that was unusual for him. 'Have your boys heard anything from the hotels? Any idea of who he was?'

'I haven't heard anything, so I guess they're still calling.'

'I hope you find out who he is so you can send him home. It's no good thing, to die in a strange country.'

'Thanks, Ettore. I'll do my best to find out who he is. And send him home.'

He set the phone down. An American. He had carried no wallet, no passport, no identification, no money aside from those few coins. All of that pointed to a street crime, one that had gone horribly wrong and ended in death instead of robbery. And the thief had a knife and had used it with either luck or skill. Street criminals in Venice had some luck, but they seldom had any skill. They grabbed and ran. In any other city, this might be taken for a mugging that had gone wrong, but here in Venice this sort of thing simply didn't happen. Skill or luck? And if it was skill, whose skill was it and why was it necessary that skill be employed?

He called down to the main office and asked if they had had any luck with the hotels. The first- and second-class hotels had only one missing guest, a man in his fifties who had not returned to the Gabriele Sandwirth the previous night. The men had begun to check the smaller hotels, one of which had an American man who had checked out the previous night but whose description didn't fit.

It was possible, Brunetti realized, that he could have been renting an apartment in the city; in that case, days could pass before he was reported missing, or he simply might not be missed.

He called the lab and asked to speak to Enzo Bocchese, the Chief Technician. When he came on the phone, Brunetti asked, 'Bocchese, have you got anything on the things in his pockets?' It wasn't necessary to specify whose pockets.

'We used the infra-red on the ticket. It was so soaked that I didn't think we'd be able to get anything. But we did.'

Bocchese, terribly proud of his technology and

the things he could do with it, always needed to be prompted, and then praised. 'Good. I don't know how you do it, but you always manage to find something.' Would that this were even close to the truth. 'Where was it from?'

'Vicenza. Round trip to Venice. Bought yesterday and cancelled for the trip from Vicenza. I've got a man coming from the station to see if he can tell us anything, from the cancellation, about what train it was, but I'm not sure he can.'

'What class was it, first or second?'

'Second.'

'Anything else? Socks? Belt?'

'Rizzardi tell you about the clothes?'

'Yes. He thinks the underwear is American.'

'It is. No question. The belt – he could have bought that anywhere. Black leather with a brass buckle. The socks are synthetic. Made in Taiwan or Korea. Sold everywhere.'

'Anything else?'

'No, nothing.'

'Good work, Bocchese, but I think we don't need more than the ticket to be sure.'

'Sure of what, Commissario?'

'That he's American.'

'Why?' the technician asked.

'Because that's where the Americans are,' Brunetti replied. Any Italian in the area knew of the base in Vicenza, Caserma Something-or-Other, the base where thousands of American soldiers and their families lived, even now, so many years after the end of the war. If he was right, this would certainly raise the spectre of terrorism, and there were certain to be questions of jurisdiction. The Americans had their own police out there, and the instant someone so much as whispered 'terrorism', there could well be NATO and possibly Interpol. Or even the CIA, at the thought of which Brunetti grimaced, thinking of how Patta would bask in the exposure, the celebrity that would follow upon their arrival. Brunetti had no idea of what acts of terrorism were supposed to feel like, but this didn't feel like one to him. A knife was too ordinary a weapon; it didn't call attention to the crime. And there had been no call to claim the murder. Surely, that might still come, but it would be too late, too convenient.

'Of course, of course,' Bocchese said. 'I should have thought of that.' He paused long enough for Brunetti to say something, but when he didn't, Bocchese asked, 'Anything else, sir?'

'Yes. After you speak to the man from the railways, let me know if he can tell you anything about the train he might have taken.'

'I doubt he can, sir. It's just an indentation in the ticket. We can't pull up anything that might identify a train. But I'll call you if he can tell us. Anything else?'

'No, nothing. And thanks, Bocchese.'

After they hung up, Brunetti sat at his desk and stared at his wall, considering the information and the possibilities. A young man, in perfect physical shape, comes to Venice on a round-trip ticket from a city where there is an American military base. He had American dental work, and he carried American coins in his pocket.

Brunetti reached for the phone and dialled the operator. 'See if you can get me the American military base in Vicenza.'

3

As he waited for the call to be put through, Brunetti found the image of that young face, eyes splayed open in death, came back into his memory. It could have been any one of the faces he had seen in the photos of the American soldiers in the Gulf War: fresh, clean-shaven, innocent, glowing with that extraordinary health that so characterized Americans. But the face of the young American on the embankment had been strangely solemn, set apart from his fellows by the mystery of death.

'Brunetti,' he said, answering the buzzing intercom.

'They're very hard to find, those Americans,' the operator said. 'There's no listing in the Vicenza phone book for American base, or for NATO, or for the United States. But I found one under Military Police. Wait just one minute, sir, and I'll put the call through.'

How strange, Brunetti thought, that a presence so strong should be all but unfindable in the phone book. He listened to the usual clicks of a long-distance call, heard it ring at the other end, and then a male voice said, 'MP station, may I help you, sir or madam?'

'Good afternoon,' Brunetti said in English. 'This is Commissario Guido Brunetti of the Venice police. I'd like to speak to the person in charge of the police there.'

'May I ask what this is in connection with, sir?'

'It's a police matter. May I speak to the person in charge?'

'Just one moment, sir.'

There was a long pause, the sound of muffled voices at the other end, then a different voice spoke. 'This is Sergeant Frolich. May I help you?'

'Good afternoon, Sergeant. This is Commissario Brunetti of the Venice police. I'd like to speak to your superior officer or to whoever is in charge.'

'Could you tell me what this is in connection with, sir?'

'As I explained to your colleague,' Brunetti said, keeping his voice level, 'this is a police matter, and I'd like to speak to your superior officer.' How long would he have to go on repeating the same formula?

'I'm sorry, sir, but he's not at the station right now.'

'When do you expect him back?'

'Couldn't say, sir. Could you give me some idea of what this is about?'

'A missing soldier.'

'I beg your pardon, sir.'

'I'd like to know if there's been any report out there of a missing soldier.'

The voice suddenly grew more serious. 'Who did you say this was, sir?'

'Commissario Brunetti. Venice police.'

'Do you have a number where we can call you?'

'You can call me at the Questura in Venice. The number is 5203222, and the city code for Venice is 041, but you'll probably want to check the number in the phone book. I'll wait for your call. Brunetti.' He hung up, certain they would now check the number and call him back. The change in the sergeant's voice had indicated interest, not alarm, so there was probably no report of a missing soldier. Not yet.

After about ten minutes, the phone rang, and the operator told him it was the American base in Vicenza calling. 'Brunetti,' he said when he heard the line open.

'Commissario Brunetti,' a different voice said, 'this is Captain Duncan of the Military Police at Vicenza. Could you tell me what it is you want to know?'

'I'd like to know if you've had a report of a missing soldier. A young man, in his mid-twenties. Light hair, blue eyes.' It took him a moment to do the calculation from metres to feet and inches. 'About five feet, nine inches tall.'

'Could you tell me why the Venice police want to

know about this? Has he gotten into trouble there?'

'You could say that, Captain. We found the body of a young man floating in a canal this morning. He had a round-trip ticket from Vicenza in his pocket, and his clothing and dental work are American, so we thought of the base and wondered if he came from there.'

'Did he drown?'

Brunetti remained silent so long that the other repeated the question. 'Did he drown?'

'No, Captain, he didn't. There were signs of violence.'

'What does that mean?'

'He was stabbed.'

'Robbed?'

'It would appear so, Captain.'

'You sound like you have some doubt about that.'

'It looks like robbery. He has no wallet, and all of his identification is missing.' Brunetti went back to his original question. 'Could you tell me if you've had a report of someone who is missing, who hasn't shown up for work?'

There was a long pause before the Captain replied. 'Can I call you back in about an hour?'

'Certainly.'

'We'll have to contact the individual duty stations and see if anyone is missing from work or their barracks. Could you repeat the description, please?'

'The man we found appears to be in his mid-twenties, has blue eyes, light hair, and is about five feet, nine inches tall.'

'Thank you, Commissario. I'll get my men working on this immediately, and we'll call you as soon as we learn anything.'

'Thank you, Captain,' Brunetti said and broke the connection.

If the young man did turn out to be an American soldier, Patta would be apoplectic with the need to find the killer. Patta, he knew, was incapable of viewing it as the taking of a human life. To him, it could be no more or less than a blow against tourism, and in protection of that civic good Patta was certain to grow ferocious.

He left his desk and walked down the flight of stairs that led to the larger offices where the uniformed men worked. Entering, he saw that Luciani was there, looking none the worse for his early-morning soaking. Brunetti shivered at the thought of entering the waters of the canals, not because of the cold but because of the filth. He'd often joked that falling into a canal was an experience he'd prefer not to survive. And yet, as a boy, he'd swum in the waters of the Grand Canal, and older people he knew talked of the way that, in the poverty of their youth, they had been forced to use the salt waters of the canals and of the *laguna* for cooking, this in the days when salt was an expensive and heavily taxed commodity, and Venetians were a poor people, tourism unknown.

Luciani was talking on the phone when Brunetti entered the office and waved him over to his desk. 'Yes, Uncle, I know that,' he said. 'But what about his son? No, not the one that was in trouble in Mestrino last year.'

As he listened to his uncle's answer, he nodded to Brunetti and signalled with an open palm that he should wait until the conversation was finished. Brunetti sat and listened to the rest of the conversation. 'When was the last time he worked? At Breda? Come on, Uncle, you know he's not able to keep any job that long.' Luciani went silent and listened for a long time, then said, 'No, no, if you hear anything about him, maybe that he suddenly has a lot of money, let me know. Yes, yes, Uncle, and give Aunt Luisa a kiss for me.' There followed a long series of those bi-syllabic 'ciaos' without which Venetians seemed incapable of ending a conversation.

When he hung up, Luciani turned to Brunetti and said, 'That was my Uncle Carlo. He lives over near Fondamente Nuove, back a bit from Santi Giovanni e Paolo. I asked him about the neighbourhood – about who sells drugs, who uses. The only one he knows about is that Vittorio Argenti.' Brunetti nodded in recognition of the name. 'We've had him here a dozen times. But my uncle said he took a job at Breda about six months ago, and now that I think about it, it's been about that long since we've seen him in here. I can check the records, but I think I would have remembered if we'd pulled him in for anything. My uncle knows the family, and he swears they're all convinced that Vittorio's changed.' Luciani lit a cigarette and blew out the match. 'From the way my uncle spoke, it sounds like he's convinced, too.'

'Aside from Argenti, is there anyone else in the neighbourhood?'

'He seems to have been the principal one. There's never been much drug traffic in that part of the city. I know the rubbish man, Noe, and he's never complained of finding syringes on the street in the morning, not like San Maurizio,' he said, naming a part of the city notorious for drug use.

'What about Rossi? He find anything?'

'Pretty much the same, sir. It's a quiet neighbourhood. Occasionally, there's a robbery or a break-in, but there's never been much in the way of drugs, and there's never been any violence,' he said, then added, 'before this.'

'What about the people in those houses? Did they hear or see anything?'

'No, sir. We spoke to all the people who were in the *campo* this morning, but no one heard or saw anything suspicious. And the same thing for the people in the houses.' He anticipated Brunetti's next question. 'Puccetti said the same thing, sir.'

'Where's Rossi?'

With no hesitation whatsoever, Luciani answered, 'He's gone out to get a coffee, sir. Ought to be back in a few minutes if you want to talk to him.'

'What about the divers?'

'They were in there for more than an hour. But they didn't bring up anything that could be a weapon. The usual mess: bottles, cups, even a refrigerator, and a screw driver, but there's nothing that even comes close.'

'What about Bonsuan? Did anyone talk to him about the tides?'

'No, sir. Not yet. We don't have a time of death yet.'

'About midnight,' Brunetti supplied.

Luciani flipped open a logbook that lay on his desk and ran one thick finger down a column of names. 'He's taking a boat to the station right now. Delivering two prisoners to the Milan train. Want me to have him go up to your office when he gets back?'

Brunetti nodded, and then they were interrupted by the return of Rossi. His story was just as Luciani had said: no one in the *campo* that morning nor in the houses facing it had seen or heard anything at all unusual.

In any other city in Italy, the fact that no one had seen or heard anything would be no more than an indication of their distrust of the police and a general unwillingness to help them. Here, however, where the people were generally law-abiding and most of the police themselves Venetians, it meant no more than that they had seen or heard nothing. If there were any serious involvement with drugs in that neighbourhood, sooner or later they would hear about it. Someone would have a cousin or a boyfriend or a mother-in-law who would make a phone call to a friend who just happened to have a cousin or a boyfriend or a mother-in-law who worked for the police, and so the word would reach him. Until that time, he would have to take it as given that there was little traffic in drugs in that part of the city, that it was not the place where a person would go to take or buy drugs, especially not a foreigner. All of that would seem to rule out drugs as having played a part in the crime, at least if it were related in any way to that neighbourhood.

'Send Bonsuan up to see me when he gets back, please,' he told them and went back to his office, careful to use the stairs in the rear of the building that avoided taking him anywhere near Patta's office. The longer he could avoid talking to his superior, the happier he would be.

In his office, he finally remembered to call Paola. He had forgotten to tell her that he wouldn't be home for lunch, but it was years since she was surprised or bothered by that. Instead of conversation, she read a book during the meal, unless the children were there. In fact, he had begun to suspect that she enjoyed her quiet lunches alone with the authors she taught at the university, for she never objected if he was delayed or kept from coming.

She answered on the third ring. '*Pronto.*'

'*Ciao*, Paola. It's me.'

'I thought it might be. How are things?' She never asked a direct question about his work or about what kept him from meals. It was not that she took no interest, only that she found it better to wait for him to talk about it. Eventually, she came to learn it all, anyway.

'I'm sorry about lunch, but I was making phone calls.'

'That's all right. I spent it with William Faulkner. Very interesting man.' Over the course of the years, they'd come to treat her lunchtime visitors as real guests, had evolved jokes about

44

the table manners of Doctor Johnson (shocking), the conversation of Melville (scurrilous), and the amount Jane Austen drank (stunning).

'I'll be back for dinner, though. All I have to do is talk to a few people here and wait for a call from Vicenza.' When she said nothing, he added, 'From the American military base there.'

'Oh, it's like that, is it?' she asked, telling him, with the question, that she had already learned about the crime and the probable identity of the victim. The barman told the postman, who told the woman on the second floor, who called her sister, and, first thing, everyone in the city knew about what had happened, long before a word appeared in the newspapers or on the evening news.

'Yes, it's like that,' he agreed.

'What time do you think you'll be back?'

'Before seven.'

'All right. I'll get off the phone now, in case your call comes.' He loved Paola for many reasons, not the least of which was the fact that he knew this to be her real motive for getting off the phone. There was no secret message, no hidden agenda in what she said; she merely wanted to free the line so that his work would be easier and he would be home sooner.

'Thanks, Paola. I'll see you about seven.'

'*Ciao*, Guido,' and she was gone, back to William Faulkner, leaving him free to work and equally free of guilt about the demands of that work.

It was almost five and still the Americans hadn't called back. For a moment, he was tempted to call them, but he resisted the impulse. If one of their soldiers was missing, they'd have to contact him. After all, to put it bluntly, he had the body.

He searched through the personnel reports that still lay in front of him until he found those of Luciani and Rossi. In both of them, he added a note that they had behaved far beyond the ordinary in going into the canal to pull the body out. They could have waited for a boat or could have used poles, but they had done something he didn't know if he would have had the courage, or the will, to do and had gone into that water to pull him ashore.

The phone rang. 'Brunetti.'

'This is Captain Duncan. We've checked all the duty stations, and we have one man who didn't show up for work today. He meets your description. I sent someone to check his apartment, but there's no sign of him, so I'd like to send someone to take a look at the body.'

'When, Captain?'

'Tonight, if possible.'

'Certainly. How will you send him?'

'I beg your pardon?'

'I'd like to know how you'll send him, by train or by car, so that I can send someone to meet him.'

'Oh, I see.' Duncan answered. 'By car.'

'Then I'll send someone to Piazzale Roma. There's a Carabinieri station there, to the right as you enter the Piazzale.'

'All right. The car will be here in about fifteen minutes, so they ought to be there in a bit less than an hour, about quarter to seven.'

'We'll have a launch waiting. He'll have to go

out to the cemetery to identify the body. Will it be someone who knew the man, Captain?' Brunetti knew from long experience how difficult it was to recognize the dead from a photograph.

'Yes, it's his commanding officer at the hospital.'

'The hospital?'

'The man who's missing is our Public Health Inspector, Sergeant Foster.'

'Could you give me the name of the man who's coming?'

'Captain Peters. Terry Peters. And Commissario,' Duncan added, 'the Captain is a woman.' There was more than a trace of smugness in his voice as he added, 'And Captain Peters is also Doctor Peters.'

What was he meant to do, Brunetti wondered, fall over on his side because the Americans allowed women into their army? Or because they also allowed them to be doctors? Instead, he decided to out-Herod Herod and become the classic Italian who couldn't resist the lure of anything, so long as it came in a skirt, even the skirt of a military uniform. 'Very good, Captain. In that case, I'll go myself to meet Captain Peters. Doctor Peters.'

Duncan took a few seconds to answer, but all he said was, 'That's very thoughtful of you, Mr Brunetti. I'll tell the Captain to ask for you.'

'Yes. Do,' Brunetti said and hung up without waiting for the other man to say goodbye. His tone, he realized without regret, had been too strong; as often happened with him, he had allowed himself to be sucked into resentment by what he thought lay between the lines of what he heard. In the past, both during Interpol seminars that had included Americans and during three months of training in Washington, he had often come up against this national sense of moral superiority, this belief so common among Americans that it had somehow been given to them to serve as a glistening moral light in a world dark with error. Perhaps that was not the case here; perhaps he was misinterpreting Duncan's tone, and the captain had meant to do no more than help Brunetti avoid embarrassment. If so, then his response had certainly done everything possible to confirm any cliché about hot-blooded, thin-skinned Italians.

Shaking his head in chagrin, he dialled an outside line and then his home number.

'*Pronto,*' Paola responded after three rings.

'This time I called,' he said without introduction.

'Which means you'll be late.'

'I've got to go to Piazzale Roma to meet an American captain who's coming from Vicenza to identify the body. I shouldn't be too late, not much past nine. She's supposed to get here by seven.'

'She?'

'Yes, *she*,' Brunetti said. 'My reaction was the same. She's also a doctor.

'It is a world of miracles in which we live,' Paola said. 'Both a captain and a doctor. She had better be very good at both because she's making you miss polenta and liver.' It was one of his favourites, and she had probably made it because he had missed lunch.

'I'll eat when I get back.'

'All right, I'll feed the kids and wait for you.'

'Thanks, Paola. I won't be late.'

'I'll wait,' she said and replaced the receiver.

As soon as the line was clear, he called down to the second floor and asked if Bonsuan had come back yet. The pilot was just coming in, and Brunetti asked that he come up to his office.

A few minutes later, Danilo Bonsuan came into Brunetti's office. Rough-hewn and robust, he looked like a man who lived on the water but who would never think of drinking the stuff. Brunetti pointed to the chair in front of his desk. Bonsuan lowered himself into the chair, stiff-jointed after decades on board and around boats. Brunetti knew better than to expect him to volunteer information, not because he was reluctant but simply because he didn't have the habit of speaking unless there was some practical purpose to be served by doing so.

'Danilo, the woman saw him at about five-thirty, dead, low tide. Doctor Rizzardi said he had been in the water about five or six hours; that's how long he was dead.' Brunetti paused, giving the other man time to begin to visualize the waterways near the hospital. 'There's no sign of a weapon in the canal where we found him.'

Bonsuan didn't bother to comment on this. No one would bother to throw away a good knife, especially not where they had just used it to kill someone.

Brunetti took this as spoken and added, 'So he might have been killed somewhere else.'

'Probably was,' Bonsuan said, breaking his silence.

'Where?'

'Five, six hours?' Bonsuan asked. When Brunetti nodded, the pilot put his head back and closed his eyes, and Brunetti could almost see the tide chart of the *laguna* that he studied. Bonsuan remained like that for a few minutes. Once he shook his head in a brief negative, dismissing some possibility that Brunetti would never learn about. Finally he opened his eyes and said, 'There are two places where it could have been. Behind Santa Marina. You know that dead *calle* that leads down to the Rio Santa Marina, behind the new hotel?'

Brunetti nodded. It was a quiet place, a dead end.

'The other is Calle Cocco.' When Brunetti seemed puzzled, Bonsuan explained, 'It's one of those two blind *calle* that lead off of Calle Lunga, where it heads out of Campo Santa Maria Formosa. Goes right down to the water.

Though Bonsuan's description made him recognize where the *calle* was, even allowed him to recall the entrance to it, past which he must have walked hundreds of times, Brunetti could not remember ever having actually walked down the *calle*. No one would, not unless they lived in it, for it was, as Bonsuan pointed out, a dead end that led to the water and ended there.

'Either one would be a perfect place,' Bonsuan

suggested. 'No one ever passes either one of them, not at that hour.'

'And the tides?'

'Last night they were very weak. No real pull in them. And a body catches on things; that slows it down. It could have been either one of those two places.'

'Any other?'

'It might have been one of the other *calle* that lead into the Canal of Santa Marina, but those are the two best places if all we've got is five or six hours for him to drift.' It seemed that Bonsuan had finished, but then he added, 'Unless he used a boat,' leaving it to Brunetti to infer that he meant the killer.

'That's possible, isn't it?' Brunetti agreed, though he thought it unlikely. Boats meant motors, and late at night that meant angry heads stuck out of windows to see who it was making all the noise.

'Thanks, Danilo. Would you tell the divers to go over those two places – it can wait until the morning – and take a look? And ask Vianello to send a team over to check both of those places to see if there's any sign that it was done there.'

Bonsuan pushed himself up from his chair, knees creaking audibly. He nodded.

'Who's down there who can take me to Piazzale Roma and then out to the cemetery?'

'Monetti,' Bonsuan responded, naming one of the other pilots.

'Could you tell him I'd like to leave in about ten minutes?'

With a nod and a mumbled, 'Yes, sir,' Bonsuan was gone.

Brunetti suddenly noticed how hungry he was. All he'd eaten since the morning were three sandwiches, well, less than that, since Orso had eaten one of them. He pulled open the bottom drawer of his desk, hoping to find something there, a box of *buranei*, the s-shaped cookies he loved and usually had to fight the children for, an old candy bar, anything, but it was as empty as it had been the last time he looked.

It would have to be coffee, then. But that would mean having Monetti stop the boat. It was a measure of his hunger, the irritation he felt at this simple problem. But then he thought of the women down in the Ufficio Stranieri; they usually had something to give him if he went begging for food.

He left his office and went down the back staircase to the ground floor, pushing his way through the large double doors and into the office. Sylvia, small and dark, and Anita, tall, blonde, and stunning, sat at their desks opposite one another, leafing through the papers that seemed never to disappear from their desks.

'*Buona sera,*' they both said as he came in, then bowed again to the green-covered files that sprawled out in front of them.

'Do you have anything to eat?' he asked with more hunger than grace.

Sylvia smiled and shook her head without speaking; he came into the office only to beg food or to tell them that one of their applicants for a work or residence permit had been arrested and could be removed from their lists and files.

'Don't you get fed at home?' Anita asked, but at the same time she was pulling open one of the drawers in her desk. From it she pulled a brown paper bag. Opening it, she took out one, then two, then three ripe pears and placed them at the front of her desk, within easy reach of his hand.

Three years ago, an Algerian who had been denied a residence permit had gone berserk in the office when he was given the news, grabbed Anita by the shoulders, and pulled her across her desk. He was holding her there, screaming in her face in hysterical Arabic, when Brunetti had come in to ask for a file. Instantly, he had wrapped an arm around the man's neck and choked him until he released Anita, who had fallen free to her desk, terrified and sobbing. No one had ever referred to the incident since then, but he knew he could always find something to eat in her desk.

'Thanks, Anita,' he said and picked up one of the pears. He plucked out the stem and bit into the pear, ripe and perfect. In five quick bites, it was gone, and he reached for the second one. A bit less ripe, it was still sweet and soft. Juggling the two damp cores in his left hand, he took the third pear, thanked her again, and went out of the office, now fortified for the ride to Piazzale Roma and his meeting with Doctor Peters. Captain Peters.

4

He got to the Carabinieri station at Piazzale Roma
at twenty minutes before seven, leaving Monetti in
the launch to wait for him to come back aboard
with the doctor. He realized, although it no doubt
made a statement about his prejudices, that he
found it more comfortable to think of her as a
doctor than as a captain. He had called ahead, so
the Carabinieri knew he was coming. It was the
usual bunch, most of them Southerners, who
seemed never to leave the smoke-filled station, the
purpose of which Brunetti could never understand. Carabinieri had nothing to do with traffic,
but traffic was all there was at Piazzale Roma: cars,
campers, taxis, and, especially during the summer,
endless rows of buses parked there just long
enough to disgorge their heavy cargoes of tourists.

Just this last summer there had been added to them a new sort of vehicle, the diesel-burning, fume-spewing buses that lumbered there over-night from a newly freed Eastern Europe and from which emerged, dazed with travel and lack of sleep, scores of thousands of very polite, very poor, very stocky tourists, who spent a single day in Venice and left it dazzled by the beauty they had seen in that one day. Here they had their first taste of capitalism triumphant, and they were too thrilled by it to realize that much of it was no more than papier mâché masks from Taiwan and lace woven in Korea.

He went into the station and exchanged friendly greetings with the two officers on duty. 'No sign of her yet, *La Capitana*,' one of them said, then added a scornful chuckle at the idea that a woman could be an officer. At the sound of it, Brunetti determined to address her, at least if she came anywhere within hearing of these two, by her rank and to give her every sign of the respect to which her rank entitled her. Not for the first time, he cringed when he saw his own prejudices manifest in other people.

He engaged in a few desultory remarks with the Carabinieri. What chance did Napoli have of winning this weekend? Would Maradona ever play again? Would the government fall? He stood looking out of the glass door and watched the waves of traffic flow into the Piazzale. Pedestrians danced and wove their way through the cars and buses. No one paid the least attention to the zebra crossing or to the white lines that were meant to indicate the separation of lanes. And yet the traffic flowed smoothly and quickly.

A light green sedan cut across the bus lane and drew up behind the two blue and white Carabinieri vehicles. It was an almost anonymous rectangle, devoid of markings or rooftop light, its only distinguishing mark a number plate which read 'AFI Official'. The driver's door opened, and a uniformed soldier emerged. He bent and opened the door behind him and held it while a young woman in a dark-green uniform got out. As soon as she stood clear of the car, she put on her uniform cap and looked around her, then over towards the Carabinieri station.

Without bothering to say goodbye to the men inside, Brunetti left the station and went towards the car. 'Doctor Peters?' he said as he approached.

She looked up at the sound of her name and took a step towards him. As he came up, she held out her hand and shook his briefly. She appeared to be in her late twenties, with curly dark-brown hair that pushed back against the pressure of her hat. Her eyes were chestnut, her skin still brown from a summer tan. Had she smiled, she would have been even prettier. Instead, she looked at him directly, mouth pulled into a tense straight line, and asked, 'Are you the police inspector?'

'Commissario Brunetti. I have a boat here. It will take us out to San Michele.' Seeing her confusion, he explained, 'The cemetery island. The body's been taken there.'

Without waiting for her reply, he pointed in the direction of the mooring and led the way across the road. She paused long enough to say something to the driver and then followed him. At the water's edge, he pointed to the blue and white police boat moored to the embankment. 'If you'll come this way, Doctor,' he said, stepping from the pavement and onto the deck of the boat. She came up close behind him and accepted his hand. The skirt of her uniform fell just a few inches below her knees. Her legs were good, tanned and muscular, the ankles slim. With no hesitation, she gripped his hand and allowed herself to be helped on board the boat. As soon as they were down in the cabin and seated, Monetti backed out of the mooring and turned the boat up the Grand Canal. He took them quickly past the railway station, blue light turning, and turned left into the Canale della Misericordia, beyond the outlet of which lay the cemetery island.

Usually, when he had to take people foreign to Venice on a police launch, Brunetti busied himself by pointing out sights and points of interest along the way. This time, however, he contented himself with the most formal of openings. 'I hope you had no trouble in getting here, Doctor.'

She looked down at the strip of green carpeting on the floor between them and muttered something he took to be a 'no' but said nothing further. He noticed that she occasionally took a deep breath in an effort to calm herself, a strange response in someone who was, after all, a doctor.

As if she had read his thoughts, she glanced up at him, smiled a very pretty smile, and said, 'It's different, when you know the person. In medical school, they're strangers, so it's easy to keep a professional distance.' She paused for a long time. 'And people my age don't usually die.'

That was certainly true enough. 'Did you work together for a long time?' Brunetti asked.

She nodded and began to answer, but before she could say anything, the boat gave a sudden lurch. She grabbed the front of her seat with both hands and shot him a frightened glance.

'We've moved out into the *laguna*, into open water. Don't worry, it's nothing to be afraid of.'

'I'm not a good sailor. I was born in North Dakota, and there's not a lot of water there. I never even learned how to swim.' Her smile was weak, but it was back in place.

'Did you and Mr Foster work together for a long time?'

'Sergeant,' she corrected him automatically. 'Yes, ever since I got to Vicenza, about seven months ago. He really runs everything. They just need an officer to be in charge. And to sign papers.'

'To take the blame?' he asked with a smile.

'Yes, yes, I suppose you could say that. But nothing's ever gone wrong. Not with Mike. He's very good at his job.' Her voice was warm. Praise? Affection?

Below them, the engine slowed to an even purr, and then there came the heavy thump as they slid into the dock at the cemetery. He stood and went up the narrow stairway to the open deck, pausing at the top to hold one side of the swinging door open to allow the doctor to pass through it. Monetti was busy wrapping the mooring lines around one of the wooden pilings that stuck up at a crazy angle from the waters of the *laguna*.

Brunetti stepped ashore and held out his arm. She placed her hand on it, then leaned heavily on it as she leaped to the shore beside him. He noticed that she carried neither handbag nor briefcase, perhaps having left it in the car or in the boat.

The cemetery closed at four, so Brunetti had to ring the bell that stood to the right of the large wooden doors. After a few minutes, the door on the right side was pulled open by a man in a dark blue uniform, and Brunetti gave his name. The man held the door open, then closed it after them. Brunetti led their way through the main entrance and paused at the watchman's window, where he announced himself and showed his warrant card. The watchman signalled for them to continue down the open arcade to the right. Brunetti nodded. He knew the way.

When they stepped through the door and into the building that held the morgue, Brunetti felt the sudden drop in temperature. Doctor Peters apparently did as well, for she brought her arms together across her chest and lowered her head. A white-uniformed attendant sat at a plain wooden desk at the end of a long corridor. He got to his feet as they approached, careful to place his book face down in front of him. 'Commissario Brunetti?' he asked.

Brunetti nodded. 'This is the doctor from the American base,' he added, nodding to the young woman at his side. To one who had looked so frequently upon the face of death, the sight of a young woman in a military uniform was hardly worthy of notice, so the attendant passed quickly in front of them and opened the heavy wooden door that stood to his left.

'I knew you were coming, so I brought him out,' he said as he led them towards a metal gurney that stood on one side of the room. All three of them recognized what was under the white cloth. When they drew up next to the body, the young man looked at Doctor Peters. She nodded. When he pulled the cloth back, she looked at the face of the dead man, and Brunetti looked at hers. For the first few moments, her own remained absolutely still and expressionless, then she closed her eyes and pulled her upper lip between her teeth. If she was trying to bite back tears, she failed, for they welled up and seeped out of her eyes. 'Mike, Mike,' she whispered and turned away from the body.

Brunetti nodded to the attendant, and he drew the cloth back across the young man's face.

Brunetti felt her hand on his arm, her grip surprisingly strong. 'What killed him?'

He stepped back, intending to turn and lead her from the room, but her grip tightened and she repeated, voice insistent, 'What killed him?'

Brunetti placed his hand on top of hers and said, 'Come outside.'

Before he had any idea what she was doing, she pushed past him and grabbed at the cloth that covered the body of the young man, ripping it away to expose his body to the waist. The giant incision of the autopsy, running from navel to neck, was sewn together with large stitches. Unsewn and seeming quite harmless when compared to the enormous incision of the autopsy was the small horizontal line that had killed him.

Her voice came out as a low moan, and she repeated the name, 'Mike, Mike,' drawing the sound out in a long, keening wail. She stood beside the body, curiously straight and rigid, and the noise continued to come from her.

The attendant stepped quickly in front of her and fastidiously replaced the cloth, covering both wounds and then the face.

She turned to face Brunetti, and he saw that her eyes were filled with tears, but he saw something else in them that looked like nothing so much as terror, sheer animal terror.

'Are you all right, Doctor?' he asked, voice low, careful not to touch her or approach her in any way.

She nodded, and the look of whatever it was passed from her eyes. Abruptly she turned and headed back towards the door of the mortuary. A few feet from it, she stopped suddenly, looked around her as if surprised to find herself where she was, and ran towards a sink that stood against the far wall. She was violently sick into it, retched repeatedly until she stood at the sink, arms braced to support herself, leaning down above it, panting.

The attendant suddenly appeared beside her and handed her a white cotton towel. She took it with a nod and wiped at her face with it. With strange gentleness, the man took her arm and led her to another sink a few metres down the same wall. He turned on the hot-water tap, then the cold, and placed his hand under the water until it reached a temperature suitable for him. When it did, he reached out and held the towel while Doctor Peters washed her face and rinsed her mouth with a handful of water, and then another. When she was done, he handed her the towel again, shut off both taps, and left the room by the door on the other side.

She folded the towel and draped it over the edge of the sink. Making her way back to Brunetti, she avoided looking to her left, where the body still lay on the gurney, covered now.

When she got near, he turned and led the way to the door, held it open for her as they passed into the warmer evening air. As they walked down under the long arcade, she said, 'I'm sorry. I don't know why that happened. I've certainly seen autopsies. I've even *done* autopsies.' She shook her head a few times as they walked. He half saw the gesture from his greater height beside her.

If only to complete the formality, he asked, 'Is that Sergeant Foster?'

'Yes, it is,' she answered with no hesitation, but he sensed that she was struggling to keep her voice calm and level. Even her walk was more rigid than it had been when they went in, as if she had let the uniform take over and direct her motions.

When they passed through the gate of the cemetery, Brunetti led her over to where Monetti had moored the boat. He sat inside the cabin, reading his newspaper. When he saw them approach, he folded it and moved to the stern, where he pulled on the mooring rope to bring the boat close enough for them to be able to climb on board easily.

This time she stepped onto the boat and went immediately down the stairs into the cabin. Pausing only long enough to whisper to Monetti, 'Take as much time as you can going back,' he followed her down into the cabin.

She sat farther forward this time, turned to face out of the front windows. The sun had already set, and the afterglow provided very little light by which to see the skyline of the city, off to their left. He took his place opposite her, noticing how straight and stiff she sat.

'There will be a lot of formalities, but I imagine we can release the body tomorrow.'

She nodded to acknowledge that she heard him.

'What will the Army do?'

'Excuse me?' she said.

'What will the Army do in a case like this?' he repeated.

'We'll send the body home, to his family.'

'No, I don't mean about the body. I mean about the investigation.'

At that, she turned and looked him in the eyes. Her confusion, he believed, was feigned. 'I don't understand. What investigation?'

'To find out why he was killed.'

'But I thought it was robbery,' she said, asking for confirmation of that belief.

'It might have been,' he said, 'but I doubt it.'

She looked away from him when he said that and stared out of the window, but the panorama of

Venice had been swallowed by the night, and all she saw there was her own reflection.

'I don't know anything about that,' she said, voice insistent.

To Brunetti, it sounded as if she believed she could make this be true, if only she repeated it often and insistently enough. 'What kind of man was he?' he asked.

For a moment, she didn't answer, but when she did, Brunetti found her answer strange. 'Honest. He was an honest man.' It was a strange thing to say about a man so young.

He waited to see if she would say anything more. When she didn't, he asked, 'How well did you know him?'

He watched, not her face, but its reflection in the window of the boat. She was no longer crying, but a fixed sadness had settled on her features. She took a deep breath and answered, 'I knew him very well.' But then her voice changed, grew more casual and offhand. 'We worked together for seven months.' And that was all she said.

'What sort of work did he do? Captain Duncan said he was the Public Health Inspector, but I'm not sure I have any idea what that means.'

She noticed that their eyes met in the window, so she turned to face him directly. 'He had to inspect the apartments where we live. We Americans, that is. Or if there were any complaints about tenants by their landlords, he had to go and investigate them.'

'Anything else?'

'He had to go to the embassies serviced by our

hospital. In Egypt, Poland, Yugoslavia, and inspect the kitchens, see that they were clean.'

'So he travelled a lot?'

'A fair amount, yes.'

'Did he like his work?'

Without hesitation and with great emphasis, she said, 'Yes, he did. He thought it was very important.'

'And you were his superior officer?'

Her smile was very small. 'You could say that, I suppose. I'm really a paediatrician; they just gave me the job in public health so that they'd have an officer's signature, and a doctor's, in the right places. Mike ran the office almost completely by himself. Occasionally, he'd give me something to sign, or he'd ask me to write a request for supplies. Things get done faster if an officer asks for them.'

'Did you ever go on any of these trips, these trips to the embassies, together?'

If she found that a strange question, he had no way of telling, for she turned away from him and again stared out of the window. 'No, Mike always went alone.' Without warning, she stood and went towards the steps at the back of the cabin. 'Does your driver, or whatever he is, know the way? It seems like it's taking us an awful long time to get back.' She pushed open one of the doors and looked carefully to either side of them, but the buildings that lined the canal were anonymous to her.

'Yes, it takes longer to get back,' Brunetti lied easily. 'Many of the canals are one way, so we have to go all the way around the station to get to

Piazzale Roma.' He saw that they were just entering the Canale di Cannaregio. In five minutes, perhaps less, they would be there.

She pushed her way outside and stood on deck. A sudden gust of wind pulled at her cap, and she crushed it to her head with one hand, then removed it and held it at her side. With its stiffness removed, she was revealed as more than pretty.

He came up the steps and stood beside her. They made the right turn into the Grand Canal. 'It's very beautiful,' she said. Then, changing her tone, she asked, 'Why do you speak English so well?'

'I studied it in school, and at the university, and I spent some time in the States.'

'You speak it very well.'

'Thank you. Do you speak Italian?'

'*Un poco*,' she replied, then smiled and added, '*molto poco*.'

Ahead of them he saw the moorings of Piazzale Roma. He stepped in front of her and grabbed the mooring rope to hold it ready while Monetti pulled up next to the piling. He flipped it over the top of the pole and tied it in an expert knot. Monetti cut the engine and Brunetti jumped to the dock. She took his hand with easy familiarity and followed him from the boat. Together, they went towards the car that was still parked in front of the Carabinieri station.

The driver, when he saw her approaching, scrambled out of the front seat, saluted, and opened the back door of the car. She pulled the skirt of her uniform under her and slipped into the back seat. Brunetti put out a restraining hand and stopped the driver from closing the door after her. 'Thank you for coming, Doctor,' he said, bowing down, one hand on the roof of the car, to speak to her.

'You're welcome,' she said and didn't bother with thanking him for having taken her to San Michele.

'I'll look forward to seeing you in Vicenza,' he said and watched for her reaction.

It was sudden and strong, and he saw a flash of that same fear he had seen when she first looked at the wound that had killed Foster. 'Why?'

His smile was bland. 'Perhaps I can find out more about why he was killed.'

She reached in front of him and pulled at the door. He had no choice but to step back from its closing weight. It slammed shut, she leaned across the seat and said something to the driver, and the car moved away. He stood and watched as it inserted itself into the traffic flowing out of Piazzale Roma, up the graded road towards the causeway. At the top, it disappeared from his sight, an anonymous pale green vehicle going back to the mainland after a trip to Venice.

5

Without bothering to glance into the Carabinieri station to see if his return with the Captain had been noticed, Brunetti went back to the boat, where he found Monetti returned to his newspaper. Years ago, a foreigner – he couldn't now remember who it was – had remarked on how slowly Italians read. Ever since then, whenever he observed someone nursing a single newspaper all the way from Venice to Milan, Brunetti thought of this; Monetti had certainly had a good deal of time, but he appeared still to be in the first pages. Perhaps boredom had forced him to begin reading through it a second time.

'Thanks, Monetti,' he said, stepping onto the deck.

The young man looked up and smiled. 'I tried to

slow her down as much as possible, sir. But it's crazy, with all these maniacs who get right on your tail and follow too closely.' Brunetti had been in his thirties when he learned to drive, forced to do it when he was posted to Naples for a three-year assignment. He did it with trepidation, and he drove badly, slowed by caution, and too often enraged by those same maniacs, the variety who drove cars, not boats.

'Would you mind taking me up to San Silvestro?' he asked.

'I'll take you right to the end of the *calle* if you'd like, sir.'

'Thanks, Monetti. I would.'

Brunetti flipped the rope up over the top of the piling and wrapped it carefully around the metal stanchion on the side of the boat. He moved ahead and stood beside Monetti as they started up the Grand Canal. Little that was to be seen down at this end of the city interested Brunetti, surely as close to a slum as the island had. They passed the railway station, a building that surprised by its drabness.

It would have been easy for Brunetti to grow indifferent to the beauty of the city, to walk in the midst of it, looking and not really seeing. But then it always happened: a window he had never noticed before would swim into his ken, or the sun would gleam in an archway, and he would actually feel his heart tighten in response to something infinitely more complex than beauty. He supposed, when he bothered to think about it, that it had something to do with language, with the fact that there were fewer than eighty thousand people who lived in the city, and perhaps with the fact that he had gone to kindergarten in a fifteenth-century *palazzo*. He missed this city when he was away from it, much in the same way he missed Paola, and he felt complete and whole only while he was here. One glance around him, as they sped up the canal, was proof of the wisdom of all of this. He had never spoken of this to anyone. No foreigner would understand; any Venetian would find it redundant.

Soon after they passed under the Rialto, Monetti pulled the boat over to the right. At the end of the long *calle* that led up to Brunetti's building, he slipped the engine into neutral, hovered for the briefest of instants beside the embankment, and let Brunetti jump to shore. Even before Brunetti could turn to wave his thanks, Monetti was gone, swinging around, back down the way he had come, blue light flashing as he took himself home to dinner.

Brunetti walked up the *calle*, legs tired with all the jumping on and off boats that he seemed to have been doing all day, since the first boat had picked him up here more than twelve hours ago. He opened the enormous door into the building and closed it quietly behind him. The narrow stairway that hairpinned its way up to the top of the building served as a perfect trumpet of sound, and they could, even four floors above, hear it whenever it slammed. Four floors. The thought burdened him.

By the time he reached the final turn in the

staircase, he could smell the onions, and that did a great deal to make the last flight easier. He glanced at his watch before he put his key into the door. Nine-thirty. Chiara would still be awake, so he could at least kiss her good night and ask her if she had done her homework. If Raffaele were there, he could hardly risk the first, and the second would be futile.

'*Ciao*, Papà,' Chiara called from the living room. He put his jacket in the cupboard and went down the corridor to the living room. Chiara lolled in an easy chair, looking up from a book that lay open in her lap.

As he walked into the room, he automatically switched on the track lighting above her. 'You want to go blind?' he asked, probably for the seven hundredth time.

'Oh, Papà, I can see enough to read.'

He bent over her and kissed her on the cheek she held up to him. 'What are you reading, Angel?'

'It's a book Mamma gave me. It's fabulous. It's about this governess who goes to work for a man, and they fall in love, but he's got this crazy wife locked up in the attic, so he can't marry her, even though they're really in love. I just got to the part where there's a fire. I hope she burns up.'

'Who, Chiara?' he asked. 'The governess or the wife?'

'The wife, silly.'

'Why?'

'So Jane Eyre,' she said, making a hash of the name, 'can marry Mister Rochester,' to whose name she did equal violence.

He was about to ask another question, but she had gone back to the fire, so he went into the kitchen, where Paola was bent over the open door of the washing-machine.

'*Ciao*, Guido,' she said, standing. 'Dinner in ten minutes.' She kissed him, turned back to the stove, where onions were browning in a pool of oil.

'I just had a literary discussion with our daughter,' he said. 'She was explaining the plot of a great classic of English literature to me. I think it might be better for her if we forced her to watch the Brazilian soap operas on television. She's in there, rooting for the fire to kill Mrs Rochester.'

'Oh, come on, Guido, everyone roots for the fire when they read *Jane Eyre*.' She stirred the onions around in the pan and added, 'Well, at least the first time they read it. It isn't until later that they realize what a cunning, self-righteous little bitch Jane Eyre really is.'

'Is that the kind of thing you tell your students?' he asked, opening a cabinet and pulling out a bottle of Pinot Noir.

The liver lay sliced and waiting on a plate beside the frying pan. Paola slipped a slotted ladle under it and flipped half into the pan, then stepped back to avoid the spitting oil. She shrugged. Classes at the university had just resumed, and she obviously didn't want to think about students on her own time.

Stirring, she asked, 'What was the captain-doctor like?'

He pulled down two glasses and poured wine into both. He leaned back against the worktop, handed her one, sipped, answered, 'Very young and very nervous.' Seeing that Paola continued to stir, he added, 'And very pretty.'

Hearing that, she sipped at the glass she held in one hand and looked at him.

'Nervous about what?' She took another sip of the wine, held the glass up to the light, and said, 'This isn't as good as what we got from Mario, is it?'

'No,' he agreed. 'But your cousin Mario is so busy making a name for himself in the international wine trade that he doesn't have time to bother with orders as small as ours.'

'He would if we paid him on time,' she snapped.

'Paola, come on. That was six months ago.'

'And it was more than six months that we kept him waiting to be paid.'

'Paola, I'm sorry. I thought I'd paid him, and then I forgot about it. I apologized to him.'

She set the glass down and gave the liver a quick jab.

'Paola, it was only two hundred thousand lire. That's not going to send your cousin Mario to the poorhouse.'

'Why do you always call him, "my cousin Mario?"'

Brunetti came within a hair's breadth of saying, 'Because he's your cousin and his name is Mario,' but, instead, set his glass down on the worktop and put his arms around her. For a long time, she remained stiff, leaning away from him. He increased the pressure of his arms around her, and she relaxed, leaned against him, and put her head back against his chest.

They stayed like that until she poked him in the ribs with the end of the spoon and said, 'Liver's burning.'

He released her and picked up his glass again.

'I don't know what she's nervous about, but it upset her to see the corpse.'

'Wouldn't anyone be upset to see a dead man, especially someone they knew?'

'No, it was more than that. I'm sure there was something between them.'

'What sort of something?'

'The usual sort.'

'Well, you said she was pretty.'

He smiled. 'Very pretty.' She smiled. 'And very,' he began, searching for the right word. The right one didn't make any sense. 'And very frightened.'

'Why do you say that?' Paola asked, carrying the pan to the table and setting it down on a ceramic tile. 'Frightened about what? That she'd be suspected of killing him?'

From beside the stove, he took the large wooden cutting board and carried it to the table. He sat and lifted the kitchen towel spread across the board and exposed the half-wheel of golden polenta that lay, still warm and now grown firm, beneath it. She brought a salad and the bottle of wine, pouring them both more before she sat down.

'No, I don't think it's that,' he said, and spooned liver and onions onto his plate, then added a broad wedge of polenta. He speared a piece of liver with his fork, pushed onions on top of it with his knife, and began to eat. As was his habit, he said nothing until his plate was empty. When the liver was gone and he was mopping the juice up with what remained of his second helping of polenta, he said, 'I think she might know, or have some idea about, who killed him. Or why he was killed.'

'Why?'

'If you'd seen her look when she saw him. No, not when she saw that he was dead and that it was really Foster, but when she saw what killed him – she was on the edge of panic. She got sick.'

'Sick?'

'Threw up.'

'Right there?'

'Yes. Strange, isn't it?'

Paola thought for a while before she answered. She finished her wine, poured herself another half-glass. 'Yes. It's a strange reaction to death. And she's a doctor?' He nodded. 'Makes no sense. What could she be afraid of?'

'Anything for dessert?'

'Figs.'

'I love you.'

'You mean you love figs,' she said and smiled.

There were six of them, perfect and moist with sweetness. He took his knife and began to peel one. When he was done, juice running down both hands, he cut it in half and handed the larger piece to her.

He crammed most of the other into his mouth and wiped at the juice that ran down his chin. He finished the fig, ate two more, wiped at his mouth again, cleaned his hands on his napkin, and said,

'If you give me a small glass of port, I'll die a happy man.'

Getting up from the table, she asked, 'What else could she be afraid of?'

'As you said, that she might be suspected of having something to do with it. Or because she did have something to do with it.'

She pulled down a squat bottle of port, but before she poured it into two tiny glasses, she took the plates from the table and placed them in the sink. When that was done, she poured them both glasses of port and brought them back to the table. Sweet, it caught up with the lingering taste of fig. A happy man. 'But I don't think it's either of those.'

'Why?'

He shrugged. 'She doesn't seem like a murderer to me.'

'Because she's pretty?' Paola asked and sipped at her port.

He was about to answer that it was because she was a doctor, but then he remembered what Rizzardi had said, that the person who killed the young man knew where to put the knife. A doctor would know that. 'Maybe,' he said, then changed the subject and asked, 'Is Raffi here?' He looked at his watch. After ten. His son knew he was supposed to be home by ten on school nights.

'Not unless he came in while we were eating,' she answered.

'No, he didn't,' Brunetti answered, sure of the answer, unsure of how he knew.

It was late, they'd had a bottle of wine, glorious

figs, and perfect port. Neither of them wanted to talk about their son. He'd still be there and still be theirs in the morning.

'Should I put those in the sink for you?' he asked, meaning the dishes but not meaning the question.

'No. I'll do it. You go and tell Chiara to go to bed.' The dishes would have been less trouble.

'Fire out?' he asked when he walked into the living room.

She didn't hear him. She was hundreds of miles and years away from him. She sat slouched low in the chair, her legs stretched out before her. On the arm of the chair were two apple cores, a packet of biscuits on the floor beside her.

'Chiara,' he said, then louder, 'Chiara.'

She glanced up from the page, not seeing him for a moment, then registering that it was her father. She looked immediately down at the page, forgetting him.

'Chiara, it's time to go to bed.'

She turned a page.

'Chiara, did you hear me? It's time to go to bed.'

Still reading, she pushed herself up from the chair with one hand. At the bottom of a page, she paused long enough to look up from the book and give him a kiss, then she was gone, finger in the page. He lacked the courage to tell her to leave the book behind. Well, if he got up in the night, he could turn her light off.

Paola came into the living room. She bent and turned off the light beside the chair, picked up the apple cores and the packet of biscuits, and went

6

Brunetti got to the Questura at eight the next morning, stopping to get the papers on the way. The murder had made the eleventh page of the *Corriere*, which gave it only two paragraphs, had not made it into *La Repubblica*, understandable enough on a day that was the anniversary of one of the bloodier terrorist bombings of the Sixties, but had made it to the front page of the second section of *Il Gazzettino*, just to the left of a story, this one with a photo, about three young men who had died when their car slammed into a tree on the state highway between Dolo and Mestre.

The article said that the young man, whose name was given as Michele Fooster, was the apparent victim of a robbery. Drugs were suspected, though the article, in the manner of the *Gazzettino*, didn't bother to specify what they were suspected of. Brunetti sometimes reflected that it was a good thing for Italy that a responsible Press was not one of the requirements for entry into the Common Market.

Inside the main door of the Questura, the usual human line snaked its way out of the Ufficio Stranieri, crowded with badly dressed and poorly shod immigrants from Northern Africa and newly freed Eastern Europe. Brunetti could never see that line without a surge of historical irony: three generations of his own family had fled Italy, seeking their fortunes in places as far apart as Australia and Argentina. And now, in a Europe transformed by recent events, Italy had become the El Dorado of new waves of still poorer, still darker immigrants. Many of his friends spoke of these people with contempt, disgust, even anger, but Brunetti could never see them without super-imposing upon them the fantasy image of his own ancestors, standing in similar lines, them-selves badly dressed, ill-shod, making a hash of the language. And, like these poor devils here, willing to clean the mess and raise the children of anyone who would pay them.

He went up the steps to his fourth-floor office, saying good-morning to one or two people, nodding to others. When he reached the office, he checked to see if there were any new papers on his desk. Nothing had arrived yet, so he considered himself free to do with the day what-ever he saw fit. And that was to reach for his phone and ask to be connected with the Carabinieri station at the American base in Vicenza.

This number proved considerably easier to find and, within minutes, he was speaking to Maggiore Ambrogiani, who told Brunetti that he had been put in charge of the Italian investigation into Foster's murder.

'Italian?' Brunetti asked.

'Well, Italian as different from the investigation that the Americans will conduct themselves.'

'Does that mean there are going to be problems of jurisdiction?' Brunetti asked.

'No, I don't think so,' the Maggiore answered. 'You people in Venice, the civil police, are in charge of the investigation there. But you'll need the permission or help of the Americans for anything you might want to do out here.'

'In Vicenza?'

Ambrogiani laughed. 'No, I don't want to give that impression. Only here, on the base. So long as you are in Vicenza, the city, then we're in charge, the Carabinieri. But once you come onto this base, they take over, and it's the Americans who will help you.'

'You make it sound as if you have some doubts about that, Maggiore,' Brunetti said.

'No, no doubts. Not at all.'

'Then I've misinterpreted your tone.' But he thought that he hadn't, not at all. 'I'd like to come out there and speak to the people who knew him, worked with him.'

'They're Americans, most of them,' Ambrogiani said, leaving it to Brunetti to infer the possibilities of difficulty with language.

'My English is all right.'

'Then you should have no trouble talking to them.'

'When would it be possible for me to come there?'

'This morning? This afternoon? Whenever you please, Commissario.'

From his bottom drawer, Brunetti grabbed a railway timetable and flipped through it, looking for the Venice–Milan line. There was a train leaving in an hour. 'I can take the nine-twenty-five.'

'Fine. I'll send a car to meet you.'

'Thank you, Maggiore.'

'A pleasure, Commissario. A pleasure. I look forward to meeting you.'

They exchanged courtesies, and Brunetti replaced the receiver. The first thing he did was go across to the cupboard that stood against the far wall. He opened it and began to hunt through the things piled and tossed on the bottom: a pair of boots, three light bulbs in separate boxes, an extension cord, a few old magazines, and a brown leather briefcase. He pulled out the briefcase and dusted it off with his hand. Carrying it back to his desk, he put the newspapers inside, then added a few files he had still to read. From his front drawer, he took a two-week-old copy of *Panorama* and threw it in.

The ride was a familiar one, along the route to Milan, through a checkered pattern of cornfields burned to painful darkness by the summer drought. He sat on the right side of the train to avoid the slanting sun that still burned through, even though it was September and the ferocity of the summer was gone. At Padova, the second stop, scores of university students crowded off the train, carrying their new text books as though they were magic talismans that would carry them to a sure, better future. He remembered that feeling, that yearly renewal of optimism that used to come to him while he was at the university, as if each year's virgin notebooks carried with them the promise of a better year, a brighter destiny.

At Vicenza, he got down from the train and looked along the platform for someone in uniform. Seeing no one, he went down the steps, through the tunnel that ran under the tracks, and up into the station. In front of it he saw the dark blue sedan marked 'Carabinieri', parked in an arrogant, unnecessary diagonal in front of the station, the driver engaged equally in a cigarette and the pink pages of the *Gazzettino dello Sport*.

Brunetti tapped on the back window. The driver turned his head languidly, stabbed out his cigarette, and reached back to unlock the door. As he opened the door, Brunetti thought about how different things were here in the North. In Southern Italy, any Carabiniere who heard an unexpected noise from the back of his car would immediately be on the floor of the car or crouched on the pavement beside it, gun in hand, perhaps already firing at the source of the noise. But here, in sleepy Vicenza, all he did was reach, without question, to allow the stranger into his car.

'Inspector Bonnini?' the driver asked.

'Commissario Brunetti.'

'From Venice?'

'Yes.'

'Good morning. I'll take you to the base.'

'Is it far?'

'Five minutes.' Saying this, the driver set the paper on the seat beside him, the latest triumph of Schilacci displayed for a soccer-loving public, and put the car in gear. Bothering to look neither right nor left, he tore out of the station car park, cutting directly into the traffic that flowed past. He skirted the city, cutting back towards the east, in the direction from which Brunetti had come.

Brunetti had not been to Vicenza for at least a decade, but he remembered it as one of the loveliest cities in Italy, its centre filled with narrow, twisting streets along which crowded Renaissance and Baroque *palazzi*, jumbled together with no regard for symmetry, chronology, or plan. Instead of this, they swung past an immense concrete football stadium, over a high railway bridge, then along one of the new *viales* that had sprung up all over mainland Italy in acknowledgement of the final triumph of the automobile.

Without signalling, the driver suddenly cut to the left and started down a narrow road lined on the right by a wire-topped cement wall. Behind it, Brunetti saw an immense dish-shaped communications antenna. The car swept in a broad curve to the right, and in front of them Brunetti saw an open gate, beside which stood a number of armed guards. There were two uniformed Carabinieri, machine guns dangling casually at their sides, and an American soldier in combat fatigues. The driver slowed, gave a desultory wave to the machine guns, which waved and dipped in acknowledgement, then followed the car onto the base with their hollow-tipped barrels. The American, Brunetti observed, followed them with his eyes but made no attempt to stop them. A quick right turn, another, and they drew up in front of a low cement building. 'This is our headquarters,' the driver said. 'Maggiore Ambrogiani's office is the fourth one on the right.'

Brunetti thanked him and went into the low building. The floor appeared to be cement, the walls lined with bulletin boards upon which notices in both English and Italian were posted. On his left, he saw a sign for 'MP Station'. A bit further on, he saw a door with the name 'Ambrogiani' printed on a card beside it. No title, just the name. He knocked, waited for the shouted *'Avanti'*, and went in. Desk, two windows, a plant in desperate need of water, a calendar, and behind the desk, a bull of a man whose neck was in open revolt against the tight collar of his uniform shirt. His broad shoulders pushed against the fabric of his uniform jacket; even his wrists seemed too tightly enclosed by the sleeves. On his shoulders, Brunetti saw the squat tower and single star of a major. He rose when Brunetti walked in, glanced at the watch that grabbed at his wrist, and said, 'Commissario Brunetti?'

'Yes.'

The smile that filled the Carabiniere's face was almost angelic in its warmth and simplicity. My

God, the man had dimples! 'I'm glad you could come all the way from Venice about this.' He came around his desk, surprisingly graceful, and pulled a chair up in front. 'Here, please have a seat. Would you like some coffee? Please put your briefcase on the desk.' He waited for Brunetti to answer.

'Yes, coffee would be good.'

The Maggiore went to the door, opened it, and said to someone in the hall, 'Pino, bring us two coffees and a bottle of mineral water.'

He came back into the room and took his place behind his desk. 'I'm sorry we couldn't send a car all the way to Venice to get you, but it's difficult, these days, to get an authorization to move out of the province. I hope your trip was comfortable.'

It was necessary, Brunetti knew from long experience, to spend the proper amount of time on these things, to poke and prod about, to take the measure of the other person, and the only way to do this was with niceties and politeness.

'No trouble at all with the train. Right on time. Padova filled with university students.'

'My son's at the university there,' Ambrogiani volunteered.

'Really? What faculty?'

'Medicine,' Ambrogiani said and shook his head.

'Isn't it a good faculty?' Brunetti asked, honestly puzzled. He'd always been told that the University of Padova had the best medical school in the country.

'No, it's not that,' the Maggiore answered and

smiled. 'I'm not pleased with his choice of medicine as a career.'

'What?' Brunetti asked. This was the Italian dream, a policeman with a son in medical school. 'Why?'

'I wanted him to be a painter.' He shook his head again, sadly. 'But, instead, he wants to be a doctor.'

'A painter?'

'Yes,' Ambrogiani answered. Then, with a dimpled smile, he added, 'And not of houses.' He gestured behind him, and Brunetti saw that the walls were patterned with small paintings, almost all seascapes, some of them of ruined castles, all of them done in a delicate style that imitated the eighteenth-century Neapolitan school.

'Your son's?'

'No,' Ambrogiani said, 'that one over there.' He pointed to the left of the door, where Brunetti saw a portrait of an old woman staring boldly at the viewer, a half-peeled apple held between her hands. It lacked the delicacy of the others, though it was good in a pretty, conventional sense.

If the others had been by the son, Brunetti would have understood the man's regret that he had chosen to study medicine. As it was, the boy had clearly made the right choice. 'It's very good,' he lied. 'And the others?'

'Oh, I did them. But years ago, when I was a student. First, the dimples, and now these soft, delicate paintings. Perhaps this American base was to be a place of surprises.

There came a quiet knock at the door, which

opened before Ambrogiani could reply. A uniformed corporal came into the room, carrying a tray
with two coffees, glasses, and a bottle of mineral
water. He set the tray on Ambrogiani's desk and
left.

'It's still hot like summer,' Ambrogiani said.
'Better to drink a lot of water.'

He leaned forward, handed Brunetti his coffee,
then took his own. When they had drunk the
coffee and each had a glass of water in his hand,
Brunetti believed they could begin to talk. 'Is
anything known about this American, Sergeant
Foster?'

Ambrogiani poked a fat finger at a slim file that
sat at the side of his desk, apparently the file on the
dead American. 'Nothing. Not from us. The
Americans won't, of course, give us the file they
have on him. That is,' he quickly amended, 'if they
have a file on him.'

'Why not?'

'It's a long story,' Ambrogiani said, with a slight
hesitation that made it evident he wanted to be
prodded.

Ever-willing to oblige, Brunetti asked, 'Why?'

Ambrogiani shifted around in his chair, body
clearly too big for it. He poked at the file, sipped at
his water, set the glass down, poked again at the
file. 'The Americans have been here, you understand, since the war ended. They've been on this
base, and it's grown bigger and continues to grow
bigger. There are thousands of them, and their
families.' Brunetti wondered what the point of this
long introduction would be. 'Because they have

been here so long, and perhaps because there are so many of them, they tend to be, well, they tend to see this base as theirs, though the treaty makes it clear that this is still Italian territory. Still. Part of Italy.' He shifted around again.

'Is there trouble?' Brunetti asked. 'With them?'

'After a long pause, Ambrogiani answered, 'No. Not exactly trouble. You know how Americans are.'

Brunetti had heard that many times, about Germans, Slavs, the British. Everyone assumed that other groups 'were' a certain way, though no one ever seemed to agree just what the way was. He raised his chin in an inquisitive gesture, prompting the Maggiore to continue.

'It's not arrogance, not really. I don't think they have the confidence it takes for real arrogance, not the way the Germans do. It's more like a sense of ownership, as if all of this, all of Italy, were somehow theirs. As if, by believing they kept it safe, they thought it was theirs.'

'Do they really keep it safe?' Brunetti asked.

Ambrogiani laughed. 'I suppose they did, after the war. And perhaps during the Sixties. But I'm not sure that, with the way the world is now, a few thousand paratroopers in Northern Italy is going to make much of a difference.'

'Are these popular feelings?' Brunetti asked. 'I mean among the military, the Carabinieri?'

'Yes, I think they are. But you have to understand the way the Americans see things.'

To Brunetti, it was a revelation to hear the man speak like this. In a country where most public institutions were no longer worthy of respect, only the Carabinieri had managed to save themselves and were still generally believed to be above corruption. This no sooner granted, than popular opinion had to compromise it and had transformed these same Carabinieri into the butt of popular myth, the classic buffoons who never understood anything and whose legendary stupidity provided glee to the entire nation. Yet here was one of them, trying to explain the other person's point of view. And apparently understanding it. Remarkable.

'What do we have as a military here in Italy?' Ambrogiani asked, his question clearly rhetorical. 'We're all volunteers, the Carabinieri. But the Army – they've all been drafted, except for the few who choose it as a career. They're kids, eighteen, nineteen, and they no more want to be soldiers than they want to . . .' Here he paused and searched for a simile that would do justice. 'Than they want to do the dishes and make their own beds, which is what they have to do, probably for the first time in their lives, while they're in the service. It's a year and a half lost, thrown away, when they could be working or studying. They go through a brutal, stupid training, and they spend a brutal, stupid year, dressed in shabby uniforms and not getting paid enough to keep themselves in cigarettes.' Brunetti knew all this. He'd done his eighteen months.

Ambrogiani was quick to sense Brunetti's waning interest. 'I say this because it explains how the Americans see us here. Their boys, and girls, I suppose, all volunteer. It's a career for them. They like it. They get paid for it, paid enough to live. And many of them take pride in it. And here, what do they see? Boys who would rather be playing soccer or going to the cinema, but who have to do work they despise instead, and who therefore do it badly. So they assume that we're all lazy.'

'And so?' Brunetti asked, cutting him short.

'And so,' Ambrogiani repeated, 'they don't understand us and therefore think badly of us for reasons that we can't understand.'

'You ought to be able to understand them. You're a military man,' Brunetti said.

Ambrogiani shrugged, as if to suggest that, first and foremost, he was an Italian.

'Is it unusual, that they wouldn't show you a file if they had one?'

'No. They tend not to help us much in things like this.'

'I'm not sure what you mean by "things like this", Maggiore.'

'Crimes that they get involved in away from the base.'

Certainly this could be said to apply to the young man lying dead in Venice, but Brunetti found the wording strange. 'Are they frequent?'

'No, not really. A few years ago, some Americans were involved in a murder. An African. They beat him to death with wooden boards. They were drunk. The African danced with a white woman.'

'Protecting their woman?' Brunetti asked, making no attempt to disguise his sarcasm.

'No,' Ambrogiani said. 'They were black. The men who killed him were black.'

'What happened to them?'

'Two of them got twelve years. One of them was found innocent and released.'

'Who tried them, them or us?' Brunetti asked.

'Luckily for them, we did.'

'Why luckily?'

'Because they were tried in a civil court. The sentences are much lighter. And the charge was manslaughter. He provoked them, beat on their car and shouted at them. So the judges ruled that they had been responding to a threat.'

'How many of them were there?'

'Three soldiers and a civilian.'

'Some threat,' Brunetti said.

'The judges ruled that it was. And took it into consideration. The Americans would have sent them away for twenty, thirty years. Military justice is nothing to joke with. Besides, they were black.'

'Does that still matter?'

A shrug. A raised eyebrow. Another shrug. 'The Americans will tell you it doesn't.' Ambrogiani took another sip of water. 'How long will you be here?'

'Today. Tomorrow. Are there other things like this?'

'Occasionally. Usually they handle crime on the base, handle it themselves, unless it gets too big or it breaks an Italian law. Then we get a part of it.'

'Like the principal?' Brunetti asked, remembering a case that had made national headlines a few years ago, something about the principal of their grammar school being accused and convicted of child abuse, the details of which were very cloudy in his memory.

'Yes, like him. But usually they handle things themselves.'

'Not this time,' Brunetti said simply.

'No, not this time. Since he was killed in Venice, he's yours, it's all yours. But they'll want to keep their hand in.'

'Why?'

'Public relations,' Ambrogiani said, using the English words. 'And things are changing. They probably suspect they aren't going to be here much longer, not here, and not anywhere in Europe, so they don't want anything to happen that might make their stay even shorter. They don't want any bad publicity.'

'It looks like a mugging,' Brunetti said.

Ambrogiani gave Brunetti a long, level stare. 'When was the last time someone was killed in a mugging in Venice?'

If Ambrogiani could ask the question like that, he knew the answer.

'Honour?' Brunetti suggested as a motive.

Ambrogiani smiled again. 'If you kill someone for honour, you don't do it a hundred kilometres from home. You do it in the bedroom, or the bar, but you don't go to Venice to do it. If it had happened here, it could have been sex or money. But it didn't happen here, so it seems that the reason has to be something else.'

7

The Maggiore pushed the slim file towards Brunetti with the tip of his blunt finger and poured himself another glass of mineral water. 'Here's what they gave us. There's a translation if you need it.'

Brunetti shook his head and opened the file. On the front cover, in red letters, was printed, 'Foster, Michael, b. 09/28/64, SSN 651 34 1054'. He opened it and saw, clipped to the inside of the front cover, a Xerox copy of a photograph. The dead man was unrecognizable. These sharp contours of black and white had nothing to do with the yellowing face of death that Brunetti had seen on the bank of the canal yesterday. Inside the folder were two type-written pages stating that Sergeant Foster worked for the Office of Public Health, that he had once been given a ticket for going through a STOP sign on the base, that he had been promoted to the rank of Sergeant one year ago, and that his family lived in Biddeford Pool, Maine.

The second page contained the summary of an interview conducted with an Italian civilian who worked in the Office of Public Health and who attested that Foster got on well with his colleagues, worked very hard at his job, and was polite and friendly with the Italian civilians who worked in the office.

'Not very much, is there?' Brunetti asked, closing the file and pushing it back towards the Maggiore. 'The perfect soldier. Hardworking. Obedient. Friendly.'

'But someone put a knife in his ribs.'

Brunetti remembered Doctor Peters and asked, 'No woman?'

'Not that we know of,' Ambrogiani answered. 'But that doesn't mean there wasn't. He was young, spoke passable Italian. So it's possible.' Ambrogiani paused for a moment and added, 'Unless he used what's for sale in front of the train station.'

'Is that where they are?'

Ambrogiani nodded. 'What about Venice?'

Brunetti shook his head. 'Not since the government closed the brothels. There are a few, but they work the hotels and don't cause us any trouble.'

'Here we have them in front of the station, but I think times are bad for some of them. There are too many women today who are willing to give it away,' Ambrogiani volunteered, then added, 'for love.'

Brunetti's daughter had just turned thirteen, so

he didn't want to think about what young women would give away for love. 'Can I talk to the Americans?' he asked.

'Yes, I think so,' Ambrogiani answered then reached for the phone. 'We'll tell them you're the Chief of Police for Venice. They'll like that rank, so they'll talk to you.' He dialled a number with easy familiarity and, while he waited for a response, pulled the file back towards him. Rather fussily, he lined up the few papers in the file and placed it squarely in front of him.

He spoke into the telephone in heavily-accented, but correct, English. 'Good afternoon, Tiffany. This is Major Ambrogiani. Is the Major there? What? Yes, I'll wait.' He put his hand over the mouthpiece and held the phone away from his ear. 'He's in conference. Americans seem to live in conference.'

'Could it be . . .' Brunetti began but stopped when Ambrogiani pulled his hand away.

'Yes, thank you. Good morning, Major Butterworth.' The name had been in the file, but when Ambrogiani said it, it sounded like 'Budderword'.

'Yes, Major. I have the Chief of the Venice police here with me now. Yes, we brought him out by helicopter for the day.' A long pause followed. 'No, he can spare us only today.' He looked down at his watch. 'In twenty minutes? Yes, he'll be there. No, I'm sorry, but I can't, Major. I have to be in conference. Yes, thank you.' He set the phone down, placed his pencil in a neat diagonal across the cover of the file, and said, 'He'll see you in twenty minutes.'

'And your conference?' Brunetti asked.

Ambrogiani dismissed the idea with a wave of the hand. 'It'll just be a waste of time. If they do know anything, they won't tell you, and if they don't know anything, then they can't. So there's no reason I should waste my time by going.' Changing the topic, he asked, 'How's your English?'

'All right.'

'Good, that'll make it much easier.'

'Who is he, this major?'

Ambrogiani repeated the name, again gliding over all of the sharper consonants. 'He's their liaison officer. Or, as they say, he "liaises"' – he used the English word – 'between them and us.' Both grinned at the ease with which English allowed its speakers to turn a noun into a verb, a familiarity which Italian would certainly not permit.

'Of what does this "liaising" consist?'

'Oh, if we have problems, he comes to us, or he goes the other way, if they have problems.'

'What sort of problems?'

'If anyone tries to get in at the gate without the proper identification. Or if we break their traffic rules. Or if they ask a Carabiniere why he's buying ten kilos of beef at their supermarket. Things like that.'

'Supermarket?' Brunetti asked with real surprise.

'Yes, supermarket. And bowling alley' – he used the English word – 'and cinema, and even a Burger King' – the name was said without a trace of an accent.

98

Fascinated, Brunetti repeated the words 'Burger King' with the same tone with which a child might say 'pony' if promised one.

Hearing him, Ambrogiani laughed. 'It's remarkable, isn't it? There's a whole little world here, one that has nothing to do with Italy.' He gestured out of his window. 'Out there lies America, Commissario. It's what we're all going to become, I think.' After a short pause, he repeated, 'America.'

That was precisely what awaited Brunetti a quarter of an hour later, when he opened the doors of the NATO command headquarters and walked up the three steps to the lobby. The walls held posters of unnamed cities which, because of the height and homogeneity of their skyscrapers, had to be American. That nation was loudly proclaimed, too, in the many signs which forbade smoking and in the notices which covered the bulletin boards along the walls. The marble floor was the only Italianate touch. As he had been directed, Brunetti climbed the steps in front of him, turned right at the top, and went into the second office on the left. The room into which he walked was divided by head-high partitions, and the walls, like those on the floor below, were covered with bulletin boards and printed notices. Backed up against one of them were two armchairs covered in what appeared to be thick grey plastic. At a desk just inside the door, to the right, sat a young woman who could only be American. She had blonde hair which was cut off in a short fringe above her blue eyes but hung down almost to her waist at the back. A rash of freckles ran across her nose, and her teeth had that perfection common to most Americans and to the wealthiest Italians. She turned to him with a bright smile; her mouth turned up at the corners, but her eyes remained curiously expressionless and flat.

'Good morning,' he said, smiling back. 'My name's Brunetti. I think the Major is expecting me.'

She came out from behind the desk, revealing a body as perfect as her teeth, and walked through an opening in the partition, though she could just as easily have phoned or called over the top. From the other side of the partition, he heard her voice answered by a deeper one. After a few seconds, she appeared at the opening and signalled to Brunetti, 'In here, please, sir.'

Behind the desk sat a blond young man who appeared to be barely into his twenties. Brunetti looked at him and as quickly away, for the man seemed to glow, glisten. When he looked back, Brunetti saw that it was not radiance but only youth, health, and someone else to care for his uniforms.

'Chief Brunetti?' he said and rose to his feet behind his desk. To Brunetti, he looked like he had just come from a shower or bath: his skin was taut, shining, as though he had set down his razor in order to take Brunetti's hand. While they shook hands, Brunetti noticed his eyes, a clear, translucent blue, the colour the *laguna* had been twenty years ago.

'I'm very glad you could come out from Venice to speak to us, Chief Brunetti, or is it Questore?'

'Vice-Questore,' Brunetti said, giving himself a

promotion in the hopes that it would assure him greater access to information. He noticed that Major Butterworth's desk held In and Out boxes; the In was empty, the Out full.

'Please have a seat,' Butterworth said and waited for Brunetti to sit before taking his own seat. The American pulled a file from his front drawer, this one just minimally thicker than the one Ambrogiani had. 'You're here about Sergeant Foster, aren't you?'

'Yes.'

'What is it you'd like to know?'

'I'd like to know who killed him,' Brunetti said impassively.

Butterworth hesitated a moment, not knowing how to take the remark, then decided to treat it as a joke. 'Yes,' he said, with a small laugh that barely passed his lips, 'we'd all like to know that. But I'm not sure we have any information that might help us find out who it was.'

'What information do you have?'

He slid the file towards Brunetti. Even though he knew it would contain the same material he had just seen, Brunetti opened it and read through the pages again. This file contained a different photograph from the one he had seen in the other. For the first time, though he had seen his dead face and naked body, Brunetti got a clear idea of what the young man looked like. More handsome in this photo, Foster here had a short moustache that he had shaved off sometime before he was killed.

'When was this photo taken?'

'Probably when he entered the service.'

'How long ago was that?'

'Seven years.'

'How long has he been here in Italy?'

'Four years. In fact, he just re-upped in order to stay here.'

'Excuse me,' Brunetti said.

'Re-enlisted. For another three years.'

'And he would have remained here?'

'Yes.'

Remembering something he had read in the file, Brunetti asked, 'How did he learn Italian?'

'I beg your pardon,' Butterworth said.

'If he had a full time job here, that wouldn't leave him a lot of time to learn a new language,' Brunetti explained.

'*Tanti di noi parliamo Italiano,*' Butterworth answered in heavily accented but understandable Italian.

'Yes, of course,' Brunetti said and smiled, as he guessed he was expected to do, at the Major's ability to speak Italian. 'Did he live here? There are barracks here, aren't there?'

'Yes, there are,' Butterworth answered. 'But Sergeant Foster had his own apartment in Vicenza.'

Brunetti knew the apartment would have been searched, so he didn't bother to ask if it had been. 'Did you find anything?'

'No.'

'Would it be possible for me to have a look at it?'

'I'm not sure that's necessary,' Butterworth said quickly.

'I'm not sure it's necessary, either,' Brunetti said

with a small smile. 'But I'd like to see where he lived.'

'It's not regular procedure, for you to see it.'

'I didn't realize there was a regular procedure here,' Brunetti said. He knew that either the Carabinieri or the Vicenza police could easily authorize his inspection of the apartment, but he wanted, at least at this point of the investigation, to remain as agreeable as possible with all of the authorities concerned.

'I suppose it could be arranged,' Butterworth conceded. 'When would you like to do it?'

'There's no hurry. This afternoon. Tomorrow.'

'I didn't realize you were planning to return tomorrow, Vice-Questore.'

'Only if I don't finish everything today, Major.'

'What else was it you wanted to do?'

'I'd like to talk to some of the people who knew him, who worked with him.' Brunetti had noticed, among the papers in the file, that the dead man had attended university classes at the base. Like the Romans, these new empire builders carried their schools with them. 'Perhaps to people he went to university with.'

'I suppose something can be arranged, though I admit I don't see the reason for it. We'll handle this end of the investigation.' He paused, as if waiting for Brunetti to challenge him. When Brunetti said nothing, Butterworth asked, 'When would you prefer to see his apartment?'

Brunetti glanced down at his watch. It was almost noon. 'Perhaps sometime this afternoon. If you could tell me where the apartment is, then I could have my driver take me there on my way back to the railway station?'

'Would you like me to go along with you, Vice-Questore?'

'That's very kind of you, Major, but I don't think that will be necessary. If you'd just give me the address.'

Major Butterworth pulled a pad towards him and, without having to open the file to find it, wrote an address and handed it to Brunetti. 'It's not far from here. I'm sure your driver won't have any trouble finding it.'

'Thank you, Major,' Brunetti said and stood. 'Would you have any objection if I spent some time here on the base?'

'Post,' Butterworth responded immediately. 'This is a post. The Air Force has bases. We have posts in the Army.'

'Ah, I see. In Italian, they're both bases. Would it be all right for me to remain here for a while?'

After no more than a moment's hesitation, Butterworth said, 'I don't see any problem with that.'

'And the apartment, Major? How will I get in?'

Major Butterworth got to his feet and started around his desk. 'We've got two men there. I'll call them and let them know you're coming.'

'Thank you, Major,' Brunetti said, standing and extending his hand.

'It's nothing. Glad to be of help in this.' Butterworth's grip was strong, forceful. But, Brunetti noted as they shook hands, the American hadn't asked to be told what he might discover about the dead man.

The blonde was no longer at her desk in the outer office. Her computer screen glimmered to one side of her desk, as blank as her expression had been.

'Where to, sir?' asked the driver when Brunetti got back into the car.

Brunetti gave him the sheet of paper with Foster's address on it. 'Do you know where that is?'

'Borgo Casale? Yes, sir. It's just behind the soccer stadium.'

'Is that the way we came?'

'Yes, sir. We passed right alongside it on the way. Would you like to go there now?'

'No, not yet. I'd like to get something to eat first.'

'Never been here before, sir?'

'No, I haven't. Have you been here long?'

'Six years. But I'm lucky to have been posted here. My family's from Schio,' he explained, naming a town about half an hour away.

'It's very strange, isn't it?' Brunetti asked, waving a hand at the buildings around them.

The driver nodded.

'What else is here, except for the offices? Maggiore Ambrogiani mentioned a supermarket.'

'And a cinema and a swimming-pool, a library, schools. It's a whole city. They even have their own hospital.'

'How many Americans are here?' Brunetti asked.

'I'm not sure. About five thousand, but that would be with wives and children, I think.'

'Do you like them?' Brunetti asked.

The driver shrugged. 'What's not to like? They're friendly.' It hardly sounded like an enthusiastic recommendation. Changing the subject, the driver asked, 'What about lunch, sir? Would you like to eat here or off-base?'

'What do you suggest?'

'The Italian *mensa* is the best place. You can get food there. Hearing this, Brunetti wondered what the Americans served in their own dining-halls. Rivets? 'But it's closed today. Strike.' Well, there was proof that it was really Italian, even on an American military installation.

'Is there anywhere else?'

Without answering, the driver slipped the car into gear and pulled away from the curb. Suddenly, he swung around in a sharp U-turn and headed back towards the main road that bisected the post. He made a series of turns around buildings and behind cars, none of which made any sense to Brunetti, and soon pulled up in front of yet another low cement building.

Brunetti looked out of the back window of the car and saw that they were stopped diagonally in front of the right angle made by two shop fronts. Above one glass door, he saw 'Food Mall'. Wasn't that what lions did to their prey? The other sign read 'Baskin Robbins'. Not at all optimistic, Brunetti asked, 'Coffee?'

The driver nodded at the second door, clearly eager for Brunetti to get out. When he did, the driver leaned back across the seat and said, 'I'll be back in ten minutes,' then shut the door and pulled away sharply, leaving Brunetti on the curb, feeling strangely abandoned and alien. To the right of the second door he could now see a sign which read, 'Capucino Bar', the sign-maker apparently an American.

Inside, he asked the woman behind the counter for a coffee then, knowing there would be no chance of lunch, asked for a brioche. It looked like pastry, felt like pastry, but tasted like cardboard. He placed three thousand-lire bills on the counter. The woman looked at the notes, looked up at him, took them, then placed on the counter the same coins he had found in the pockets of the dead man. For an instant, Brunetti wondered if she was attempting to give him some private signal, but a closer look at her face showed him that all she was doing was giving him the proper change.

He left the place and went to stand outside, content to get a sense of the post while waiting for his driver to return. He sat on a bench in front of the shops and watched the people walking past.

A few glanced at him as he sat there, dressed in suit and tie and clearly out of place among them. Many of the people who walked past him, men and women alike, wore uniform. Most of the others wore shorts and tennis shoes, and many of the women, too often those who shouldn't have, wore halter tops. They appeared to be dressed either for war or for the beach. Most of the men were fit and powerful; many of the women were enormously, terrifyingly fat.

Cars drove by slowly, their drivers searching for parking spaces: big cars, Japanese cars, cars with that same AFI number plate. Most had the windows raised, while from the air-conditioned interiors blared rock music in varying degrees of loudness.

They strolled by, amiable and friendly, greeting one another and exchanging pleasant words, thoroughly at home in their little American village here in Italy.

Ten minutes later, the driver pulled up in front of him. Brunetti got into the back seat. 'Would you like to go to that address now, sir?' the driver asked.

'Yes,' Brunetti said, a little tired of America.

Driving more quickly than the other cars on the base, they headed towards the front gate and passed through it. Outside, they turned right and headed back towards the city, again passing over the railway bridge. At the bottom, they turned left, then right, and pulled up in front of a five-storey building set back a few metres from the street. Parked opposite the gate they saw a dark-green Jeep, two soldiers in American uniform sitting in the front seat. Brunetti approached them. One of them climbed down from the Jeep.

'I'm Commissario Brunetti, from Venice,' he said, resuming his real rank, then added, 'Major Butterworth sent me out to take a look at Foster's apartment.' Perhaps not the truth, but certainly related to it.

The soldier sketched out something that might have been a salute, reached into his pocket, and handed Brunetti a set of keys. 'The red one is the front door, sir,' the soldier said. 'Apartment 3B, on the third floor. Elevator to your right as you go in.'

Inside this building, he took the elevator, feeling hemmed in and uncomfortable in its closeness. The door to 3B stood directly opposite the elevator and opened easily with the key.

He pushed open the door and noticed the usual marble floors. Doors opened off a central corridor at the end of which another door stood ajar. The room on the right was a bathroom, the one on the left a small kitchen. Both were clean, the objects in them well-ordered. He noticed, however, that the kitchen held an enormous refrigerator and a large four-ring stove, beside which stood an equally outsized washing-machine, both of the electrical appliances plugged into a transformer that broke down the 220 Italian current to the 110 of America. Did they bring these appliances all the way from America with them? Little space was left in the kitchen for a small square table, at which only two chairs stood. The wall held the gas-burning heater which seemed to provide both hot water and heat for the radiators in the apartment.

The next doors opened into two bedrooms. One held a double bed and a large cupboard. The other had been turned into a study and held a desk with a computer keyboard and screen attached to a printer. Shelves held books and some stereo equipment, under which was neatly lined a row of compact discs. He checked the books: most appeared to be textbooks, the rest books about travel and – could it be? – religion. He pulled down some of these and took a closer look. *The Christian Life in an Age of Doubt*, *Spiritual Transcendence*, and

Jesus: the Ideal Life. The author of the last was Revd Michael Foster. His father?

The music was, he thought, rock. Some of the names he recognized from having heard Raffaele and Chiara mention them; he doubted that he would recognize the music.

He switched on the CD player and pushed the 'Eject' button on the control panel. Like a patient showing his tongue to a doctor, it opened and slid out the playing panel. Empty. He closed the panel and switched off the machine. He switched on the amplifier and tape deck. Panel lights glowed, showing they both worked. He turned them off. He switched the computer on, watched the letters appear on the screen, then switched it off.

The clothes in the closet were no more forthcoming. He found three complete uniforms, jackets still in the plastic laundry bags, each carefully lined up beside a pair of dark-green trousers. The rack also held a few pairs of jeans, neatly folded over hangers, three or four shirts, and a dark blue suit made out of some synthetic material. Almost absent-mindedly, Brunetti checked the pockets of the jacket and all the trousers, but there was nothing; no loose change, no papers, no comb. Either Sergeant Foster was a very neat young man, or the Americans had been here before him.

He went back into the bathroom, removed the lid from the top of the toilet, glanced into the empty tank, then replaced the lid. He opened the door to the mirror-fronted medicine chest, opened a bottle or two.

In the kitchen, he opened the top section of the outsized refrigerator. Ice. Nothing more. Below, a few apples, an open bottle of white wine, and some ageing cheese in a plastic wrapper. The oven held only three empty pans; the washing-machine was empty. He stood with his back against the worktop and looked slowly around the room. From the top drawer under the worktop he took a knife, then pulled one of the wooden chairs from the table and placed it under the water heater. He climbed up onto the chair and used the knife to loosen the screws that held the front panel to the heater. As they came loose, he dropped the screws into his jacket pocket. When he pulled the last one out, he slipped the knife into his pocket and shifted the panel from side to side until it came loose in his hands. He set it down on the chair, leaning it against his leg.

Two plastic bags were taped to the inside of the wall of the water heater. They contained fine white powder, about a kilo of it, he judged. He took his handkerchief from his pocket and, wrapping his hand in it, pulled first one bag loose, then the other. Just to be sure of what he already knew, he pulled open the ziplock top of one of the bags, wet the tip of his index finger and tapped it onto the powder. When he put his finger to his tongue, he tasted the slightly metallic, unmistakable tang of cocaine.

He leaned down and set the two bags on the counter. Then he lifted the front panel back into place, careful to line it up accurately with the holes in the body of the heater. Slowly, he fitted in the four screws and turned them back into place. Carefully, he turned the grooves in the top screws to perfect horizontals, the two below into equally precise verticals.

He glanced at his watch. He had been inside the apartment fifteen minutes. The Americans had had a day and a half to go through the apartment; the Italian police had had just as much time. Yet Brunetti had found the two packages in less than quarter of an hour.

He opened the door to one of the wall cabinets and saw only three or four dinner plates. He looked under the sink and found what he wanted, two plastic bags. Still covering his hand with his handkerchief, he placed a bag of cocaine inside each of the larger plastic bags and placed them in the two inner pockets of his jacket. He wiped the knife clean on the sleeve of his jacket and replaced it in the drawer, then used his handkerchief to wipe the surface of the heater clean of all prints.

He left the apartment, locking the door behind him. Outside, he approached the American soldiers in the Jeep, smiling comfortably at them. 'Thank you,' he said and handed the key back to the man who had given it to him.

'Well?' the soldier asked.

'Nothing. I just wanted to see how he lived.' If the soldier was surprised by Brunetti's answer, he gave no indication of it.

Brunetti walked back to his car, got in, and told the driver to take him to the train station. He caught the three-fifteen Intercity train from Milan and prepared to spend the trip back to Venice as he had spent the trip out, sitting and looking out of the window of the train while thinking about why a young American soldier would have been murdered. But now he had a new thought to add to that one: why would drugs have been planted in his apartment after his death? And who would have planted them?

8

As his train pulled out of the Vicenza train station, Brunetti walked towards the front, searching for an empty compartment in the first-class section. The two plastic packages weighed down his inner pockets, and he hunched forward in an attempt to disguise their bulk. Finally, in the first car, he found an empty compartment and sat near the window, then got up to slide the door closed. He put his briefcase on the seat beside him and debated whether to transfer the packages or not. As he sat debating, the door to the compartment was abruptly pulled open by a man in uniform. For a hallucinogenic instant, Brunetti saw his career in ruins, himself in jail, but then the man asked for his ticket, and Brunetti was saved.

When the conductor left, Brunetti concentrated

on keeping himself from reaching inside his jacket or from checking with his elbows to see that the two packages were still in place. He seldom had to deal with drugs in his work, but he knew enough to realize that he was carrying at least a few hundred million lire in each pocket: a new apartment in one and early retirement in the other. The idea had little attraction for him. He would gladly have traded both packages to know who had put them where he found them. Though he had no idea of who, the reason why was pretty clear: what better motive for murder than drugs and drug dealing, and what better proof of drug dealing than the presence of a kilo of cocaine hidden in a man's home? And who better to find it than the policeman from Venice, who, if only because of geography, could not possibly have had any involvement with the crime or the dead man? And what could that young soldier have been involved in that a kilo of cocaine would be used to call attention away from it?

At Padova, an elderly woman came into the compartment and sat, reading a magazine, until Mestre station, where she got out, without even having spoken to or looked at Brunetti. When the train pulled into Venice station, Brunetti picked up his briefcase and left the train, checking to see if any of the people who had got onto the train in Vicenza got down from the train with him. In front of the station, he walked to the right, towards the number one boat, got as far as the landing dock, then stopped and looked back at the clock that stood on the other side of the station. Abruptly, he changed direction and walked towards the other side of the *piazza* in front of the station, to the dock where the number two boat stopped. No one followed him.

A few minutes later, the boat came from the right, and he was the only person to get on. At four-thirty, there were few people on the boat. He walked down the steps and through the rear cabin, out to the aft deck, where he was alone. The boat pulled away from the embankment and under the Bridge of the Scalzi, up the Grand Canal towards the Rialto and its final stop.

Through the glass doors, Brunetti saw that the four people sitting in the inner cabin were all busy reading their newspapers. He set his briefcase on the chair beside him, propped the lid open, and reached into his inner pocket, pulling out one of the envelopes. Carefully, touching only its corners, he peeled it open. Turning sideways, the better to examine the façade of the Natural History Museum, he slid his hand under the railing and emptied the white powder into the waters of the canal. He slipped the empty bag into his briefcase and repeated the process with the second. During the golden age of the Most Serene Republic, the Doge used to perform an elaborate yearly ceremony, tossing a gold ring into the waters of the Grand Canal to solemnize the wedding of the city to the waters that gave it life, wealth, and power. But never, Brunetti thought, had such great wealth been deliberately offered to any waters.

From the Rialto, he walked back to the Questura and went directly to the lab. Bocchese was there, sharpening a pair of scissors at one of the many machines that only he seemed able to operate. He turned the machine off when he saw Brunetti and set the scissors on the counter in front of him.

Brunetti put his briefcase beside the scissors, opened it, and pulled out, careful to touch them only at the corners, the two plastic bags. He set them beside the scissors. 'Could you see if the American's prints are on these?' he asked. Bocchese nodded. 'I'll come down and you can tell me, all right?' Brunetti said.

The technician nodded again. 'It's like that, huh?'

'Yes.'

'Would you like me to lose the bags after I get the prints off them?' Bocchese asked.

'What bags?'

Bocchese reached for the scissors. 'As soon as I finish this,' he said. He flipped a switch, and the wheel of the machine spun into life again. Brunetti's muttered thanks were drowned out by the high-pitched rasp of metal against metal as Bocchese went back to sharpening the scissors.

Deciding that it would be better to go and speak to Patta than be told to do so, Brunetti took the front steps and stopped outside his superior's door. He knocked, heard a noise, and opened the door. As he did so, he realized, belatedly, that the sound he had heard had not been an invitation to enter.

The scene was a blending of cartoon cliché and every bureaucrat's worst nightmare: in front of the window, the top two buttons of her blouse open, stood Anita, from the Ufficio Stranieri; a single step from her, and moving backward, stood a red-faced Vice-Questore Patta. Brunetti caught this in a glance and dropped his briefcase in an attempt to give Anita time to turn her back on the two men and button her blouse. As she did this, Brunetti knelt to retrieve the papers that had spilled from the briefcase, and Patta went to sit behind his desk. It took Anita as long to button her blouse as it did Brunetti to stuff the papers back into his briefcase.

When everything was back where it should be, Patta said, using the formal 'lei', 'Thank you, Signorina. I'll have these papers taken down to you as soon as I sign them.'

She nodded and made towards the door. As she walked past Brunetti, she gave him a wink and an enormous smile, both of which he ignored.

When she was gone, Brunetti walked over to Patta's desk. 'I've just got back from Vicenza, sir. From the American base.'

'Yes? What did you find?' Patta asked, face still suffused with a residual blush that Brunetti had to force himself to ignore.

'Nothing much. I took a look at his apartment.'

'Did you find anything?'

'No, sir. Nothing. I'd like to go back there tomorrow.'

'Why?'

'To speak to some of the people who knew him.'

'What difference will that make? It's clear that this is a simple case of a mugging that went too far. Who cares who knew him or what they have to say about him?'

Brunetti recognized the signs of Patta's growing indignation. If left unleashed, he would work himself up to forbidding Brunetti to continue the investigation at Vicenza. Since a simple mugging was the most convenient explanation, it would be the one towards which Patta would direct his hopes and, consequently, the investigation.

'I'm sure you're right, sir. But I thought that, until we could find the person who did it, it wouldn't hurt if we could give the impression that the source of the crime lay outside the city. You know how tourists are. Just the least little thing will frighten them and keep them away.'

Did Patta's rosy blush diminish discernibly at that, or was it just his imagination? 'I'm glad to see you agree with me, Commissario. After a pause that could only be called pregnant, Patta added, 'For once.' He extended a well-manicured hand and straightened the folder at the centre of his desk. 'Do you think there's any connection with Vicenza?'

Brunetti paused before he answered, delighted at the ease with which Patta was transferring the responsibility of the decision to him. 'I don't know, sir. But I don't think it could hurt us here if we gave the impression that there was.'

The pause with which his superior greeted this was artistic, his hesitation against any irregularity of procedure perfectly balanced against his desire to leave no stone unturned in the search for truth. He pulled his Mont Blanc Meisterstück from his breast pocket, opened the folder, and signed the three papers there, managing to make each repetition of the name more thoughtful and, at the same time, more decisive. 'All right, Brunetti, if you think this is the best way to handle it, go to Vicenza again. We can't have people afraid to come to Venice, can we?'

'No, sir,' Brunetti answered, his voice the very pattern of earnestness, 'we certainly can't.' Maintaining the same level voice, Brunetti asked, 'Will there be anything else, sir?'

'No, that's all, Brunetti. Give me a full report on what you find.'

'Of course, sir,' Brunetti said and turned towards the door, wondering what bromide Patta would find to hurl at his departing back.

'We'll bring the man to justice,' Patta said.

'We certainly will, sir,' Brunetti said, only too eager to abet his superior's use of the plural.

He went back up to his office, leafed through the issue of *Panorama* that had been in the briefcase, and gave Bocchese about half an hour to check the prints. At the end of that time, he went back down to the lab, this time to find Bocchese holding the blade of a bread-knife up against the whirling disc of the machine. When he saw Brunetti, he switched off the machine but kept the knife in his hand, testing the blade against his thumb.

'Is this an extra job you've got?' Brunetti asked.

'No. My wife asks me to sharpen things every few months, and this is the best way to do it. If your wife would like me to sharpen anything for her, I'd be glad to.'

Brunetti nodded his thanks. 'Find anything?'

'Yes. There's a good set of prints on one of the bags.'

'His?'

'Yes.'

'Anyone else's?'

'There are one or two other prints, probably a woman's.'

'What about the second bag?'

'Nothing. Clean. Wiped clean or handled only with gloves.' Bocchese picked up a piece of paper and shaved a slice from it with the bread-knife. Satisfied, he set it down on the desk and turned to Brunetti. 'I think the first bag had been used for something else before the . . .' Bocchese stopped himself, not sure what could be said here. '. . . before the other substance was put in it.'

'Used for what, originally?'

'I can't be sure, but it might have been cheese. There was a trace of some sort of oily residue on the inside. And that bag had clearly been handled more than the other, had creases in it, so I'd say it had been used for something else, then had the, uh, powder put in it.'

When Brunetti said nothing, Bocchese asked, 'Aren't you surprised?'

'No, I'm not.'

Bocchese pulled a wooden-handled steak-knife from a paper bag to the left of the machine and felt its blade with his thumb. 'Well, if there's anything else I can do, just let me know. And tell your wife about the knives.'

'Yes, thanks, Bocchese,' Brunetti said. 'What did you do with the bags?'

Bocchese switched on the machine, raised the knife towards it, and looked up at Brunetti. 'What bags?'

9

He saw no reason to remain in the Questura since there was little chance that he would get any new information until he returned to Vicenza, so he put his briefcase back in the bottom of the cupboard and left his office. As he walked from the front door, he quickly glanced both ways, searching for someone who seemed out of place. He cut to the left, heading towards Campo Maria Formosa and then to Rialto, using narrow back streets that would allow him to evade anyone who might be following him as well as the battalions of ravening tourists who invariably centred their attacks on the area around San Marco. Each year, it grew harder to have patience with them, to put up with their stop-and-go walking, with their insistence on walking three abreast, even in the narrowest *calle*.

There were times when he wanted to scream at them, even push them aside, but he contented himself by taking out all of his aggression through the single expedient of refusing to stop or in any way alter his walking in order to allow them a photo opportunity. Because of this, he was sure his body, back, face, elbow appeared in hundreds of photos and videos; he sometimes contemplated the disappointed Germans, looking at their summer videos during the violence of a North Sea storm, as they watched a purposeful, dark-suited Italian walk in front of Tante Gerda or Onkel Fritz, blurring, if only for an instant, the vision of sun-burned, Lederhosen-clad, sturdy thighs as they posed upon the Rialto Bridge, in front of the doors of the Basilica of San Marco, or beside a particularly charming cat. He lived here, damn it, so they could wait for their stupid pictures until he got past them, or they could take home a picture of a real Venetian, probably the closest any of them would come to making contact with the city in any significant way. And, oh yes, wasn't he a happy man to take home to Paola? Especially during her first week of classes.

To avoid this, he stopped in at Do Mori, his favourite bar, just a few steps from Rialto, and said hello to Roberto, the grey-haired proprietor. They exchanged a few words, and Brunetti asked for a glass of Cabernet, the only thing he felt like drinking. With it, he ate a few of the fried shrimp that were always available at the bar, then decided to have a *tramezzino*, thick with ham and artichoke. He had another glass of wine and, after it, he began to feel human, for the first time that day. Paola always accused him of becoming foul-tempered when he didn't eat for a long time, and he was beginning to believe she might be right. He paid and left, cut back to Rugetta and continued towards his home.

In front of Biancat, he stopped to study the flowers in the window. Signor Biancat saw him through the immense glass window, smiled and nodded, so Brunetti went inside and asked for ten blue irises. As he wrapped them, Biancat talked about Thailand, from which he had just returned after a week-long conference of orchid breeders and growers. It seemed to Brunetti a strange way to spend a week, but then he reflected that he had, in the past, gone to both Dallas and Los Angeles for police seminars. Who was he to say that it was stranger to spend a week talking about orchids than about the incidence of sodomy among serial killers or the various objects used in rapes?

The stairs to his apartment generally served as an accurate gauge of the state of his being. When he felt good, they hardly seemed to be there; when he felt tired, his legs counted out each of the ninety-four. Tonight, someone had clearly slipped in an extra flight or two.

He opened the door, anticipating the smell of home, of food, of the varied odours he had come to attribute to this place where they lived. Instead, upon entering, he smelled only the odour of freshly-made coffee, hardly the thing longed for by a man who had just spent the whole day working in – yes – America.

'Paola?' he called and glanced down the corridor towards the kitchen. Her voice answered him from the other direction, from the bathroom, and then he smelled the sweet scent of bath salts that was carried down the hall towards him on a sea of moist, warm air. Almost eight at night, and she was taking a bath?

He walked down the hall and stood outside the partly-open door. 'You in there?' he asked. The question was so stupid that she didn't bother to answer it. Instead, she asked, 'You going to wear your grey suit?'

'Grey suit?' he repeated, stepping into the steam-filled room. He saw her towel-wrapped head, floating disembodied on a cloud of suds, as though it had been carefully placed there by the person who had decapitated her. 'Grey suit?' he repeated, thinking what an odd couple they would appear, he in his grey suit and she in her suds.

Her eyes opened, the head turned towards him, and she gave him The Look, the one that always made him wonder if she was looking through him to where his suitcase lay in the attic, estimating how long it would take her to pack it for him. It was enough to remind him that tonight was the night when they were to go to the Casinò, invited there, with her parents, by an old friend of her family. It meant a late dinner, hideously expensive, made worse, or better – he could never decide which – by the fact that the family friend paid for it with his golden, or was it platinum, credit card. And then there always followed an hour or so of gambling or, worse, watching other people gamble.

Having been the investigating officer both times that the staff of the Casinò had been discovered at various sorts of peculation and having been, in both cases, the arresting officer, Brunetti hated the unctuous politeness with which he was treated by the Director and the staff. If he gambled and won, he wondered if the game had been fixed in his favour; if he lost, he had to consider the possibility that vengeance had been taken. In neither scenario did Brunetti bother to speculate on the nature of luck.

'I thought I'd wear the dark blue one,' he said, holding out the flowers and bending over the tub. 'I brought you these.'

The Look changed into The Smile, which could still, even after twenty years with her, occasionally reduce his knees to jelly. A hand, then an arm, lifted out of the water. She touched the back of his wrist, leaving it wet and warm, then pulled her arm back under the surface of bubbles. 'I'll be out in five minutes.' Her eyes caught his and held. 'If you'd been earlier, then you could have had a bath, too.'

He laughed and broke the mood. 'But then we would have been late for dinner.' True enough. True enough. But he cursed the time he had lost by stopping for a drink. He left the bathroom and went down the long hall to the kitchen and placed the flowers in the sink, plugged it, and added enough water to cover their stems.

In their bedroom, he saw that she had placed a long red dress across the bed. He didn't remember the dress, but he seldom did remember them, and he thought it best not to mention it. If it turned out to be a new dress and he remarked on it, he would sound like he thought she was buying too many clothes, and if it was something she had worn before, he would sound like he paid no attention to her and hadn't bothered to notice it before. He sighed at the eternal inequality of marriage, opened the closet, and decided that the grey suit would be better. He removed his trousers and jacket, took off his tie, and studied his shirt in the mirror, wondering if he could wear it that evening. Deciding against it, he took it off and draped it across the back of a chair, then began dressing himself anew, vaguely bothered with having to do it but too much an Italian to consider the possibility of not doing so.

A few minutes later, Paola came into the bedroom, golden hair free, the towel now wrapped around her body, and walked to the dresser where she kept her underwear and sweaters. Casually, carelessly, she tossed the towel onto the bed and bent to open a drawer. Slipping a new tie under his collar and beginning to knot it, he studied her as she stepped into a pair of black panties, then pulled a bra around herself and hooked it. To distract himself, he thought of physics, which he had studied at the university. He doubted that he would ever understand the dynamics and stress forces of female undergarments: so many things to hold, support, keep in place. He finished knotting his tie and pulled his jacket from the closet. By the time he had it on, she was zipping the side of her dress and stepping into a pair of black shoes. His friends often complained of waiting eternities while their wives dressed or put on make-up; Paola always beat him to the door.

She reached into her side of the closet and drew out a floor-length coat that looked like it was made of fish scales. For a moment, he caught her looking at the mink that hung at the end of a row of clothing, but she ignored it and closed the door. Her father had given her the mink for Christmas a few years ago, but she had not worn it for the last two years. Brunetti didn't know if this was because it was already out of style – he assumed that furs *did* go out of style; certainly everything else his wife or daughter wore did – or because of the growing anti-fur sentiment expressed both in the Press and at his dinner-table.

Two months ago, a quiet family dinner had exploded into a heated confrontation about the rights of animals, his children insisting that it was wrong to wear furs, that animals had the same rights as humans, and to deny this was to engage in 'speciescentricity', a term Brunetti was sure they had made up just to use against him in the argument. He had listened for ten minutes as the argument went back and forth between them and Paola, they demanding equal rights for all the species on the planet, she attempting to make a distinction between animals capable of reason and those which were not. Finally, out of patience with Paola for attempting rational opposition to an argument that seemed to him idiotic, he had reached over the table and poked with his fork at the chicken bones that lay at the side of his daughter's plate. 'We can't wear them, but we can eat them, eh?' he asked, got up, and went inside to read the paper and drink a grappa.

In any case, the mink remained in the closet and they set out for the Casinò.

They got off the vaporetto at the San Marcuola stop and walked down the narrow streets and over the hump-backed bridge that led to the iron gates of the Casinò, open now and extending a welcoming embrace to all who chose to enter. On the outer walls, the ones visible from the Grand Canal, were inscribed the words *'Non Nobis'*, Not For Us, which, during the ages of the Republic, had declared the Casinò off-limits to Venetians. Only foreigners were to be fleeced; Venetians were to invest their money wisely and not squander it on dice and gaming. How he wished, this endless evening yawning out before him, that the rules of the Republic still pertained and could free him of the next few hours. They entered the marble-paved lobby, and immediately a tuxedoed assistant manager came from the entrance desk and greeted him by name. 'Dottor Brunetti. Signora,' – this with a bow that put a neat horizontal pleat in his red cummerbund. 'We are honoured to have you here. Your party is in the restaurant.' With a wave as graceful as the bow, he pointed to the right, to the single elevator that stood there, open and waiting. 'If you'd come this way, I'll take you to them.'

Paola's hand grabbed at his, squeezing it hard, cutting him off from saying that they knew the way. Instead, all three crowded into the tiny box of the elevator and smiled pleasant smiles at one another as it inched itself towards the top floor of the building.

The elevator racketed to a halt, the assistant manager opened the twin doors and held them while Brunetti and Paola got off, then led them into the brightly lit restaurant. Brunetti looked around as he walked in, checking for the nearest exit and for anyone who looked capable of violence, a survey which he gave, entirely automatically, to any public room he entered. In a corner near a window that gave over the Grand Canal, he saw his parents-in-law and their friends, the Pastores, an elderly couple from Milan who were Paola's Godparents and the oldest friends of her parents and who were, because of that, placed utterly beyond reproach or criticism.

As he and Paola drew near the round table, both of the older men, dressed in dark suits which were identical in quality, however different in colour, rose to their feet. Paola's father kissed her on the cheek, then shook Brunetti's hand, while Doctor Pastore bent to kiss Paola's hand and then embraced Brunetti and kissed him on both cheeks. Because he never felt fully at ease with the man, this display of intimacy always made Brunetti uncomfortable.

One of the things that spoiled these dinners, this yearly ritual that he had inherited upon marrying Paola, was that he always arrived to find that dinner had been ordered by Doctor Pastore. The Doctor was, of course, solicitous, insisting that he hoped no one minded if he took the liberty of ordering, but it was the season for this, the season for that, truffles were at their best, the first mushrooms were just beginning to come in. And he was always right, and the meal was always delicious, but Brunetti disliked not being able to order what he wanted to eat, even if what he wanted turned out to be less good than what they ended up eating. And, each year, he chided himself for being stupid and pigheaded, yet he could not conquer the flash of irritation he felt when he arrived to find that the meal was already planned and ordered, and he had not been consulted in the ordering of it. Male ego against male ego? Surely, it was nothing more than that. Questions of palate and cuisine had nothing whatsoever to do with it.

There were the usual compliments, then the matter of where to sit. Brunetti ended up with his back to the window, Doctor Pastore to his left and Paola's father directly opposite him.

'How nice to see you again, Guido,' Doctor Pastore said. 'Orazio and I were just talking about you.'

'Badly, I hope,' Paola said and laughed, but then she turned her attention to her mother, who was fingering the material of her dress, a sign that it must be a new one, and to Signora Pastore, who sat with one of Paola's hands still in hers.

He gave the Doctor a polite, inquisitive glance. 'We were talking about this American. You're in charge of it, aren't you?'

'Yes, Dottore, I am.'

'Why would someone want to kill an American?

He was a soldier, wasn't he? Robbery? Revenge? Jealousy?' Because the Doctor was Italian, nothing else came to his mind.

'Perhaps,' Brunetti said, answering all five questions with one word. He paused as two waiters approached the table with two large platters of seafood antipasto. They offered the platters, serving each person in turn. Idly, more interested in murder than the meal, the Doctor waited until everyone had been served and the food complimented and then returned to the initial subject.

'Have you any ideas?'

'Nothing definite,' Brunetti answered and ate a shrimp.

'Drugs?' asked Paola's father, displaying a worldliness superior to his friend's.

Brunetti repeated his 'Perhaps', and ate a few more shrimp, delighted to find them fresh and sweet.

At the sound of the word 'drugs', Paola's mother turned to them and asked them what they were talking about.

'Guido's latest murder,' her husband said, making it sound, somehow, as though it were one he had committed rather than one he had been sent to solve. 'I'm sure it will turn out to have been a street crime. What do they call them in America – a "mugging"?' He sounded surprisingly like Patta.

Because Signora Pastore had heard nothing about the murder, her husband had to repeat the whole story, turning to Brunetti occasionally to ask about details or for confirmation of fact. Brunetti didn't mind this at all, for it made the meal pass more quickly than it usually did. And so, with talk of murder and mayhem, they ate their way through risotto, mixed grilled fish, four vegetables, salad, *tiramisù*, and coffee.

While the men sipped at their grappa, Doctor Pastore, as he did each year, asked the ladies if they cared to join him in the Casinò below. When they agreed, he responded with a delight new-minted each year and pulled from the inner pocket of his jacket three small suede bags, which he placed in front of them.

As she did each year, Paola protested, 'Oh, Dottore, you shouldn't,' which, as usual, she said while busily opening the bag to reveal the Casinò chips which the bags always contained. Brunetti noticed the same combination he did each year and knew that the total would be two hundred thousand lire for each woman, enough to divert them while Doctor Pastore spent an hour or two playing blackjack and usually winning back far more than he had provided for the ladies' amusement.

The three men rose from the table, held the chairs of the women, and the six of them started for the Casinò gaming rooms on the floor below.

Because they couldn't all fit into the elevator, the women were put inside while the men decided to use the main staircase to go down to the main gambling hall. Brunetti found Count Orazio on his right and tried to think of something to say to his father-in-law.

'Did you know that Richard Wagner died here?'

134

he asked, forgetting now how it was that he knew this, since Wagner was hardly a composer he liked.

'Yes,' the Count answered. 'Hardly soon enough.'

And then, luckily, they were in the main gaming room, and Count Orazio joined his wife to watch as she played roulette, taking leave of Brunetti with a friendly smile and something that flirted with being a bow.

Brunetti had first been to a casino not in his native Venice, where no one but compulsive or professional gamblers paid any attention to the tables, but in Las Vegas, where he had stopped while driving across America many years ago. Because his first experience of gambling had been there, he always associated the practice with bright lights, loud music, and the high whoops of those who won or lost. He remembered a stage show, helium-filled balloons bouncing against the ceilings, people dressed in T-shirts, jeans, shorts. Consequently, though he came here to the Casinò each year, he was always surprised to find the atmosphere somewhere between that of an art museum and, worse, a church. Few people smiled, voices were never raised above a whisper, and no one ever appeared to be having any fun. In the midst of this solemnity, he missed the honest shouts of victory or defeat, the wild shrieks of joy that came with changes of fortune.

None of that here, no indeed. Men and women, all well-dressed, hushed to reverent silence, ringed the roulette table, putting down chips across the felt board. Silence, pause, then the croupier gave the wheel a sharp turn, dropped the ball in, and all eyes riveted themselves upon the whirl of metal and colour, stuck there as it slowed, slowed, slowed to a halt. Snake-like, the croupier's rake crept up and down the board, sweeping in the losers' chips and nudging a few to the winner. And then again the same motions, the flurry, the spin, and those eyes, fixed, nailed to the spinning wheel. Why, he wondered, did so many of these men wear rings on their little fingers?

He drifted into the next room, vaguely aware that he had become separated from his party, curious to observe. In an inner room, he came upon the blackjack tables and saw Doctor Pastore already seated there, a middling pile of chips stacked with surgical neatness in front of him. As Brunetti watched, he called for a card, drew a six, stopped, waited while the other players drew, then flipped his cards over to display a seven and an eight to accompany the six. His pile of chips grew; Brunetti turned away.

Everyone seemed to be smoking. One player at the baccarat table had two cigarettes burning in an ashtray in front of him, a third hanging from his lower lip. Smoke was everywhere: in his eyes, his hair, his clothing; it floated in a cloud that could be cut and stirred by a hand. He moved to the bar and bought himself a grappa, not really wanting it, but bored with watching the play.

He sat on a plush velvet sofa and watched the players in the room, occasionally sipping at the glass in his hand. He closed his eyes and allowed himself to drift for a few minutes. He felt the sofa move beside him and, without opening his eyes or moving his head from where it rested against the back of the sofa, he knew it was Paola. She took his glass, sipped at it, then gave it back to him.

'Tired?' she asked.

He nodded, suddenly too tired to speak.

'All right. Come with me and we'll have one more round at roulette, and then we can go home.'

He turned his head, opened his eyes, and smiled at her. 'I love you, Paola,' he said, then bowed his head and sipped at his grappa. How many years had it been since he had said that? He glanced up at her, almost shyly. She grinned and leaned over and kissed him on the mouth. 'Come on,' she said, getting to her feet and reaching down to pull him up. 'Let's lose this money, and then we'll go home.' She had five chips in her hand, each worth fifty thousand lire, which meant she had been winning. She handed him two, keeping the others for herself.

Back in the main gaming room, they had to wait a few minutes before they could worm themselves up beside the roulette table and, when they were there, he waited two turns until, for no reason he could name, it seemed the right time to play. Stacking the two chips one on top of the other in his hand, he placed them blindly on the board, then looked down and saw that they rested on number 28, a number that had no significance whatsoever for him. Paola placed hers on the black.

Spin, watch, wait, and, as he knew it would, the ball slipped into its rightful place in number 28, and he won more than three million lire. Almost a month's salary, a vacation for them this summer, a computer for Chiara. He watched as the croupier's rake came sliding towards him, chugging those chips across the felt until they stopped in front of him. He scooped them up, smiled at Paola, and, in the loudest voice heard in the Casinò in years, shouted, in English, 'Hot damn.'

10

He saw no sense in bothering to go to the Questura the next morning and, instead, stayed at home until it was time to get the train to Vicenza. He did, however, call Maggiore Ambrogiani and ask that the driver be sent to get him at the station.

As the train crossed over the causeway and away from the city, he looked off into the distance and saw, visible only rarely these days, the mountains, not yet snow-covered but, he hoped, soon to be. This was the third dry year, with little rain in the spring, none in the summer, and bad harvests in the autumn. The farmers had their hopes pinned on winter snows this year, and he recalled the saying of the peasants of the Friuli, a grim, hard-working people: *'Sotto la neve, pane; sotto la pioggia, fame.'* Yes, the winter snows would bring bread, releasing their trapped waters slowly during the growing season, while rain, which ran off quickly, brought only hunger.

He hadn't bothered with a briefcase today; it was unlikely he would find bags of cocaine two days in a row, but he had bought a paper at the train station, and he read through it as the train took him across the flat plain towards Vicenza. There was no mention of the dead American today, his place taken by a crime of passion in Modena, a dentist who had strangled a woman who refused to marry him and then shot himself. He spent the rest of the trip reading the political news, knowing as much when he arrived in Vicenza as when he left Venice.

The same driver was waiting for him in front of the station, but this time he got out to open the door for Brunetti. At the gate, he stopped without being told to do so and waited while the Carabiniere wrote out a pass for Brunetti. 'Where would you like to go, sir?'

'Where's the Office of Public Health?' he asked.

'In the hospital.'

'Then let's go there.'

The driver took him up the long main street of the base, and Brunetti felt himself to be in a foreign country. Pine trees lined the street on both sides. The car rode past men and women in shorts, riding bicycles or pushing babies in pushchairs. Joggers loped by; they even drove past a swimming-pool, still filled with water but empty of swimmers.

The driver pulled up in front of yet another undistinguished cement building. 'Vicenza Field

Hospital', Brunetti read. 'In there, sir,' the driver said, pulling into a parking space designated for the handicapped and cutting the engine.

Inside, he found himself in front of a low, curved reception desk. A young woman looked up, smiled, and asked, 'Yes, sir, may I help you?'

'I'm looking for the Office of Public Health.'

'Take the corridor behind me, turn right, then it's the third door on the left,' she said, then turned to a pregnant woman in uniform who had come in and stood beside him. Brunetti walked away from the desk in the direction given and did not, he thought proudly to himself, did not turn to look at the woman in uniform, the pregnant woman in uniform.

He stopped in front of the third door, clearly marked 'Public Health', and knocked. No one answered, so he knocked again. Still no one answered, so he tried the knob, and, noting that it was a knob and not a handle, opened the door and went in. The small room held three metal desks, each with a chair drawn up in front of it, and two filing cabinets, from the top of both of which straggled long, tired-looking plants much in need of both water and dusting. On the wall hung the now predictable bulletin board, this one covered with notices and charts. Two of the desks were covered with the normal detritus of office work: papers, forms, folders, pens, pencils. The third held a computer terminal and keyboard but, for the rest, was conspicuously bare. Brunetti seated himself in the chair that was clearly intended for visitors. One of the phones – each desk had one –

rang and went on ringing seven times, then stopped. Brunetti waited a few minutes then went to the door and stepped back out into the corridor. A nurse was walking by, and Brunetti asked her if she knew where the people from the office were.

'Should be right back, sir,' she answered in the internationally recognized code by which fellow workers cover for one another with strangers who might or might not have been sent there to find out who was at work and who was not. He stepped back inside and closed the door.

As in any office, there were the usual cartoons, postcards, and handwritten notes interspersed with official notices. The cartoons all seemed to have soldiers or doctors, and many of the post-cards had either minarets or archaeological sites. He unpinned the first and found that Bob said hello from the Blue Mosque. The second told him that Bob liked the Colosseum. But the third, which showed a camel in front of the Pyramids, revealed, far more interestingly, that M and T were finished with the inspection of the kitchens and would be back on Tuesday. He pinned this one back and stepped away from the board.

'May I help you?' a voice said behind him.

He recognized her voice, turned, and she recognized him. 'Mr Brunetti, what are you doing here?' Her surprise was both genuine and strong.

'Good morning, Doctor Peters. I told you I'd come out to see if I could learn more about Sergeant Foster. I was told this was the Office of Public Health, so I came down here in the hopes of meeting someone who worked with him. But, as you can see,' he said, gesturing around the empty office and taking two steps that further distanced him from the board, 'no one is here.'

'They're all at a meeting,' she explained. 'Trying to figure out a way to divide up the work until we get a replacement for Mike.'

'Aren't you at the meeting?' he asked.

In response, she pulled a stethoscope out of the breast pocket of her white lab coat and said, 'Remember, I'm a paediatrician.

'I see.'

'They ought to be back here very soon,' she volunteered. 'Who did you want to speak to?'

'I don't know. Whoever worked most closely with him.'

'I told you, Mike pretty much had charge of the office himself.'

'So it wouldn't help me to talk to anyone?'

'I can't answer that for you, Mr Brunetti, since I don't know what it is you want to find out.'

Brunetti assumed her irritation was the result of nervousness, so he dropped the subject and asked, instead, 'Do you know if Sergeant Foster drank?'

'Drank?'

'Alcohol.'

'Very little.'

'And drugs?'

'What sort of drugs?'

'Illegal drugs.'

'No.' Her voice was firm, her conviction absolute.

'You sound very certain.'

'I'm certain because I knew him, and I'm also

certain because I'm his commanding officer, and I see his medical record.'

'Is that something that would normally appear in a medical report?' Brunetti asked.

She nodded. 'We can be tested, any of us in the Army, at any time, for drug use. Most of us get a urine test once a year.'

'Even officers?'

'Even officers.'

'Even doctors?'

'Even doctors.'

'And you saw the results of his?'

'Yes.'

'When was the last one?'

'I don't remember. Sometime this summer, I think.' She shifted some folders from one hand to the other. 'I don't know why you're asking this. Mike never used drugs. Just the opposite. He was dead set against them. We used to argue about it.'

'How? Why?'

'I see no problem with them. I'm not interested in them myself, but if people want to use them, then I think they ought to be allowed to.' When Brunetti said nothing, she continued, 'Look, I'm supposed to be taking care of little kids, but we're short-staffed here, so I see a lot of their mothers as well, and a lot of them ask me to renew their prescription for Valium and Librium. If I refuse because I think they're taking too much of them, they just wait a day or two and go down the hall and have an appointment with a different doctor, and sooner or later, someone's going to give them what they want. A lot of them would be better off if they could just smoke a joint now and then.'

Brunetti wondered how well these opinions were received by both medical and military authorities, but he thought it best to keep the question to himself. After all, it was not Doctor Peters' opinion about the use of drugs that he was interested in; it was whether Sergeant Foster had used them or not. And, not at all incidentally, why she had lied about going on a trip with him.

Behind her, the door opened and a stocky middle-aged man in a green uniform came in. He seemed to be surprised to see Brunetti there, but he clearly recognized the doctor.

'Is the meeting over, Ron?' she asked.

'Yes,' he said, paused, looked up at Brunetti and, not sure who he might be, added, 'm'am.'

Doctor Peters turned to Brunetti. 'This is First Sergeant Wolf,' she said. 'Sergeant, this is Commissario Brunetti, from the Venice police. He's come out to ask some questions about Mike.'

After the two men had shaken hands and exchanged pleasantries, Doctor Peters said, 'Perhaps Sergeant Wolf can give you a clearer idea of what Sergeant Foster did, Mr Brunetti. He's in charge of all of the contacts that the hospital has off-post.' She turned towards the door. 'I'll leave you with him and get back to my patients.' Brunetti nodded in her direction, but she had turned away from them and left the office quickly.

'What is it you wanted to know, Commissario?' Sergeant Wolf asked, then added, less formally, 'Would you like to come back to my office?'

'Don't you work here?'

'No. I'm part of the administrative staff of the hospital. Our offices are on the other side of the building.'

'Then who else works here?' he asked, pointing to the three desks.

'This desk is Mike's. Was Mike's,' he corrected himself. 'The other desk is Sergeant Dostie's, but he's in Warsaw. They shared the computer.'

How wide this American eagle spread its wings. 'When will he be back?' Brunetti asked.

'Sometime next week, I think,' Wolf answered.

'And how long has he been away?' Brunetti thought this less direct than asking when he had left.

'Since before this happened,' Wolf responded, effectively answering Brunetti's question and eliminating Sergeant Dostie as a suspect.

'Would you like to come down to my office?'

Brunetti followed him from the room and down the halls of the hospital, trying to remember the way they went. They passed through a set of swinging double doors, down a spotlessly clean corridor, through another set of doors, and then Wolf stopped in front of an open door.

'Not much, but I call it home,' he said with surprising warmth. He stepped back to let Brunetti go into the office first, then came in and pulled the door closed behind them. 'Don't want us to be disturbed,' he said and smiled. He walked behind his desk and sat in an imitation-leather swivel chair. Most of the surface was covered with an enormous desk calendar, and on that rested files, an In- and Out-tray, and a telephone. To the right, in a brass frame, was a photo of an Oriental woman and three young children, apparently the children of this mixed marriage.

'Your wife?' Brunetti asked, taking a seat in front of the desk.

'Yes, beautiful, isn't she?'

'Very,' Brunetti answered.

'And those are our three kids. Joshua's ten, Melissa's six, and Jessica is only one.'

'It's a very handsome family,' Brunetti volunteered.

'Yes, they are. I don't know what I'd do if I didn't have them. I often told Mike that's what he needed, to marry and settle down.'

'Did he need to settle down?' Brunetti asked, interested in the fact that it was always married men with numerous children who wished this on single men.

'Well, I don't know,' Wolf said, leaning forward and propping his elbows on his desk. 'He was twenty-five, after all. Time to start a family.'

'Did he have a girlfriend to start it with?' Brunetti asked cordially.

Wolf looked across at him, then down at his desk. 'Not that I knew about.'

'Did he like women?' If Wolf understood that the corollary of this was whether he liked men, he gave no sign.

'I suppose so. I really didn't know him all that well. Just here at work.'

'Was anyone here a special friend?' When Wolf shook his head, Brunetti added, 'Doctor Peters was very upset when she saw the body.'

'Well, they'd worked together for a half a year or so. Don't you think it's normal she'd be upset to see him?'

'Yes, I suppose,' Brunetti answered, offering no explanation. 'Anyone else?'

'No, not that I can think of.'

'Perhaps I could ask Mr Dostie when he gets back.'

'Sergeant Dostie,' Wolf corrected automatically.

'Did he know Sergeant Foster well?'

'I really don't know, Commissario.' It seemed to Brunetti that this man didn't know very much at all, not about a man who had worked for him for . . . 'How long did Sergeant Foster work for you?' he asked.

Wolf pushed himself back in his chair, glanced at the picture, as if his wife would tell him, then answered, 'Three years, ever since he got here.'

'I see. And how long has Sergeant Dostie been here?'

'About four years.'

'What kind of man was he, Sergeant Wolf?' Brunetti asked, turning the conversation back to the dead man.

This time, Wolf checked with his children before he answered. 'He was an excellent troop. His record will tell you that. He tended pretty much to keep to himself, but that might be because he was going to school, and he was very serious about that.' Wolf paused, as if looking for something more profound to say. 'He was a very caring individual.'

'I beg your pardon?' Brunetti asked, utterly lost.

Caring? What did Foster care about? 'I'm afraid I don't understand.'

Wolf was glad to explain. 'You know, what you Italians call "*simpatico*".'

'Oh,' Brunetti muttered. What a strange language these people spoke. More directly, he asked, 'Did you like him?'

The soldier was clearly surprised by the question. 'Well, yes, I suppose I did. I mean, like, we weren't friends or anything, but he was a nice guy.'

'What were his exact duties?' Brunetti asked, taking his notebook from his pocket.

'Well,' Sergeant Wolf began, latching his hands behind his head and sitting back more comfortably in his chair, 'he had to see about housing, that landlords kept up standards. You know, enough hot water, enough heat in the winter. And he had to see that, when we were tenants, we didn't do any damage to the apartments or the houses. If a landlord calls us and tells us his tenants are creating a health hazard, we go out and investigate it.'

'What sort of a health hazard?' Brunetti asked, honestly curious. 'Oh, lots of things. Not taking the garbage out, or putting the garbage too near the house. Or not cleaning up after their animals. There's a lot of that.'

'What do you do?'

'We have permission to, no, we have the right to go into their houses.'

'Even if they object?'

'Especially if they object,' Wolf said with an easy

laugh. 'That's generally a sure sign the place will be a mess.'

'Then what do you do?'

'We inspect the house to see if there's any danger to health.'

'Does this happen often?'

Wolf started to answer, then checked himself, and Brunetti realized that the man was weighing up how much of this he could tell an Italian, what his response would be to such tales regarding Americans. 'We get a few,' he said neutrally.

'And then?'

'We tell them to clean it up, and we report it to their commander, and they're given a certain time to clean it up.'

'And if they don't?'

'They get an Article Fifteen.'

Brunetti smiled that bland old smile again. 'An Article Fifteen?'

'It's a sort of official reprimand. It goes into the permanent file, and it can cause someone a lot of trouble.'

'Such as?'

'It can cost them salary, or demotion, or sometimes it can get them thrown out of the Army.'

'For having a dirty house?' Brunetti asked, unable to restrain his surprise.

'Mr Brunetti, if you saw some of these houses, you'd want to throw them out of the country.' He paused for a moment, then began again, 'And he had to go and check out the kitchens in the embassies, especially if someone got sick there, or, worse, if a lot of people started getting sick. We had hepatitis in Belgrade last year, and he had to go and check it out.'

'Anything else?' Brunetti asked.

'No, nothing important.'

Brunetti smiled. 'I'm not sure now what is and isn't important at this point, Sergeant Wolf, but I'd like to have a clear idea of his duties.'

Sergeant Wolf returned his smile. 'Of course. I understand. He also had to see that the kids at the school all had the proper vaccinations. You know, against things like measles and chickenpox. And he had to see that the rays got disposed of, them and some other stuff that we can't dispose of in the normal way. And there was a certain amount of public health information that he was in charge of.' He looked up, finished. 'That's about it, I think.'

'Rays?' Brunetti asked.

'Yes, the X-rays from the dental clinic, and even some of them from here in the hospital. They have to be disposed of specially. We can't put them in the trash.'

'How is that done?'

'Oh, we've got a contract with an Italian haulier who comes in once a month and takes them away. Mike had to see to that, check to see that the containers got picked up.' Wolf smiled. 'That's about it.'

Brunetti returned his smile and stood. 'Thank you, Sergeant Wolf. You've been very helpful.'

'Well, I hope it does some good. We all liked Mike here, and we certainly want to see you get the person who did this.'

'Yes. Certainly,' Brunetti said, extending his

hand. 'I don't want to keep you from your work, Sergeant.'

The American stood to shake Brunetti's hand. His grasp was firm, confident. 'Glad to be of help, sir. If you have any more questions, please come and ask.'

'Thank you, Sergeant. I just might.'

When he was back in the corridor, he traced his way back to the Public Health Office and knocked on the door again. He waited a few seconds and, hearing nothing, let himself into the office. As he had expected, the Blue Mosque and the Colosseum were still there. The Pyramids were gone.

11

Back in the hall, he asked the first person passing by, a young black woman in a nurse's uniform, where he might find Doctor Peters. She told him that she was going to Ward B, where Doctor Peters worked, and said she would take him there. This time, they branched off in the opposite direction, through still another set of double doors, but this time the people coming towards him wore white uniforms or light-green scrub suits, not the darker green of military uniforms. They passed a room with a sign that said it was a recovery room, then off to his right he heard the squalling of babies. He glanced down at the nurse, who smiled and nodded her head. 'Three, all born this week.'

It seemed to Brunetti that babies had no business being born here, on a military installation, surrounded by guns, uniforms, and the business of killing. But then he remembered that, so far, he had seen a library, chapel, swimming-pool, and Baskin Robbins ice-cream parlour on this same military installation, so maybe it did make sense that babies were born here, too. How little of what he had seen here, in fact, had anything to do with the business of war or killing or being an army. Did the Americans realize, he wondered, where their money went? Did they realize the profligacy with which it was spent? Because he was an Italian, he assumed that his government was serious only about the business of tossing money away, usually in the general direction of the friends of those in government, but it had never occurred to him that the American government might be equally intent upon doing the same thing.

'This is Doctor Peters' office, sir. I think she's with a patient now, but she ought to be back soon.' She smiled and left him standing there, never having bothered to ask who he was or what he wanted.

The office looked like any doctor's office he had ever been in. One wall was covered with thick books with thicker titles; there was a scale in one corner with a sliding metal pole for measuring height. He stepped on the scale and slid the metal weight back and forth on the horizontal pole until it clicked into place at 193. He did the arithmetic in his head, dividing by 2.2, and sighed at the result. He measured his height, 5 feet, 10 inches, but he had never been able to do that conversion without pencil and paper. Besides, he assumed that his height would be less likely to betray him, the way his weight had.

There were some posters on the wall: one of Fulvio Roiter's predictable photos of Carnevale; a reproduction of the mosaics in San Vitale in Ravenna; an enlarged photo of mountains that looked like the jagged-toothed Dolomites. The wall to the right, as was the case in so many doctors' offices, was covered with framed diplomas, as if doctors were afraid no one would believe them unless tangible proof of their training were plastered up on the wall for all to see. 'Emory University.' That meant nothing to him. *'Phi Beta Kappa.'* Nor did that. *'Summa Cum Laude.'* Well, that certainly did.

A magazine lay closed on the desk. *Family Practice Journal.* He picked it up and leafed through, then stopped at an article that carried coloured photos of what he thought were human feet, but feet distorted beyond all recognition, with toes that grew every which way, toes that curled up and back towards the top of the foot, or, worse, toes that curved down towards the soles. He stared at the photos for a while, then, just as he began to read the article, he sensed motion beside him and looked up to see Doctor Peters standing just inside the door. With no preamble, she took the magazine from his hands, slapped it closed, and placed it on the other side of the desk from him.

'What are you doing here?' she asked, hiding neither surprise nor anger.

He stood. 'I apologize for touching your things,

Doctor. I came here to talk to you, if you have time. I saw the magazine there and looked through it while I was waiting. I hope you don't mind.'

Clearly, she realized that her reaction had been too strong. He watched while she tried to gain control of herself. Finally, she sat in the chair in front of her desk and said, trying to smile, 'Well, better that than my mail.' That said, her smile seemed to become genuine. She pointed to the now closed magazine. 'It happens in old people. They get too stiff to bend down and cut their toenails, but they continue to grow, and, as you saw, the feet become horribly distorted.'

'Better paediatrics,' he said.

She smiled again. 'Yes, far better. I think it's better to invest your time in children.' She placed her stethoscope on top of the magazine and said, 'I don't think you came here to discuss my career choices, Commissario. What is it you'd like to know?'

'I'd like to know why you lied about your trip to Cairo with Sergeant Foster.'

He saw that she wasn't surprised, had perhaps been expecting it. She crossed her legs, her knees just visible under the hem of the uniform skirt she wore beneath the white jacket. 'So you do read my mail?' she asked. When he didn't say anything, she continued, 'I didn't want anyone here to know what happened.'

'Doctor, you sent the postcard here, with both your names, well, initials, on it. It would hardly be a secret to anyone here that you went to Cairo together.'

'Please, you know what I mean. I didn't want anyone here to know what happened,' she repeated. 'You were there when I saw his body. So you know.'

'Why don't you want anyone here to know? Are you married to someone else?'

'No,' she said, shaking her head tiredly at his failure to understand. 'It wouldn't be so bad if it were only that. But I'm an officer, and Mike was an enlisted man.' She saw his confusion. 'That's fraternization, and it's one of the things we are forbidden to do.' She paused for a long time. 'One of many things.'

'What would happen to you if they found out?' he asked, not thinking it necessary to define 'they'.

She shrugged. 'I have no idea. One of us would have been spoken to, perhaps disciplined. Maybe even transferred to some other place. But that's hardly a concern now, is it?' she asked, looking at him directly.

'No, I'm afraid it isn't. Could it still hurt your career?' he asked.

'I'll be out of the Army in six months, Mr Brunetti. They wouldn't bother with it now, and if they did, I don't think I'd much care. I don't want a career, not with the Army, but I still don't want them to know. I just want to get out and go back to my life.' She paused for a moment, gave him a diagnostic glance, then continued. 'The Army sent me to medical school. I could never have afforded it myself and neither could my family. So they gave me six years of school, and now I've given them four years of work. That's ten years, Mr Brunetti, ten years. So I guess I shouldn't even say I want to go back to my life. I want to start to have one.'

'What are you going to do? With that life, I mean.'

She pursed her lips and raised her eyebrows. 'I don't know. I've applied to some hospitals. There's always private practice. Or I could go back to school. I don't think about that much.'

'Is that because of Sergeant Foster's death?'

She prodded the stethoscope with one finger, looked at him, then back down at her hand.

'Doctor Peters,' he began, feeling awkward about how speech-like this was going to sound in English. 'I'm not sure what's going on here, but I know that Sergeant Foster wasn't killed by a mugger or in some bungled robbery attempt. He was murdered, and whoever murdered him has something to do with the American military, or with the Italian police. And I believe that you know something about whatever it was that caused him to be killed. I'd like you to tell me what it is you know, or what it is you suspect. Or what you're afraid of.' The words sounded leaden and artificial in his ears.

She looked over at him when he said that, and he saw a phantom of what he had seen in her eyes that night on the island of San Michele. She started to speak, stopped, and looked back down at the stethoscope. After a long time, she shook her head and said, 'I think you're exaggerating my reaction, Mr Brunetti. I don't know what you're talking about when you say I'm afraid of something.' And then, to convince them both, 'I don't know anything about why Mike would have been killed or who might have wanted to kill him.'

He glanced at her hand and saw that she had bent the black rubber tube that led down to the flat disc at the end of the instrument until the rubber was grey with tension. She caught the direction of his eyes, looked down at her own hand, and slowly released it, until the tube was again straight, the rubber black. 'And now, if you'll excuse me, I have another patient to see.'

'Certainly, Doctor,' he said, knowing that he had lost. 'If you think of anything you want to tell me or if you want to talk to me, you can reach me at the Questura in Venice.'

'Thank you,' she said, stood and went to the door. 'Do you want to finish the article?'

'No,' he said, scrambling to his feet and going to the door. He put out his hand. 'If you think of anything, Doctor.'

She took his hand, smiled, but said nothing. He watched as she went down the corridor to the left and into the next room, from which he could hear the voice of a woman talking in a low, crooning voice, probably to a sick child.

Outside, the driver was waiting, busy with a magazine. He looked up when Brunetti opened the back door of the car. 'Where to, sir?'

'Is that dining-hall open today?' He was very hungry, realized only now that it was after one.

'Yes, sir. Strike's been settled.'

'Who was on strike?'

'CGL,' he explained, naming the biggest of the Communist labour unions.

'CGL?' Brunetti repeated in amazement. 'On an American military base?'

'Yes, sir,' the driver said and laughed. 'After the war, they hired people who spoke some English, and they let the unions form without paying any attention to them. But once they realized that CGL was Communist, they refused to hire anyone else who was a member. But they can't get rid of the people who still are. Lots of them work in the dining-hall. Food's good.'

'All right, take me there. How far?'

'Oh, about two minutes,' he said, pulling away from the kerb and cutting the car into another tight U-turn that took them back up what Brunetti was sure was a one-way street.

On their left, they passed two larger-than-life statues that he hadn't noticed before. 'Who are those two?' he asked.

'I don't know who the angel with the sword is, but the other one is Saint Barbara.'

'Saint Barbara? What's she doing here?'

'She's the patron saint of the artillery, sir. Remember, her father was struck by lightning when he tried to cut her head off?'

Although he had been raised a Catholic, Brunetti had never felt much interest in religion and found it difficult to keep the different saints straight, rather, he believed, in the manner the pagans must have found it hard to remember which god was in charge of what. Besides, it had always seemed to him that the saints spent entirely too much time misplacing various body parts: eyes, breasts, arms, and now, with Saint

Barbara, her head. 'I don't know the legend. What happened?'

The driver swerved through a STOP sign and around a corner, looked back at Brunetti, and explained. 'Her father was a pagan, and she was a Christian. Her father wanted her to marry a pagan, but she wanted to stay a virgin.' He added, under his breath, 'Silly girl.' He looked back at the road, just in time to brake sharply to avoid running into a truck. 'So the father decided to punish her by cutting off her head. He raised his sword over her, giving her one last chance to obey him, and *zacketay!* lightning struck the sword and killed him.'

'What happened to her?'

'Oh, they never tell you that part of the story. In any case, because of the explosion of the lightning, she's the patron saint of the artillery.' He pulled up in front of another low building. 'Here we are, sir.' Then he added, puzzled. 'I'm surprised you didn't know that, sir. About Saint Barbara.'

'I wasn't assigned the case,' Brunetti said.

After lunch, he had the driver take him back to Foster's apartment. The same two soldiers were sitting in their Jeep in front of the apartment. They both got out when Brunetti approached them and waited for him to draw up to them. 'Good afternoon,' he said, smiling pleasantly. 'I'd like to have another look inside the apartment if that's possible.'

'Have you spoken to Major Butterworth about this, sir?' the one with more stripes asked.

'No, not today. But he gave me permission yesterday.'

'Could you tell me why you want to go back, sir?'

'My notebook. I was jotting down the names of his books yesterday, and I must have set it down on the bookcase inside. I didn't have it when I got on the train, and this was the last place I'd been.' He saw that the soldier was about to refuse, so he added, 'You're welcome to come inside with me if you'd like. All I want to do is pick up the notebook if it's there. I don't think the apartment is going to be any help to me, but I have notes on other things in there, and they're important to me.' He was talking too much, he realized.

The two soldiers exchanged glances, and apparently one of them decided that it would be all right. The one he had spoken to handed his rifle to his companion and said, 'If you'll come along with me, sir, I'll let you into the apartment.'

Smiling his gratitude, Brunetti followed him towards the front entrance and into the elevator. Neither of them spoke during the short ride to the third floor nor while the soldier opened the door. He stepped back and allowed Brunetti to walk past him into the apartment, then closed the door behind them.

Brunetti went into the living room and up to the bookcase. He made a show of looking for the notebook, which was in his jacket pocket, even stooped down and looked behind a chair that stood beside the bookcase. 'That's strange. I'm sure I had it here.' He pulled a few books forward and looked behind them. Nothing. He paused, reflecting on where else he might have set it down.

'I got myself a drink of water in the kitchen,' he said to the soldier. 'I might have set it down in there.' Then, as if he had just thought of it, 'Is there any chance that someone might have come in and found it?'

'No, sir. No one's been in here since you left.'

'Good,' Brunetti answered with his friendliest smile, 'then it's got to be here.' He preceded the soldier into the kitchen and went to the worktop beside the sink. He looked around him, bent down to look under the kitchen table, then stood. As he did, he placed himself directly in front of the water heater. The screws on the front panel which he had replaced yesterday, careful to leave them at exact verticals and horizontals, had all been moved and were all slightly out of true. So someone had checked and found that the bags were missing.

'It doesn't seem to be here, sir.'

'No, it doesn't,' Brunetti agreed in a voice into which he put real confusion. 'Very strange. I'm sure I had it while I was here.'

'Could you have dropped it in your car, sir?' the soldier suggested.

'The driver would have told me,' Brunetti said, then, as if the idea had just come to him, 'if he found it.'

'Better check your vehicle, sir.'

They left the apartment together, the soldier careful to lock the door behind him. As they descended in the elevator, Brunetti decided that it would be far too coincidental for him to find the notebook hidden behind the back seat of the car. Consequently, when they emerged from the building, he thanked the soldier for his help and went back to his own car.

Not sure if the American was within hearing distance and not certain about whether he understood Italian, he played it straight and asked his driver if he had found a notebook in the car. Obviously, he had not. Brunetti opened the back door, stuck his hand behind the back seat, and felt around in the empty space. He found, not at all to his surprise, nothing. He pulled himself from the car and turned back towards the Jeep. He opened his hands in an empty, significant gesture, and then got into the back seat and asked the driver to take him to the station.

a place called Biloxi, a city he believed to be in Bangladesh. No, in America, but how could that name be explained? There was a large picture of houses and cars overturned, trees shoved over onto one another. He turned a page and read that a pit bull had bitten off the hand of a sleeping child in Detroit, a city he was certain was in America. There was no picture. The Secretary of Defense had assured Congress that all those contractors who had defrauded the government would be prosecuted to the full extent of the law. Remarkable, the similarity between the rhetoric of American politics and Italian. He had no doubt that the illusory nature of that promise would be the same in both countries.

There were three pages of cartoons, none of which made the least bit of sense to him, and six of sports news, which made even less. In one of the cartoons, a caveman swung a club, and on one of the sports pages, a man in a striped uniform did the same. Beyond that, all was arcana to Brunetti. The last page carried a continuation of the report on the hurricane, but then the train pulled into Venice station and he abandoned the story. He left the paper on the seat beside him; perhaps someone else could profit from it better than he.

It was after seven when they arrived, but the sky was still light. That would end this weekend, he thought, when the clocks were set back an hour, and it got dark earlier. Or was it the other way, and it stayed bright longer? He hoped that it took most people as long to figure this out each year as it did him. He crossed the Bridge of the Scalzi and entered the rabbit warren of streets that wove their way back towards his apartment. Few people, even at this hour, passed him, since most went to the station or to the bus depot at Piazzale Roma by boat. Usually as he walked, he glanced at the fronts of buildings, up at their windows, down narrow streets, always alert to something he might not have noticed before. Like many of his townsmen, Brunetti never tired of studying the city, every so often delighting himself by discovering something he had never noticed before. Over the course of the years, he had worked out a system that allowed him to reward himself for each discovery: a new window earned him a coffee; a new statue of a saint, however small, got him a glass of wine; and once, years ago, he had noticed on a wall he must have passed five times a week since he was a child a lapidary stone that commemorated the site of the Aldine Publishing House, the oldest in Italy, founded in the fourteenth century. He had gone right around the corner and into a bar in Campo San Luca and ordered himself a Brandy Alexander, though it was ten in the morning and the barman had given Brunetti a strange look when he placed the glass in front of him.

Tonight, however, the streets failed to capture his interest; he was still back in Vicenza, still seeing the grooves in the four screws that held the front panel of the water heater in Foster's apartment, each of them slightly moved from the careful straight lines in which Brunetti had left them the day before, each giving the lie to the soldier's assertion that no one had been in the apartment after Brunetti. So now they – whoever 'they' were – knew that Brunetti had taken the drugs from the apartment and had said nothing about it.

He let himself into the building and had unlocked their mailbox before he remembered that Paola would have been home hours ago and would have checked the post. He began the ascent to his home, grateful for the first flight, low and gentle, a remnant of the original fifteenth-century *palazzo*. At the top, the stairs jogged off to the left and rose up, in two steep flights, to the next floor. A door awaited him there, which he unlocked and closed behind him. Another flight, these dangerous and steep. They doubled back above themselves and carried him up the last twenty-five steps to the door of his apartment. He unlocked the door and let himself in, finally home.

There was the smell of cooking to welcome him, one scent mingling with another. Tonight he could make out the faint odour of squash, which meant that Paola was making *risotto con zucca*, available only in this season, when the dark green, squat *barucca* squash were brought from Chioggia, across the *laguna*. And after that? Shank of veal? Roasted with olives and white wine?

He hung his jacket in the cupboard and went down the hall to the kitchen. The room was hotter than usual, which meant the oven was on. The large frying pan on the stove revealed, when he lifted the lid, bright orange chunks of *zucca*, frying slowly with minced onions. He took a glass from the rack beside the sink and pulled a bottle of Ribolla from the refrigerator. He poured a little more than a mouthful, tasted, drank it down, then filled the glass and replaced the bottle. The warmth of the kitchen swept up about him. He loosened his tie and went back down the corridor. 'Paola?'

'I'm here, in the back,' he heard her answering call.

He didn't answer but went into the long living room and then out onto the balcony. This was the best time of day for Brunetti, for he could see, from their terrace, the sunset off in the West. On the clearest of days, he could see the Dolomites from the small window in the kitchen, but it was so late in the day now that they would be hazed over and invisible. He stayed where he was, forearms propped on the railing, studying the rooftops and towers that never ceased to please him. He heard Paola move down the hall, back into the kitchen, heard the clang of shifted pots, but he stayed where he was, listening to the eight o'clock bells ring out from San Polo, then to the answering resonance of San Marco, a few seconds late, as always, come booming across the city. When all the bells were silent, he went back into the house, closing the door against the growing evening chill.

In the kitchen, Paola stood at the stove, stirring the risotto, pausing now and again to add more boiling broth. 'Glass of wine?' he asked. She shook her head, still stirring. He passed behind her, paused long enough to kiss her on the back of the neck, and poured himself another glass of wine.

'How was Vicenza?' she asked.

'Better to ask me how was America.'

169

'Yes, I know,' she said. 'It's incredible, isn't it?'

'Were you ever there?'

'Years ago. With the Alvises.' Seeing his puzzled look, she explained. 'The Colonel, when he was stationed in Padova. There was some sort of party at the officers' club, for Italian and American officers. About ten years ago.'

'I don't remember.'

'No, you didn't go. It was when you were in Naples. I think. Is it still the same?'

'Depends on what it was like then,' he said, smiling.

'Don't be smart with me, Guido. What was it like?'

'It was very clean, and everyone smiled a great deal.'

'Good,' she said, stirring again. 'Then it hasn't changed.'

'I wonder why it is, that they always smile so much.' He had noticed the same thing, each time he was in America.

She turned away from the risotto and stared at him. 'Why shouldn't they smile, Guido? Think about it. They're the richest people in the world. Everyone has to defer to them in politics, and they have convinced themselves, somehow, that everything they have ever done in their very brief history has been done for no purpose other than to further the general good of mankind. Why shouldn't they smile?' She turned back to the pan and muttered darkly as she felt the rice sticking to the bottom. She poured more broth into it and stirred quickly for a moment.

'Is this going to turn into a cell meeting?' he asked blandly. Though they generally agreed about politics, Brunetti had always voted Socialist, while Paola voted, fiercely, Communist. But now, with the demise of the system and the death of the party, he had begun to take tentative shots at her.

She didn't bother to grace him with an answer.

He started to pull down plates in order to set the table. 'Where are the kids?'

'Both with friends.' Then, before he could ask, she added, 'Yes, they both called and asked permission.' She turned off the flame under the risotto, added a substantial chunk of butter that stood on the worktop, and poured in a small dish of finely grated Parmigiano Reggiano. She stirred it around until both were dissolved into the rice, poured the risotto into a serving bowl, and set it on the table. She pulled out her chair, sat down, and turned the spoon towards him, saying, *'Mangia, ti fa bene,'* a command that had filled Brunetti with joy for as long as he could remember.

He filled his dish, abundantly. He'd worked hard, spent the day in a foreign country, so who cared how much risotto he ate? Starting from the centre, he worked his fork in a neat concentric circle and pushed the risotto to the edge of his dish to help it cool faster. He took two forkfuls, sighed in appreciation, and continued to eat.

When Paola saw that he had passed beyond the point of hunger and was eating for the pleasure of the act, she said, 'You haven't told me how your trip to America was.'

He spoke through the risotto. 'Confusing. The

Americans are very polite and say they want to help, but no one seems to know anything that might help me.'

'And the doctor?'

'The pretty one?' he asked, grinning.

'Yes, Guido, the pretty one.'

Seeing he had run that one into the ground, he answered simply, 'I still think she's the person who knows what I want to know. But she's not saying anything. She gets out of the Army in six months, so she'll go back to America and all of this will be behind her.'

'And he was her lover?' Paola asked with a snort to show that she refused to believe the doctor wouldn't help if she could.

'It would seem so.'

'Then I'm not so sure she'll just pack up and forget about him.'

'Maybe it's something she doesn't want to know.'

'Like what?'

'Nothing. Well, nothing I can explain.' He had decided not to tell her about the two plastic bags he had found in Foster's apartment; that was something no one was to know. Except for the person who had opened the water heater, seen that the bags were gone, and then tightened those screws. He pulled the bowl of risotto towards him. 'Should I finish this?' he asked, not having to be a detective to know the answer.

'Go ahead. I don't like it left over, and neither do you.'

While he finished the risotto, she took the bowl

from the table and placed it in the sink. He shifted two wicker mats about on the table to make a place for the roasting pan Paola took from the oven.

'What are you going to do?'

'I don't know. See what Patta does,' he said, cutting a piece of meat from the shank and placing it on her plate. With a motion of her hand, she signalled that she didn't want any more. He cut himself two large pieces, reached for some bread, and started to eat again.

'What difference does it make what Patta does?' she asked.

'Ah, my sweet innocent,' he replied. 'If he tries to shift me away from this, then I'll be sure that someone wants it covered up. And since our Vice-Questore responds only to voices that come from high places – the higher the place, the faster he moves – then I'll know that whoever wants this thing shut down has a certain amount of power.'

'Like who?'

He took another piece of bread and wiped at the gravy on his plate. 'Your guess is as good as mine, but it makes me very uncomfortable, thinking about who it might be.'

'Who?'

'I don't know, not exactly. But if the American military is involved, then you can be sure it's political, and that means the government. Theirs. And that means ours, as well.'

'And hence a phone call to Patta?'

'Yes.'

'And hence trouble?'

Brunetti was not given to remarking upon the self-evident.

'And if Patta doesn't try to stop you?'

Brunetti shrugged. He'd wait and see.

Paola removed the plates. 'Dessert?'

He shook his head. 'What time will the kids be home?'

Moving about the kitchen, she answered, 'Chiara will be here by nine. I told Raffaele to be home by ten.' The difference in the way she expressed it told the whole story.

'You speak to his teachers?' Brunetti asked.

'No. It's too soon in the year.'

'When's the first meeting for the parents?'

'I don't know. I've got the letter from the school around here somewhere. In October, I think.'

'How is he?' Even as he asked it, he hoped Paola would just answer the question, not ask him what he meant, because he didn't know what he meant.

'I don't know, Guido. He never talks to me, not about school or about his friends or what he's doing. Were you like that when you were his age?'

He thought about being sixteen and what it had been like. 'I don't know. I suppose I was. But then I discovered girls, and I forgot all about being angry or lost, or whatever I was. I just wanted them to like me. That's the only thing that was important to me.'

'Were there a lot of them?' she asked.

He shrugged.

'And did they like you?'

He grinned.

'Oh, go away, Guido, and find yourself something to do. Watch television.'

'I hate television.'

'Then help me do the dishes.'

'I love television.'

'Guido,' she repeated, not exasperated, but on the way, 'just get up and go away from me.'

Both of them heard the sound of a key in the lock. It was Chiara, banging the door open and dropping a school book as she came into the apartment. She came down the hall to the kitchen, kissed both of her parents, and went to stand next to Brunetti, arm draped on his shoulder. 'Is there anything to eat, Mamma?' she asked.

'Didn't Luisa's mother feed you?'

'Yes, but that was hours ago. I'm starved.'

Brunetti wrapped his arm around her and pulled her onto his lap. In his bad cop voice he said, harshly, 'All right, I've got you. Confess. Where do you put it?'

'Oh, Papà, stop it,' she said, squirming with delight. 'I just eat it. But then I get hungry again. Don't you?'

'Your father usually waits at least an hour, Chiara.' Then, more kindly, Paola asked, 'Fruit? A sandwich?'

'Both?' she pleaded.

By the time Chiara had eaten a sandwich, a massive thing filled with prosciutto, tomato, and mayonnaise, then devoured two apples, it was time for all of them to go to bed. Raffaele had not returned by eleven-thirty, but Brunetti, waking in the night, heard the door open and close and his son's footsteps in the hall. After that, he slept deeply.

13

Ordinarily, Brunetti would not bother to go to the Questura on a Saturday, but this morning he did, more to see who else turned up than for any other reason. He made no attempt to get there on time, ambled through Campo San Luca and had a cappuccino at Rosa Salva, the bar Paola insisted had the best coffee in the city.

He continued towards the Questura, cutting parallel to San Marco but avoiding the Piazza itself. When he arrived, he went to the second floor, where he found Rossi talking to Riverre, an officer he thought was out on sick leave. When he walked in, Rossi signalled for him to come over to his desk.

'I'm glad you're here, sir. We've got something new.'

'What?'

'A break-in. On the Grand Canal. That big *palazzo* that's just been restored, over by San Stae.'

'The one that belongs to the Milanese?'

'Yes, sir. When he got there last night, he found two men, maybe there were three, he wasn't sure, in the place.'

'What happened?'

'Vianello's over at the hospital, talking to him now. What I've got, I got from the men who answered the call and took him to the hospital.'

'What did they say?'

'He tried to get out, but they grabbed him and gave him a going over. He had to be taken to the hospital, but it's nothing too bad. Cuts and bruises.'

'And the three men? Two men?'

'No sign of them. The men who answered the call went back to the place after they took him to the hospital. It looks like they got away with a couple of paintings and some of his wife's jewellery.'

'Any description of the men who did it?'

'He didn't see them clearly, couldn't say much, except that one of them was very tall, and he thought one of them might have a beard. But,' Rossi added, looking up and smiling, 'there was a pair of tourists sitting on the edge of the canal, and they saw three men come out of the *palazzo*. One of them was carrying a suitcase. These kids were still there when our men arrived, and they gave us a description.' He paused and smiled as if sure

178

Brunetti would enjoy what was coming next. 'One of them sounds like Ruffolo.'

Brunetti's response was immediate. 'I thought he was in prison.'

'He was, sir, until two weeks ago.'

'Have you shown them photos?'

'Yes, sir. And they think it's him. They noticed the big ears.'

'What about the owner? Have you shown him the photo?'

'Not yet, sir. I just got back from talking to these Belgian kids. Sounds like Ruffolo to me.'

'And what about the other two men? Are the descriptions these Belgian kids gave you the same as his?'

'Well, sir, it was dark, and they weren't really paying attention.'

'But?'

'But they're pretty sure neither one of them had a beard.'

Brunetti thought about this for a moment, then told Rossi, 'Take the photo over to the hospital and see if he recognizes him. Can he talk, the Milanese?'

'Oh, yes, sir. He's all right. A couple of bruises, a black eye, but he's all right. Place is fully insured.'

Why was it that it always seemed less a crime if the place was insured?

'If he gives you a positive identification of Ruffolo, let me know, and I'll go over to his mother's place and see if she knows where he is.'

Rossi snorted at this.

'I know, I know. She'd lie to the Pope if it would save her little Peppino. Well, who's to blame her? He *is* her only son. Besides, I'd like to see the old battle-axe again; I don't think I've seen her more than twice since the last time I arrested him.'

'She tried to get you with scissors then, didn't she, sir?' Rossi asked.

'Well, her heart really wasn't in it, and Peppino was there to stop her.' He grinned outright at the memory, certainly one of the most absurd moments in his career. 'Besides, they were only pinking shears.'

'She's a piece of work, Signora Concetta.'

'Indeed,' Brunetti agreed. 'And get someone to keep an eye on that girlfriend of his. What's her name?'

'Ivana Something-or-Other.'

'Yes, her.'

'You want us to talk to her, sir?'

'No, she'd just say she hasn't seen him. Speak to those people who live under her. They turned Ruffolo in last time. Maybe they'd let us put someone in the apartment until he shows up. Ask them.'

'Yes, sir.'

'Anything else?'

'No, nothing.'

'I'll be in my office for an hour or so. Let me know what happens in the hospital, if it's Ruffolo.' He started to leave the office, but Rossi called out after him.

'One thing, sir, a phone call came for you last night.'

'Who was it?'

'I don't know, sir. The operator said the call came at about eleven. A woman. She asked for you by name, but she didn't speak Italian, or very little. He said something else, but I don't remember what it was.'

'I'll stop and talk to him on the way up,' Brunetti said and left the office. Instead of taking the stairs, he stopped at the end of the corridor and went into the cubicle where the telephone operator sat. He was a young police recruit, fresh-faced and probably all of eighteen. Brunetti couldn't remember his name.

When he saw Brunetti, he leaped to his feet, dragging with him the wire that attached his headphones to the switchboard. 'Good morning, sir.'

'Good morning. Please sit down.'

The young man did, poised nervously on the edge of his chair.

'Rossi tells me a phone call came for me last night.'

'Yes, sir,' the recruit said, fighting the urge to jump to his feet when addressing a superior.

'Did you take the call?'

'Yes sir.' Then, to prevent Brunetti from asking why he was still there twelve hours later, the young man explained, 'I was taking Monico's shift, sir. He's sick.'

Uninterested in this detail, Brunetti asked, 'What did she say?'

'She asked for you by name, sir. But she didn't speak more than a little bit of Italian.'

'Do you remember exactly what she said?'

'Yes, sir,' he said, fumbling at some papers on the desk in front of the switchboard. 'I have it written down here.' He pushed papers aside and came up with a single sheet, from which he read, 'She asked for you, but she didn't give her name or anything. I asked her for her name, but she didn't answer me, or she didn't understand. I told her that you weren't here, but then she asked for you again.'

'Was she speaking English?'

'I think so, sir, but she only spoke a few words and I couldn't understand her. I told her to speak in Italian.'

'What else did she say?'

'She said something that sounded like "*basta*", or it could have been "*pasta*", or "*posta*".'

'Anything else?'

'No, sir. Just that. And then she hung up.'

'How did she sound?'

The boy thought about this for a while and finally answered, 'She didn't sound anything in particular, sir. Just disappointed that you weren't here, I'd say.'

'All right. If she calls back, put her call through to me or to Rossi. He speaks English.'

'Yes, sir,' the young man said. When Brunetti turned to leave the room, the temptation proved irresistible, and the young man jumped to his feet to salute Brunetti's retreating back.

A woman, one who spoke very little Italian. '*Molto poco*', he remembered the doctor saying. He also remembered something his father had once told him about fishing, when it had been possible to fish in the *laguna*, that it was bad to flick the bait, that it scared the fish away. So he would wait. She was there for six months, at any rate, and he wasn't going anywhere. If she didn't call again, he'd call the hospital on Monday and ask to speak to her.

And now Ruffolo was out and back in business. A petty thief and burglar, Ruffolo had been in and out of jail for the last ten years, twice put there by Brunetti. His parents had moved up from Naples years ago, bringing with them this delinquent child. His father had drunk himself to death, but not before instilling in his only son the principle that the Ruffolos were not meant for things as ordinary as work, or trade, not even study. True fruit of his father's loins, Giuseppe had never worked, the only trade he had ever practised was in stolen objects, and all he had ever studied was how best to open a lock or break into a house. If he was back at work so soon after being released, two years in prison had apparently not been wasted on him.

Brunetti, however, couldn't keep himself from liking both the mother and the son. Peppino seemed not to hold Brunetti personally responsible for having arrested him, and Signora Concetta, once the pinking shears incident was forgotten, had been grateful for Brunetti's testimony at Ruffolo's trial that he had avoided the use of any force or threat of violence in the commission of his crimes. It was probably that testimony that had helped limit the sentence for burglary to only two years.

He didn't have to send down to the record office for Ruffolo's file. Sooner or later, he would turn up at his mother's apartment, or at Ivana's, and Giuseppe would soon be back inside, there to become more practised in crime, more fully confirmed in his doom.

As soon as he got to his office, he began to look for Rizzardi's report on the autopsy of the young American. When they spoke, the pathologist had said nothing about the presence of drugs in the blood, and Brunetti had not asked that question specifically at the time of the autopsy. He found the report on his desk, opened it, and began to page through. Just as Rizzardi had threatened, its language was virtually impenetrable. On the second page, he found what he thought might be the answer, though it was hard to tell in the midst of the long Latin terms and tortured syntax. He read it through three times and, by then, was reasonably sure that it meant that there had been no traces of drugs of any sort in his blood. He would have been surprised if the autopsy had discovered anything different.

The intercom buzzer on his phone sounded. He answered with a prompt, 'Yes, sir.'

Patta didn't bother asking him how he knew who was calling, a sure sign that the call was important. 'I'd like to speak to you, Commissario.' The use of the title, rather than his name, emphasized the importance of the call.

Brunetti said that he would go immediately down to the Vice-Questore's office. Patta was a man of limited moods, each one clearly legible, and this was one that Brunetti needed to read carefully.

When he went into Patta's office, Brunetti found his superior sitting behind his empty desk, hands folded in front of him. Usually, Patta made the attempt to create the appearance of diligence, even if it was no more than an empty file in front of him. Today there was nothing, just a serious, one might even say solemn, face and a pair of folded hands. The spicy odour of some omnisexual cologne wafted out from Patta, whose face, this morning, appeared to have been oiled rather than shaved. Brunetti walked over to the desk and stood in front of it, wondering how long Patta would remain silent, a technique he frequently employed when he wanted to stress the importance of what he had to say.

At least a full minute passed before Patta said, 'Sit down, Commissario.' The repeated use of the title told Brunetti that what he was going to hear would be unpleasant in some way and that Patta knew it.

'I'd like to talk to you about this robbery,' Patta said with no preamble as soon as Brunetti was seated.

Brunetti suspected he did not mean this most recent one, on the Grand Canal, even though the victim was an industrialist from Milan. An assault on a person of that importance would usually be enough to drive Patta to almost any excess in the appearance of diligence.

'Yes, sir,' Brunetti said.

'I learned today that you made another trip out to Vicenza.'

'Yes, sir.'

'Why was that necessary? Don't you have enough to do here in Venice?'

Brunetti steeled himself, knowing that, despite their previous conversation, he would have to explain everything all over again. 'I wanted to speak to some of the people who knew him, sir.'

'Didn't you do that the first day you were there?'

'No, sir, there wasn't time.'

'You didn't say anything about that when you came back that afternoon.' When Brunetti didn't respond, Patta asked, 'Why didn't you do that the first day?'

'There wasn't time, sir.'

'You were back here by six. There would have been plenty of time to stay out there and finish things up that afternoon.'

Only with difficulty did Brunetti stop himself from displaying his astonishment that Patta would recall a detail such as the time Brunetti had returned from Vicenza. This was the man, after all, who could not be depended upon to name more than two or three of the uniformed police.

'I didn't get to it, sir.'

'What happened when you went back?'

'I spoke to Foster's commanding officer and to one of the men who worked with him.'

'And what did you learn?'

'Nothing substantial, sir.'

Patta glared across the desk at him. 'What's that supposed to mean?'

'I didn't learn anything about why a person would want to kill him.'

186

Patta threw his hands up in the air and let out a great sigh of exasperation. 'That's exactly the point, Brunetti. There is no reason why anyone would want to kill him, which is why you didn't find it. And, I might add, why you aren't going to find it. Because it isn't there. He was killed for his money, and the proof of that is the fact that his wallet wasn't found on him.' One of his shoes wasn't found with him, either. Did that mean he was killed for a size 11 Reebok?

Patta opened his top drawer and pulled out a few sheets of paper. 'I think you've wasted more than enough time chasing out to Vicenza, Brunetti. I don't like the idea of your bothering the Americans about this. The crime happened here, and the killer will be found here.' Patta made that last sound firmly terminal. He picked up one of the papers and glanced at it. 'I'd like you to make better use of your time from now on.'

'And how might I do that, sir?'

Patta peered at him, then back at the paper. 'I'm assigning you to the investigation of this break-in on the Grand Canal.' Brunetti was certain that the location of that crime, and the suggestion it made about the wealth of the victim, was more than enough to make it seem, to Patta, far more important in real terms than mere murder, especially when that victim was not even an officer.

'And what about the American, sir?'

'We'll go through the usual procedures. We'll see if any of our bad boys talk about it or suddenly seem to have more money than they should.'

'And if they don't?'

'The Americans are looking into it, as well,' Patta said, as if that put an end to it.

'I beg your pardon, sir. How can the Americans look into something here in Venice?'

Patta narrowed his eyes. 'They have their ways, Brunetti. They have their ways.'

Brunetti was in no doubt as to that, but he was in some doubt as to whether those ways would necessarily be directed towards finding the murderer. 'I'd prefer to continue with this, sir. I don't believe it was a mugging.'

'I've decided it was, Commissario, and that's how we're going to treat it.'

'What does that mean, sir?'

Patta tried astonishment. 'It means, Commissario, and I want you to pay attention to this, it means precisely what I said, that we are going to treat it as a murder that happened during a robbery attempt.'

'Officially?'

'Officially,' Patta repeated, then added, with heavy emphasis, 'and unofficially.'

There was no need for Brunetti to ask what that meant.

Gracious in his victory, Patta said, 'Of course, your interest and enthusiasm in this will be appreciated by the Americans.' Brunetti thought it would make more sense for them to appreciate success, but this was not an opinion that could be offered now when Patta was at his most quixotic and had to be handled with greatest delicacy.

'Well, I'm still not convinced, sir,' Brunetti began, letting doubt and resignation struggle in his voice. 'But I suppose it's possible. I certainly found nothing about him that would suggest anything else.' That is, if he discounted the odd few hundred million in cocaine.

'I'm glad you see it that way, Brunetti. I think it shows that you're growing more realistic about police work.' Patta looked down at the papers on his desk. 'They had a Guardi.'

Brunetti, left behind by his superior's chamois-like leap from one subject to another, could only ask, 'A what?'

'A Guardi, Commissario. Francesco Guardi. I would think you'd at least recognize the name: he's one of your most famous Venetian painters.'

'Oh, sorry, sir. I thought it was a kind of German television.'

Patta gave a firm and disapproving 'No,' before he looked down at the papers on his desk. 'All I have is a list from Signor Viscardi. A Guardi, a Monet, and a Gauguin.'

'Is he still in hospital, this Signor Viscardi?' Brunetti asked.

'Yes, I believe so. Why?'

'He seems pretty certain about which paintings they had, even if he didn't see the men who took them.'

'What are you suggesting?'

'I'm not suggesting anything, sir,' Brunetti answered. 'Maybe he had only three paintings.' But if all he had were three paintings, this case would not have moved so quickly to the top of

Patta's list. 'What does Signor Viscardi do in Milan, if I might ask?'

'He directs a number of factories.'

'Directs, or owns and directs?'

Patta made no attempt to disguise his irritation. 'He's an important citizen, and he has spent an enormous amount of money on the restoration of that *palazzo*. He's an asset to the city, and I think we should see that, if nothing else, the man is safe while he's here.'

'He and his possessions,' Brunetti added.

'Yes, and his possessions.' Patta repeated the word but not the dry tone. 'I'd like you to see to this investigation, Commissario, and I expect Signor Viscardi to be treated with every respect.'

'Certainly, sir.' Brunetti got up to leave. 'Do you know what sort of factories he directs, sir?'

'I believe they manufacture armaments.'

'Thank you, sir.'

'And I don't want you bothering the Americans any more, Brunetti. Is that clear?'

'Yes, sir.' It certainly was clear, but the reason was not.

'Good, then get to it. I'd like this sorted out as quickly as possible.'

Brunetti smiled and left Patta's office, wondering what strings had been pulled, and by whom. With Viscardi, it was pretty easy to figure out: armaments, enough money to buy and restore a *palazzo* on the Grand Canal – the mingled odours of money and power had come wafting out of every phrase Patta spoke. With the American, the scents were less easy to trace back to their source, but that difficulty made them no less tangible than the others. But it was clear that the word had been passed to Patta: the death of the American was to be treated as a robbery gone wrong, nothing more. But from whom?

Instead of going up to his office, he went back down the stairs and into the main office. Vianello had returned from the hospital and was at his desk, leaning back in his chair, telephone pressed to his ear. When he saw Brunetti come in, he cut the conversation short and hung up.

'Yes, sir?' he said.

Brunetti leaned against the side of Vianello's desk. 'This Viscardi, how did he seem when you spoke to him?'

'Upset. He'd been in a ward all night, had just managed to get himself put into a private room . . .'

Brunetti interrupted. 'How'd he manage that?'

Vianello shrugged. The Casinò was not the only public institution in the city that carried a 'Non Nobis' sign in front of it. The hospital's, although visible only to the wealthy, was no less real. 'I suppose he knows someone there or knows someone to call. People like him always do.' From Vianello's tone, it didn't sound like Viscardi had made a hit.

'What's he like?' Brunetti asked.

Vianello smiled, then grimaced. 'You know. Typical Milanese. Wouldn't say 'R' if he had a mouthful of them,' he said, eliding all of the 'R's in the sentence, imitating perfectly this Milanese affectation in speech, so popular among the most *arriviste* politicians and the comedians who delighted in mocking them. 'First thing he did was tell me how important the paintings are, which, I suppose, means how important he is. Then he complained about having to spend the night in a ward. I think that meant he was afraid of picking up some low-class disease.'

'Did he give you a description of the men?'

'He said that one of them was very tall, taller than I am.' Vianello was one of the tallest men on the force. 'And the other one had a beard.'

'How many were there, two or three?'

'He wasn't sure. They grabbed him when he went in, and he was so surprised that he didn't see, or he doesn't remember.'

'How badly is he hurt?'

'Not bad enough for a private room,' Vianello said, making no attempt to disguise his disapproval.

'Could you be a bit more specific?' Brunetti asked with a smile.

Vianello took no offence and answered, 'He's got a black eye. That will get worse today. Someone really gave him a good shot there. And he's got a cut lip, some bruises on his arms.'

'That's all?'

'Yes, sir.'

'I agree; hardly seems like the sort of thing to require a private room. Or a hospital at all.'

Vianello responded immediately to Brunetti's tone. 'Are you thinking what I think you are, sir?'

'Vice-Questore Patta knows what the three missing paintings are. What time did the call come in?'

'Just a little past midnight, sir.'

Brunetti looked at his watch. 'Twelve hours. The paintings are by Guardi, Monet, and Gauguin.'

'Sorry, sir, I don't know about that sort of thing. But do the names mean money?'

Brunetti gave a very affirmative nod. 'Rossi told me that the place was insured. How'd he come to know that?'

'The agent called us at about ten and asked if he could go and have a look at the *palazzo*.'

Vianello took a pack of cigarettes from his desk and lit one. 'Rossi told me these Belgian kids think Ruffolo was there.' Brunetti nodded. 'Ruffolo's just a little runt of a guy, isn't he, sir? Not very tall at all.' He blew out a thin stream of smoke, then waved it away.

'And he certainly didn't grow a beard while he was in prison,' Brunetti observed.

'So that means that neither of the men Viscardi says he saw could have been Ruffolo, doesn't it, sir?'

'That certainly would seem to be the case,' Brunetti said. 'I asked Rossi to go over to the hospital and ask Viscardi if he recognizes a picture of Ruffolo.'

'Probably won't,' Vianello remarked laconically.

Brunetti pushed himself away from the desk. 'I think I'll go and make a few phone calls. If you'll excuse me, officer.'

'Certainly, sir,' Vianello said, then added, 'Zero two,' giving Brunetti the dialling prefix for Milan.

14

In his office, Brunetti took a spiral-bound notebook from his desk and began to leaf through it. For years he had been telling himself, then promising himself, that he would take the names and numbers in this book and arrange them in some sort of order. He renewed the vow each time, such as now, he had to hunt through it for a number he had not called in months or years. In a way, paging through it was like strolling through a museum in which he saw many familiar paintings, allowing each to summon up the flash of memory before he passed on in search of the one he had come to see. Finally he found it, the home number of Riccardo Fosco, the Financial Editor of one of the major weekly news magazines.

Until a few years ago, Fosco had been the bright

light of the news media, unearthing financial scandals in the most unlikely places, had been one of the first to begin asking questions about the Banco Ambrosiano. His office had become the centre of a web of information about the real nature of business in Italy, his columns the place to look for the first suggestions that something might not be right with a company, a buy-out, or a takeover. Two years ago, as he emerged from that same office at five in the afternoon, on his way to meet friends for a drink, someone in a parked car opened up with a machine gun, aimed carefully at his knees, shattering them both, and now Fosco's home was his office, and walking was something he did only with the help of two canes, one knee permanently stiffened and the other with a range of motion of only thirty degrees. No arrest had ever been made in the crime.

'Fosco,' he said, answering as he always did.

'*Ciao*, Riccardo. It's Guido Brunetti.'

'*Ciao*, Guido. I haven't heard from you in a long time. Are you still trying to find out about the money that was supposed to save Venice?'

It was a long-standing joke between them, the ease with which the millions of dollars – no one ever knew exactly how much – that had been raised by UNESCO to 'save' Venice had disappeared in the offices and deep pockets of the 'projectors' who had rushed forward with their plans and programmes after the devastating flood of 1966. There was a foundation with a full working staff, an archive full of blueprints, there were even fund-raising galas and balls, but there was no more money, and the tides, unimpeded, continued to do whatever they chose with the city. This story, with threads leading to the UN, to the Common Market, and to various governments and financial institutions, had proven too complicated even for Fosco, who had never written about it, fearing that his audience would accuse him of having turned to fiction. Brunetti, for his part, had worked on the assumption that, since most of the people who had been involved in the projects were Venetian, the money had indeed gone to save the city, though perhaps not in the manner originally intended.

'No, Riccardo, it's about one of yours, a Milanese. Viscardi. I don't even know his first name, but he's in armaments, and he's just finished spending a fortune restoring a *palazzo* here.'

'Augusto,' Fosco replied instantly, then repeated the name for the sheer beauty of it, 'Augusto Viscardi.'

'That was quick,' Brunetti said.

'Oh, yes. Signor Viscardi's is a name I hear quite often.'

'And what sort of things do you hear?'

'The munitions factories are out in Monza. There are four of them. The word is he had enormous contracts with Iraq, in fact, with a number of countries in the Middle East. Somehow, he managed to continue deliveries even during the war, through the Yemen, I think.' Fosco paused for a moment, then added, 'But I've heard that he had trouble during the war.'

'What sort of trouble?' Brunetti asked.

'Well, not enough to do him serious harm, or at least that's what I heard. None of those factories closed during the war, and I don't mean only his. From what I've heard, the whole zone remained at full production. There'll always be someone to buy what they make.'

'But what was the trouble he had?'

'I'm not sure. I'll have to make some calls out here. But the rumours were that he got hit pretty hard. Most of them make sure the payments are made in some place safe like Panama or Lichtenstein before they make delivery, but Viscardi had been doing business with them for so long – I think he even went there a few times, talked to the boss man – that he didn't bother, sure he'd be given best-dealer treatment.'

'And that didn't happen?'

'No, that didn't happen. A lot of the stuff got blown up before it was delivered. I think a whole shipload might have been hijacked by pirates in the Gulf. Let me call around, Guido. I'll get back to you soon, within an hour.'

'Is there anything personal?'

'Nothing I've heard, but I'll ask.'

'Thanks, Riccardo.'

'Can you tell me what this is about?'

Brunetti saw no reason why he couldn't. 'His place was robbed last night, and he walked in on the robbery. He couldn't identify the three men, but he knew what three paintings they took.'

'Sounds like Viscardi,' Fosco said.

'Is he that stupid?'

'No, he's not stupid, not at all. But he is arrogant,

and he's willing to take chances. It's those two things that have made him his fortune.' Fosco's voice changed. 'Sorry, Guido, I've got a call on another line. I'll call you later this morning, all right?'

'Thanks, Riccardo,' he repeated, but before he could add, 'I appreciate it,' the line was dead.

The secret of police success lay, Brunetti knew, not in brilliant deductions or the psychological manipulation of suspects but in the simple fact that human beings tended to assume that their own level of intelligence was the norm, the standard, and to work on that assumption. Hence the stupid were quickly caught, for their idea of what was cunning was so lamentably impoverished as to make them obvious prey. This same rule, unfortunately, made his job all the more difficult when he had to deal with criminals possessed of intelligence or courage.

During the next hour, Brunetti called down to Vianello and got the name of the insurance agent who had asked to inspect the scene of the crime. When he finally found the man at his office, he assured Brunetti that the paintings were all genuine and had all disappeared in the robbery. Copies of papers of authenticity were on his desk, even as they spoke. The current value of the three paintings? Well, they were insured for a total of five billion lire, but their current real market value had perhaps increased in the last year, with the rise in prices for Impressionists. No, there had never been a robbery before. Some jewellery had also been taken, but it was nothing in value when compared to the paintings: a few hundred million lire. Ah, how sweet the world in which a few hundred million lire were viewed as nothing.

By the time he was finished talking to the agent, Rossi was back from the hospital, telling him that Signor Viscardi had been very surprised to see the picture of Ruffolo. He had quickly overcome that emotion, however, and said that the photo bore no resemblance to either of the two men he had seen, now insistent, upon further reflection, that there had been only two.

'What do you think?' Brunetti asked.

There was no uncertainty in Rossi's voice when he answered, 'He's lying. I don't know what else he's lying about, but he's lying about not knowing Ruffolo. He couldn't have been more surprised if I'd shown him a picture of his own mother.'

'I guess that means I'll go over and have a talk with Ruffolo's mother,' Brunetti said.

'Would you like me to go down to the supply room and get you a bullet-proof vest?' Rossi asked with a laugh.

'No, Rossi, the widow Ruffolo and I are on the best of terms now. After I spoke up for him at the trial, she decided to forgive and forget. She even smiles when she sees me on the street.' He didn't mention that he had gone to see her a few times during the last two years, apparently the only person in the city who had.

'Lucky you. Does she talk to you, too?'

'Yes.'

'In *Siciliano*?'

'I don't think she knows how to speak anything else.'

'How much do you understand?'

'About half,' Brunetti answered, then added, for truth's sake, 'but only if she talks very, very slowly.' Though Signora Ruffolo could not be said to have adapted to life in Venice, she had, in her own way, become part of the police legend of the city, a woman who would attack a commissario of police to protect her son.

Soon after Rossi left, Fosco called back. 'Guido, I spoke to a few people here. The word is that he lost a fortune in the Gulf business. A ship that was carrying an entire cargo – and no one knew what was in the cargo – disappeared, probably taken by pirates. Because the boycott was in effect, he couldn't get insurance.'

'So he lost the whole lot?'

'Yes.'

'Any idea how much?'

'No one's sure. I've heard estimates that range from five to fifteen billion, but no one could give me an exact amount. In any case, the word is that he managed to hold things together for a while, but now he's got serious cash-flow problems. One friend of mine at *Corriere* said Viscardi's really got nothing to worry about because he's tied into some sort of government contract. And he's got holdings in other countries. My contact wasn't certain where. Do you want me to try to find out more?'

Signor Viscardi was beginning to sound to Brunetti like any one of the rising generation of businessmen, those who had replaced hard work with boldness, and honesty with connections. 'No, I don't think so, Riccardo. I just wanted to get an idea of whether he'd try something like this.'

'And?'

'Well, it looks like he might be in a position to want to give it a try, doesn't it?'

Fosco offered a bit more information. 'The word is that he's very well connected, but the person I spoke to wasn't sure just how. Do you want me to ask around some more?'

'Did it sound like it might be Mafia?' Brunetti asked.

'It looks that way.' Fosco gave a resigned laugh. 'But when doesn't it? It seems, though, that he's also connected to people in the government.'

Brunetti resisted, in his turn, the temptation to ask when didn't it sound that way and, instead, asked, 'What about his personal life?'

'He's got a wife and a couple of kids here. She's some sort of den mother for the Knights of Malta – you know, charity balls and visits to hospitals. And a mistress in Verona; I think it's Verona. Some place out your way.'

'You said he's arrogant.'

'Yes. A few people I spoke to say he's more than that.'

'What does that mean?' Brunetti asked.

'Two said he could be dangerous.'

'Personally?'

'You mean, will he pull a knife?' Fosco asked with a laugh.

'Something like that.'

'No, that's not the impression I got. Not

personally, at any rate. But he likes to take chances; at least that's the reputation he has here. And, as I said, he's a very well-protected man, and he has no hesitation about asking his friends to help him.' Fosco paused for a moment and then added, 'One person I spoke to was even more outspoken, but he wouldn't tell me anything exact. He just said that anyone who dealt with Viscardi should be very careful.'

Brunetti decided to treat this last lightly and said, 'I'm not afraid of knives.'

Fosco's response was immediate. 'I used not to be afraid of machine guns, Guido.' Then, embarrassed at the remark, he added, 'I mean it, Guido, be careful with him.

'All right, I will. And thanks,' he said, then added, 'I still haven't heard anything, but when I do, I'll let you know.' Most of the police who knew Fosco had put out the word that they were interested in knowing who had done the shooting and who had done the sending, but whoever it was had been very cautious, knowing how well-liked Fosco was with the police, and years had passed in silence. Brunetti believed it was hopeless, but he still asked the occasional question, dropped a hint here and there, spoke vaguely to suspects about the chance of a trade-off in exchange for the information he wanted. But, in all these years, he had never got close.

'I appreciate it, Guido. But I'm not so sure it's all that important any more.' Was this wisdom or resignation he was hearing.

'Why?'

'I'm getting married.' Love, then, better than either.

'Congratulations, Riccardo. Who?'

'I don't think you know her, Guido. She works on the magazine, but she's just been here a year or so.'

'When is it?'

'Next month.'

Brunetti didn't bother with false promises to try to attend, but he spoke from the heart when he said, 'I hope you'll both be happy, Riccardo.'

'Thanks, Guido. Look, if I hear anything more about this guy, I'll call, all right?'

'I'd appreciate it.' With more good wishes for the future, Brunetti said goodbye and hung up. Could it be this simple? Could his business losses have driven Viscardi to organize something as rash as a fake robbery? Only a stranger to Venice could have chosen Ruffolo, a young man infinitely better at being caught than at being criminal. But perhaps the fact that he was so recently out of prison had served as sufficient recommendation.

There was nothing more he could do here today, and Patta would be the first to scream police brutality if a millionaire was questioned on the same day by three different policemen, especially if the questioning took place while the man was still in hospital. There was no sense in going to Vicenza on a day when the American offices would be closed, though it might be easier to defy Patta's order if he went in his own time. No, let the doctor swim towards the bait until next week, when he could easily give another gentle tug on the line. For today, he would drop his line in Venetian waters and go after different prey.

Signora Concetta Ruffolo lived, her son Giuseppe sharing it with her during those brief periods when he was not incarcerated, in a two-room apartment near Campo San Boldo, an area of the city characterized by proximity to the severed tower of that church, to no convenient vaporetto stop, and, if one is but willing to expand the definition of the word 'proximity', to the church of San Simeone Piccolo, where Sunday Mass is still said, in open protest to concepts such as modernity or relevance, in Latin. The widow lived in an apartment owned by a public foundation, IRE, which rents its many apartments to those people judged sufficiently needy to be awarded them. Often, they were given to Venetians; how Signora Ruffolo had been given one remained a mystery, though no mystery surrounded the reality of her need.

Brunetti crossed the Rialto Bridge and went down past San Cassiano, then cut to his left, soon to find the squat tower of San Boldo on his right. He turned into a narrow *calle* and stopped in front of a low building. The name 'Ruffolo' was engraved in delicate script on a metal nameplate to the right of the bell; rust streaked down from both and discoloured the plaster that slowly peeled from the front wall of the building. He rang the bell, waited a moment, rang it again, waited, and rang it a third time.

A full two minutes after his last ring, he heard a voice ask from inside, *'Sì, chi è?'*

'It's me, Signora Concetta. Brunetti.'

The door was quickly pulled open and, looking into the dark hall, he had his usual sensation that he was looking at a barrel and not a woman. Signora Concetta, her family history recounted, had forty years ago been the reigning beauty of Caltanisetta. Young men, it was maintained, would spend hours walking up and down Corso Vittorio Emmanuele in the hope of no more than a glimpse of the fair Concetta. She could have had her pick of them, from the mayor's son to the doctor's younger brother, but instead she had chosen the third son of the family which had once ruled the entire province with an iron fist. She had become a Ruffolo by marriage, and when Annuziato's debts had driven them from Sicily, she had become an alien in this cold and inhospitable city. And, in quick succession, she had become a widow, living on a pension paid by the State and the charity of her husband's family, and, even before Giuseppe could finish school, she had become the mother of a felon.

From the day of her husband's death, to which event her emotional response was unfathomable, even to her son, perhaps even to her herself – she had clothed herself solidly in black: dress, shoes, stockings, even a scarf for those times she left the house. Though she grew stouter with the years, her face more lined with the grief of her son's life, the black remained unchanged: she would wear it to her grave, perhaps beyond.

'*Buon giorno*, Signora Concetta,' Brunetti said, smiling and offering her his hand.

He watched her face, read her expression as a child would the quickly-turning pages of a comic book. There was the instant recognition, the instinctive chill of disgust at what he represented, but then he saw her remember the kindness he had shown to her son, her star, her sun, and with that her face softened and her mouth turned up in a smile of real pleasure. 'Ah, Dottore, you've come to visit me again. How nice, how nice. But you should have called so that I could give the house a real cleaning, make you some fresh pastries.' He understood 'called', 'house', 'cleaning', and 'pastries', so he constructed her speech to mean that.

'Signora, a cup of your good coffee is more than I could hope to have.'

'Come in, come in,' she said, putting her hand under his arm and pulling him towards her. She backed through the open door of her apartment, keeping her hold on his arm, as if she were afraid he would try to escape her.

When they were inside the apartment, she closed the door with one hand and continued to pull him forward with the other. The apartment was so small that no one could be lost in it, and yet she kept her hand on his arm and led him into the small living room. 'Take this chair, Dottore,' she said, leading him to an overstuffed armchair covered in shiny orange cloth, where she finally released him. When he hesitated, she insisted, 'Sit, sit. I'll make us some coffee.'

He did as she commanded, sinking down until his knees were on a level almost with his chin. She switched on the light that stood beside his chair;

the Ruffolos lived in the endless twilight of ground-floor apartments, but even lights at midday could do nothing to work against the damp.

'Don't move,' she commanded and went to the other side of the room, where she pushed aside a flowered curtain, behind which lay a sink and stove. From his side of the room, he could see that the taps gleamed and the surface of the stove was almost radiant in its whiteness. She opened a cabinet and pulled down the straight cylindrical espresso pot he always associated with the South, he didn't know why. She unscrewed it, rinsed it carefully, rinsed it again, filled it with water, and then reached down a glass canister filled with coffee. With gestures grown rhythmic with decades of repetition, she filled the pot, lit the stove, and placed the pot over the flame.

The room was unchanged from the last time he was there. Yellow plastic flowers stood in front of the plaster statue of the Madonna; embroidered lace ovals, rectangles, and circles covered every surface; on top of them stood ranks of family photos, in all of which appeared Peppino: Peppino dressed as a tiny sailor, Peppino in the brilliant white of his First Communion, Peppino held on the back of a donkey, grinning through his fear. In all of the photos, the child's outsized ears were visible, making him look almost like a cartoon figure. In one corner stood what could only be described as a shrine to her late husband: their wedding photo, in which Brunetti could see her long-gone beauty; her husband's walking stick propped in a corner, ivory knob aglow even in this dim light; his *lupara*, its deadly short barrels kept polished and oiled, more than a decade after his death, as if even death had not freed him from the need to live up to the cliché of the Sicilian male, ever ready to defend with his shotgun any offence to his honour or his family.

He continued to watch as, seeming to ignore him, she pulled down a tray, plates, and, from another cabinet, a metal tin that she prised open with a knife. From it, she removed pastries, and then more pastries, piling them high on one of the plates. From another tin, she took sweets wrapped in violent-coloured foil and stacked them on another plate. The coffee boiled up, and she quickly grabbed the pot, flipped it upside down in one swift motion, and carried the tray to the large table that took up most of one side of the room. Like a dealer, she passed out plates and saucers, spoons and cups, setting them carefully on the plastic tablecloth, and then went back to bring the coffee to the table. When everything was done, she turned to him and waved her hand towards the table.

Brunetti had to push himself up out of the low chair, both hands pressing firmly down upon the arms. When he was at the table, she pulled his chair out for him and then, when he was seated, sat opposite him. The Capodimonte saucers both had hairline cracks in them, radiating from the edges to the centres like the papery wrinkles he remembered in his grandmother's cheeks. The spoons gleamed, and beside his plate lay a linen napkin ironed into a state of rectangular submission.

Signora Ruffolo poured two cups of coffee, placed one in front of Brunetti, and then put the silver sugar bowl beside his plate. Using silver tongs, she piled six pastries, each the size of an apricot, on his plate, and then used the same tongs to set four of the foil-wrapped sweets beside it.

He added sugar to his coffee and sipped at it. 'It's the best coffee in Venice, Signora. You still won't tell me your secret?'

She smiled at that, and Brunetti saw that she had lost another tooth, this the right front one. He bit into a pastry, felt the sugar surge out into his mouth. Ground almonds, sugar, the finest of pastry dough, and yet more sugar. The next had ground pistachios. The third was chocolate, and the fourth exploded with pastry creme. He took a bite of the fifth and set half of it down on his plate.

'Eat. You're too thin, Dottore. Eat. Sugar gives energy. And it's good for your blood.' The nouns conveyed the message.

'They're wonderful, Signora Concetta. But I just had lunch, and if I eat too many of them, I won't eat my dinner, and then my wife will be angry with me.'

She nodded. She understood the anger of wives.

He finished his coffee and set the cup down on the saucer. Not three seconds passed before she was up, across the room, and back with a carved glass decanter and two glasses no bigger than olives. 'Marsala. From home,' she said, pouring him a thimbleful. He took the glass from her, waited while she poured no more than a few drops into her own glass, tapped his glass to hers, and sipped at it. It tasted of sun, and the sea, and songs that told of love and death.

He set his glass down, looked across the table at her, and said, 'Signora Concetta, I think you know why I've come.'

She nodded. 'Peppino?'

'Yes, Signora.'

She held her hand up, palm towards him, as if to ward off his words or perhaps to protect herself from the *malocchio*.

'Signora, I think Peppino is involved in something very bad.'

'But this time . . .' she began, but then she remembered who Brunetti was, and she said only, 'he is not a bad boy.'

Brunetti waited until he was sure she was not going to say anything else, and then he continued. 'Signora, I spoke to a friend of mine today. He tells me that a man I think Peppino might be involved with is a very bad man. Do you know anything about this? About what Peppino is doing, about the people he's been seeing since . . .' He wasn't sure how to phrase it. 'Since he came home?'

She considered this for a long time before she answered. 'Peppino was with very bad people when he was in that place.' Even now, after all these years, she could not bring herself to name that place. 'He talked about those people.'

'What did he say about them, Signora?'

'He said that they were important, that his luck was going to change.' Yes, Brunetti remembered this about Peppino: his luck was always going to change.

'Did he tell you anything more, Signora?'

She shook her head. It was a negation, but he wasn't sure what she was denying. Brunetti had never been sure in the past just how much Signora Concetta knew of what her son actually did. He imagined she knew far more than she indicated, but he feared she probably kept that knowledge hidden even from herself. There is only so much truth a mother can permit herself.

'Did you meet any of them, Signora?'

She shook her head fiercely. 'He will not bring them here, not to my home.' This, beyond question, was the truth.

'Signora, we are looking for Peppino now.'

She closed her eyes and bowed her head. He had been out of that place for only two weeks, and already the police were looking for him.

'What did he do, Dottore?'

'We're not sure, Signora. We want to talk to him. Some people say they saw him where a crime took place. But all they saw is a photo of Peppino.'

'So maybe it wasn't my son?'

'We don't know, Signora. That's why we want to talk to him. Do you know where he is?'

She shook her head, but, again, Brunetti didn't know if that meant she didn't know or she didn't want to say.

'Signora, if you talk to Peppino, will you tell him two things for me?'

'Yes, Dottore.'

'Please tell him that we need to talk to him. And tell him that these people are bad people, and they might be dangerous.'

'Dottore, you're a guest in my house, so I shouldn't ask you this.'

'What, Signora?'

'Is this the truth or is this a trick?'

'Signora, you tell me something to swear on, and I'll swear this is the truth.'

With no hesitation, she demanded, 'Will you swear on your mother's heart?'

'Signora, I swear on my mother's heart that this is the truth. Peppino should come and talk to us. And he should be very careful with these people.'

She set her glass down, untasted. 'I'll try to talk to him, Dottore. But maybe it will be different this time?' She couldn't keep the hope from her voice. Brunetti realized that Peppino must have told his mother a great deal about his important friends, about this new chance, when everything would be different, and they would finally be rich.

'I'm sorry, Signora,' he said, meaning it. He got to his feet. 'Thank you for the coffee, and for the pastries. No one in Venice knows how to make them like you do.'

She pushed herself to her feet and grabbed a handful of the sweets. She slipped them into the pocket of his jacket. 'For your children. They're growing. Sugar's good for them.'

'You're very kind, Signora,' he said, painfully aware of how true this was.

She walked with him to the door, again leading him by the arm, as if he were a blind man or liable to lose his way. At the door to the street, they shook hands formally, and she stood at the door, watching him as he walked away.

15

The next morning, Sunday, was the day of the week Paola dreaded, for it was the day when she woke up with a stranger. During the years of their marriage, she had grown accustomed to waking up with her husband, a grim, foul creature incapable of civility for at least an hour after waking, a surly presence from whom she expected grunts and dark looks. Not the brightest bed partner, perhaps, but at least he left her alone and let her sleep. On Sunday, however, his place was taken by someone who, she hated the very word, chirped. Liberated from work and responsibility, a different man emerged: friendly, playful, often amorous. She loathed him.

This Sunday, he was awake at seven, thinking of what he could do with the money he had won at the Casinò. He could beat his father-in-law to the purchase of a computer for Chiara. He could get himself a new winter coat. They could all go to the mountains for a week in January. He lay in bed for half an hour, spending and respending the money, then was finally driven out of bed by his desire for coffee.

He hummed his way to the kitchen and pulled down the largest pot, filled it, set it on the stove, and put a saucepan of milk next to it, then went into the bathroom while they heated. When he emerged, teeth brushed and face glowing from the shock of cold water, the coffee was bubbling up, filling the house with its aroma. He poured it into two large cups, added the sugar and the milk, and went back towards the bedroom. He set the cups on the table beside their bed, got back down under the covers, and fought with his pillow until he had beaten it into a position that would allow him to sit up enough to drink his coffee. He took a loud sip, wiggled himself into a more comfortable position, and said softly, 'Paola.'

From the long lump beside him, his fair consort made no response.

'Paola,' he repeated, voice a little louder. Silence. 'Humm, such good coffee. Think I'll have another sip,' which he proceeded to do, loudly. A hand emerged from the lump, turned itself into a fist, and poked at his shoulder. 'Wonderful, wonderful coffee. Think I'll have another sip.' A distinctly threatening noise emerged. He ignored it and sipped at his coffee. Knowing what was about to come, he placed the cup on the table beside the bed so that it would not be spilled. 'Umm,' was all he said before the lump erupted and Paola flipped herself onto her back, in the manner of a large fish, extending her left arm across his chest. Turning, he took the second cup from the table and placed it into her hand, then took it back and held it for her while she pushed herself up onto her pillow.

This scene had first taken place the second Sunday of their marriage, they still on their honeymoon, when he had bent over his still-sleeping wife to nuzzle at her ear. The voice that had said, steel-like, 'If you don't stop that, I'll rip out your liver and eat it,' had informed him that the honeymoon was over.

Try as he might, which wasn't very hard, he could never understand her lack of sympathy with what he insisted upon seeing as his real self. Sunday was the only day he had during the week, the only day when he didn't have to concern himself directly with death and disaster, so the person who woke up, he maintained, was the real man, the true Brunetti, and he could dismiss that other, Hyde-like creature as being in no way representative of his spirit. Paola was having none of this.

While she sipped at her coffee and worked at getting her eyes open, he switched on the radio and listened to the morning news, though he knew it was likely to turn his mood until it resembled hers. Three more murders in Calabria, all members of the Mafia, one a wanted killer (one for us, he thought); talk of the imminent collapse of the government (when was it not imminent?); a boatload of toxic waste docked at Genoa, turned back from Africa (and why not?); and a priest, murdered in his garden, shot eight times in the head (had he given too severe a penance in confession?). He switched it off while there was still time to save his day and turned to Paola. 'You awake?'

She nodded, still incapable of speech.

'What will we do with the money?'

She shook her head, nose buried in the fumes of the coffee.

'Anything you'd like?'

She finished the coffee, handed the cup to him without comment, and fell back on her pillow. Looking at her, he didn't know whether to give her more coffee or artificial respiration. 'Kids need anything?'

Eyes still closed, she shook her head.

'Sure there's nothing you'd like?'

It cost her inhuman effort, but she got the words out. 'Go away for an hour, then bring me a brioche and more coffee.' That said, she flipped herself over onto her stomach and was asleep before he was out of the room.

He took a long shower, shaving under the flood of hot water, glad that he didn't have to fear the responses of the varied ecological sensibilities of the other members of the household, always ready to decry what they saw as waste or misuse of the environment. Brunetti believed himself to be a man whose family always chose enthusiasms and causes that contributed directly to his inconvenience. Other men, he was sure, managed to have children who contented themselves with worrying about things that were far away – the rainforest, nuclear testing, the plight of the Kurds. Yet here he was, a city official, a man the newspapers had even once praised, and he was forbidden, by members of his own family, from buying mineral water that came in plastic bottles. Instead, he had to buy water in glass bottles, then haul those bottles up and down ninety-four steps. And if he stayed under the shower for more time than it took the average human being to wash his hands, he had to listen to endless denunciations of the thoughtlessness of the West, its devouring of the resources of the world. When he was a child, waste was condemned because they were poor; now it was condemned because they were rich. At this point, he discovered how difficult it was to shave while grinning, so he abandoned the catalogue of his woes and finished his shower.

When he emerged from the house twenty minutes later, he found himself swept by a boundless feeling of unspecified delight. Though the morning was cool, the day would be warm, one of those glorious sun-swept days that graced the city in the autumn. The air was so dry that it was impossible to believe the city was built on water, though a glance to the right as he walked past any of the side streets on his way towards Rialto was ample proof of that fact.

Arriving at the major cross-street, he turned left and headed down towards the fish market, closed now on Sunday but still giving off the faintest odour of the fish that had been sold there for hundreds of years. He crossed a bridge, turned to the left, and went into a *pasticceria*. He ordered a dozen pastries. Even if they didn't eat them all for breakfast, Chiara was sure to knock them off during the course of the day. Probably the morning. Balancing the rectangular package on his outstretched palm, he went back towards Rialto, then turned right and back up towards San Polo. At Sant' Aponal, he stopped at the newsstand and bought two papers, *Corriere* and *Il Manifesto*, which he thought were the ones Paola wanted to read that day. Back home, the steps seemed almost not to be there as he climbed up to the apartment.

He found Paola in the kitchen, coffee just brimming up in the pot. From down the hall, he heard Raffaele shouting to Chiara through the bathroom door, 'Come on, hurry up. You've been in there all morning.' Ah, the water police, back on duty.

He set the package down on the table and tore back the white paper. The mound of pastries glistened with melted sugar, and some fine powdered sugar floated out to settle on the dark wood of the table. He grabbed a piece of apple strudel and took a bite.

'Where'd they come from?' Paola asked, pouring coffee.

'That place down by Carampane.'

'You went all the way there?'

'It's a beautiful day, Paola. After we eat, let's go for a walk. We could go out to Burano for lunch. Come on, let's do it. It's a perfect day for the ride out.' Even the thought of it, the long boat ride out to the island, the sun glimmering on the crazy patchwork of riotously coloured houses as they grew nearer, lifted his heart even higher.

'Good idea,' she agreed. 'What about the kids?'

'Ask them. Chiara will want to come.'

'All right. Maybe Raffi will, too.'

Maybe.

Paola shoved the *Manifesto* towards him and picked up *Corriere*. Nothing would be done, no move to embrace this glorious day, until she had at least two more cups of coffee and read the papers. He took the newspaper in one hand, his cup in the other, and went back through the living room to the terrace. He set those things down on the balcony and went back into the living room for a straight-backed chair, which he propped up just the right distance from the railing. He sat, pushed the chair back, and rested his feet on the railing. Grabbing the paper, he opened it and began to read.

Church bells sounded, the sun rained down abundantly upon his face, and Brunetti knew a moment of absolute peace.

Paola spoke from the doorway to the terrace. 'Guido, what was that doctor's name?'

'The pretty one?' he asked, not looking up from his paper, not really paying attention to her voice.

'Guido, what was her name?'

He lowered his paper and turned to look at her. When he saw her face, he took his feet from the railing and set the chair down. 'Peters.' She closed her eyes for a moment, then handed him the *Corriere*, turned back to a page in the middle.

'American Doctor Dead of Overdose', he read. The article was a small one, easily overlooked, no more than six or seven lines. The body of Captain Terry Peters, a paediatrician in the US Army, had been found late Saturday afternoon, in her apartment in Due Ville, in the province of Vicenza. Doctor Peters, who worked at the Army hospital at Caserme Ederle, had been found by a friend, who had gone to see why the doctor had not shown up for work that morning. A used syringe was found by the doctor's body, and there were signs of other drug use, as well as evidence that the doctor had been drinking. The Carabinieri and the American military police were handling the investigation.

He read the article again, then again. He looked through the newspaper he had, but *Il Manifesto* had made no mention of it.

'Is this possible, Guido?'

He shook his head. No, an overdose was impossible, but she was dead; the paper gave proof of that.

'What will you do?'

He looked off towards the bell tower of San Polo, the closest church. He had no idea. Patta would see this as an unrelated event or, if related, either an unfortunate accident or, at worst, a suicide. Since only Brunetti knew she had destroyed the postcard from Cairo, and only he had seen her reaction to the body of her lover, there was nothing to link the two of them together as anything other than colleagues, and that surely was no reason for suicide. Drugs and alcohol, and a woman living alone; that was enough to tell how the Press would treat this one – unless, unless the same sort of call that Brunetti was sure had been made to Patta were to be made to editors' offices. In that case, the story would die a quick death, as many stories did. As Doctor Peters had.

'I don't know,' he said, finally answering Paola's question. 'Patta's warned me off, told me not to go back to Vicenza.'

'But certainly this changes things.'

'Not for Patta. It's an overdose. The Carabinieri and the American military police will handle it. They'll do an autopsy, then they'll send her body back to America.'

'Just like the other one,' Paola said, giving voice to his thoughts. 'Why kill them both?'

Brunetti shook his head. 'I have no idea.' But he knew. She had been silenced. Her casual remark that she wasn't interested in drugs had not been a lie: the idea of an overdose was ludicrous. She'd been killed because of whatever she knew about Foster, because of whatever it was that had sent her careening across the room, away from her lover's body. Killed by drugs. He wondered if that was meant to be a message to him but dismissed the idea as vainglorious. Whoever had killed her hadn't had enough time to arrange an accident, and a second murder would have been too obvious, a suicide unexplained and therefore suspicious. So an accidental overdose was the perfect solution: she did it to herself, nowhere else to look, another dead end. And Brunetti didn't even know if it was she who had called to say, *'Basta'*.

Paola came closer to him and put a hand on his shoulder. 'I'm sorry, Guido. Sorry for her.'

'She couldn't have been thirty yet,' he said. 'All those years in school, all that work.' It seemed to him that her death would have been less unfair if she had had time for more fun. 'I hope her family doesn't believe it.'

Paola spoke his thoughts. 'If the police and the Army tell you something, you're likely to believe it. And I'm sure it looked very real, very convincing.'

'Poor people,' he said.

'Could you . . .' she broke off, remembering that Patta had told him to stay clear of this.

'If I can. It's bad enough that she's dead. They don't need to believe this.'

'That she was murdered isn't going to be any better,' Paola said.

'At least she didn't do that.'

Both of them stayed there in the late autumn sunshine, thinking about parents and being a parent, and what parents want and need to know about their children. He had no idea which would be better, worse. At least, if you knew that your child had been murdered, your life would have the grim hope of someday being able to kill the person who had done it, but that hardly seemed any sort of consolation.

'I should have called her.'

'Guido,' she said, voice growing firm. 'Don't start that. Because all it means is that you should have been a mind-reader. And you're not. So don't even start thinking that.' He was surprised by the real anger in her voice.

He wrapped an arm around her waist and pulled her closer to him. They remained like that, without speaking, until the bells of San Marco boomed out ten o'clock.

'What are you going to do? Will you go to Vicenza?'

'No, not yet. I'm going to wait.'

'What do you mean?'

'Whatever they knew, they knew because of where they worked. It's the link they had. There have got to be other people who know or suspect or have access to what they learned. So I'm going to wait.'

'Guido, now you're asking other people to be mind-readers. How are they going to know to come to you?'

'I'll go out there, but not for a week, and then I'll make myself conspicuous. Speak to that major, to the sergeant who worked with them, to other doctors. It's a small world there. People will talk to one another; they'll know something.' And to hell with Patta.

'Let's forget Burano, all right, Guido?'

He nodded then got to his feet. 'I think I'll go for a walk. I'll be back for lunch.' He squeezed her arm. 'I just need to walk.' He glanced out over the rooftops of the city. How strange; the glory of the day was undiminished. Sparrows swooped and played tag with one another almost within his grasp, chirping for the joy of flight. And off in the far distance, the gold on the wings of the angel atop the bell tower of San Marco flashed in the sun, bathing the entire city in its glistening benediction.

16

On Monday morning, he went into his office at the
regular time and stood looking at the façade of the
church of San Lorenzo for more than an hour.
During that entire time, he saw no sign of motion
or activity, neither on the scaffolding nor on the
roof, which was stacked with neat rows of
terracotta tiles. Twice he heard people come into
his office, but when they didn't speak to him, he
didn't bother to turn around, and they left,
presumably after having placed things on his desk.

At ten-thirty, his phone rang, and he turned
away from the window to answer it.

'Good morning, Commissario. This is Maggiore
Ambrogiani.'

'Good morning, Maggiore. I'm glad you called.
In fact, I was going to call you this afternoon.'

'They did it this morning,' Ambrogiani said with no prelude.

'And?' Brunetti asked, knowing what he meant.

'It was an overdose of heroin, enough to kill someone twice her size.'

'Who did the autopsy?'

'Doctor Franceso Urbani. One of ours.'

'Where?'

'Here at the hospital in Vicenza.

'Were any of the Americans present?'

'They sent one of their doctors. Sent him down from Germany. A colonel, this doctor.'

'Did he assist or only observe?'

'He merely observed the autopsy.'

'Who's Urbani?'

'Our pathologist.'

'Reliable?'

'Very.'

Aware of the potential ambiguity of the last question, Brunetti rephrased it. 'Believable?'

'Yes.'

'So that means it was really an overdose?'

'Yes, I'm afraid it does.'

'What else did he find?'

'Urbani?'

'Yes.'

'There were no signs of violence in the apartment. There were no signs of prior drug use, but there was a bruise on her upper right arm and one on her left wrist. It was suggested to Doctor Urbani that these bruises were consistent with a fall.'

'Who made that suggestion?'

The length of the pause before Ambrogiani

answered was probably meant as a reproach to Brunetti's even having to ask. 'The American doctor. The colonel.'

'And what was Doctor Urbani's opinion?'

'That the marks are not inconsistent with a fall.'

'Any other needle marks?'

'No, none.'

'So she overdosed the first time she did it?'

'Strange coincidence, isn't it?' Ambrogiani asked.

'Did you know her?'

'No, I didn't. But one of my men works with an American policeman whose son was her patient. He said she was very good with the little boy. He broke his arm last year and got bad treatment at the beginning. Doctors and nurses rushed, too busy to tell him what they were doing; you know the story, so he was afraid of doctors, afraid they'd hurt him again. She was very kind with him, spent a lot of time. It seems she always made sure to schedule a double appointment for the boy, so she wouldn't have to rush him.'

'That doesn't mean she didn't use drugs, Maggiore,' Brunetti said, trying to make it sound like he believed it.

'No, it doesn't, does it?' Ambrogiani agreed.

'What else did the report say?'

'I don't know. I haven't seen a copy of it.'

'Then how do you know what you've told me?'

'I called Urbani.'

'Why?'

'Dottor Brunetti. An American soldier was murdered in Venice. Less than a week later, his commanding officer dies under mysterious circumstances. I'd be a fool if I didn't suspect some sort of connection between the two events.'

'When will you have a copy of the autopsy report?'

'Probably this afternoon. Would you like me to call you?'

'Yes. I'd appreciate that, Maggiore.'

'Is there anything you think I should know?' Ambrogiani asked.

Ambrogiani was there, in daily contact with the Americans. Anything Brunetti told him was sure to become a fair trade. 'They were lovers, and she was very frightened when she saw his body.'

'Saw his body?'

'Yes. She was sent to identify his body.'

Ambrogiani's silence suggested that he, too, saw this as a particularly subtle touch. 'Did you speak to her after it?' he finally asked.

'Yes and no. I came back to the city on the boat with her, but she didn't want to talk about it. It seemed to me at the time that she was afraid of something. She had the same reaction when I saw her out there.'

'Was that when you came out here?' Ambrogiani asked.

'Yes. Friday.'

'Do you have any idea what she was afraid of?'

'No. None. She might have tried to call me here on Friday night. There was a phone message here at the Questura, from a woman who didn't speak Italian. The operator who took the call doesn't speak English and all he could understand was that she said, '*Basta.*'

'Do you think it was she?'

'It could have been. I've no idea. But the message makes no sense.' Brunetti thought of Patta's order and asked, 'What's going to happen out there?'

'Their military police are going to try to find out where she got the heroin. There were other signs of drugs found with her, the ends of marijuana cigarettes, some hashish. And the autopsy showed that she had been drinking.'

'They certainly didn't leave any doubt, did they?' Brunetti asked.

'There's no sign that she was forced to take the injection.'

'Those bruises?' Brunetti asked.

'She fell.'

'So it looks like she did it?'

'Yes.' Neither of them spoke for a while, then Ambrogiani asked, 'Are you going to come out here?'

'I've been told not to bother the Americans.'

'Who told you?'

'The Vice-Questore here in Venice.'

'What are you going to do?'

'I'll wait a few days, a week, then I'd like to come out there and speak to you. Do your men have contact with the Americans?'

'Not much. We each keep to ourselves. But I'll see what I can find out about her.'

'Did any Italians work with them?'

'I don't think so. Why?'

'I'm not sure. But both of them, especially Foster, had to travel for his job, going back and forth to places like Egypt.'

'Drugs?' Ambrogiani asked.

'Could be. Or it could be something else.'

'What?'

'I don't know. Drugs don't feel right, somehow.'

'What does feel right?'

'I don't know.' He looked up and saw Vianello at the door to his office. 'Look, Maggiore, I've got someone here now. I'll call you in a few days. We can decide then when I can go out there.'

'All right. I'll see what I can find out here.'

Brunetti hung up and waved Vianello into the office. 'Anything on Ruffolo?' he asked.

'Yes, sir. Those people who live below his girlfriend said he was there last week. They saw him a few times on the steps, but they haven't seen him for three or four days. Do you want me to speak to her, sir?'

'Yes, maybe you'd better. Tell her that it's different from the other times. Viscardi has been assaulted, so that changes everything, especially for her if she's hiding him or knows where he is.'

'You think it will work?'

'On Ivana?' Brunetti asked sarcastically.

'Well, no, I suppose it won't,' Vianello agreed. 'But I'll try it anyway. Besides, I'd rather talk to her than to the mother. At least I can understand what she says, even though every word of it is a lie.'

When Vianello had left to go and try to interview Ivana, Brunetti went back to the window, but after a few minutes he found that unsatisfactory and went to sit at his desk. Ignoring the files that had been placed there during the morning, he sat and considered the various possibilities. The first one, that it had been an overdose, he dismissed out of hand. Suicide, too, was impossible. In the past, he had seen distraught lovers who saw no possibility of a future life without the other person, but she was not one of them. Those two possibilities excluded, the only one that remained was murder.

To accomplish it, however, would have taken some planning, for he ruled out luck in these things. There were those bruises – not for a second did he believe in a fall – someone could have held her while she was given the injection. The autopsy showed that she had been drinking; how much did a person have to drink to be so deeply asleep as not to feel a needle or to be so fuddled as not to be able to resist it? More importantly, who would she have drunk with, who would she have felt so comfortable with? Not a lover; hers had just been killed. A friend, then, and who were the friends of Americans abroad? Who did they trust if not other Americans? And all of that pointed back to the base and her job, for Brunetti was certain that the answer, whatever it was, lay there.

17

Three days passed during which Brunetti did almost nothing. At the Questura, he went through the motions of his job: looking at papers, signing them, filling out a staffing projection for the next year without giving a thought to the fact that Patta was supposed to do it. At home, he talked to Paola and the children, who were all too busy with the start of the new school year to realize how inattentive he was. Even the search for Ruffolo didn't interest him much at all, certain as he was that someone so foolish and rash was sure soon to make a mistake that would put him in the hands of the police yet again.

He did not call Ambrogiani, and in his meetings with Patta, he made no mention of the murders, one that had so quickly been forgotten by the

Press, and one that had never been called a murder, or of the base in Vicenza. So frequently as to be almost obsessive, he played over scenes with the young doctor, caught flashes of her in his memory: stepping up out of the boat and giving him her hand; arms braced against the sink in the morgue, body racked by the spasms of her shock; smiling when she told him that, in six months, she would begin her life.

It was the nature of police work that he never knew the victims whose deaths he investigated. Much as he came to know them intimately, to know about them in work, in bed, and in death, he had never known any of them in this life, and so he felt a special link to Doctor Peters and, because of that link, a special responsibility to find her murderer.

On Thursday morning, he checked with Vianello and Rossi when he got to the Questura, but there had still been no sign of Ruffolo. Viscardi had gone back to Milan, after giving written descriptions of the two men, one very tall and one with a beard, to both the insurance company and the police. It appeared that they had forced their way into the *palazzo*, for the locks on the side door had been picked, the padlock that held a metal grating in place filed through. Though Brunetti had not spoken to Viscardi, his talks with Vianello and Fosco had been enough to persuade him that there had been no robbery, well, not a robbery of anything other than the insurance company's money.

A little after ten, one of the secretaries from

downstairs brought the mail around to the offices on the top floor and placed a few letters and a magazine-sized manila envelope on his desk.

The letters were the usual things: invitations to conferences, attempts to sell him special life insurance, responses to questions he had sent to various police departments in other parts of the country. After he read them, he picked up the envelope and examined it. A narrow band of stamps ran across the top of the envelope; there must have been twenty of them. All the same, they carried a small American flag and were marked with the denomination of twenty-nine cents. The envelope was addressed to him, by his name, but the only address was 'Questura, Venice, Italy'. He could think of no one in America who would be writing to him. There was no return address.

He tore the envelope open, reached in, and pulled out a magazine. He glanced at the cover and recognized the medical review Doctor Peters had pulled from his hands when she found him reading it in her office. He leafed through it, paused for a moment at those grotesque photos, then continued through the magazine. Towards the end, he found three sheets of paper, obviously a Xerox copy of some other original, slipped between the pages of the magazine. He took them out and placed them on his desk.

At the top, he read 'Medical Report' and then, below it, saw the boxes meant to hold information about the name, age, and rank of the patient. This one carried the name of Daniel Kayman, whose year of birth was given as 1984. There followed three pages of information about his medical history, starting with measles in 1989, a series of bloody noses in the winter of 1990, a broken finger in 1991, and, on the last two pages, a series of visits, starting two months ago, for a skin rash on his left arm. As Brunetti read, he watched the rash grow larger, deeper, and more confusing to the three doctors who had attempted to deal with it.

On 8 July, the boy had been seen for the first time by Doctor Peters. Her neat, slanted handwriting said that the rash was 'of unknown origin' but had broken out after the boy got home from a picnic with his parents. It covered the underside of his arm from wrist to elbow, was dark purple, but did not itch. The prescribed treatment was a medicated skin cream.

Three days later, the boy was back, the rash worse. It was now oozing a yellow liquid and had grown painful, and the boy was running a high fever. Doctor Peters suggested a consultation with a dermatologist at the local Vicenza hospital, but the parents refused to let the child see an Italian doctor. She prescribed a new cream, this one with cortisone, and an antibiotic to bring the fever down.

After only two days, the boy was brought back to the hospital and seen by a different doctor, Girrard, who noted in the record that the boy was in considerable pain. The rash now seemed to be a burn and had moved up his arm, spreading towards his shoulder. His hand was swollen and painful. The fever was unchanged.

A Doctor Grancheck, apparently a dermatologist, had looked at the boy and suggested he be immediately transferred to the Army hospital in Landstuhl, Germany.

The day after this visit, the boy was sent to Germany on a medical evacuation flight. Nothing else was written in the body of the report, but Doctor Peters' neat script had pencilled a single notation in the margin, next to the remark that the boy's rash now appeared to be a burn. It read 'PCB' and carried after it 'FPJ, March.'

He checked the date, but he knew what it would be even before he looked at it. *Family Practice Journal*, the March issue. He opened the magazine and began to read. He noticed that the editorial board was almost all men, that men had written most of the articles, and that the articles listed in the Table of Contents dealt with everything from the article about feet that had so horrified him to one that dealt with the increase in the incidence of tuberculosis as a result of the AIDS epidemic. There was even an article about the transmission of parasites from domestic pets to children.

Seeing no help in the Table of Contents, he began to read from the first page, including all the ads and the letters to the editors. It was on page 62, a brief reference to a case that had been reported in Newark, New Jersey, of a young child, a girl, who had been playing in an empty car park and had stepped into what she thought was a puddle of oil leaked from an abandoned car. The liquid had spilled over the top of her shoe and soaked through her sock. The next day, she developed a rash on the foot, which soon changed into something that had every appearance of a burn and which gradually spread up her leg to her knee. The child had a high fever. All treatment proved futile until a public health official went to the car park and took a sample of the liquid, which proved to be heavy in PCBs, which had leaked there from barrels of toxic waste dumped there. Though the burns eventually healed, the child's doctors were fearful for her future because of the neurological and genetic damage that had often been noted in animal experimentation with substances containing PCBs.

He set the magazine aside and went back to the medical record, reading it through a second time. The symptoms were identical, though no mention was made of where or how the child had made the original contact with the substance that must have produced the rash. 'While on a picnic with his family,' was the only thing the record said. Nor did the record carry any report of the treatment given to the child in Germany.

He picked up the envelope and examined it. The stamps were cancelled by a circular imprint that bore, within it, the words 'Army Postal System' and Saturday's date. So, sometime on Friday or Saturday, she had put this in the mail for him, then tried to call him. It hadn't been *'Basta'* or *'Pasta'*, but *'Posta'*, to alert him to its arrival in the mail. What had happened to warn her? To make her send these papers off to him?

He remembered something Butterworth had

said about Foster; it was his job to see that used X-rays were taken away from the hospital. He had said something about other objects and substances, but he had said nothing about what they were or where they were dumped. Surely, the Americans would have to know.

This had to be the connecting link between the two deaths or else she would not have sent the envelope to him, then tried to call. The child had been her patient, but then he had been taken away and sent up to Germany, and there the medical record ended. He had the child's last name, and Ambrogiani would certainly have access to a list of all the Americans stationed at the base, so it would be easy enough to learn if the boy's family was still there. And if they weren't?

He picked up the phone and asked the operator to get him Maggiore Ambrogiani at the American base in Vicenza. While he waited for the call to go through, he tried to think of a way all of this could be made to connect, hoping that it would lead him to whoever it was had pushed the needle into the doctor's arm.

Ambrogiani answered by giving his name. He showed no surprise when Brunetti told him who it was, merely held the line and allowed the silence to lengthen.

'Has there been any progress there?' Brunetti asked.

'They seem to have instituted a whole new series of drug tests. Everyone is subject to it, even the commander of the hospital. The rumour is he had to go into the men's room and give a urine sample while one of the doctors waited outside. Apparently, they've done more than a hundred this week.'

'With what results?'

'Oh, none yet. All of the samples have to be sent up to Germany, to the hospitals there, to be tested. Then the results come down after a month or so.'

'And they're accurate?' Brunetti asked, amazed that any organization could or would trust results that passed through so many hands, over so long a period of time.

'They seem to believe so. If the test is positive, they simply throw you out.'

'Who's being tested?'

'There's no pattern. The only ones they're leaving alone are the ones who keep coming back from the Middle East.'

'Because they're heroes?' Brunetti asked.

No, because they're afraid too many of them will test positive. Drugs are as easy to get in that part of the world as they were in Vietnam, and apparently they're afraid it will create too much bad publicity if all of their heroes come back with souvenirs in their bloodstreams.'

'Is it still given out that it was an overdose?'

'Absolutely. One of my men told me her family wouldn't even come to accompany the body back to America.'

'So what happened?'

'They sent it back. But it went back alone.'

Brunetti told himself it didn't matter. The dead didn't care about such things; it made no difference to them how they were treated or what the living thought of them. But he didn't believe this.

'I'd like you to try to get some information for me, Maggiore.'

'If I can. Gladly.'

'I'd like to know if there's a soldier stationed there named Kayman.' He spelled the name for Ambrogiani. 'He has a son, nine years old, who was a patient of Doctor Peters. The boy was sent up to a hospital in Germany, at Landstuhl. I'd like to know if the parents are still there, and if they are, I'd like to be able to speak to them.'

'Unofficial, all of this?'

'Very.'

'Can you tell me what it's about?'

'I'm not sure. She sent me a copy of the boy's medical file, and an article about PCBs.'

'About what?'

'Toxic chemicals. I'm not sure what they're made of or what they do, but I know disposing of them is difficult. And they're corrosive. The child had a rash on his arm, probably caused by exposure to them.'

'What's that got to do with the Americans?'

'I don't know. That's why I want to speak to the boy's parents.'

'All right. I'll get busy with this now and call you this afternoon.'

'Can you find him without the Americans finding out?'

'I think so,' Ambrogiani answered. 'We have copies of the vehicle registrations, and almost all of them have cars, so I can find out if he's still here without having to ask them any questions.'

'Good,' Brunetti said. 'I think it would be best if this stayed with us.'

'You mean, as opposed to the Americans?'

'For now, yes.'

'Fine. I'll call you after I check the records.'

'Thanks, Maggiore.'

'Giancarlo,' the Carabiniere said. 'I think we can call one another by our first names if we're going to do something like this.'

'I agree,' Brunetti said, glad to find an ally. 'Guido.'

When he hung up, Brunetti found himself wishing he were in America. One of the great revelations to him when he was there was the system of public libraries: a person could simply walk in and ask questions, read any book he wanted, easily find a catalogue of magazines. Here in Italy, either one bought the book or found it in a university library, and even there it was difficult to gain access without the proper cards, permissions, identification. And so how to find out about PCBs, what they were, where they came from, and what they did to a human body that came in contact with them?

He glanced at his watch. There was still time to get to the bookshop at San Luca if he hurried; it was likely to have the sort of book that might be useful to him.

He got there fifteen minutes before it closed and explained what he wanted to the sales assistant. He said that there were two basic books on toxic substances and pollution, though one had more to do with emissions that went directly into the atmosphere. There was a third book, a sort of general guide to chemistry for the layman. After glancing through them, Brunetti bought the first and the third, then added a rather strident-looking text, published by the Green party, that bore the title, *Global Suicide*. He hoped that the treatment of the subject would be more serious than either the title or the cover promised.

He stopped at a restaurant and had a proper lunch, then went back to the office and opened the first book. Three hours later, he had begun to see, with mounting shock and horror, the extent of the problem that industrial man had created for himself and, worse, for those who would follow him on the planet.

These chemicals, it seemed, were essential in many of the processes necessary to modern man, among them refrigeration, for they served as the coolant in domestic refrigerators and air conditioners. They were also used in the oil for transformers, but the PCBs were only a single flower in the deadly bouquet industry had presented to mankind. He read the chemical names with difficulty, the formulae with incomprehension. What remained were the numbers given for the half-life of the substances involved. He thought this was the time it took the substance to become half as deadly as it was when measured. In some cases, the number was hundreds of years; in some it was thousands. And it was these substances which were produced in enormous

241

quantities by the industrialized world as it hurtled towards the future.

For decades, the Third World had been the rubbish dump of the industrialized nations, taking in shiploads of toxic substances, which were scattered around on their pampas, savannahs, and plateaux, placed there in exchange for current wealth, no thought given to the future price that would come due and be paid by future generations. And now, with some of the countries in the Third World refusing any longer to serve as the dumping ground of the First, the industrial countries were constrained to devise systems of disposal, many of them ruinously expensive. As a result, fleets of phantom trucks with false manifests travelled up and down the Italian peninsula, seeking and finding places to unload their lethal cargoes. Or boats sailed from Genoa or Taranto, holds filled with barrels of solvents, chemicals, God alone knew what, and when they arrived at their final ports, those barrels were no longer on board, as though the god who knew their contents had decided to take them to his bosom. Occasionally, they washed ashore in North Africa or Calabria, but no one, of course, had any idea where they might have come from, nor did anyone notice when they were delivered back to the waves that had brought them to the beaches.

The tone of the book published by the Green party irritated him; the facts terrified him. They named the shippers, named the companies that paid them, and, worst, showed photos of the places where these illegal dumps had been found.

The rhetoric was accusatory, and the culprit, according to the authors, was the entire government, hand in glove with the companies which produced these products and were not constrained by law to account for their disposal. The last chapter of the book dealt with Vietnam and the results that were just now beginning to be seen of the genetic cost of the tons of dioxin that had been dumped on that country during its war with the United States. The descriptions of birth defects, elevated rates of miscarriage, and the lingering presence of dioxin in fish, water, the very land itself were clear and, even allowing for the inevitable exaggerations of the writers, staggering. These same chemicals, the authors maintained, were being dumped all over Italy on a day-to-day, business-as-usual basis.

When Brunetti stopped reading, he realized that he had been manipulated, that the books all had enormous flaws in their reasoning, that they assumed connections where none could be shown, placed guilt where the evidence didn't. But he realized as well that one of the basic assumptions made in all of the books was probably true: a violation of the law this widespread and un-punished – and the refusal of the government to pass more stringent laws – argued for a strong link between the offenders and the government whose job it was to prevent or prosecute them. Was it into this vortex that those two innocents at the base had stepped, brought there by a child with a rash on his arm?

18

Ambrogiani called him back about five to tell him that the boy's father, a sergeant who worked in the contracting office, was still stationed at Vicenza; at least his car was still there and had had its registration renewed only two weeks before, and since that process required the signature of the owner of the vehicle, it was safe to assume that he was still in Vicenza.

'Where does he live?'

'I don't know,' answered Ambrogiani. 'The papers have only his mailing address, a postbox here at the base, but not his home address.'

'Can you get it?'

'Not without their learning that I'm interested in him.'

'No. I don't want that,' Brunetti said. 'But I

want to be able to talk to him, away from there.'

'Give me a day. I'll have one of my men go into the office where he works and find out who he is. Luckily, they all wear those name tags on their uniforms. Then I'll see about having him followed. It shouldn't be too difficult. I'll call you tomorrow, and then you can think about setting up a meeting with him. Most of them live off the base. In fact, if he's got children, he's certain to. I'll call you tomorrow and let you know what I manage, all right?'

Brunetti could see no better way. He realized how much he wanted to get on a train to Vicenza immediately, speak to the boy's father, and begin to piece together the puzzle of how the picnic and the rash and that pencilled notation in the margin of the medical record had led to the murder of those two young people. He had some of the pieces; the boy's father must have another one; sooner or later, by putting them together and examining them, switching them to new positions, he would be sure to see the pattern that now lay hidden.

Seeing no other solution, he agreed to Ambrogiani's suggestion that he wait for his call the following day. He opened the third book again, drew a piece of paper from his desk, and began to make a list of all of the companies which were suspected of hauling or shipping toxic wastes without the proper authorization and another of all of the companies which were named as having already been formally accused of illegal dumping. Most of them were located in the North and most of those in Lombardy, the manufacturing heart of the country.

He checked the copyright of the book and saw that it had been printed only the year before, so the list was current. He turned to the back and saw a region-by-region map of the places where illegal dumping sites had been found. The provinces of Vicenza and Verona were heavily dotted, especially the region just north of both cities, leading up to the foothills of the Alps.

He closed the book, folding the list carefully inside it. There was nothing more he could do until he spoke to the boy's father, but still he burned with the desire to go there now, futile as he knew that desire to be.

The intercom buzzed. 'Brunetti,' he said, picking it up.

'Commissario,' Patta's voice said, 'I'd like you to come down to my office right now.'

For a fleeting instant, Brunetti wondered if Patta was having his phone tapped or a record kept of his calls and somehow knew that he was still in contact with the American base. Even this new information about the toxins, Brunetti knew, would not deflect the other man from his attempt to keep things quiet. And the instant he learned that Brunetti suspected that so lofty an institution as something that could be graced with the name of 'company' might be involved, Patta was sure to threaten to reprimand him officially if he persisted in his attempt to learn what had happened. If the forces of law were not to defer to the desires of business, then surely the Republic was imperilled.

He went immediately down to Patta's office, knocked, and was told to enter. Patta was poised at his desk, looking as though he had just come from a film audition. A successful one. As Brunetti entered, Patta was busy fitting one of his Russian cigarettes into his onyx holder, careful to hold both away from his desk, lest a particle of tobacco fall upon and somehow diminish the gleaming perfection of the Renaissance desk behind which he sat. The cigarette proving resistant, Patta kept Brunetti waiting in front of him until he had managed to fit it carefully within the gold circle of the holder. 'Brunetti,' he said, lighting the cigarette and taking a few cautious exploratory puffs, perhaps seeking to taste the effect of the gold, 'I've had a very upsetting phone call.'

'Not your wife, I hope, sir,' Brunetti said in what he hoped was a meek voice.

Patta rested the cigarette on the edge of his malachite ashtray, then grabbed quickly at it as the weight of the holder caused it to topple back onto the desk. He replaced it, this time resting it level, burning end and mouthpiece balanced on opposing sides of the round ashtray. As soon as he took his hand from it, the weight of the head of the holder pressed it down. The end of the cigarette slipped out, and both cigarette and holder fell, the holder with a rich clatter, into the bowl of the ashtray.

Brunetti folded his hands behind him and looked out of the window, bouncing up and down a few times on the balls of his feet. When he looked back, the cigarette was extinguished, the holder gone.

'Sit down, Brunetti.'

'Thank you, sir,' he said, ever-polite, taking his usual place in the chair in front of the desk.

'I've had,' Patta resumed, 'a phone call.' He paused just long enough to dare Brunetti to repeat his suggestion, then continued, 'From Signor Viscardi, from Milan.' When Brunetti asked nothing, he added, 'He called to tell me that you are calling his good name into question.' Brunetti did not jump to his own defence, so Patta was forced to explain. 'He said that his insurance agent has received a phone call, from you, I might add, asking how he knew so quickly that certain things had been taken from the *palazzo*.' Had Patta been in love with the most desirable woman in the world, he could not have whispered her name with more adoration than he devoted to that last word. 'Further, Signor Viscardi has learned that Riccardo Fosco, a known leftist' – and what did this mean, Brunetti wondered, in a country where the President of the Chamber of Deputies was a Communist? – 'has been asking suggestive questions about Signor Viscardi's financial position.'

Patta paused here to give Brunetti an opportunity to jump to his own defence, but he said nothing. 'Signor Viscardi,' Patta continued, voice growing more indicative of the concern he felt, 'did not volunteer this information; I had to ask him very specific questions about his treatment here. But he said that the policeman who questioned him, the second one, though I see no reason why it was necessary to send two, that this policeman seemed not to believe some of his answers.

Understandably, Signor Viscardi, who is a well-respected businessman, and a fellow member of the Rotary International' – it was not necessary here to specify who his fellow member was – 'found this treatment upsetting, especially as it came so soon after his brutal treatment at the hands of the men who broke into his palace and made off with paintings and jewellery of great value. Are you listening, Brunetti?' Patta suddenly asked.

'Oh, yes, sir.'

'Then why don't you have anything to say?'

'I was waiting to learn about the upsetting phone call, sir.'

'Damn it,' Patta shouted, slamming his hand down on the desk. 'This was the upsetting call. Signor Viscardi is an important man, both here and in Milan. He has a great deal of political influence, and I won't have him thinking, and saying, that he has been treated badly by the police of this city.'

'I don't understand how he has been badly treated, sir.'

'You understand nothing, Brunetti,' Patta said in tight-lipped anger. 'You call the man's insurance agent the same day the claim is made, as if you suspected there was something strange about the claim. And two separate policemen go to the hospital to question him and show him photos of people who had nothing to do with the crime.'

'Did he tell you that?'

'Yes, after we'd been speaking a while and I assured him that I had every confidence in him.'

'What did he say, exactly, about the photo?'

'That the second policeman had shown him a photo of a young criminal and had seemed not to believe him when he said he didn't recognize the man.'

'How did he know the man in the photo was a criminal?'

'What?'

Brunetti repeated himself. 'How did he know that the photo of the man he was shown was the photo of a criminal? It could have been a photo of anyone, the policeman's son, anyone.'

'Commissario, who else would they show him a picture of if not of a criminal?' When Brunetti didn't answer, Patta repeated his exasperated sigh. 'You're being ridiculous, Brunetti.' Brunetti started to speak but Patta cut him off. 'And don't try to stick up for your men when you know they're in the wrong.' At Patta's insistence that the offending police were 'his', there slipped into Brunetti's mind a vision of what it must be like when Patta and his wife tried to portion out responsibility for the failures and achievements of their two sons. 'My' son would win a prize at school, while 'yours' would be disrespectful to teachers or fail an exam.

'Have you anything to say?' Patta finally asked.

'He couldn't describe the men who attacked him, but he knew which pictures they were carrying.'

Once again, Brunetti's insistence did no more than display to Patta the poverty of the background from which he came. 'Obviously, you're not accustomed to living with precious objects, Brunetti. If a person lives for years with objects of great value, and here I mean aesthetic value, not just material price' – his voice urged Brunetti to stretch his imagination to encompass the concept – 'then they come to recognize them, just as they would members of their own family. So, even in a flashing moment, even under stress such as Signor Viscardi experienced, he would recognize those paintings, just as he would recognize his wife.' From what Fosco had said, Brunetti suspected Viscardi would have less trouble recognizing the paintings.

Patta leaned forward, paternally, and asked, 'Are you capable of understanding any of this?'

'I'll understand a lot more when we speak to Ruffolo.'

'Ruffolo? Who's he?'

'The young criminal in the photo.'

Patta said no more than Brunetti's name, but he said it so softly that it called for an explanation.

'Two tourists were sitting on a bridge and saw three men leave the house with a suitcase. Both of them identified the photo of Ruffolo.'

Because he had not bothered to read the report on the case, Patta didn't ask why this information wasn't contained in it. 'He could have been hiding outside,' he suggested.

'That's entirely possible,' Brunetti agreed, though it was far more likely to him that Ruffolo had been inside, and not hiding.

'And what about this Fosco person? What about his phone calls?'

'All I know about Fosco is that he's the Financial Editor of one of the most important magazines in the country. I called him to get an idea of how important Signor Viscardi was. So we'd know how to treat him.' This so precisely mirrored Patta's thinking that he was incapable of questioning Brunetti's sincerity. Brunetti hardly thought it necessary to make an excuse for the seriousness with which the policemen had seen fit to question Viscardi. Instead, he said, 'All we've got to do is get our hands on this Ruffolo, and everything will be straightened out. Signor Viscardi will get his paintings back, the insurance company will thank us, and I imagine the *Gazzettino* would run a story on the front page of the second section. After all, Signor Viscardi is a very important man, and the quicker this is settled, the better it will be for all of us.' Suddenly Brunetti felt himself overwhelmed with a wave of disgust at having to do this, go through this stupid charade every time they spoke. He looked away, then back at his superior.

Patta's smile was as broad as it was genuine. Could it be that Brunetti was finally beginning to have some sense, to take some heed of political realities? If so, then Patta believed that the credit for this might not unjustly be laid at his own door. They were a headstrong people, these Venetians, clinging to their own ways, outdated ways. Lucky for them that his appointment as Vice-Questore had brought them some exposure to the larger, more modern world, the world of tomorrow. Brunetti was right. All they had to do was find this Ruffolo character, get the paintings back, and Viscardi would be firmly behind him.

'Right,' he said, speaking crisply, the way policemen in American films spoke, 'let me know as soon as this Ruffolo is in custody. Do you need any more men assigned to this?'

'No, sir,' Brunetti said after a reflective pause. 'I think we've got enough on it right now. It's just a question of waiting until he makes a false step. That's bound to happen soon enough.'

Patta was completely uninterested in what it was or was not a question of. He wanted an arrest, the return of the paintings, and Viscardi's support should he decide to run for city councillor. 'Fine, let me know when you have something,' he said, dismissing Brunetti with the tone, if not with the words. Patta reached for another cigarette and Brunetti, unwilling to wait and watch the ceremony, excused himself and went down to speak to Vianello.

'Any word on Ruffolo?' Brunetti asked when he went into the office.

'There is and there isn't,' Vianello answered, rising minimally from his chair in deference to his superior, then lowering himself back into it.

'Meaning?'

'Meaning that the word is that he'd like to talk.'

'Where'd the word come from?'

'From someone who knows someone who knows him.'

'And who spoke to this someone?'

'I did. It's one of those kids out on Burano. You know, the ones who stole the fishing boat last year. Ever since we let them off on that, I've figured he's owed me a favour, so I went out to talk to him yesterday. I remembered that he went to school with Ruffolo. And he called me back about an hour ago. No questions asked. He just said that this other person had talked to someone who saw Ruffolo, and he wants to talk to us.'

'To anyone in particular?'

'Not to you, I'd imagine, sir. After all, you've put him away twice.'

'You want to do it, Vianello?'

The other man shrugged. 'Why not? I just don't want it to be a lot of bother. He's had nothing to do for the last two years but sit in jail and watch American police movies, so he'll probably suggest that we meet at midnight in a boat on the *laguna*.'

'Or in the cemetery at dawn, just when the vampires are flying back to nest.'

'Why can't he just make it a bar, so we can be comfortable and have a glass of wine?'

'Well, wherever it is, go and meet him.'

'Should I arrest him when he shows up?'

'No, don't try it. Just ask him what he wants to tell us, see what sort of deal he wants to make.'

'Do you want me to have someone there to follow him?'

'No. He'll probably be expecting that. And he'd panic if he thought he was being followed. Just see what he wants. If it isn't too much, make a deal with him.'

'You think he's going to tell us about Viscardi?'

'There's no other reason for him to want to talk to us, is there?'

'No, I suppose not.'

When Brunetti turned to leave, Vianello asked, 'What about the deal I make with him? Will we keep our part of it?'

At this, Brunetti turned back and gave Vianello a long look. 'Of course. If criminals can't believe in an illegal deal with the police, what can they believe in?'

19

He heard nothing from Ambrogiani that afternoon, nor did Vianello manage to make contact
with the boy on Burano. The next morning, no call
had come in, nor had there been any by the time he
got back from lunch. Vianello came in at about five
to tell him that the boy had called and a meeting
had been set up for Saturday afternoon, at Piazzale
Roma. A car would come to meet Vianello, who
was not to be in uniform, and would take him to
where Ruffolo would talk to him. After he
explained this to Brunetti, Vianello grinned and
added, 'Hollywood.'

'It probably means they'll have to steal a car to
do it, too.'

'And no chance of a drink, either, I suppose,'
said Vianello resignedly.

'Pity they pulled down the Pullman Bar; at least that way you could have had one before you left.'

'No such luck. I have to stand where the number five bus stops. They'll pull up and I have to get in.'

'How are they going to recognize you?'

Did Vianello blush? 'I have to be carrying a bouquet of red carnations.'

At this, Brunetti could not restrain himself and exploded into laughter. 'Red carnations? You? My God, I hope no one who knows you sees you, standing at a bus stop, leaving the city, with a bouquet of red carnations.'

'I've told my wife. She doesn't like it, not one bit, especially that I have to use my Saturday afternoon to do it. We were supposed to go out to dinner, and I won't hear the end of this for months.'

'Vianello, I'll make a deal. Do this, we'll even pay for the carnations, but you'll have to get a receipt, but do it and I'll fix the duty rosters so that you get next Friday and Saturday off, all right?' It seemed the least he could do for the man who was willing to take the risk of putting himself into the hands of known criminals and who, more courageously, was willing to take the risk of angering his wife.

'It's all right, sir, but I don't like it.'

'Look, you don't have to do this, Vianello. We're bound to get our hands on him sooner or later.'

'That's all right, sir. He's never been stupid enough to do anything to one of us before. And I know him from the last time.'

Vianello, Brunetti remembered, had two children

and a third on the way. 'If this works, you get the credit for it. It'll help towards a promotion.'

'Oh, fine, and how's he going to like that?' Vianello lowered his eyes in the direction of Patta's office. 'How's he going to like our arresting his friend, Signor Politically Important Viscardi?'

'Oh, come on, Vianello, you know what he'll do. Once Viscardi's behind bars and the case looks strong enough, Patta'll talk about the way he was suspicious from the very beginning but remained friendly with Viscardi, the better to lead him into the trap that he himself had devised.' Both of them knew from long experience that this was true.

Further ruminations on the behaviour of their superior were cut short by Vianello's phone. He answered it with his name, listened for a moment, then handed it to Brunetti. 'For you, sir.'

'Yes,' he said, then felt a rush of excitement when he recognized Ambrogiani's voice.

'He's still here. One of my men followed him to his home; it's in Grisignano, about twenty minutes from the base.'

'The train stops there, doesn't it?' Brunetti asked, already planning.

'Only the local. When do you want to see him?'

'Tomorrow morning.'

'Hold on a minute; I've got the schedule here.' While Brunetti waited, he heard the phone being set down for a moment, then Ambrogiani's voice. 'There's one that leaves Venice at eight; gets into Grisignano at eight-forty-three.'

'And before that?'

'Six-twenty-four.'

'Can you have someone meet that?'

'Guido, that gets in at seven-thirty,' Ambrogiani said, voice almost pleading.

'I want to speak to him at his house, and I don't want him to leave before I get a chance to talk to him.'

'Guido, you can't go barging in on people's homes at seven-thirty in the morning, even if they are Americans.'

'If you give me the address, maybe I can get a car here.' Even as he said it, he knew it was impossible; news of the request was bound to get back to Patta, and that was bound to cause nothing but trouble.

'You're a stubborn devil, aren't you?' Ambrogiani asked, but with more respect than anger in his voice. 'All right, I'll meet the train. I'll bring my own car; that way we can park near his house and not have the entire neighbourhood wondering what we're doing there.' Brunetti, to whom cars were alien, strange things, hadn't stopped to consider this, how a car that clearly belonged either to the Carabinieri or the police was bound to cause a stir in any small neighbourhood.

'Thanks, Giancarlo. I appreciate it.'

'I would certainly hope so. Seven-thirty on Saturday morning,' Ambrogiani said with disbelief and replaced the receiver before Brunetti could say anything else. Well, at least he didn't have to carry a dozen red carnations.

The next morning, he managed to get to the station on time to have a coffee before the train left, so he was reasonably civil to Ambrogiani when he met him at the tiny station of Grisignano. The Maggiore looked surprisingly fresh and alert, as though he had been up for hours, something that Brunetti found, in his current mood, faintly annoying. Opposite the station, they stopped at a bar, and each had a coffee and a brioche, the Maggiore signalling to the barman with his chin that he wanted a dash of grappa added to his coffee. 'It's not far from here,' Ambrogiani said. 'A few kilometres. They live in a semi-detached house. On the other side there's the landlord and his family.' Seeing Brunetti's inquisitive gaze, he explained. 'I had someone come out and ask a few questions. Not much to say. Three kids. They've lived there for more than three years, always pay their rent on time, get on well with the landlord. His wife's Italian, so that helps things in the neighbourhood.'

'And the boy?'

'He's here, back from the hospital in Germany.'

'And how is he?'

'He began school in September. Nothing seems to be wrong with him, but one of the neighbours says he has a nasty scar on his arm. Like he was burned.'

Brunetti finished his coffee, put the cup down on the counter, and said, 'Let's go out to their house, and I'll tell you what I know.'

As they drove though the sleepy lanes and tree-lined roads, Brunetti explained to Ambrogiani what he had learned from the books he read, told him about the Xerox copy of the medical report on Kayman's son, and about the article in the medical journal.

'It sounds like she, or Foster, put it together. But that still doesn't explain why they were both killed.'

'You think they were, too?' Brunetti asked.

Ambrogiani turned his attention from the road and looked at Brunetti. 'I never believed Foster was killed in a robbery, and I don't believe in an overdose. No matter how good both of them were made to look.'

Ambrogiani turned into an even smaller road and pulled up a hundred metres before a white cement house that stood back from the road, surrounded by a metal fence. The double entry doors to the semi-detached house opened from a porch raised above the doors of twin garages. In the driveway two bicycles lay, one beside the other, with the complete abandon that only bicycles could achieve.

'Tell me more about these chemicals,' Ambrogiani said when he turned off the engine. 'I tried to find out something about them last night, but no one I asked seemed to know anything precise about them, except that they were dangerous.'

'I don't know that I learned much more from what I read,' Brunetti admitted. 'There's a whole spectrum of them, a real death cocktail. It's easy to produce them, and most factories seem to need some of them, or create them doing whatever it is they do, but the trouble comes in getting rid of them. It used to be possible to dump them just about anywhere, but now it's harder. Too many people complained about having them in their back yards.'

'Wasn't there something in the paper a few years ago, about a ship, *Karen B* or something like that, that got as far as Africa and got turned around, ended up in Genoa?'

When Ambrogiani mentioned it, Brunetti remembered it and remembered the headlines about the 'Ship of Poisons', a freighter that had tried to unload its cargo in some African port but was refused permission to dock. So the boat sailed around in the Mediterranean for what seemed like weeks, the Press as fond of it as it was of those crazy porpoises who tried to swim up the Tiber every couple of years. Finally, the *Karen B* had docked at Genoa, and that had been the end of it. As efficiently as if she had gone down in the waters of the Mediterranean, the *Karen B* sank off the pages of the newspapers and from the screens of Italian television. And the poisons she had been carrying, an entire boatload of lethal substances, had just as completely disappeared, no one to know or ask how. Or where.

'Yes. But I don't remember what her cargo was,' Brunetti said.

'We've never had a case of it out here,' Ambrogiani said, not feeling it necessary to explain that 'we' were the Carabinieri and 'it' illegal dumping. 'I don't even know if it's our job to look for it or arrest for it.'

Neither of them wanted to be the first to break the silence that thought led to. Finally, Brunetti said, 'Interesting, isn't it?'

'That no one seems responsible to enforce the law? If there are laws?' Ambrogiani asked.

'Yes.'

Before they could follow this up, the front door on the left side of the house they were watching opened and a man stepped out onto the porch. He walked down the steps, pulled open the garage door, then bent to move both bicycles to the grass at the side of the driveway. When he disappeared back into the garage, both Brunetti and Ambrogiani got out of the car and started to walk towards the house.

Just as they got to the gate in the fence, a car came backing slowly out of the garage. It backed towards the gate, and the man got out, leaving the engine running, and moved to the gate to open it. Either he didn't see the two men there or he chose to ignore them. He unlatched the gate, shoved it open, and then headed back towards the open door of his car.

'Sergeant Kayman?' Brunetti called over the sound of the engine.

At the sound of his name, the man turned and looked at them. Both policemen stepped forward but stopped at the gate, careful not to pass onto the man's property uninvited. Seeing this, the man waved them ahead with his hand and bent into the car to switch off the engine.

He was a tall blond man with a slight stoop that might once have been intended to disguise his height but which had now become habitual. He moved with that loose-limbed ease so common to Americans, the ease that made them look so good in casual clothing, so awkward in formal dress. He walked towards them, face open and quizzical, not smiling but certainly not suspicious.

'Yes?' he asked in English. 'You guys looking for me?'

'Sergeant Edward Kayman?' Ambrogiani asked.

'Yeah. What can I do for you? Sort of early, isn't it?'

Brunetti stepped forward and extended his hand. 'Good morning, Sergeant. I'm Guido Brunetti, from the Venice police.'

The American shook Brunetti's hand, his grasp firm and strong. 'Long way from home, aren't you, Mr Brunetti?' he asked, turning the last two consonants into 'D's.

It was meant as a pleasantry, so Brunetti smiled at him. 'I suppose I am. But there are a few things I wanted to ask you, Sergeant.' Ambrogiani smiled and nodded but made no attempt to introduce himself, leaving the conversation to Brunetti.

'Well, ask away,' said the American, then added, 'sorry I can't invite you gentlemen into the house for a cup of coffee, but the wife's still asleep, and she'd kill me if I woke the kids up. Saturday's her only morning to sleep in.'

'I understand,' Brunetti said. 'Same thing at my house. I had to sneak out like a burglar myself this morning.' They shared a grin at the unreasonable tyranny of sleeping women, and Brunetti began, 'I'd like to ask you about your son.'

'Daniel?' the American asked.

'Yes.'

'I thought so.'

'You don't seem surprised,' Brunetti remarked.

Before he answered, the soldier moved over and leaned back against his car, bracing his weight against it. Brunetti took this opportunity to turn to Ambrogiani and asked in Italian, 'Are you following what we say?' The Carabiniere nodded.

The American crossed his feet at the ankles and pulled a packet of cigarettes from his shirt pocket. He held the pack towards the Italians, but both shook their heads. He lit a cigarette with a lighter, careful to cup it between both hands from the nonexistent breeze, then slipped both packet and lighter back into his pocket.

'It's about this doctor business, isn't it?' he asked, putting his head back and blowing a stream of smoke up into the air.

'What makes you say that, Sergeant?'

'Doesn't take much figuring, does it? She was Danny's doctor, and she sure as heck was all upset when his arm got so bad. Kept asking him what happened, and then that boyfriend of hers, the one that got himself killed in Venice, then he started bein' all over me with questions.'

'You knew he was her boyfriend?' Brunetti asked, honestly surprised.

'Well, it wasn't until after he was killed that anyone said anything, but I suspect a fair number of people must have known before. I didn't, for one, but I didn't work with them. Heck, there aren't but a few thousand of us, all living and working cheek by jowl. Nobody gets to keep any secrets, leastways not for very long.'

'What sort of questions did he ask you?'

'About where it was that Danny had been

walking that day. And what else we saw there. Stuff like that.'

'What did you tell him?'

'I told him I didn't know.'

'You didn't know?'

'Well, not exactly. We were up above Aviano that day, up near Lake Barcis, but we stopped at another place on the way back down from the mountains; that's where we had our picnic. Danny went off for a while into the woods by himself, but he couldn't remember where it was he fell down, which place it was. I told Foster, tried to describe where it was, but I couldn't remember real clear where we parked the car that day. With three kids and a dog to keep an eye on, you don't pay much attention to things like that.'

'What did he do when you said you couldn't remember?'

'Heck, he wanted me to go up there with him, drive all the way up there with him some Saturday and look for the place, see if I could remember where it was we parked the car.'

'And did you go back with him.'

'Not on your life. I've got three kids, a wife, and, if I'm lucky, one day off a week. I'm not going to go spend one of them running around the mountains, looking for some place I once had a picnic in. Besides, that was the time when Danny was in the hospital, and I wasn't about to leave my wife alone all day, just to go on some wild-goose chase.'

'How did he behave when you told him?'

'Well, I could see that he was pretty angry, but I just told him I couldn't do it, and he seemed to quiet down. He stopped asking me to go with him, but I think he went up there, looking, by himself, or maybe with Doctor Peters.'

'Why do you say that?'

'Well, he went and talked to a friend of mine who works in the dental clinic. He's the X-ray technician, and he told me that, one Friday afternoon, Foster went into the lab and asked him to lend him his tab for the weekend.'

'His what?'

'His tab. At least that's what he calls it. You know, that little card thing they all have to wear, the people who work with X-rays. You get overexposed, it turns a different colour. I don't know what you call it.' Brunetti nodded his head, knowing what it was. 'Well, this guy lent it to him for the weekend, and he had it back to him on Monday morning, in time for work. Good as his word.'

'And the sensor?'

'Wasn't changed at all. Same colour it was when he gave it to him.'

'Why do you think that was why he borrowed it?'

'You didn't know him, did you?' he asked Brunetti, who shook his head. 'He was a funny guy. Real serious. Real serious about his work, well, about just about everything. I think he was religious, too, but not like those crazy born-agains. When he decided that something was right, there was no stopping him from doing it. And he had it in his head that . . .' He paused here. 'I'm not sure what he had in his head, but he wanted to find out where it was Danny touched that stuff he's allergic to.'

'Is that what it was? An allergy?'

'That's what they told me when he came down from Germany. His arm's an awful mess, but the doctors up there said it would heal up pretty good. Might take a year or so, but the scar'll go away, or at least it'll fade a fair bit.'

Ambrogiani spoke for the first time. 'Did they tell you what he was allergic to?'

'No, they couldn't find out. Said it was probably sap from some sort of tree that grows up in those mountains. They did all sorts of tests on the boy.' Here his face softened and his eyes lit up with real pride. 'Never complained, not once, that boy. Got the makings of a real man. I'm not half proud of him.'

'But they didn't tell you what he was allergic to?' the Carabiniere repeated.

'Nope. And then the dang fools went and lost Danny's medical records, leastwise the records from Germany.'

At this, Brunetti and Ambrogiani exchanged a look, and Brunetti asked, 'Do you know if Foster ever found the place?'

'Couldn't say. He got killed two weeks after he borrowed that sensor thing, and I never had occasion to talk to him again. So I don't know. I'm sorry that happened to him. He was an OK guy, and I'm sorry his doctor friend had to take it so hard. I didn't know they were that . . .' Here he failed to find the right word, so he stopped.

'Is that what people here believe, that Doctor

Peters gave herself that overdose because of Foster?'

This time, it was the soldier who was surprised. 'Doesn't make sense any other way, does it? She was a doctor, wasn't she? If anybody knew how much of that stuff to put in a needle, it should have been her.'

'Yes, I suppose so,' Brunetti said, feeling his disloyalty even as he spoke.

'Funny thing, though,' began the American. 'If I hadn't 've been so bothered with worryin' about Danny, I maybe would have thought of something to tell Foster. Might have helped him find the place he was looking for.'

'What's that?' Brunetti asked, making the question casual.

'While we were up there that day, I saw two of the trucks that come here, saw them turning into a dirt road off down the hill a ways from where we were. I just didn't think of it when Foster asked me. Wish I had. Could have saved him a lot of trouble. All he'd have to do is go ask Mr Gamberetto where his trucks were that day, and he would have found the place.'

'Mr Gamberetto?' Brunetti inquired politely.

'Yeah, he's the fellow's got the haulage contract from the post. His trucks pull in here twice a week and take away the restricted stuff. You know, the medical waste from the hospital, and from the dental clinic. I think he picks up stuff from the motor pool, too. The oil they take out of the transformers and from the oil changes they do. The trucks don't have his name on them or anything, but they have this red stripe down the side, and that's the kind of trucks I saw up by Lake Barcis that day.' He paused and grew reflective. 'I don't know why I didn't think of it that day, when Foster asked me. But Danny had just gone up to Germany, and I guess I wasn't thinking all that clear.'

'You work in the contracting office, don't you, Sergeant?' Ambrogiani asked.

If the American found it strange that Ambrogiani would know this, he gave no sign of it. 'Yes, I do.'

'Do you ever have occasion to speak to this Mr Gamberetto?'

'Nope. Never laid eyes on the man. I just know his name from seeing the contract in the office.'

'Doesn't he come in to sign the contract?' Ambrogiani asked.

'No, one of the officers goes out to his office. I imagine he gets a free lunch out of him, then comes back with the signed contract, and we process it.' Brunetti didn't have to look at Ambrogiani to know he was thinking that someone might be getting a lot more out of Mr Gamberetto than a free lunch.

'Is that the only contract Mr Gamberetto has?'

'No, sir. He's got the contract to build the new hospital. That was supposed to start a while back, but then we had the Gulf War, and all building projects got put on hold. But it looks like things are beginning to loosen up, and I imagine work will begin in the spring, soon as the ground is ready to be broke open.'

'Is it a big contract?' Brunetti asked. 'Certainly sounds like it, a hospital.'

'I don't remember the exact figures, it's been so long since we handled the contract, but I think it was something in the neighbourhood of ten million dollars. But that was three years ago, when it was signed. I imagine it's increased a fair bit since then.'

'Yes, I should certainly think so,' Brunetti said. Suddenly they all turned towards the sound of wild barking from the house. As they watched, the front door opened a crack and a large black dog came catapulting from the door and down the steps. Barking dementedly, she ran directly to Kayman and jumped up at him, licking at his face. She turned to the two men, checked them over, then ran off a few metres to squat on the grass and relieve herself. That done, she was back at Kayman, leaping up, aiming her nose at his.

'Get down, Kitty Kat,' he said, no firmness at all in his voice. She soared up again and made contact. 'Get down now, girl. Stop that.' She ignored him, ran off, the better to gain momentum for her next leap, turned, and raced back. 'Bad dog,' Kayman said in a tone that meant the opposite. He pushed the dog down with both hands and latched them in the fur at her neck, where he began to scratch her roughly. 'Sorry. I wanted to get away without her. Once she sees me get into the car, she goes crazy if she can't come along. Loves the car.'

'I don't want to keep you, Sergeant. You've been very helpful,' Brunetti said, putting out his hand. The dog followed his hand with her eyes, tongue lolling to the left of her mouth. Kayman freed one hand and shook Brunetti's hand, but he did it awkwardly, still bent down over the dog. He shook Ambrogiani's, then, when they turned away and went back towards the gate, he opened the door to the car and allowed the dog to leap in ahead of him.

As the car backed towards them, Brunetti stood by the metal gate. He waved to Sergeant Kayman to indicate that he would see to closing the gate and did just that. The American waited long enough to see that the gate was closed, put his car in gear, and drove off slowly. The last they saw was the head of the dog, poking out of the rear window of the car, nose prodding at the wind.

20

As the head of the dog disappeared up the narrow road, Ambrogiani turned to Brunetti and asked, 'Well?'

Brunetti began to walk towards the parked car. When they were both inside and the doors closed, Ambrogiani sat behind the wheel without starting the engine.

'Big job, building a hospital,' Brunetti finally said. 'Big job for Signor Gamberetto.'

'Very,' the other agreed.

'The name mean anything to you?' Brunetti asked.

'Oh, yes,' Ambrogiani said, then added, 'he's someone we've been told to stay away from.'

When Brunetti gave him a puzzled glance, Ambrogiani explained, 'Well, it's never been given

273

as a specific order – nothing like that ever is – but the word has filtered down that Signor Gamberetto and his affairs are not to be examined too closely.'

'Or else?' Brunetti asked.

'Oh,' Ambrogiani said with a bitter chuckle, 'it's never as crude as that. It is simply suggested, and anyone who has any sense understands what it means.'

'And stays away from Signor Gamberetto?'

'Precisely.'

'Interesting,' Brunetti offered.

'Very.'

'So you treat him like he's just a simple businessman with dealings in the area?'

Ambrogiani nodded.

'And by Lake Barcis, it seems.'

'Yes, it does, doesn't it?'

'You think you could find out about him?'

'Well, I think I could try.'

'Meaning?'

'Meaning that, if he's a medium-sized fish, then I'll be able to find out about him. But if he's a big fish, then there won't be much to find out. Or what I do find out will tell me that he's no more than a respectable local businessman, well-connected politically. And that will merely confirm what we know already, that he is a man with Friends in High Places.'

'Mafia?'

Ambrogiani shrugged one shoulder by way of answer.

'Even up here?'

'Why not? They've got to go somewhere. All

they do is kill one another down South. How many murders have there been so far this year? Two hundred? Two hundred and fifty? So they've started moving up here.'

'The government?'

Ambrogiani gave the special snort of disgust that Italians reserve for use only when speaking of their government. 'Who can tell them apart anymore, Mafia and government?'

This vision was more severe than Brunetti's, but perhaps the nationwide network of the Carabinieri had access to more information than he did.

'What about you?' Ambrogiani asked.

'I can make some phone calls when I get back. Call in some favours.' He didn't tell Ambrogiani of the one call he thought would be most successful, one that had nothing to do with calling in a favour; quite the opposite.

They sat there for a long time. Finally, Ambrogiani reached forward and opened the glove compartment. He began to rifle though the stack of maps that lay inside until he finally pulled one out. 'Have you got time?' he asked.

'Yes. How long will it take to get there?'

Instead of answering, Ambrogiani pulled open a map and spread it open in front of him, braced against the steering wheel. With a thick finger, he roved around the map until he found what he was looking for. 'Here it is. Lake Barcis.' His finger snaked to the right on the lake and then cut sharply down in a straight line leading to Pordenone. 'An hour and a half. Maybe two. Most of it is *autostrada*. What do you say?'

By way of answer, Brunetti reached behind him and pulled his seat belt across his chest, snapping it into place between the seats.

Two hours later, they were driving up the snake-like road that led to Lake Barcis, one of at least twenty cars caught behind an immense gravel-filled truck that crawled along at about ten kilometres an hour, forcing Ambrogiani constantly to switch gears from second to first as they stopped on curves to allow the truck to manoeuvre its way around them. Every so often, a car swept past them on the left, then cut narrowly between two of the cars crammed behind the truck, forcing an opening with its front end and horn. Occasionally, a car pulled sharply to the right and sought a parking space on the too-narrow shoulder. The driver would pop out, pull open the bonnet, and sometimes make the mistake of opening the radiator.

Brunetti wanted to suggest that they pull over, since they were in no hurry, had no destination, but, even though he wasn't really a driver, he knew enough not to suggest what to do. After about twenty minutes of this, the truck pulled off the road into a long parking area, no doubt designed for just this purpose, and the cars shot past, some waving their thanks, most not bothering. Ten minutes later, they pulled into the small town of Barcis, and Ambrogiani turned off to the left and down a sharp driveway that led to the lake.

Ambrogiani hauled himself out of the car, obviously rattled by the drive. 'Let's have something to drink,' he said, walking towards a café that filled an enormous veranda behind one of the buildings beside the lake. He pulled out a chair at one of the umbrella-shaded tables and dropped into it. Before them stretched the lake, water eerily blue, mountains shooting up behind it. A waiter came and took their order, returned a few minutes later with two coffees and two glasses of mineral water.

After Brunetti had finished his coffee and taken a sip of the water, he asked, 'Well?'

Ambrogiani smiled. 'Pretty lake, isn't it?'

'Yes, beautiful. What are we, tourists?'

'I suppose so. Pity we can't stay here and look at the lake all day, isn't it?'

It unsettled Brunetti not to know if the other man was serious or not. But, yes it would be nice. He found himself hoping that the two young Americans had been able to spend the weekend up here, regardless of the reason for their trip. If they were in love, this would be a beautiful place to be. Himself his own editor, he corrected that to read, if they were in love, anywhere would be beautiful.

Brunetti summoned the waiter and paid him. They had decided on the ride up not to call attention to themselves by asking questions about trucks with red stripes turning onto side roads. They were tourists, even if they were in tie and jacket, and tourists certainly had the right to pull off at a picnic site on the way down and look at the mountains as the traffic sped past them. Because he didn't know how long they would be, he stopped at the counter inside and asked if the barman could make a few sandwiches to take with them. The best he could do was prosciutto and cheese. Ambrogiani nodded, told him to make four and to put in a bottle of red wine and two plastic cups.

With this in hand, they returned to Ambrogiani's car and drove down the hill, back in the direction of Pordenone. About two kilometres from Barcis, they saw a broad parking area on the right-hand side and pulled into it. Ambrogiani swung the car around so that they could see the road, not the mountains, killed the engine and said, 'Here we are.'

'It wasn't my idea of how I'd spend my Saturday,' Brunetti admitted.

'I've had worse,' Ambrogiani said and then talked about a time when he had been assigned to look for a kidnap victim in Aspromonte and had spent three days up in the hills, lying on the ground, watching through a pair of field glasses as people went into and out of a shepherd's hut.

'What happened?' Brunetti asked.

'Oh, we got them.' And then he laughed. 'But it was someone else, not the one we were looking for. This girl's family had never called us, never reported it. They were willing to pay the ransom, only we got there before they had the chance to pay a lira.'

'What happened to the other one? The one you were looking for?'

'They killed him. We found him a week after we found the girl. They'd cut his throat. The smell led us to him. And the birds.'

'Why did they do it?'

'Probably because we found the girl. We warned her family, when we took her back to them, not to say anything. But someone called the papers, and it was all over the front pages. You know, "Joyous Liberation", complete with pictures of her with her mother, eating her first dish of pasta in two months. They must have read about it and figured we were looking for them, getting close. So they killed him.'

'Why not just let him go?' Then, because it had not been said, Brunetti asked, 'How old was he?'

'Twelve.' There followed a long pause, then Ambrogiani answered the first question. 'Letting him go would be bad business. It would let other people know that if we got close enough, there might be a chance for them. By killing him, they made the message clear: we mean business, and if you don't pay, we kill.'

Ambrogiani opened the bottle of wine and poured some into the plastic cups. They each ate a sandwich, then, because there was nothing else to do, another. During all of this, Brunetti had kept himself from looking at his watch, knowing that it would be later, the longer he waited. Unable to resist, he looked. Noon. The hours stretched ahead. He rolled down the window, looked over at the mountains for a long time. When he glanced back, Ambrogiani was asleep, head canted to the left, resting against the window. Brunetti watched the traffic going down and coming up the steep gradient. All of the cars looked pretty much the same to him, different only in colour and, if they were moving slowly enough, in number plate.

After an hour, the traffic began to taper off, everyone had stopped to eat. Soon after he noticed this, he heard the sharp exhalation of air from the brakes of a truck and looked up to see a large truck with a red stripe along the side pass down the hill.

He poked Ambrogiani in the arm. The Carabiniere was instantly awake, his hand turning the key. He pulled onto the road and followed the truck. About two kilometres from where they had been parked, the truck signalled and then turned off to the right, disappearing down a narrow dirt-covered road. They drove past, continuing down the hill, but Brunetti saw Ambrogiani reach out to the dashboard and push the button that moved the mileometer back to zero. After he had gone a full kilometre, he pulled off the road and cut the engine.

'What was the number plate?'

'Vicenza,' Brunetti said and pulled out his notebook to write the numbers down while they were still fresh in his memory. 'What do you think?'

'We stay here until the truck passes us on the way down or we wait half an hour and go back.'

After half an hour, the truck had not passed the place where they were parked, so Ambrogiani drove back up towards the road the truck had turned into. They passed it and he pulled off to the right a bit beyond it, angling the car in between two cement road markers.

Ambrogiani got out and went around to the boot of the car. He opened it and reached in. Slipped in next to the tyre was a large calibre pistol, which he pushed into the waistband of his trousers. 'You have one?' he asked.

Brunetti shook his head. 'I didn't bring it today.'

'I've got another one in here. Want it?'

Brunetti shook his head again.

Ambrogiani slammed the boot closed and together they walked across the road and onto the dirt path that led off towards the mountains.

Trucks had worn a double groove into the dirt of the path; with the first heavy rain, the dirt would turn to mud, and the road would be impassable to vehicles the size of the truck they had seen turn into it. After a few hundred metres, the path widened minimally and curved to run alongside a stream that had to be coming down from the lake. Soon the path branched off to the left, leaving the stream and now following a long line of trees. Ahead, the path took another sharp turn to the left and up a sharp incline, where it seemed to come to an end. With no warning, Ambrogiani stepped behind one of the trees and pulled Brunetti after him. With a single motion, the Carabiniere reached inside his jacket and pulled out his gun with one hand and, with the other, gave Brunetti a brutal push in the centre of his back that sent him spinning away, completely off-balance.

Brunetti flailed at the air with his arms, unable to stop his forward motion. For an instant, he hung between motion and collapse, but then the ground sloped away under him and he knew he was going to fall. As he did, he turned his head and saw Ambrogiani coming directly after him, gun in hand. His heart contracted in sudden terror. He had trusted this man, never stopping to think that the person at the American base who had learned about Foster's curiosity and who had learned about Doctor Peters' affair with him could just as easily be an Italian as an American. And he had even offered Brunetti a gun.

He crashed forward onto the ground, stunned, wind knocked from him. He tried to push himself to his knees, he thought of Paola, and he was conscious of the blaze of sunlight all around him. Ambrogiani crashed to the ground beside him, threw an arm over his back, and pushed him back down to the ground. 'Stay down. Keep your head down,' he said into Brunetti's ear, lying beside him, arm across his back.

Brunetti lay on the earth, digging his hands into the grass beneath him, eyes closed, conscious only of the weight of Ambrogiani's arm and of the sweat that covered his entire body. Through the torrent of his pulse, he heard the sound of a truck coming towards them from what had seemed the end of the road. As he listened, its motor drummed past them then grew dimmer as it made its way back towards the main road. When it was gone, Ambrogiani pushed himself heavily to his knees and started to brush off his clothing. 'Sorry,' he said, smiling down at Brunetti and extending his hand. 'I just did it, didn't have time to think. You all right?'

Brunetti took his hand, pulled himself up, and stood beside the other man, knees trembling uncontrollably. 'Sure, fine,' he said, and bent to swipe the worst of the dust off his trousers. His underclothing stuck to his body, glued there by the sudden wave of animal terror that had overcome him.

Ambrogiani turned and went back towards the path, either in complete ignorance of Brunetti's fear or in an exquisite gesture of feigned ignorance. Brunetti finished dusting himself off, took a few deep breaths, and followed Ambrogiani down the path to where it started to rise. It did not end but, instead, twisted suddenly to the right and stopped abruptly at the edge of a small bluff. Together, the two men walked up to the edge and looked down over it. Below them spread an area about half the size of a soccer field, most of it covered with creeping vines that could easily have grown up that same summer. The end nearest them, spreading out from the rise of land they stood on, contained about a hundred metal barrels that must once have contained kerosene. Mixed in with them were large black plastic bags, industrial strength, sealed closed at one end. At some point, a bulldozer must have been used, for the barrels at the far end disappeared under a heap of vine-covered earth that had been piled over them. There was no telling how far back the covered barrels extended, no hope of counting them.

'Well, it seems like we've found what the American was looking for,' Ambrogiani said.

'I'd guess he found it, too.'

Ambrogiani nodded. 'No need to kill him if he didn't. What do you think he did, confront Gamberetto directly?'

'I don't know,' Brunetti said. It didn't make

sense, so severe a response. What was the worst that could have happened to Gamberetto? A fine? Surely, he'd blame the drivers, even pay one of them to say he did it on his own. He would hardly lose a contract to build a hospital if something like this was discovered; Italian law treated it as little more than a misdemeanour. He would be in more serious danger if he were caught driving an unregistered car. That, after all, deprived the government directly of income; this merely poisoned the earth.

'Do you think we can get down there?' he asked.

Ambrogiani stared at him. 'You want to go and look at that stuff?'

'I'd like to see what's written on the barrels.'

'Maybe if we cut down to the left, over there,' Ambrogiani said, pointing off in that direction to a narrow path that led down towards the dumping ground. Together, they walked down the sharp incline, occasionally sliding in the dust, grabbing at one another to stop their skidding descent. Finally, at the bottom, they found themselves only a few metres from the first of the barrels.

Brunetti looked down at the earth. The dust was dry and loose here, on the outskirts of the dump; inside, it seemed to thicken and turn to paste. He walked towards the barrels, careful where he placed his feet. Nothing was written on the top or sides; no labels, no stickers, no identification of any sort. Moving along the outskirts of the dump, careful not to step too close to them, he studied the tops and visible sides of the barrels that stood there. They came almost to his hip, each with a metal cap hammered tightly into place on the top. Whoever had placed them there had at least been careful enough to place them upright.

When he reached the end of the rows of exposed barrels without seeing any identification, he looked back along the row he had walked beside, searching for a place where enough room stood between them to allow him to move about among them. He went back a few metres and found a place that would allow him to slip between them. The stuff under his feet was more than paste now; it had turned to a thin layer of oily mud that came up the sides of the soles of his shoes. He moved deeper into the standing barrels, bending down now and again to search for any sign of identification. His foot came up against one of the black plastic bags. The barrel it rested against had a flap of paper hanging from it. Taking his handkerchief, Brunetti reached out and turned the paper over. 'US Air Force. Ramst . . .' Part of the last word was missing, but, ever since the Italian Air Force flying squad had hurled their planes madly into one another, raining death on the hundreds of German and American civilians below them, everyone in Italy knew that the largest American military air base in Germany was at Ramstein.

He kicked at the bag. It shifted over on its side, and, from the shapes that protruded inside the plastic, it seemed to be filled with cans. He took his keys from his pocket and slashed at the bag, ripping it open all down one side. Cans and cardboard boxes spilled out. As a can rolled towards him, he stepped back involuntarily.

From behind him, Ambrogiani called out, 'What is it?'

Brunetti waved his arm above his head to signal that he was all right and bent to examine the writing on the cans and boxes. 'Government issue. Not for resale or private use', was written on some of them, in English. A few of the boxes had labels in German. Most of them had the skull and crossbones that warned of poison or other danger. He lifted his foot and prodded at a can with his foot. The label, also in English, read, 'If found, contact your NBC officer. Do not touch.'

Brunetti turned and walked delicately towards the edge of the dumping ground, even more cautious now where he placed his feet. A few metres from the edge, he dropped his handkerchief to the earth and left it there. When he emerged from the barrels, Ambrogiani came up to him.

'Well?' the Carabiniere asked.

'The labels are in English and German. Some of them come from one of their air force bases in Germany. I have no idea where the rest of it comes from.' They started to walk away from the dump. 'What's an NBC officer?' Brunetti asked, hoping that Ambrogiani would know.

'Nuclear, biological, and chemical.'

'Mother of God,' Brunetti whispered.

There was no need for Foster to have gone to Gamberetto to put himself in jeopardy. He was a young man who kept books like *Christian Life in an Age of Doubt* on his shelf. He probably would have done what any innocent young soldier would have done – reported it to his superior officer. American waste. American military waste. Shipped to Italy so that it could be dumped there. Secretly.

They walked back along the path, meeting no trucks on the way. When they got to the car, Brunetti sat on the seat, feet still outside the car. With two quick motions, he kicked his shoes off and far into the grass at the side of the road. Careful to hold them by the top, he peeled off his socks and hurled them after the shoes. Turning to Ambrogiani, he said, 'Do you think we could stop at a shoe shop on the way to the station?'

21

On the drive back to Mestre train station, Ambrogiani gave Brunetti an idea of how the dumping would be possible. Though the Italian customs police had the right to inspect every truck that came down from Germany to the American base, there were so many that some did not get inspected, and what inspection was given was often cursory, at best. As to planes, don't even speak; they flew in and out of the military airports at Villafranca and Aviano at will, loading and unloading whatever they chose. When Brunetti asked why there were so many deliveries, Ambrogiani explained the extent to which America saw that its soldiers and airmen, their wives and children, were kept happy. Ice cream, frozen pizza, spaghetti sauce, crisps, spirits,

California wines, beer: all of this, and more, was flown in to stock the shelves of the supermarket, and this was to make no mention of the shops that sold stereo equipment, televisions, racing bicycles, potting soil, underwear. Then there were the transports that brought in heavy equipment, tanks, Jeeps. He remembered the navy base at Naples and the base at Livorno; anything could be brought in by ship.

'It sounds like they'd have no trouble doing it,' Brunetti said.

'But why bring it down here?' Ambrogiani asked.

It seemed pretty simple to Brunetti. 'The Germans are more careful about this sort of thing. The environmentalists are a real power there. If anyone got wind of something like this in Germany, there'd be a scandal. Now that they're united, someone would start to talk about throwing the Americans out, not just waiting for them to leave on their own. But here in Italy, no one cares what gets dumped, anywhere, so all they have to do is remove the identification. Then, if what they dump is found, it can't be tied to anyone, everyone can deny all knowledge, and no one will care enough to find out. And no one here is going to talk about throwing the Americans out.'

'But they haven't removed all identification,' Ambrogiani corrected.

'Maybe they thought they'd get it covered before anyone found it. It's easy enough to bring in a bulldozer and finish piling the dirt over it. It looked like they were running out of room there, anyway.'

'Why not just ship it back to America?'

Brunetti gave him a long look. Surely, he couldn't be this innocent. 'We try to unload ours on Third World countries, Giancarlo. To the Americans, maybe we're a Third World country. Or maybe all countries that aren't America are Third World.'

Ambrogiani muttered something under his breath.

Up ahead of them, the traffic slowed at the toll booths at the end of the *autostrada*. Brunetti pulled out his wallet and handed Ambrogiani ten thousand lire, pocketed the change, and put his wallet back in his pocket. At the third exit, Ambrogiani pulled to the right and down into the chaotic Saturday afternoon traffic. They crawled towards Mestre train station, battling the aggression of various cars. Ambrogiani pulled up across from it, ignoring the No Parking sign and the angry honk from a car that wanted to pull in behind him. 'Well?' he asked, looking over at Brunetti.

'See what you can find out about Gamberetto, and I'll speak to a few people here.'

'Should I call you?'

'Not from the base.' Brunetti scribbled his home number on a piece of paper and handed it to the other man. 'This is my own number. You can get me there early in the morning or at night. Call from a phone booth, I think.'

'Yes,' Ambrogiani agreed, voice sombre, as if

this small suggestion had suddenly warned him of the magnitude of what they were involved with.

Brunetti opened the door and got out of the car. He came around to the other side and leaned down towards the open window. 'Thanks, Giancarlo.'

They shook hands through the open window, saying nothing more, and Brunetti crossed the road to the station while Ambrogiani drove away.

By the time he got to his house, his feet hurt from the new shoes that Ambrogiani had bought for him in a place on the motorway. A hundred and sixty thousand lire and they hurt his feet! As soon as he got inside the door, he kicked them off, then walked towards the bathroom, peeling off his clothing as he walked, dropping it carelessly behind him. He stood in the shower for a long time, soaping his body repeatedly, rubbing at his feet and between his toes with a cloth, rinsing and washing them again and again. He dried himself and sat on the edge of the tub to examine his feet closely. Though they were red from the hot water and scrubbing, he saw no sign of rash or burning on them; they felt like feet, though he wasn't at all sure how feet were supposed to feel.

He wrapped a second towel around himself and went towards the bedroom. As he did, he heard Paola call from the kitchen, 'This place doesn't come with maid service, Guido.' Her voice was raised over the rush of water into the washing-machine.

He ignored her, went to the closet and got dressed, sitting on the bed while he pulled on a new pair of socks, again examining his feet. They still looked like feet. He pulled a pair of brown shoes from the bottom of the closet, tied them, and walked down towards the kitchen. As soon as she heard him coming, she continued, 'How do you expect me to get the kids to pick up after themselves if you drop things anywhere you want?'

When he walked into the kitchen, he found her kneeling in front of the washing-machine, thumb poised over the button that turned it on and off. Through the clear glass window, he could see a sodden heap of clothes being swirled first one way, then another.

'What's the matter with that thing?' he asked.

She didn't look up at him as she answered, kept her mesmerized stare on the swirling clothing. 'It's unbalanced somehow. If I put towels in it, anything that absorbs a lot of water, the weight of the initial spin tilts it out of balance, and it blows out all of the electricity in the house. So I've got to wait for it to start, see that it doesn't happen. If it does, then I've got to turn it off before it happens and wring the clothes out.'

'Paola, do you have to do this every time you do a wash?'

'No. Only if there are towels or those flannel sheets from Chiara's bed.' She stopped talking here, raised her thumb over the button as the machine made a click. Suddenly, it jolted into sudden motion and the clothing inside began to spin around, pressed against the side of the swirling drum. Paola got to her feet, smiled, and said, 'Well, no trouble that time.'

'How long has it been like that?'

'Oh, I don't know. Couple of years.'

'And you have to do that every time you do a wash?'

'If I wash towels. I told you.' She smiled, irritation forgotten. 'Where have you been since the crack of dawn? Did you have anything to eat?'

'Up at Lake Barcis.'

'Doing what, playing army? Your clothes were filthy. It looks like you've been rolling around in the dirt.'

'I have been rolling around in the dirt,' he began and told her about his day with Ambrogiani. It took a long time because he had to keep going back to explain about Kayman, his son, the way the boy's medical records had been 'lost', the medical journal that he had received in the post. And, finally, he told her about the drugs that had been hidden in Foster's apartment.

When he finished, Paola asked, 'And they told those people that their son was allergic to something from a tree? That everything was all right?' He nodded and she exploded. 'Bastards! And what happens when the boy develops other symptoms? What do they tell the parents then?'

'Maybe he won't develop other symptoms.'

'And maybe he will, Guido. What happens then? What do they tell him then, that he's got something they can't figure out? Do they lose his medical records again?'

Brunetti wanted to tell her that none of this was his fault, but that seemed too feeble a protest, so he said nothing.

After her outburst, Paola realized how futile it

was and turned to more practical things. 'What are you going to do?' she asked.

'I don't know.' He paused, then said, 'I want to talk to your father.'

'To Papà? Why?' Her surprise was real.

Brunetti knew how inflammatory his answer would be, but he said it anyway, knowing it was true. 'Because he'd know about this.'

She attacked before she thought. 'What do you mean, know about it? How could he? What do you think my father is, some sort of international criminal?'

In the face of Brunetti's silence, she stopped. Behind them, the washing-machine stopped spinning and clicked itself off. The room was silent save for the echo of her question. She turned and bent to empty it, filling her arms with damp clothing. Saying nothing, she passed in front of him and went onto the terrace, where she dumped the washing onto a chair, then pegged it to the clothesline piece by piece. When she came back inside, all she said was, 'Well, it's possible that he might know people who might know something about it. Do you want to call him or do you want me to?'

'I think I'd better do it.'

'Better do it now, Guido. My mother said they're going to Capri for a week, leaving tomorrow.'

'All right,' Brunetti said and went into the living room, where the phone was.

He dialled the number from memory, having no idea why this number, that he might call twice a year, was one he never forgot. His mother-in-law answered and, if she was surprised to hear Brunetti's voice, gave no sign of it. She said Count Orazio was home, asked no questions, and said she would call her husband to the phone.

'Yes, Guido,' the Count said when he picked up the phone.

'I wonder if you have some time free this afternoon,' Brunetti said. 'I'd like to speak to you about something that's come up.'

'Viscardi?' the Count asked, surprising Brunetti that he knew about that case.

'No, not about that,' Brunetti answered, thinking only then of how much easier it would have been to have asked his father-in-law, instead of Fosco, about Viscardi, and perhaps how much more accurate. 'It's about something else I'm working on.'

The Count was far too polite to ask what but said, instead, 'We're invited to dinner, but if you could come over now, we would have an hour or so free. Is that convenient, Guido?'

'Yes, it is. I'll come over now. And thank you.'

'Well?' Paola asked when he went back into the kitchen, where another load of washing was busily swimming about in a sea of white suds.

'I'm going over there now. Would you like to come along and see your mother?'

By way of answer, she pointed with her chin to the washing-machine.

'All right. I'll go now. They have to go to dinner, so I imagine I'll be back before eight. Would you like to go out to dinner tonight?'

She smiled at him, nodding.

'All right. You choose the place and call for a reservation. Any place you like.'

'Al Covo?'

Manfully, he did not wince at what he knew that would cost. First, the shoes, and now dinner at Al Covo. The food was glorious; to hell with what it cost. He smiled. 'Reserve for eight-thirty. And ask the kids if they want to come.' After all, he was a man who had been given back his life that afternoon. Why not celebrate?

When he got to the Faliers' *palazzo*, Brunetti was faced with the decision that always awaited him there, whether to use the immense iron ring that hung from the wooden door, dropping it against the metal plate beneath and sending the message of his arrival booming across the open courtyard, or to use the more prosaic doorbell. He chose the second, and a moment later a voice spoke through the intercom, asking who it was. After he gave his name, the door jolted open. He pushed it back, slammed it closed behind him, and walked across the courtyard towards the part of the *palazzo* that fronted onto the Grand Canal. From an upstairs window, a uniformed maid looked out, checking to see who had come in. Apparently satisfied that Brunetti was not a malefactor, she pulled her head inside the window and disappeared. The Count was waiting at the top of the outside staircase that led into the part of the *palazzo* where he and his wife lived.

Though Brunetti knew that the Count would soon be seventy, it was hard, seeing him, to think that he was Paola's father. Older brother, perhaps, or the youngest of her uncles, but certainly not a man almost thirty years older than she. The thinning hair, cut short around the shining oval of his head, suggested his age, but that impression was dispelled by the taut skin of his face and the clear intelligence shining from his eyes. 'How nice to see you, Guido. You're looking well. We'll go into the study, shall we?' the Count said, turning and leading Brunetti back towards the front of the house. They passed through a few rooms until they finally arrived at the glass-fronted study that looked out over the Grand Canal as it curved up towards the Accademia Bridge. 'Would you like a drink?' the Count asked, going to the sideboard where a bottle of Dom Perignon stood, already open, in a silver bucket filled with ice.

Brunetti knew the Count well enough to know that there was absolutely no affectation in this. If the Count had preferred to drink Coca-Cola, he would have kept a litre-and-a-half plastic bottle in the same ice bucket and offered it in the same manner to his guests. The Count had been born having no one he needed to impress.

'Yes, thanks,' Brunetti answered. This way, he could set the tone for an evening at Al Covo. If the Count turned his back, perhaps he could get away with the ice bucket and thus pay for that dinner.

The Count poured champagne into a fresh glass, added some to his own, and handed the first glass to Brunetti. 'Shall we sit, Guido?' he asked, leading him towards two easy chairs that were turned to face out over the water.

When they were both seated and Brunetti had tasted his wine, the Count asked, 'In what way can I be of service?'

'I'd like to ask you for some information, but I'm not sure just what questions I have to ask,' Brunetti began, deciding to tell the truth. He couldn't ask the Count not to repeat what he told him; an insult like that would be difficult for the Count to forgive, even of the father of his only grandchildren. 'I'd like to know whatever you could tell me about a Signor Gamberetto, of Vicenza, who has both a hauling company and, apparently, a construction company. I don't know anything more about him other than his name. And that he might be involved in something illegal.'

The Count nodded, suggesting that the name was familiar but that he preferred to wait until he knew what else his son-in-law wanted to know before saying anything.

'And then I'd like to know about the involvement of the American military, first with Signor Gamberetto, and second with the illegal dumping of toxic substances that seems to be taking place in this country.' He sipped at his wine. 'Anything you can tell me, I'll be very grateful for.'

The Count finished his wine and placed the empty glass on an inlaid table at his side. He crossed his long legs, exposing an expanse of black silk sock, and brought his fingers together in a pyramid under his chin. 'Signor Gamberetto is a particularly nasty, and particularly well-connected, businessman. Not only does he have the two companies you refer to, Guido, but he is also the owner of a large chain of hotels, travel agencies, and resorts, many of which are not in this country. He is also believed to have recently branched out into armaments and munitions, buying into partnership with one of the most important arms manufacturers in Lombardy. Many of these companies are owned by his wife; therefore, his name is not anywhere present in the papers that deal with them, nor does it appear in the contracts made by those businesses. I believe the construction business is under his uncle's name, but I could be wrong there.

'Like many of our new businessmen,' the Count continued, 'he is strangely invisible. He happens, however, to be more powerfully connected than are most. He has influential friends in both the Socialist and Christian Democratic party, no mean feat, so he is very well-protected.'

The Count got up and walked over to the sideboard, came back and filled both their glasses, then went and replaced the bottle in the ice bucket. When he was comfortable in his chair again, he continued. 'Signor Gamberetto is from the South, and his father was, if memory serves, a janitor in a public school. Consequently, there are not many social occasions when we are likely to meet. I know nothing about his personal life.'

He sipped. 'As to your second question, about the Americans, I'd like to know what prompts your curiosity in this matter.' When Brunetti didn't answer, the Count added, 'There exists a great deal of rumour.' Brunetti could do no more than speculate about the dizzy heights at which such things were rumoured, but still he said nothing.

The Count twirled the stem of his glass between his thin fingers. When it became evident that Brunetti intended to say nothing, he continued, 'I know that certain extraordinary rights have been extended to them, rights which are not stipulated in the treaty we signed with them at the end of the war. Various of our many short-lived and variously incompetent governments have seen fit to offer them preferential treatment of one sort or another. This, you realize, extends not only to things like allowing them to peppercorn our hills with missile silos, information to be had from any resident of the province of Vicenza, but to allowing them to bring into this country just about anything they wish.'

'Including toxic substances?' Brunetti asked directly.

The Count bowed his head. 'It is rumoured.'

'But why? We'd have to be insane to accept them.'

'Guido, it is not the business of a government to be sane; it is their business only to be successful.' Dismissing what he must have perceived as a pedantic tone, the Count became more direct and particular. 'The rumours say that, in the past, the cargoes were merely transshipped through Italy. That they came down from the bases in Germany, were unloaded here, and immediately loaded onto Italian vessels that took them off to Africa or South America, where no questions were asked about what got dropped into the middle of the jungle or the forest or the lake. But since many of these countries have experienced radical changes of government in recent years, these outlets have been cut off, and they refuse any longer to accept our deadly rubbish. Or they are willing to accept it, but now the price they put upon doing so has become exorbitant. At any rate, those who receive the ongoing shipments at this end are unwilling to cease doing so – and thus cease to profit from them – merely because they can no longer dispose of them in other places, on other continents. So they continue to arrive, and room is found for them here.'

'You know all of this?' Brunetti asked, making no attempt to hide his surprise, or was it something stronger?

'Guido, this much – or this little – is common knowledge, at least at the level of rumour. You could easily discover it in a few hours on the phone. But no one *knows* it except the people who are directly involved, and they are not the sort of people who talk about these things. Nor, I might add, are they the sort of people one talks to.'

'Snubbing them at cocktail parties can hardly be enough to make them stop,' Brunetti snapped. 'Nor will it make the things they've already dumped suddenly disappear.'

'Your sarcasm is not lost on me, Guido, but I'm afraid that this is a situation in which one is helpless.'

'Who is "one"?' Brunetti asked.

'Those who know about the government and

what it does but are not part of it, not in any active sense. There is also the not inconsiderable fact that it is not only our own government which is involved, but that of America, as well.'

'To make no mention of the gentlemen from the South?'

'Ah, yes, the Mafia,' the Count said with a tired sigh. 'It would seem that this is a web woven by all three of them, and, because of that, triply strong and, if I might add as a note of warning, triply dangerous.' He looked over at Brunetti and asked, 'How closely are you involved in this, Guido?' His concern was audible.

'Do you remember that American who was murdered here over a week ago?'

'Ah, yes, during a robbery. Most unfortunate.' Then, tiring of his pose, the Count added, soberly, 'You've discovered some connection between him and this Signor Gamberetto, I assume.'

'Yes.'

'There was another strange death among the Americans, a doctor at the Vicenza hospital. Is that correct?'

'Yes. She was his lover.'

'It was an overdose, as I recall.'

'It was a murder,' Brunetti corrected but offered no explanation.

The Count sought none and remained silent for a long time, sitting and staring at the boats that travelled up and down the canal. Finally he asked, 'What are you going to do?'

'I don't know,' Brunetti answered and then asked in his turn, bringing himself close to the reason for his coming, 'Is this something over which you have any influence?'

The Count considered this question for a long time. 'I'm not sure what you mean by that, Guido,' he finally said.

Brunetti, to whom the question was sufficiently clear, ignored the Count's remark and provided him, instead, with more information. 'There's a dumping site up near Lake Barcis. The barrels and cans are from the Americans' base in Ramstein, in Germany; the labels are in English and German.'

'Did those two Americans find this place?'

'I think so.'

'And they died after they found it?'

'Yes.'

'Does anyone else know about this?'

'A Carabiniere officer who works at the American base.' There was no need to bring Ambrogiani's name into this, nor did Brunetti see fit to tell the Count that the only other person who knew anything about this was his only child.

'Can he be trusted?'

'To do what?'

'Don't be intentionally ignorant, Guido,' the Count said. 'I'm trying to help you here.' Not without difficulty, the Count gained control of himself and asked, 'Can he be trusted to keep his mouth shut?'

'Until what?'

'Until something is done about this.'

'What does that mean?'

'It means that I'll call some people this evening and see what can be done.'

'Done about what?'

'About seeing that this dump is cleared up, that the things are taken away.'

'And moved where?' Brunetti asked, voice sharp.

'Moved away from where they are, Guido.'

'To some other part of Italy?'

Brunetti watched as the Count considered whether to lie to him or not. Finally, deciding against it, Brunetti would never understand why, the Count said, 'Perhaps. But more likely out of the country.' Before Brunetti could ask any more questions, the Count held up his hand to stop him. 'Guido, please try to understand. I can't promise you any more than I just have. I think that this dump can be disposed of, but, beyond that, I would be afraid to move.'

'Do you mean that literally, afraid?'

The Count's voice was ice. 'Literally. Afraid.'

'Why?'

'I would prefer not to explain that, Guido.'

Brunetti thought he would try one more tack. 'The reason they found out about the dump was that a little boy fell into it and burned his arm on the things leaking from those barrels. It could have been any child. It could have been Chiara.'

The Count's glance was cool. 'Please, Guido, now you're being mawkishly sentimental.'

It was true, Brunetti knew it. 'Don't you care about any of this?' he asked, unable to keep the passion from his voice.

The Count dipped his finger into the trace of wine left in his glass and began to run the tip of his moistened finger around the rim. As his finger moved ever faster, a high-pitched whining emerged from the crystal and filled the room. Suddenly, he lifted his finger from the glass, but the sound continued, hanging in the room, just as did their conversation. He looked from the glass to Brunetti. 'Yes, I care about it, Guido, but not in the same way you do. You have managed to retain remnants of optimism, even in the midst of the work you do. I have none. Not for myself, nor for my future, and not for this country or its future.'

He looked down at the glass again. 'I care that these things happen, that we poison ourselves and our progeny, that we knowingly destroy our future, but I do not believe that there is anything – and I repeat, anything – that can be done to prevent it. We are a nation of egoists. It is our glory, but it will be our destruction, for none of us can be made to concern ourselves about something as abstract as "the common good". The best of us can rise to feeling concern for our families, but as a nation we are incapable of more.'

'I refuse to believe that,' Brunetti said.

'Your refusal to believe it,' the Count said with a smile that was almost tender, 'makes it no less true, Guido.'

'Your daughter doesn't believe it,' Brunetti added.

'And for that grace I give daily thanks,' the Count said in a soft voice. 'That is perhaps the finest thing I've achieved in my life, that my daughter does not share my beliefs.'

Brunetti sought irony or sarcasm in the Count's tone, but found only pained truth.

'You said you'd do this, see that this dump is cleared up, taken away. Why can't you do more?'

Again, the Count bestowed that same smile upon his son-in-law. 'I believe this is the first time we've talked to one another in all these years, Guido.' Then, changing his voice, he added, 'Because there are too many dumps and too many men like Gamberetto.'

'Can you do anything about him?'

'Ah, there I can do nothing.'

'Can or will do nothing?'

'From some positions, Guido, can and will are the same.'

'That's sophistry,' Brunetti shot back.

The Count laughed outright. 'Yes, it is, isn't it? Then let me say it like this: I prefer to do nothing else about this matter save what I've told you I will do.'

'And why is that?' Brunetti asked.

'Because,' the Count replied, 'I can bring myself to care for nothing beyond my family.' The tone of his voice was terminal; Brunetti would get no explanation beyond that.

'May I ask you one more question?' Brunetti asked.

'Yes.'

'When I called and asked if I could talk to you, you asked if I wanted to talk about Viscardi. Why was that?'

The Count looked at him in involuntary surprise, then returned his attention to the boats on the canal. When a few had gone past, he answered, 'Signor Viscardi and I have common business interests.'

'What is that supposed to mean?'

'Precisely what I said, that we have interests in common.'

'And may I ask what those interests are?'

The Count faced him before he answered, 'Guido, my business interests are a subject I do not discuss, except with those who are involved in them directly.'

Before Brunetti could protest, the Count added, 'Upon my death, interest in those matters will pass beyond my control. Many will pass to your wife,' he paused here, then added, 'and to you. But until that time, I will discuss them only with those people who are concerned with them.'

Brunetti wanted to ask the Count if his dealings with Signor Viscardi were legitimate dealings, but he didn't know how to ask this without offending him. Worse, Brunetti feared he didn't himself any longer know what the word 'legitimate' meant.

'Can you tell me anything about Signor Viscardi?'

The Count's answer was a long time in coming. 'He has business interests in common with a number of other people. Many of them are very powerful people.'

Brunetti heard the warning in the Count's voice, but he also saw the connection that lurked there, as well.

'Have we just been talking about one of them?'

The Count said nothing.

'Have we just been talking about one of them?' he repeated.

The Count nodded.

'Will you tell me about the interests they have in common?'

'I can – I will – tell you no more than that you should have nothing to do with either one of them.'

'And if I choose to do so?'

'I would prefer that you didn't.'

'I would prefer that you tell me about their business interests.'

Brunetti couldn't resist saying, 'And I prefer that you tell me about their business interests.'

'Then we seem to be at an impasse, don't we?' the Count asked in a voice that was artificially light and conversational. Before Brunetti could answer, they heard a noise behind them and both turned to see the Countess come into the room. She hurried quickly over to Brunetti, high heels tapping out a happy message on the parquet. Both men stood. 'Guido, how nice to see you,' she said, leaning up to kiss him on both cheeks.

'Ah, my dearest,' the Count said, bending over her hand. Married for forty years, Brunetti thought, and still he kisses her hand when she comes into the room. At least he doesn't click his heels.

'We were just talking about Chiara,' the Count said, smiling benignly at his wife.

'Yes,' agreed Brunetti, 'we were just saying how lucky Paola and I are that both of the children are so healthy.' The Count shot him a look over his wife's head, but she smiled up at both of them, saying, 'Yes, thank God for that. We're so lucky we live in a healthy country like Italy.'

'Indeed,' agreed the Count.

'What can I bring her from Capri?' asked the Countess.

'Only your safe return,' Brunetti said gallantly. 'You know what it's like down there in the South.'

She smiled up at him. 'Oh, Guido, all that talk about the Mafia can't be true. It's just stories. All my friends say it is.' She turned to her husband for confirmation.

'If your friends say so, my dear, then I'm certain it is,' the Count said. To Brunetti, 'I'll take care of those things for you, Guido. I'll make the calls tonight. And please speak to your friend at Vicenza. There's no need for either one of you to preoccupy yourself with this.'

His wife gave him a questioning look. 'Nothing, my dearest,' he said. Just some business Guido asked me to look into for him. Nothing important. Just some paperwork that I might be able to get through more quickly than he can.'

'How kind of you, Orazio. And Guido,' she said, positively aglow with this vision of happy families, 'I'm so glad you'd think to ask.'

The Count put his hand under her arm and said, 'We might think about leaving now, dearest. Is the launch here?'

'Oh, yes, that's what I came to tell you. But I forgot about it with all this talk of business.' She turned to Brunetti. 'Give my love to Paola and kiss the children for me. I'll call when we get to Capri. Or is it Ischia? Orazio, which is it?'

'Capri, my dearest.'

'I'll call, then. Goodbye, Guido,' she said, standing on tiptoe to kiss him again.

The Count and Brunetti shook hands. All three of them walked down into the courtyard together. The Count and Countess turned and walked through the water gate and stepped into the launch that waited for them at the landing stage of the *palazzo*. Brunetti let himself out of the main door, careful to slam it closed behind him.

22

Monday was a normal day at the Questura: three North Africans were brought in for selling purses and sunglasses on the street without a licence; two break-ins were reported in various parts of the city; four summonses were given to boats caught without the proper safety equipment aboard; and two known drug addicts were brought in for threatening a doctor who refused to write them prescriptions. Patta appeared at eleven, called up to Brunetti to learn if there was any progress on the Viscardi case, made no attempt to disguise his irritation that there had not been, and went to lunch half an hour later, not to return until well past three.

Vianello came up to report to Brunetti that the car had not shown up on Saturday, and he had been left waiting at Piazzale Roma for an hour, standing at the number five bus stop with a bouquet of red carnations in his arms. He had finally given up and gone home and given his wife the flowers. Keeping his part of the bargain, even if the criminals couldn't be depended on, Brunetti changed the duty roster to give Vianello the following Friday and Saturday free, asking him to get in touch with the boy on Burano to see what had gone wrong and why Ruffolo's friends had not shown up for the meeting.

He had bought all of the major papers on the way to his office and passed the better part of the morning reading through them, searching for any reference to the dump near Lake Barcis, Gamberetto, or anything that had to do with the deaths of the two Americans. History, however, refused to concern itself with any of these topics, so he ended up reading the soccer news and calling it work.

He bought the papers again the next morning and began to read through them carefully. Riots in Albania, the Kurds, a volcano, Indians killing one another, this time for politics, instead of religion, but there was no mention of the finding of toxic waste near Lake Barcis.

Knowing it was foolish but unable to stop himself from doing it, he went down to the switchboard and asked the operator for the number of the American base. If Ambrogiani had been able to find out anything about Gamberetto, Brunetti wanted to know what it was and found himself incapable of waiting for the other man to call. The operator gave him both the central number and that of the Carabinieri office. Brunetti had to walk to Riva degli Schiavoni before he found a public phone that would take a magnetic phone card. He dialled the number of the Carabinieri station and asked for Maggiore Ambrogiani. The Maggiore was not at his desk at the moment. Who was calling, please? 'Signor Rossi, from the Generali Insurance Company. I'll call back this afternoon.'

Ambrogiani's absence could mean nothing. Or anything.

As he did whenever he was overcome by nervousness, Brunetti walked. He turned left and walked along the water until he came to the bridge that took him to Sant' Elena, crossed it, and walked around this farthest part of the city, finding it no more interesting than he ever had in the past. He cut back through Castello, along the wall of the Arsenale, and back towards Santi Giovanni e Paolo, where all of this had begun. Intentionally, he avoided the *campo*, refusing to look at the place where Foster's body had been pulled out of the water. He cut directly towards the Fondamente Nuove and followed the water until he had to turn away from it and head back into the city. He passed the Madonna dell' Orto, noticed that work was still being done on the hotel, and suddenly found himself in Campo del Ghetto. He sat on a bench and watched the people going past him. They had no idea, none at all. They distrusted the government, feared the Mafia, resented the Americans, but they were all generalized, unfocused ideas.

They sensed conspiracy, as Italians always have, but they lacked the details, the proofs. They had learned enough, from long centuries of experience, to know that the proof was there, amply, but those same brutal centuries had also taught the people that whatever government happened to be in power would always succeed in hiding any and all proof of its evildoing from its citizens.

He closed his eyes, sank lower on the bench, glad of the sun. When he opened them, he saw the two Mariani sisters walking across the *campo*. They must be in their seventies now, both of them, with their shoulder-length hair, high heels, and bright carmined lips. No one any longer remembered the facts, but everyone remembered the story. During the war, the Christian husband of one of them had denounced her to the police, and both of them were taken away to one of the camps. No one remembered which it had been, Auschwitz, Bergen-Belsen, Dachau; the name hardly mattered. After the war, they had returned to the city, having survived no one knew what horrors, and here they were, almost fifty years later, walking across the Campo del Ghetto, arm in arm, each with a bright yellow ribbon in her hair. For the Mariani sisters, there had been conspiracy, and certainly they had seen the proof of human evil, and yet here they walked in the rich sunshine of a peaceful afternoon in Venice, sun dappled on their flowered dresses.

Brunetti knew that he was being unnecessarily sentimental. He was tempted to go home directly, but he went back to the Questura instead, walking slowly, in no hurry to get there.

When he arrived, he found a note on his desk, 'See me about Ruffolo. V', and went down immediately to Vianello.

The officer was at his desk, talking to a young man who sat in a chair facing him. When Brunetti approached, Vianello said to the young man, 'This is Commissario Brunetti. He can answer your questions better than I can.'

The young man stood but made no attempt to shake hands. 'Good afternoon, Dottore,' he said. 'I came because he called me,' leaving it to Brunetti to figure out who the 'he' was. The boy was short, stocky, and had hands that were a few sizes too big for his body, already red and swollen, even though he couldn't have been more than seventeen. If his hands were not enough to show that he was a fisherman, his accent, the rugged undulance of Burano, was. On Burano, you either fished or made lace; the boy's hands excluded the second possibility.

'Sit down, please,' Brunetti said, drawing up a second chair for himself. Obviously the boy's mother had trained him well, for he continued to stand until both men were seated, then took his place, sitting up straight, hands wrapped around the sides of the seat of his chair.

When he began to speak in the rough dialect of the outer islands, no Italian not born in Venice could have understood him. Brunetti wondered if the boy could, in fact, speak Italian at all. But his curiosity about dialect was soon lost when the boy continued, 'Ruffolo called my friend again, and my friend called me, and since I told the Sergeant

315

here that I would tell him if I heard from my friend again, I came in to tell him.'

'What did your friend say?'

'Ruffolo wants to talk to someone. He's frightened.' He stopped at that and looked sharply up at the two policemen to see if they had noticed his slip. It seemed that they had not, so he continued, 'I mean my friend said that he sounded frightened, but all he, this friend of mine, would say is that Peppino wanted to talk to someone, but he said that a sergeant isn't enough. He wants to talk to someone high up.'

'Did your friend say why Ruffolo wants to do this?'

'No, sir, he didn't. But I think his mother told him to do it.'

'Do you know Ruffolo?'

The boy shrugged.

'What would frighten him?'

This time, the shrug was probably meant to mean that the boy didn't know. 'He thinks he's smart. Ruffolo. He always talks big, talks about the people he met inside and about his important friends. When he called, he told me,' the boy said, forgetting about the existence of the imaginary friend, the supposed intermediary in all of this, 'that he wanted to give himself up but that he had some things to trade. He said that you'd be glad to get them, that it was a good trade.'

'Did he say what that was?' Brunetti asked.

'No, but he said to tell you that there are three of them, that you'd understand that.'

Brunetti did. Guardi, Monet, and Gauguin.

'And where does he want this person to meet him?'

As if he suddenly realized that the imaginary friend was no longer there to serve as a buffer between himself and the forces of authority, the boy stopped and looked around the room, but the friend was gone; not a sign of him remained.

'You know that catwalk that goes along the front of the Arsenale?' the boy asked.

Both Brunetti and Vianello nodded. At least half a kilometre long, the elevated cement walkway led from the shipyards within the Arsenale to the Celestia vaporetto stop, running about two metres above the waters of the *laguna*.

'He said he'd be there, at the part where there's that little beach, the one on the Arsenale side of the bridge. At midnight, tomorrow night.' Brunetti and Vianello exchanged a glance over the boy's lowered head, and Vianello mouthed the word 'Hollywood'.

'And who does he want to meet him there?'

'Somebody important. He said that's why he didn't show up on Saturday, not for just a sergeant.' Vianello, it appeared, took this with good grace.

Brunetti allowed himself a moment's fantasy, picturing Patta, complete with onyx cigarette holder and walking stick and, because these late nights were foggy, his Burberry raincoat, collar artfully raised, waiting on the Arsenale catwalk as the bells of San Marco boomed out midnight. Because it was his fantasy, Brunetti had Patta meet, not Ruffolo, who spoke Italian, but this simple boy from Burano, and the fantasy petered out amidst the garbled sound of the boy's heavy dialect and Patta's slurred Sicilian pronunciation, both whipped away from their mouths by the midnight winds from the *laguna*.

'Will a Commissario be important enough?' Brunetti asked.

The boy looked up at that, not certain how to take it. 'Yes, sir,' he said, deciding to take it seriously.

'At midnight tomorrow night?'

'Yes, sir.'

'Did Ruffolo say, did he tell your friend, that he'd bring those things with him?'

'No, sir, he didn't say. He just said he'd be on the catwalk at midnight, near the bridge. By the little beach.' It wasn't really a beach, Brunetti remembered, more a place where the tides had driven enough sand and gravel up against one of the walls of the Arsenale to allow a place where plastic bottles and old boots could wash up and be covered with slimy seaweed.

'If your friend speaks to Ruffolo again, tell him I'll be there.'

Satisfied that he had done what he came for, the boy got to his feet, nodded his head awkwardly to both men, and left the office.

'Probably going to go and look for a phone so he can call Ruffolo and tell him the deal's on,' Vianello said.

'I hope so. I don't want to spend an hour standing out there waiting for him if he doesn't show up.

318

'Would you like me to come along, sir?' Vianello volunteered.

'Yes, I think I would,' Brunetti said, realizing he was not the stuff of heroes. But then he added, more practically, 'But it's probably a bad idea. He'll have friends planted at either end of the catwalk, and there's no place at either end where you could be without being seen. Besides, there's no meanness in Ruffolo. He's never been violent.'

'I could go down there and ask if I could stay in one of the houses.'

'No, I don't think it's a good idea. He'd think of that, and his friends will probably be wandering around there, watching out for just that.' Brunetti tried for a moment to form a mental image of the area around the Celestia stop, but all he could remember were anonymous blocks of public housing, an area almost completely devoid of shops or bars. In fact, if it were not for the presence of the *laguna*, there would be no telling it was in Venice, all of the apartments were so new, utterly without character or individuality. Might as well be in Mestre or Marghera.

'What about the other two?' Vianello asked, meaning the other two men involved in the robbery.

'I imagine they want a part of Ruffolo's deal. Or else he's a lot smarter now than he was two years ago, and he managed to get the paintings away from them.'

'Maybe they got the jewellery,' Vianello suggested.

'Possibly. But it's more likely that Ruffolo's the spokesman for all three.'

319

'Doesn't make any sense, does it?' Vianello asked. 'I mean, they got away with it, they've go the paintings and the jewellery. What's th advantage to them if they just give up, give it a back?'

'Maybe the paintings are too hard to sell.'

'Come on, sir. You know the market as well as do. You look hard enough, you can find a buyer fo anything, no matter how hot it is. I could sell th Pietà if I could get it out of Saint Peter's.'

Vianello was right. It didn't make any sense Ruffolo was hardly the type to reform, and ther was always a market for paintings, no matte where they came from. The moon had just turne full, he remembered, and he thought of what clear target he would be, dark jacket outline against the pale wall of the Arsenale. He dismisse the idea as ridiculous.

'Well, I'll go along and see what Ruffolo has t offer,' he said, sounding to himself like one c those nitwit heroes in a British film.

'If you change your mind, sir, let me knov tomorrow. I'll be home tomorrow night. All yo have to do is call.'

'Thanks, Vianello. But I think it will be all righ I appreciate it, really I do.'

Vianello waved his hand and went back to th papers on his desk.

If he had to be a midnight hero, even if it was day away, Brunetti saw no reason to stay in hi office any longer.

When he got home, Paola told him that she ha spoken to her parents that afternoon. They wer well, enjoying what her mother persisted in believing was Ischia. Her father's only message to Brunetti was that he had begun to take care of that matter for him and that it ought to be fully resolved by the end of the week. Though Brunetti was convinced it was a matter that would never be fully resolved, he thanked Paola for the information and told her to extend his greetings to her parents the next time they called.

Dinner was a strangely tranquil meal, chiefly because of Raffaele's behaviour. He seemed, though Brunetti was astonished when he found himself thinking the word, he seemed cleaner, though it had never occurred to Brunetti that he might have been dirty. His hair had been recently cut, and the jeans he wore had a discernible crease down the front of both legs. He listened to what his parents said without objecting and, very strangely, did not fight Chiara for the last helping of pasta. When the meal was over, he protested at being told it was his turn to do the dishes, which reassured Brunetti, but then he did them without sighs and grumbles of dissatisfaction, and that silence caused Brunetti to ask Paola, 'Is anything wrong with Raffi?' They were sitting on the sofa in the living room, and the silence that came in from the kitchen filled the entire room.

She smiled. 'Strange, isn't it? I felt like it was the calm before the storm.'

'Do you think we should lock our door at night?' he asked. They both laughed but neither was sure if it was at the remark or at the possibility that it might be over. For them, as for the parents of all adolescents, 'it' needed no clarification: that awful brooding cloud of resentment and righteous indignation that drifted into their lives with certain hormonal levels and remained there until those levels changed.

'He asked me if I'd read over an essay he had to write for his English class,' Paola said. Seeing his surprise, she added, 'Brace yourself. He also asked if he could have a new jacket for the autumn.'

'New, like you buy it in a shop?' Brunetti asked, amazed. This from the boy who had, two weeks ago, delivered a ringing condemnation of the capitalist system and its creation of false consumer needs, that had invented the idea of fashion just to create the unending demand for new clothing.

Paola nodded. 'New. From a shop.'

'I don't know if I'm ready for this,' Brunetti said. 'Are we going to lose our rough-mannered anarchist?'

'I think so, Guido. The jacket he said he wanted is in the window of Duca d'Aosta and costs four hundred thousand lire.'

'Well, tell him Karl Marx never went shopping at Duca D'Aosta. Let him go to Benetton with the rest of the proletariat.' Four hundred thousand lire; he'd won almost ten times that at the Casinò. In a family of four, Raffi's fair share? No, not for a jacket. This must be it, the first crack in the ice, the beginning of the end of adolescence. And adolescence over, that meant the next step his son would take was into young manhood. Manhood.

'Do you have any idea why this is happening?' he asked her. If it occurred to Paola to say that he

322

would be a better person to understand the phenomenon of male adolescence, she didn't say it, and instead, answered, 'Signora Pizzutti spoke to me on the stairs today.'

He gave her a puzzled stare, and then it registered. 'Sara's mother.'

Paola nodded. 'Sara's mother.'

'Oh my God! No!'

'Yes, Guido, and she's a nice girl.'

'He's only sixteen, Paola.' He heard the bleat in his voice, but he couldn't stop it.

Paola put her hand on his arm, then up to her mouth, and then burst into loud peals of laughter. 'Oh, Guido, you should hear yourself. "He's only sixteen." No, I don't believe it.' She continued to laugh, had to lean back against the arm of the sofa, so helpless did her mirth render her.

What was he supposed to do, he wondered, grin and tell dirty jokes? Raffaele was his only son, and he didn't know anything about what was out there: AIDS, prostitutes, girls who got pregnant and made you marry them. And then, suddenly, he saw it through Paola's eyes, and he laughed until tears came into his.

Raffaele came in then to ask his mother to help him with his Greek homework and, finding them like that, he wondered what all this talk about adulthood was.

23

Neither that night nor the following day did Ambrogiani call, and Brunetti had to fight the constant temptation to call the American base and try to get in touch with him. He called Fosco in Milan and got only his answering machine. Feeling not a little foolish at being reduced to talking to a machine, he told Riccardo what Ambrogiani had told him about Gamberetto, asked him to see what else he could find out, and asked him to call. Beyond this, he could think of little to do, so he read and commented on reports, read the newspapers, and found himself constantly distracted by the thought of that night's meeting with Ruffolo.

Just as he was preparing to leave to go home for lunch, the intercom rang. 'Yes, Vice-Questore,' he answered automatically, too preoccupied to be able to savour Patta's inevitable moment of unease when he was recognized before he identified himself.

'Brunetti,' he began, 'I'd like you to step down to my office for a moment.'

'Immediately, sir,' Brunetti answered, pulling yet another report towards him, opening it, and beginning to read.

'I'd like you to come now, not "immediately",' Commissario,' Patta said, so sternly that Brunetti realized he must have someone, someone important, in his office with him.

'Yes, sir. This instant,' he answered and turned the page he was reading face down, the better to resume his place when he came back. After lunch, he thought, and went to the window to see if it still looked like rain. The sky above San Lorenzo was grey and ominous, and the leaves of the trees in the small *campo* flipped over with the force of the wind that swirled around them. He went over to the cupboard to hunt for an umbrella: he hadn't bothered to bring one with him this morning. He pulled open the door and looked inside. There was the usual jumble of abandoned objects: a single yellow boot, a shopping bag filled with old newspapers, two large, padded envelopes, and a pink umbrella. Pink. Chiara's, left there months ago. If he remembered correctly, it had large, happy elephants on it, but he didn't want to open it to find out. Pink was bad enough. He looked deeper, shifting things aside delicately with his toe, but there was no second umbrella.

He took the umbrella from the closet and went back to his desk. If he rolled *La Repubblica* the long way, he could wrap it around most of the umbrella, leaving only the handle exposed, the handle and a handsbreadth of pink. He did this to his satisfaction, left his office, and took the steps down to Patta's. He knocked, waited until he was sure he heard his superior call *'Avanti'*, and went in.

Usually, when Brunetti entered, he found Patta behind his desk – 'enthroned' was the word that sprang most easily to mind – but today he was seated in one of the smaller chairs that sat in front of the desk, seated to the right of a dark-haired man who sat entirely at his ease, legs crossed at the knees, one hand dangling from the arm of the chair, cigarette held between the first two fingers. Neither man bothered to stand when Brunetti came in, though the visitor did uncross his legs and lean forward to stab out his cigarette in the malachite ashtray.

'Ah, Brunetti,' Patta said. Had he been expecting someone else? He gestured to the man beside him. 'This is Signor Viscardi. He's in Venice for the day and stopped by to bring me an invitation to the gala dinner at Palazzo Pisani Moretta next week, and I asked him to stay. I thought he might like to have a word with you.'

Viscardi got to his feet then and approached Brunetti, hand extended. 'I'd like to thank you, Commissario, for your attention to this case.' As Rossi had noted, the man spoke with the elided R of Milan, the consonant slithering unpronounced from his tongue. He was a tall man with dark brown eyes, soft and peaceful eyes, and an easy, relaxed smile. The skin under his left eye was slightly discoloured and appeared to be covered with something, perhaps make-up.

Brunetti shook his hand and returned his smile.

Patta interrupted here. 'I'm afraid there isn't much progress, Augusto, but we hope to have some information about your paintings soon.' He used the familiar 'tu' with Viscardi, an intimacy Brunetti assumed he was meant to register. And respect.

'I certainly hope so. My wife is very attached to those paintings, especially the Monet.' He made it sound like the enthusiasm children had for their toys. He turned his attention, and his charm, to Brunetti. 'Perhaps you could tell me if you have had any, I think they're called "leads", Commissario. I'd like to be able to take good news back to my wife.'

'Unfortunately, we have very little to report, Signor Viscardi. We've passed the descriptions you gave us of the men you saw to our officers, and we've sent copies of your photos of the paintings to the Art Fraud Police. But beyond that, nothing.' Signor Viscardi smiled when he heard this, and Brunetti knew he didn't want him to learn about Ruffolo's attempt to speak to the police.

'But haven't you,' Patta interrupted, 'got a suspect? I remember reading something in your report about Vianello, that he was going to talk to him last weekend. What happened?'

'A suspect?' Viscardi asked, eyes bright with interest.

327

'It turned out to be nothing, sir,' Brunetti said, addressing Patta. 'A false lead.'

'I thought it was that man in the photograph,' Patta insisted. 'I read his name in the report, but I forget it.'

'Would that be the same man your sergeant showed me a picture of?' Viscardi asked.

'It seems it was a false lead,' Brunetti said, smiling apologetically. 'It turns out he couldn't have had anything to do with it. At least we're convinced that he couldn't have.'

'It seems you were right, Augusto,' Patta said, insistent upon the repetition of his first name. He turned to Brunetti and made his voice firm. What have you got on the two men whose descriptions you do have?'

'Unfortunately, nothing, sir.'

'Have you checked . . .' Patta began, and Brunetti gave him his undivided attention, waiting to see what concrete suggestions would follow. 'Have you checked the usual sources?' Underlings knew details.

'Oh, yes, sir. It was the first thing we did.'

Viscardi shot back his starched cuff, glanced down at a gleaming fleck of gold, and said, turning to Patta, 'I don't want to keep you from your lunch appointment, Pippo.' As soon as Brunetti heard the nickname, he found himself turning it in his mind like a mantra: Pippo Patta, Pippo Patta, Pippo Patta.

'Perhaps you'll join us, Augusto,' he asked, ignoring Brunetti.

'No, no, I've got to get to the airport. My wife

expects me for cocktails, and then, as I told you, we have guests for dinner.' He must have told Patta the names of these guests, as well, for the mere reminder of their magic power was enough to cause Patta to smile broadly and clasp his hands together, as if in vicarious enjoyment of their presence, here in his office.

Patta glanced at his own watch, and Brunetti was witness to his agony, having to leave one rich and powerful man to go and dine with others. 'Yes, I really must go. Can't keep the minister waiting.' He didn't bother to waste the minister's name on Brunetti and Brunetti wondered if it was because Patta assumed he wouldn't be impressed or because he wouldn't recognize it. Little matter, he was not to learn it.

Patta went to the fifteenth-century Tuscan *armadio* that stood beside the door and took his Burberry from it. He slipped it on, then helped Viscardi into his coat. 'Are you leaving now?' Viscardi asked Brunetti, who answered that he was. 'The Vice-Questore is going to Corte Sconta for lunch, but I'm going up towards San Marco, where I can get a boat to the airport. Are you walking that way, by any chance?'

'Why, yes, I am, Signor Viscardi,' Brunetti lied.

Patta walked ahead with Viscardi until they got to the front door of the Questura. There, the two men shook hands, and Patta said something about seeing Brunetti after lunch. Outside, Patta turned up the collar of his raincoat and hurried off to the left. Viscardi turned right, waited a moment for Brunetti to position himself beside him, and started towards Ponte dei Greci and, beyond it, San Marco.

'I certainly hope this case can be quickly ended,' Viscardi said by way of beginning.

'Yes, so do I,' Brunetti agreed.

'I had hoped to find a safer city here, after Milan.'

'It certainly was an unusual crime,' Brunetti offered.

Viscardi paused for a moment, glanced sideways at Brunetti, then continued walking. 'Before I moved here, I had believed that all crime would be unusual in Venice.'

'It's certainly less common here than in other cities, but we do have crime,' Brunetti explained, and then added, 'and we have criminals.'

'Could I offer you a drink, Commissario. What do you Venetians call it, "un' ombra"?'

'Yes, "un' ombra", and yes, I'd like one.' Together, they turned into a bar they were passing, and Viscardi ordered them two glasses of white wine. When they came, he handed one to Brunetti and lifted his own. He tilted up his glass and said, 'Cin, cin.' Brunetti responded with a nod.

The wine was sharp, not good at all. Had he been alone, Brunetti would have left it. Instead, he took another sip, met Viscardi's glance, and smiled.

'I spoke to your father-in-law last week,' Viscardi said.

Brunetti had wondered how long it would take him to get around to this. He took another sip. 'Yes?'

'There were a number of matters we had to discuss.'

'Yes?'

'When we finished with our discussion of business, the Count mentioned his relationship with you. I admit that I was at first surprised.' Viscardi's tone suggested that his surprise was the result of his discovery that the Count would have allowed his daughter to marry a policeman, especially this one. 'By the coincidence, you understand,' Viscardi added, just a beat too late, and smiled again.

'Of course.'

'I was, quite frankly, encouraged to learn that you were related to the Count.' Brunetti gave him an inquiring look. 'I mean, that offered me the possibility of speaking frankly to you. That is, if I might.'

'Please, Signore.'

'Then I must admit that a number of things about this investigation are upsetting to me.'

'In what way, Signor Viscardi?'

'Not the least,' he began, turning to Brunetti with a smile of candid friendliness, 'are my feelings about the way I was treated by your policemen.' He paused, sipped at his wine, tried another smile, this time a consciously tentative one. 'I may speak frankly, I hope, Commissario.'

'Certainly, Signor Viscardi. I desire nothing else.'

'Then, let me say that I felt, at the time, as if your policemen were treating me more as a suspect than as a victim.' When Brunetti said nothing to this,

Viscardi added, 'That is, two of them came to the hospital, and both of them asked questions that had little bearing on the crime.'

'And what is it that they asked you?' Brunetti enquired.

'One asked how I knew what the paintings were. As if I wouldn't recognize them. And the second asked me if I recognized that young man in the photo and seemed sceptical when I said that I did not.'

'Well, that's been sorted out,' Brunetti said. 'He had nothing to do with it.'

'But you've got no new suspects?'

'Unfortunately not,' Brunetti answered, wondering why it was that Viscardi was willing so quickly to abandon interest in the young man in the photo. 'You said that there were a number of things that bothered you, Signor Viscardi. That is only one. Might I ask what the others are?'

Viscardi raised his glass towards his lips, then lowered it without drinking and said, 'I've learned that certain questions have been asked about me and about my affairs.'

Brunetti opened his eyes in feigned surprise. 'I hope you don't suspect that I would pry into your private life, Signor Viscardi.'

Viscardi suddenly set his glass, still almost completely full, back onto the counter and said, quite clearly, 'Swill.' When he saw Brunetti's surprise, he added, 'The wine, of course. I'm afraid we haven't chosen the right place to have a drink.'

'No, it isn't very good, is it?' Brunetti agreed,

setting his empty glass down on the counter beside Viscardi's.

'I repeat, Commissario, that questions have been asked about my business dealings. No good can come of asking those questions. I'm afraid that any further invasion of my privacy will force me to seek the aid of certain friends of mine.'

'And what friends are those, Signor Viscardi?'

'It would be presumptuous of me to mention their names. But they are sufficiently well-placed to see that I am not the victim of bureaucratic persecution. Should that be the case, I am sure they would step in to see that it was stopped.'

'That sounds very much like a threat, Signor Viscardi.'

'Don't be melodramatic, Dottor Brunetti. It would be better to call it a suggestion. Further, it is a suggestion in which your father-in-law joins me. I know I speak for him when I say that you would be wise not to ask those questions. I repeat, no good will come to anyone who asks them.'

'I'm not sure that I would expect much good at all to come of anything that has to do with your business dealings, Signor Viscardi.'

Viscardi suddenly pulled some loose bills from his pocket and threw them onto the counter, not bothering to ask how much the wine cost. Saying nothing to Brunetti, he turned and walked to the door of the bar. Brunetti followed him. Outside, it had begun to rain, the wind-shoved sheets of autumn. Viscardi paused at the door but only long enough to pull up the collar of his coat. Saying nothing, not bothering to glance back at Brunetti, he stepped out into the rain and quickly disappeared around a corner.

Brunetti stood in the doorway for a moment. Finally, seeing no other way, he reached down and unwrapped *La Repubblica* from around the umbrella, exposing its full length. He refolded the newspaper into a more easily handled shape and stepped out into the rain. He pressed the release and slid the umbrella open, looked up and saw it extend its plastic protection over him. Elephants, happy, dancing pink elephants. With the taste of the sour wine in his mouth, he hurried towards home and lunch.

At eleven, he went out onto the balcony, looked up at the sky, and saw the stars. Half an hour later, he left the house, assuring Paola that he would probably be home by one and telling her not to bother waiting up for him. If Ruffolo gave himself up, they would have to go down to the Questura, and then there would be the business of writing up a statement and having Ruffolo sign it, and that could take hours. He said he would try to call her if this happened, but he knew she was so accustomed to his being out at odd hours that she would probably sleep through the call, and he didn't want to wake the children.

The number five stopped running at nine, so he had no choice but to walk. He didn't mind, especially on this splendid moonlit night. As so often happened, he gave no conscious thought to where he was going, simply allowed his feet, made wise by decades of walking, to take him there the shortest way. He crossed Rialto, passed through Santa Marina and down towards San Francesco della Vigna. As always at this hour, the city was virtually deserted; he passed a night watchman, slipping little orange paper rectangles into the gratings in front of shops, proof that he had gone by in the night. He passed a restaurant and glanced in to see the white-jacketed staff crowded around a table, having a last drink before going home. And cats. Sitting, lying, serpentining themselves around fountains, padding. No hunting for these cats, though rats there were in plenty. They ignored him, knowing the precise hours of the people who came to feed them, certain that this stranger was not one of them.

He passed along the right side of the church of San Francesco della Vigna, then cut to the left and back to the Celestia vaporetto stop. Clearly outlined ahead of him he saw the metal-railed walkway and the steps leading up to it. He climbed them and when he got to the beginning of the walkway, he looked ahead at the bridge that rose up, like the hump on a camel, over the opening in the Arsenale wall that let the number five boat cut through the middle of the island and come out in the Bacino of San Marco.

The top of the bridge, he could see clearly, was empty. Not even Ruffolo would be so foolish as to make himself visible to any passing boat, not when the police were looking for him. He had probably jumped down onto the small beach on the other side of the bridge. Brunetti started towards the bridge, allowing himself a flash of irritation that he found himself here, walking around in the evening chill when any sensible person would be at home in bed. Why did crazy Ruffolo have to see an important person? He wants to see an important person, let him come into the Questura and talk to Patta.

He passed the first of the small beaches, no more than a few metres long, and glanced down onto it, looking for Ruffolo. In the ensilvering light of the moon, he could see that it was empty, but he could also see that its surface was covered with fragments of discarded bricks, shards of broken bottles, all covered with a layer of slimy green seaweed. Signorino Ruffolo had another thought coming if he believed that Brunetti was going to jump down onto that other filth-covered beach to have a little chat with him. He'd already lost one pair of shoes this week, and it wasn't going to happen again. If Ruffolo wanted to talk, he could climb back up onto the walkway or he could stay down there and see that he spoke loud enough for Brunetti to hear.

He climbed the stairs on his side of the cement bridge, stood on the top for a moment, then walked down the stairs on the other side. Ahead of him, he saw the small beach, its far side hidden by a curve in the massive brick wall of the Arsenale that rose up ten metres above Brunetti's head on his right.

A few metres from the island, he stopped and called in a low voice, 'Ruffolo. It's Brunetti.' There was no answer. 'Peppino, it's Brunetti.' Still no answer. The moonlight was so strong that it actually cast a shadow, hiding the part of the little island that lay under the walkway. But the foot was visible, one foot, wearing a brown leather shoe, and above it a leg. Brunetti leaned over the railing, but all he could see was the foot and the part of the leg that disappeared into the shadow under the walkway. He climbed over the railing, dropped to the stones below, slipped as he landed in seaweed, and broke his fall with both hands. When he stood, he could see the body more clearly, though the head and shoulders rested in the shadows. That didn't matter at all; he knew who it was. One arm lay flung out beyond the body, hand just at the edge of the water, tiny waves lapping at it delicately. The other arm was crumpled under the body. Brunetti bent down and felt at the wrist, but he could find no pulse. The flesh was cold, damp with the moisture that had risen up from the *laguna*. He moved a step closer, slipping into the shadow, and placed his hand at the base of the boy's neck. There was no pulse. When he stepped back into the moonlight, Brunetti saw that there was blood on his fingers. He stooped down at the edge of the water and waved his hand back and forth quickly in the water of the *laguna*, water so filthy that the thought of it usually disgusted him.

Standing, he dried his hand on his handkerchief, then took a small pencil flash from his pocket and bent back under the walkway. The blood came from a large open wound on the left side of Ruffolo's head. Not far from him there lay a conveniently-placed rock. Just think of that; it looked precisely like he had jumped from the walkway, slipped on the slick rocks, and fallen backwards to smash his head in the fall. Brunetti had little doubt that there would be blood on the rock, Ruffolo's blood.

Above him, he heard a soft footfall, and he ducked instinctively under the walkway. Even as he did, the stones and bricks shifted around under his feet, sending off a noise that deafened him. He crouched low, back placed up against the seaweed-covered sea wall of the Arsenale. Again, he heard the footsteps, now directly above his head. He drew his pistol.

'Commissario Brunetti?'

His panic receded, pushed back by that familiar voice. 'Vianello,' Brunetti said, coming out from under the walkway, 'what the Devil are you doing here?'

Vianello's head appeared above him, leaning over the railing and looking down to where Brunetti stood on the rubble that covered the surface of the beach.

'I've been behind you, sir, since you went past the church, about fifteen minutes ago.' Brunetti had heard and seen nothing, even though he had believed all his senses fully alert.

'Did you see anyone?'

'No, sir. I've been down there, reading the timetable at the boat stop, trying to look like I missed the last boat and couldn't understand when the next one came. I mean, I had to have some excuse to be here at this time of night.' Vianello suddenly stopped speaking, and Brunetti knew he had seen the leg sticking out from under the walkway.

'That Ruffolo?' he asked, surprised. This was too much like those Hollywood movies.

'Yes.' Brunetti moved away from the body and stood directly under Vianello.

'What happened, sir?'

'He's dead. It looks like he fell.' Brunetti grimaced at the precision of the words. That's exactly what it looked like.

The policeman knelt and stretched his hand out to Brunetti. 'You want a hand up, sir?'

Brunetti glanced up at him and then down at Ruffolo's leg. 'No, Vianello, I'll stay here with him.

There's a phone down at the Celestia stop. Go and call for a boat.'

Vianello moved off quickly, amazing Brunetti with the racket his feet made, echoing all through the space under the walkway. How silently he must have come, if Brunetti hadn't heard him until he was directly overhead.

Left alone, Brunetti took his flashlight out of his pocket again and bent back over Ruffolo's body. He wore a heavy sweater, no jacket, so the only pockets were those in his jeans. In his back pocket, he had a wallet. It held the usual things: identity card (Ruffolo was only twenty-six), driver's licence (not a Venetian, he had one), twenty thousand lire, and the usual assortment of plastic cards and scraps of paper with phone numbers scribbled on them. He'd look at them later. He wore a watch, but there was no change in his pockets. Brunetti slipped the wallet back into Ruffolo's pocket and turned away from the body. He looked out over the shimmering water, off to where the lights of Murano and Burano were visible in the distance. The moonlight lay softly upon the waters of the *laguna*, and no boats moved upon it to disturb its peace. A single glimmering sheet of silver connected the mainland with the outer islands. It reminded him of something Paola had read to him once, the night she told him she was pregnant with Raffaele, something about gold being beaten to a fine thinness. No, not fine, airy; that was the way they loved one another. He hadn't really understood it then, too excited with the news to try to understand the English. But the image struck him now, as the moonlight lay upon the *laguna* like silver beaten to airy thinness. And Ruffolo, poor, stupid Ruffolo, lay dead at his feet.

The boat was audible a long way off, and then it came shooting out of the Rio di Santa Giustina, blue light twirling around on the forward cabin. He turned on his flashlight and pointed it in their direction, giving them a beacon for approaching the beach. They got as close as they could, and then two policemen had to put on high waders and walk in the low water up to the island. They brought Brunetti a third pair, and he slipped them on over his shoes and trousers. He waited on the small beach while the others came, trapped there with Ruffolo, the presence of death, and the smell of rotting seaweed.

By the time they took photos of the body, removed it, and went back to the Questura to make out a full report, it was three in the morning. Brunetti was preparing to go home when Vianello came in and put a neatly typewritten sheet of paper on his desk. 'If you'd be kind enough to sign this, sir,' he said, 'I'll see that it gets where it's supposed to go.'

Brunetti looked down at the paper and saw that it was a full report of his plan to meet Ruffolo, but it was phrased in the future tense. He looked at the top of the sheet and saw that it bore yesterday's date and was addressed to Vice-Questore Patta.

One of the rules that Patta had introduced to the Questura when he took up his command there some years ago was one that ordered the three commissarios to have on his desk, before seven-thirty in the evening, a complete report of what they had accomplished that day and a projected idea of what they would do the following day. Since Patta was never to be seen in the Questura that late, and was certainly not to be seen before ten in the morning, it would have been an easy thing to slip it on his desk, were it not for the fact that there were only two keys to Patta's office. He kept one on a gold key chain attached to the bottom buttonhole of the vests of the three-piece British suits he affected. The other was in the charge of Lieutenant Scarpa, a leather-faced Sicilian whom Patta had brought up with him from Palermo and who was fiercely loyal to his superior. It was Scarpa who locked the office at seven-thirty and unlocked it at eight-thirty each morning. He also checked to see what was on his superior's desk when he unlocked the office.

'I appreciate it, Vianello,' Brunetti said when he read the first two paragraphs of the report, which explained in detail what he intended to do in meeting Ruffolo and why he thought it important that Patta be kept informed. He smiled tiredly and held it out without bothering to read the rest. 'But I think there's no way to keep him from finding out that I did this on my own, that I had no intention of telling him about it.'

Vianello didn't move. 'If you'd just sign the report, sir, I'll take care of it.'

'Vianello, what are you going to do with this?'

Ignoring the question, Vianello said, 'He kept me on burglary for two years, didn't he, sir? Even when I asked for a transfer.' He tapped the back of

25

Even though he didn't get to sleep until after four, Brunetti still managed to arrive at the Questura at ten. He found notes on his desk telling him that the autopsy on Ruffolo was scheduled for that afternoon, that his mother had been informed of her son's death, and that Vice-Questore Patta would like Brunetti to see him in his office when he came in.

Patta here before ten. Let angelic hosts proclaim!

When he went into Patta's office, the Cavaliere looked up and, Brunetti blamed it on his own lack of sleep, seemed to smile at him. 'Good morning, Brunetti. Please have a seat. You really didn't have to get here this early, not after your exploits of last night.' Exploits?

'Thank you, sir. It's nice to see you here so early.'

Patta ignored the remark and continued to smile. 'You did very well with this Ruffolo thing. I'm glad you finally came to see it the same way I did.'

Brunetti had no idea what he was talking about, so he chose the course of greatest wisdom. 'Thank you, sir.'

'That just about ties it up, doesn't it? I mean, we don't have a confession, but I think the Procuratore will see the case the way we do and believe that Ruffolo was on his way to try to make a deal. He was foolish to bring the evidence with him, but I'm sure he thought all you were going to do was talk.'

None of the paintings had been on that tiny beach; Brunetti was sure of that. But he might have had some of Signora Viscardi's jewellery hidden somewhere on him. All Brunetti had done was check his pockets, so it was possible.

'Where was it?' he asked.

'In his wallet, Brunetti. Don't tell me you didn't see it. It was in the list of the things he had on him when we found his body. Didn't you stay long enough to make out the list?'

'Sergeant Vianello took care of that, sir.'

'I see.' At the first sign of what was an oversight on Brunetti's part, Patta's mood grew even sweeter. 'Then you didn't see it?'

'No, sir. I'm sorry, but I must have overlooked it. The light was very bad out there last night.' This was beginning to make no sense. There had been no jewellery in Ruffolo's wallet, not unless he had sold one of the pieces for twenty thousand lire.

'The Americans are sending someone here to

take a look at it today, but I don't think there's any doubt. Foster's name is on it, and Rossi tells me the photo looks like him.'

'His passport?'

Patta's smile was broad. 'His military identification card.' Of course. The plastic cards that were in Ruffolo's wallet, that he had stuffed back inside without bothering to examine. Patta continued, 'It's sure proof that Ruffolo was the one who killed him. The American probably made some sort of false move. Foolish thing to do when a man has a knife. And Ruffolo would have panicked, so soon out of prison.' Patta shook his head at the rashness of criminals.

'Coincidentally, Signor Viscardi called me yesterday afternoon to tell me that it's possible the young man in the photograph might have been there that night. He said he was too surprised at the time to think clearly.' Patta pursed his lips in disapproval as he added, 'And I'm sure the treatment he received at the hands of your officers didn't help him remember.' His expression changed, the smile reblossomed. 'But that's all in the past, and he certainly seems to bear no ill will. So it seems those Belgian people were right, and Ruffolo was there. I assume he didn't get much money from the American and thought he'd try to arrange a more profitable robbery.'

Patta was expansive. 'I've already spoken to the Press about this, explaining that we were in no doubt from the very beginning. The murder of the American had to be a random thing. And now, thank God, that's proved.' As he listened to Patta so blandly lay Foster's murder at Ruffolo's door, Brunetti saw that Doctor Peters' death would never be seen as anything other than an accidental overdose.

He had no choice but to hurl himself under the juggernaut of Patta's certainty. 'But why would he take the chance of carrying the American's card? That doesn't make any sense.'

Patta rolled right over him. 'He could outrun you easily, Commissario, so there was no chance he would be found with it. Or perhaps he forgot about it.'

'People don't often forget about evidence that links them to murder, sir.'

Patta ignored him. 'I've told the Press we had reason to suspect him in the killing of the American from the very beginning, that this was why you wanted to talk to him. He was probably afraid we were onto him and thought he could make a deal with us about a lesser crime. Or perhaps he was going to try to blame someone else for the American's death. The fact that he had the American's card with him leaves no doubt that he killed him.' Well, Brunetti was sure of that: it surely would remove all doubt. 'That, after all, is why you went to meet him, isn't it? About the American?' When Brunetti didn't answer, Patta repeated his question, 'Isn't it, Commissario?'

Brunetti brushed aside the question with a motion of his head and asked, 'Have you said any of this to the Procuratore, sir?'

'Of course I have. What do you think I've been doing all morning? Like me, he believes it's an

pen-and-shut case. Ruffolo killed the American
n a robbery attempt, then tried to make more
money by robbing the Viscardi *palazzo*.'

Brunetti tried one last time to interject some
ense into this. 'They're very different sorts of
rime, a mugging and the theft of paintings.'

Patta's voice grew louder. 'There's evidence that
e was involved in both crimes, Commissario.
here's the identification card, and there are your
Belgian witnesses. You were willing enough to
elieve in them before, that they saw Ruffolo the
ight of the robbery. And now Signor Viscardi
hinks he remembers Ruffolo. He's asked to take
nother look at the photo, and if he recognizes
im, there will be no doubt. There's more than
nough evidence for me, and more than enough to
onvince the Procuratore.'

Brunetti pushed his chair back abruptly and
tood. 'Will that be all, sir?'

'I thought you'd be more pleased, Brunetti,'
Patta said with real surprise. 'This closes the case
of the American, but it will make it harder to find
Signor Viscardi's paintings and see that they're
eturned to him. You're not exactly a hero, since
ou didn't bring Ruffolo in. But I'm sure you
vould have, if only he hadn't fallen from the
valkway. I've mentioned your name to the Press.'

That was probably harder for Patta to do than it
vould be for him to give Brunetti his own first-
orn son. Take the gift as given. 'Thank you, sir.'

'Of course, I made it clear that you were
ollowing my suggestions, mind you, that I'd been
uspicious of Ruffolo from the very first. After all,

he was let out of prison only a week before he killed the American.'

'Yes, sir.'

Patta grew expansive. 'It's unfortunate that we haven't found Signor Viscardi's paintings. I'll try to stop by to see him sometime today to tell him about this myself.'

'He's here?'

'Yes, when I spoke to him yesterday, he mentioned he would be coming to Venice today. He said he was willing to stop by and take another look at that photograph. As I told you, that would remove all doubts.'

'Do you think he'll be bothered that we didn't get the paintings back?'

'Oh,' Patta said, clearly having considered this. 'Of course he will be. A person who has a collection feels that way about their paintings. Art comes alive to some people.'

'I suppose that's the way Paola feels about that Canaletto.'

'That what?' Patta asked.

'Canaletto. He was a Venetian painter. Paola's uncle gave us one of his paintings as a wedding present. Not a very big one, sir. But she seems very attached to it. I keep telling her to put it in the living room, but she likes to keep it in the kitchen. As revenge, it wasn't much, but it was something.

Patta's voice was strangled. 'In the kitchen?'

'Yes, I'm glad you think it's a strange place to keep it, sir. I'll tell her you think so, too. I think I'll go down and see what Vianello's done. He had a few things he has to take care of for me.'

'Fine, Brunetti. I wanted to compliment you on job well done. Signor Viscardi was very pleased.'

'Thank you, sir,' Brunetti said, moving towards the door.

'He's a friend of the mayor's, you know.'

'Ah,' Brunetti said, 'no, I didn't know that, sir.' But he should have.

Downstairs, Vianello was at his desk. He looked up when Brunetti came in and smiled. 'I hear you're a hero this morning.'

'What else was in that paper I signed last night?' Brunetti asked with no prelude.

'It said that you thought Ruffolo was involved with the death of the American.'

'That's ridiculous. You know what Ruffolo was like. He would have cut and run if anyone had so little as yelled at him.'

'He'd just done two years inside, sir. It's possible he changed.'

'Do you really think that?'

'It's possible, sir.'

'That's not what I asked you, Vianello. I asked you if you believed he did it.'

'If he didn't, then how did the American's identity card get into his wallet?'

'You believe it, then?'

'Yes. At least I think it's possible. Why don't you believe it, sir?'

Because of the Count's warning – Brunetti could only now see it as the warning it had been – about the connection between Gamberetto and Viscardi. He saw now, as well, that Viscardi's threat had had nothing to do with Brunetti's investigation of the

robbery at the *palazzo*. It was his investigatio
into the murders of the two Americans tha
Viscardi had warned him away from, murder
with which poor, stupid Ruffolo had nothing t
do, murders which he knew, now, would go fo
ever unpunished.

His thoughts turned from the two dea
Americans to Ruffolo, finally hitting what h
thought was the big time, boasting to his mothe
about his important friends. He had robbed th
palazzo, even done what the important man tol
him to do, roughed him up a little, though that wa
not at all like Ruffolo. When had Ruffolo learne
that Signor Viscardi was involved in far more tha
stealing his own paintings? He had mentione
three things that would interest Brunetti – the
must have been the paintings – yet, in his walle
there had been only one. Who had put it there
Had Ruffolo somehow come into possession of th
identity card and kept it to use as a bargaining chi
in his conversation with Brunetti? Worse, had h
tried to threaten Viscardi with his knowledge of i
and what it meant? Or had he merely been a
innocent, ignorant pawn, one of the countless littl
players in the game, like Foster and Peters, use
for a while and then tossed away when the
learned something that would threaten the majo
players? Had the card been slipped into his walle
by the same person who had used the rock to kil
him?

Vianello still sat at his desk, looking at hin
strangely, but there was no answer Brunetti coul
give him, none that he would believe. Because h

as almost a hero, he went back upstairs, closed
ne door to his office, and looked out of the
window for an hour. A few workers had finally
ppeared on the scaffolding of San Lorenzo, but
nere was no way of telling what they were doing.
None of them ever went as high as the roof, so the
les remained untouched. Nor did they appear to
e carrying tools of any sort. They walked along
ne various layers of scaffolding, climbed up and
own between them on the several ladders that
onnected them, came together and spoke to one
nother, then separated and went back to climbing
ne ladders. It was very much like watching the
usy activity of ants: it appeared to have a
urpose, if only because they were so energetic,
ut no human was capable of understanding that
urpose.

His phone rang, and he turned away from the
window to answer it. 'Brunetti.'

'Commissario Brunetti. This is Maggiore
mbrogiani at the American base in Vicenza. We
net some time ago in regard to the death of that
oldier in Venice.'

'Ah yes, Maggiore,' Brunetti said after a pause
ong enough to suggest to whoever was listening
n that he recalled the Maggiore only with
ifficulty. 'How can I help you?'

'You've already done that, Signor Brunetti, at
east for my American colleagues, by finding the
nurderer of that young man. I've called to give
ou my personal thanks and extend those of the
merican authorities here at the base.'

'Ah, that's most kind of you, Maggiore. I do

appreciate it. Of course, anything we can do to b
of assistance to America, especially the agencies ⟨
its government, is gladly done.'

'How nicely put, Signor Brunetti. I'll be sure t
convey your exact words to them.'

'Yes, do that, Maggiore. Is there anything else
can do for you?'

'Wish me good luck, I suppose,' Ambrogia
said with an artificial laugh.

'Gladly, Maggiore, but why?'

'I've been given a new assignment.'

'Where?'

'Sicily.' Ambrogiani's voice was absolutely lev
and without emotion when he pronounced th
name.

'Ah, how very nice for you, Maggiore. I'm told
has an excellent climate. When will you be going

'This weekend.'

'Ah, as soon as that? When will your family b
joining you?'

'I'm afraid that's not going to be possible. I'v
been given command of a small unit in th
mountains, and it's not possible for us to bring ou
families with us.'

'I'm sorry to hear that, Maggiore.'

'Well, it's all in the nature of the service,
suppose.'

'Yes, I suppose it is. Anything else we can do fc
you here, Maggiore?'

'No, Commissario. Again, I extend my thank
and those of my American colleagues.'

'Thank you, Maggiore. And good luck,' Brunet
said, the only honest words he had said in th

onversation. He hung up and went back to xamining the scaffolding. The men were no onger on it. Had they, he wondered, been sent to iicily, as well? How long does one survive in iicily? A month? Two? He forgot how long \mbrogiani had said he had until he could retire. 3runetti hoped he made it that long.

He thought again of those three young people, ll gone to their violent deaths, pawns tossed aside y a brutal hand. Until now, that hand could have een Viscardi's alone, but Ambrogiani's transfer neant that other, more powerful, players were nvolved, players to whom both he and \mbrogiani could just as easily be swept from the)oard. He recalled the lettering on one of those leath-filled plastic bags, 'Property of US iovernment'. He shivered.

He had no need to check the file for the address. Ie left the Questura and walked towards the Rialto, seeing nothing, insensible to what he)assed. At Rialto, suddenly overcome with weari-iess at the thought of walking any further, he vaited for the number one vaporetto and got off at he second stop, San Stae. Though he had never)een there, his feet guided him to the door; /ianello had told him — it seemed months ago – vhere it was. He rang the bell, gave his name, and he door snapped open.

The courtyard was small, devoid of plants, the iteps leading up from it a dull grey. Brunetti eached the top of the stairs and raised his hand to knock on the wooden door, but Viscardi opened it)efore he could do so.

The mark under his eye was lighter, the bruisin almost entirely gone. The smile, however, was th same. 'What a pleasant surprise to see yo Commissario. Do come in.' He held out his han but when Brunetti ignored it, he lowered it as naturally and used it to pull back the door.

Brunetti stepped into the entrance hall an allowed Viscardi to close the door behind him. H felt a compelling desire to strike this man, to d some sort of physical violence to him, hurt hi somehow. Instead, he followed Viscardi into large, airy salon that looked out across what mu: be a back garden.

'What may I do for you, Commissario?' Viscar asked, still maintaining his politeness, but not t the point of offering Brunetti either a seat or drink.

'Where were you last night, Signor Viscardi?'

Viscardi smiled, letting his eyes grow soft an warm. The question surprised him not in the leas 'I was where any decent man is at night, Dottore: was at home with my wife and children.'

'Here?'

'No, I was in Milan. And if I might anticipat your next question, there were other people ther two guests and three servants.'

'When did you get here?'

'This morning, on the early plane.' He smile and, reaching into his pocket, pulled out a sma blue card. 'Ah, how very fortunate, I still have th boarding pass with me.' He held it toward Brunetti. 'Would you like to inspect i Commissario?'

Brunetti ignored the gesture. 'We found that young man who was in the photo,' Brunetti said.

'The young man?' Viscardi asked, paused, and then let remembrance play across his face. 'Ah yes, the young criminal your sergeant showed me the picture of. Has Vice-Questore Patta told you that I think I might remember him now?' Brunetti ignored the question so Viscardi continued, 'Does this mean you've arrested him? If this means you'll be getting my pictures back, my wife will be thrilled.'

'He's dead.'

'Dead?' Viscardi asked, letting one brow arch in surprise. 'How unfortunate. Was it a natural death?' he asked, then paused as if weighing his next question. 'A drug overdose, perhaps? I'm told that accidents like that happen, especially with young people.'

'No, it wasn't a drug overdose. He was murdered.'

'Oh, I am sorry to hear that, but there does seem to be an awful lot of that going around, doesn't there?' He smiled at his little joke and asked, 'And was he, after all, responsible for the robbery here?'

'There is evidence that connects him to it.'

Viscardi contracted his eyes, no doubt intending to display dawning realization. 'Then it really was him I saw that night?'

'Yes, you saw him.'

'Does that mean I'll be getting the pictures back soon?'

'No.'

'Ah, too bad. My wife will be so disappointed.'

'We found evidence that he was connected to another crime.'

'Really? What crime?'

'The murder of the American soldier.'

'You and Vice-Questore Patta must be pleased to be able to solve that crime, as well.'

'The Vice-Questore is.'

'And you are not? Why is that, Commissario?'

'Because he wasn't the killer.'

'You sound very certain of that fact.'

'I am very certain of that fact.'

Viscardi tried another smile, a very narrow one. 'I'm afraid, Dottore, that I'd be far more pleased if you could be equally certain that you'd find my paintings.'

'You may be certain I will, Signor Viscardi.'

'That's very encouraging, Commissario.' He pushed back his cuff, glanced fleetingly at his watch, and said, 'But I'm afraid you must excuse me. I'm expecting friends for lunch. And then have a business appointment and really must get to the station.'

'Your appointment isn't in Venice?' Brunetti asked.

A smile of pure delight bubbled up into Viscardi's eyes. He tried to suppress it but failed. 'No, Commissario. It's not in Venice. It's in Vicenza.'

Brunetti took his rage home with him, and it sat between him and his family as they ate. He tried to respond to their questions, tried to pay attention to what they said, but in the midst of Chiara's account of something that happened in class that morning, he saw Viscardi's sly smile of gleeful triumph; when Raffi smiled at something his mother said, Brunetti remembered only Ruffolo's goofy, apologetic smile, two years ago, when he had taken the scissors from his mother's upraised hand and begged her to understand that the Commissario was only doing his job.

Ruffolo's body, he knew, would be turned over to her this afternoon, when the autopsy was completed and the cause of death determined. Brunetti was in no doubt as to what that would be: the marks of the blow to Ruffolo's head would match exactly the configuration of the rock found beside his body on the small beach; who to determine whether the blow was struck in a fall or in some other way? And who, since Ruffolo's death resolved everything so neatly, to care? Perhaps, as in the case of Doctor Peters, signs of alcohol would be found in Ruffolo's blood, and that surely would account even more for the fall. Brunetti's case was solved. Both, in fact, were solved, for the murderer of the American had turned out to be, most fortuitously, the thief of Viscardi's paintings. With that thought, he pushed his chair back from the table, ignoring the six eyes that followed his progress from the room. Giving no explanation, he left the house and started towards the Civil Hospital, where he knew Ruffolo's body would be.

When he got to Campo Santi Giovanni e Paolo, familiar, too familiar, with where he had to go, he walked towards the back part of the hospital, not really seeing the people around him. When he passed the radiology department and started down the narrow corridor that led to pathology, he could no longer ignore the people, so many seemed crowded into the narrow hallway. They weren't going anywhere, just standing around in small groups, heads together, talking. Some clearly patients, wore pyjamas and dressing gowns; others wore suits; some the white jackets of orderlies. Just outside the door to the pathology department, he saw a uniform he was more familiar with: Rossi stood in front of the closed door, one hand held up in a gesture meant to keep the crowd from coming any closer.

'What is it, Rossi?' Brunetti asked, pushing himself through the front row of bystanders.

'I'm not sure, sir. We got a call about half an hour ago. Whoever called said one of the old women from the rest home next door had gone mad and was breaking up the place. I came over here with Vianello and Miotti. They went inside and I stayed out here to try to keep these people from going in.'

Brunetti moved around Rossi and pushed open the door to the pathology department. Inside, the scene was remarkably like that outside: people stood in small groups and talked, heads close together. All of these people, however, were dressed in the white jackets of the hospital staff. Words and phrases floated across the room to him: 'Impazzita', 'terribile', 'che paura', 'vecchiaccia'. That certainly corresponded with what Rossi had said, but it didn't give Brunetti any idea of what had gone on.

He started towards the door that led back into

the examining rooms. Seeing this, one of the orderlies broke away from the people he was talking to and moved in front of him. 'You can't go in there. The police are here.'

'I'm police,' Brunetti said and moved around him.

'Not until you show me some identification,' the man said, putting a restraining hand on Brunetti's chest.

The man's opposition reignited all of the rage Brunetti had felt at Viscardi; he pulled his hand back, fingers closing in an involuntary fist. The man moved back a step from him, and this slight motion was enough to bring Brunetti back to his senses. He forced his fingers open, reached into his pocket, took out his wallet, and showed his warrant card to the orderly. The man was just doing his job.

'I'm just doing my job, sir,' he said and turned to open the door for Brunetti.

'Thank you,' Brunetti told him as he walked past, but without meeting his eyes.

Inside, he saw Vianello and Miotti on the other side of the room. They were both leaning over a short man who was sitting on a chair, holding a white towel to his head. Vianello had his notebook in his hand and appeared to be questioning him. When Brunetti approached, all three looked at him. He recognized the third man then, Doctor Ottavio Bonaventura, Rizzardi's assistant. The young doctor nodded in greeting, then closed his eyes and leaned his head back, pressing the towel to his forehead.

'What's going on?' Brunetti asked.

'That's what we're trying to find out, sir,' Vianello answered, nodding down at Bonaventura. 'We got a call about half an hour ago, from the nurse at the desk out there,' he said, apparently meaning the outer office. 'She said that a madwoman had attacked one of the doctors, so we came over here as fast as we could. Apparently, the orderlies couldn't restrain her, even though there were two of them.'

'Three,' Bonaventura said, eyes still closed.

'What happened?'

'We don't know, sir. That's what we're trying to find out. She was gone by the time we got here, but we don't know if the orderlies took her away. We don't know anything,' he said, making no attempt to disguise his exasperation. Three men and they couldn't restrain a woman.

'Dottor Bonaventura,' Brunetti said, 'could you tell us what happened here? Are you all right?'

Bonaventura gave a small nod. He pulled the towel away from his head, and Brunetti saw a deep, bloody gouge that ran from his eyebrow and disappeared into his hairline just above his ear. The doctor turned the towel to expose a fresh clean place and pressed it against the wound.

'I was at the desk over there,' he began, not bothering to point to the only desk in the room, 'doing some paperwork, and suddenly this old woman was in the room, screaming, out of her mind. She came at me with something in her hand. I don't know what it was; it might just have been her purse. She was screaming, but I don't know what she said. I couldn't understand her, or maybe I was too surprised. Or frightened.' He turned the towel again; the bleeding refused to stop.

'She came up to the desk, and she hit me, then she started tearing at all the papers on the desk. That was when the orderlies came in, but she was wild, hysterical. She knocked one of them down, and then another one of them tripped over him. I don't know what happened then because I had blood in my eye. But when I wiped it away, she was gone. Two of the orderlies were still here, on the floor, but she was gone.'

Brunetti looked at Vianello, who answered, 'No, sir. She's not outside. She just disappeared. I spoke to two of the orderlies, but they don't know what happened to her. We called over to the *Casa di Riposo* to see if any of their patients are missing, but they said no. It was lunch time, so it was easy for them to count them all.'

Brunetti turned his attention back to Bonaventura. 'Do you have any idea who she might be, Dottore?'

'No. None. I'd never seen her before. I don't have any idea how she got in here.'

'Were you seeing patients?'

'No, I told you, I was doing paperwork, writing up my notes. And I don't think she came in from the waiting room. I think she came in from there,' he said, pointing to the door at the other side of the room.

'What's back there?'

'The mortuary. I'd finished in there about half an hour before and was writing up my notes.'

In the confusion of Bonaventura's story, Brunetti had forgotten his rage. Now he was suddenly cold, chilled to the bone, but the emotion was not rage.

'What did she look like, Dottore?'

'Just a little fat old lady, all in black.'

'What notes were you writing up, Dottore?'

'I told you, from the autopsy.'

'Which autopsy?' Brunetti asked, though he knew there was no need for the question.

'What was his name? That young man they brought in last night. Rigetti? Ribelli?'

'No, Dottore. Ruffolo.'

'Yes, that's it. I'd just finished. He's all sewn up. The family was supposed to come and get him at two, but I finished a little bit early, and I was trying to write up the notes before I began the next one.'

'Can you remember anything she said, Dottore?'

'I told you. I couldn't understand her.'

'Please try to think, Dottore,' Brunetti said, voice straining for calm. 'It might be important. Any words? Phrases.' Bonaventura said nothing so Brunetti prompted, 'Did she speak Italian, Dottore?'

'Sort of. Some of the words were Italian, but the rest was dialect, worst I've ever heard.' There were no more clean places on Bonaventura's towel. 'I think I'd like to go and get this taken care of,' he said.

'In just a moment, Dottore. Did you understand any words?'

'Well, of course, she was screaming, "*Bambino*,

bambino", but that young man wasn't her bambino. She must be too old.' She wasn't, but Brunetti saw no reason to tell him this.

'Is there anything else you understood, Dottore?' Brunetti asked again.

Bonaventura closed his eyes with the combined weight of pain and memory. 'She said, "*assassino*", but that's what she was calling me, I think. She threatened to kill me, but all she did was hit me. None of it made any sense. No words or anything, just noise, like an animal. I think that's when the orderlies came in.'

Turning away from him and nodding towards the door to the mortuary, Brunetti asked, 'Is the body in there?'

'Yes, I told you. The family was told to come and get it at two.'

Brunetti went over to the door and pushed it open. Inside, only a few metres into the room, the body of Ruffolo lay, naked and exposed, on a metal gurney. The sheet that had covered his body lay crumpled on the floor, as though it had been torn off and flung there.

Brunetti took a few steps into the room and looked across at the young man. The body lay with the head turned away, so Brunetti could see the jagged line that ran through the hair, showing where the crown of the head had been severed so that Bonaventura could examine the damage to the brain. The front of the body bore the long butterfly incision, the same horrible line that had run down the strong young body of the American. Like a line drawn with a compass, the circle of death had been drawn just and true, bringing Brunetti back to where he had begun.

He backed away from what had been Ruffolo into the office. Another man in a white jacket was bending down over Bonaventura, fingering delicately at the edges of the wound. Brunetti nodded to Vianello and Miotti, but before either man could move, Bonaventura looked across at Brunetti and said, 'There's one strange thing.'

'What is that, Dottore?' Brunetti asked.

'She thought I was from Milan.'

'I don't understand. What do you mean?'

'When she said she'd kill me, she called me *'milanese traditore'*, but all she did was hit me. She kept screaming she'd kill me, kept calling me *'milanese traditore'*. It doesn't make any sense to me.'

Suddenly it made sense to Brunetti. 'Vianello, have you got a boat?'

'Yes, sir, it's outside.'

'Miotti, call the Questura and have them send the Squadra Mobile, right now, to Viscardi's *palazzo*. Come on, Vianello.'

The police launch was tied up at the left of the hospital, engine idling. Brunetti leapt down onto the deck, Vianello close behind him. 'Bonsuan,' Brunetti said, glad to find him at the wheel, 'over near San Stae, that new *palazzo*, by Palazzo Duodo.'

There was no need for Bonsuan to ask for more. Brunetti's fear was contagious. He hit the switch for the two-pitched siren, shoved the throttle forward, and swung the boat out into the canal. A

he end, he turned into Rio San Giovanni
Crisostomo, siren wailing, and towards the Grand
Canal. Minutes later, the boat shot out into the
broad waters of the Grand Canal, narrowly
missing a taxi and sending out on either side a
violent wake that slapped at boats and buildings.
They sped past a vaporetto that was just docking at
San Stae, their wake slamming it into the
mbarcadero and causing more than one tourist to
dance about, footing temporarily lost.

Just beyond Palazzo Duodo, Bonsuan pulled the
boat to the *riva*, and Brunetti and Vianello leapt
ashore, leaving it to the pilot to moor the boat.
Brunetti ran up the narrow *calle*, paused for a
moment to orient himself to this unexpected
arrival from the waterside, and then turned
towards the left and the *palazzo*.

When he saw the heavy wooden door to the
courtyard standing open, he knew it would be too
late: too late for Viscardi, and too late for Signora
Concetta. He found her there, at the bottom of the
steps that led up from the courtyard, her arms held
behind her back by two of Viscardi's luncheon
guests, one of them, Brunetti noticed, still with his
napkin stuffed into the neck of his shirt.

They were both very large men, Signor
Viscardi's guests, and it seemed to Brunetti that it
was not necessary for them to hold Signora
Concetta's arms like that, pulled roughly behind
her back. For one thing, it was too late, and for
another, she offered them no resistance, was
content, one would almost say happy, to look
down at what lay at her feet in the courtyard.

Viscardi had fallen on his face, so the gaping holes the shotgun had blasted in his chest were hidden, though the blood could not be stopped from seeping out across the granite paving stones. Beside his body, but closer to Signora Concetta, the shotgun lay where she had dropped it. Her late husband's *lupara* had served its purpose and avenged the family honour.

Brunetti approached the woman. She looked up at him, recognized him, but did not smile: her face could have been made of steel. Brunetti spoke to the men. 'Let her go.' They did nothing, so he repeated, voice still neutral, 'Let her go.' This time they obeyed him and released her arms, both careful to step away from her as they did so.

'Signora Concetta,' Brunetti said, 'how did you know?' To ask her why she had done it was unnecessary.

Awkwardly, as though it hurt her to move them, she brought her arms forward and crossed them over her chest. 'My Peppino told me everything.'

'What did he tell you, Signora?'

'That this time he would make enough money for us to go home. To go home. It's been so long since I've been home.'

'What else did he tell you, Signora? Did he tell you about the pictures?'

The man with the napkin in his shirt interrupted him, speaking in a high-pitched, insistent voice. 'Whoever you are, I want to warn you that I am Signor Viscardi's lawyer. And I warn you that you are giving information to this woman. I'm a

368

witness to this crime, and she is not to be spoken to until the police arrive.'

Brunetti glanced at him briefly and then down at Viscardi. 'He doesn't need a lawyer any more.' He turned his attention back to Signora Concetta. 'What did Peppino tell you, Signora?'

She struggled to speak clearly, forcing herself away from dialect. These, after all, were the police. 'I knew everything. The pictures. Everything. I knew my Peppino was going to meet you. He was very frightened, my Peppino. He was afraid of that man,' she said pointing down to Viscardi. 'He found something that made him have much fear.' She looked away from Viscardi and up at Brunetti. 'Can I go away from here now, Dottore? My work is finished.'

The man with the napkin spoke again. 'You are asking leading questions of this woman, and I'm a witness to that fact.'

Brunetti put out his hand and placed it under Signora Concetta's elbow. 'Come with me, Signora.' He nodded to Vianello, who was quickly beside him. 'Go with this man, Signora. He has a boat, and he'll take you to the Questura.'

'Not on a boat,' she said. 'I'm afraid of the water.'

'It's a very safe boat, Signora,' Vianello offered.

She turned to Brunetti. 'Will you come with us, Dottore?'

'No, Signora, I must stay here.'

She pointed to Vianello, spoke to Brunetti. 'Can I trust him?'

'Yes, Signora, you can trust him.'

'You swear?'

'Yes, Signora. I swear.'

'*Va bene*, we go in the boat.'

She started to walk away, led by Vianello, who had to bend down to keep his hand under her elbow. She took two steps, stopped, and turned back to Brunetti. 'Dottore?'

'Yes, Signora Concetta?'

'The paintings are at my house.' She turned away and continued towards the door with Vianello.

Later, Brunetti was to discover that, after twenty years in Venice, she had never been on a boat: like many people from the mountains of Sicily, she had a deadly fear of the water, and in twenty years, she had never overcome it. But before that he was to learn what she had done with the paintings. When the police got to her apartment that afternoon, they found the three paintings, the Monet, the Gauguin, and the Guardi, hacked to pieces with the same scissors with which she had tried to attack Brunetti, years ago. This time, there had been no Peppino to stop her, and she had destroyed them utterly, leaving only jagged tatters of canvas and colour in the wake of her grief. It came as no surprise to Brunetti to learn that many people considered this the sure proof of her madness: anyone could kill a man; only a madwoman would destroy a Guardi.

Two nights later, after dinner, Paola answered the ringing phone. He could tell from the warmth of her voice and the frequent laughter with which she greeted what she heard that it was her parents.

After a long time, almost half an hour, she came out onto the terrace and said, 'Guido, my father would like to speak to you for a moment.'

He went back into the living room and picked up the phone. 'Good evening,' he said.

'Good evening, Guido,' the Count said. 'I've got some news for you.'

'About the dump?'

'Dump?' the Count repeated, managing to sound confused.

'The dump by Lake Barcis.'

'Ah, you mean the building site. A private hauling contractor was up there earlier this week. The whole site has been cleaned up, everything removed, earth bulldozed over it.'

'Building site?'

'Yes, the Army has decided to conduct tests on radon emissions in the area. So they're going to close off the area and build some sort of testing facility there. Unmanned, of course.'

'Whose army, theirs or ours?'

'Why ours, of course.'

'Where was the material taken?'

'I believe the trucks went to Genoa. But the friend who told me about it wasn't too clear.'

'You knew Viscardi was involved in this, didn't you?'

'Guido, I don't like your accusatory tone,' the Count said sharply. Brunetti didn't apologize and the Count continued, 'I knew a great deal about Signor Viscardi, Guido, but he was beyond my reach.'

'He's beyond everyone's reach now,' Brunetti

said, but he took no satisfaction in being able to say it.

'I attempted to tell you.'

'I didn't realize he was so powerful.'

'He was. And his uncle,' the Count named a cabinet minister, 'remains even more so. Do you understand?'

He understood more than he wanted to. 'I have another favour.'

'I've done a lot for you this week, Guido. Much of it has been against my own best interests.'

'It's not for me.'

'Guido, favours are always for ourselves. Especially when we ask for things for other people.'

Brunetti said nothing for so long that the Count finally asked, 'What is it?'

'There's a Carabiniere officer, Ambrogiani. He's just been reassigned to Sicily. Can you see that nothing happens to him while he's there?'

'Ambrogiani?' the Count asked, as if interested in knowing no more than the name.

'Yes.'

'I'll see what I can do, Guido.'

'I'd be very grateful.'

'So, I imagine, will Maggiore Ambrogiani.'

'Thank you.'

'You're welcome, Guido. We'll be home next week.'

'Good. Have a nice holiday.'

'Yes, I shall. Good night, Guido.'

'Good night.'

As he replaced the phone, a detail of the

conversation came flashing into Brunetti's mind, and he stood frozen in place, staring down at his hand, unable to pry it loose from the receiver. The Count had known Ambrogiani's rank. He had called him an officer, but the Count had called him 'Maggiore Ambrogiani'. The Count knew about Gamberetto. He had business dealings with Viscardi. And now he knew Ambrogiani's rank. What else did the Count know? And in what else was he involved?

Paola had replaced him on the terrace. He opened the door and went out to stand beside her, putting his arm over her shoulder. The sky in the West gave off the last glimmerings of light; it would soon be dark.

'The days are getting shorter, aren't they?' she asked.

He tightened his hold on her and nodded.

They stood together like that. The bells started to ring, first the light bells of San Polo and then, from across the city, the canals, the centuries, they heard the magisterial boom of San Marco.

'Guido, I think Raffi's in love,' she said, hoping this was the right moment.

Brunetti stood beside the mother of his only son, thinking of parents and the way they love their children. He said nothing for so long that she turned and looked up at him. 'Guido, why are you crying?'

Penguin will publish another
Commissario Guido Brunetti
mystery in May 2005.

Read on for the first chapter of
Doctored Evidence . . .

1

She was an old cow and he hated her. Because he was a doctor and she his patient, he felt guilty about hating her, but not so guilty as to make him hate her any the less. Nasty, greedy, ill-tempered, forever complaining about her health and the few people who still had the stomach for her company, Maria Grazia Battestini was a woman about whom nothing good could be said, not even by the most generous of souls. The priest had given up on her long ago, and her neighbours spoke of her with distaste, sometimes with open animosity. Her family remained connected to her only by means of the laws governing inheritance. But he was a doctor, so he had no choice but to make his weekly visit, even though it now consisted of nothing more than a perfunctory inquiry as to how she felt, followed by the speedy measuring of her pulse and blood pressure. He'd been coming for more than four years now, and his aversion had become so strong that he had lost the fight against his repeated disappointment at the continued absence of signs of illness. Just past eighty, she looked and acted a decade older, but she'd live to bury him; she'd live to bury them all.

He had a key and used it to let himself into the building. The whole place was hers, all three floors, though she occupied only half of the second. Spite and meanness caused her to maintain the fiction that she occupied all of it, for by so doing she kept her sister Santina's daughter from moving into either the floor above or the one below. He forgot how many times, in the years since the death of her son, she had hurled abuse upon her sister and told him how much pleasure it gave her perpetually to frustrate her family's designs upon the house. She spoke of her sister with malice that had gathered momentum ever since their shared childhood.

He turned the key to the right, and because it is in the nature of Venetian doors not to open at first try, he automatically pulled the door towards him as he turned the key. He pushed the door open, stepping into the dim entrance hall. No sunlight could penetrate the decades of grease and dirt that covered the two narrow windows above the door to the *calle*. He no longer noticed the dimness, and it had been years since Signora Battestini had been able to come down the steps, so the windows were unlikely to be cleaned any time soon. Damp had fused the wires years before, but she refused to pay for an electrician, and he had lost the habit of trying to switch the light on.

He started up the first flight of stairs, glad that this was his last call of the morning. He'd finish with the old horror and go and have a drink, then get some lunch. He didn't have to be at his surgery to see patients until five; had no plans after lunch and nothing he particularly wanted to do, so long as he could be free of the sight and sound of their wasted and bloated bodies.

As he started up the second flight, he found himself hoping that the new woman – he thought this one was Romanian, for that was how the old woman referred to her, though they never stayed long enough for him to remember their names – would last. Since her arrival, the old shrew was at least clean and no longer stank of urine. Over the years he'd watched them come and go; come because they were drawn by the prospect of work, even if it meant cleaning and feeding Signora Battestini and submitting to her unrelenting abuse; go because each had eventually been so worn down that even the most abject need could not resist the assault of the woman's nastiness.

From the habit of politeness, he knocked at her door, though he knew it a futile courtesy. The blaring of her television, which had been audible even from outside the building, drowned out the sound: even the younger ears of the Romanian – what *was* her name? – seldom registered his arrival.

3

He took the second key and turned it twice, then stepped into the apartment. At least it was clean. There had been a time, he thought it was about a year after her son died, when no one had come for more than a week, and the old woman had been left alone in the apartment. He still remembered the smell of the place when he'd opened the door for his then bi-monthly visit, and, when he'd gone into the kitchen, the sight of the plates of decomposing food left on the table for a week in the July heat. And the sight of her, body encased in layers of fat, naked and covered with the drips and dribbles of what she had tried to eat, hunched in a chair in front of the eternally blaring television. She'd ended up in hospital that time, dehydrated and disoriented, but they'd wanted quit of her after only three days, and since she demanded to be in her own home, they'd gladly taken the option and had her carried there. The Ukrainian woman had come then, the one who'd disappeared after three weeks, taking a silver serving plate with her, and his visits had been increased to once a week. But the old woman had not changed: her heart pounded on, her lungs pulled in the air of the apartment, and the layers of fat grew ever thicker.

He set his bag on the table by the door, glad to see that its surface was clean, a sure sign that the Romanian was still there. He took the stethoscope, hooked it behind his ears, and went into the living room.

Had the television not been on, he probably would have heard the noise before he went in. But n the screen the much-lifted blonde with the hirley Temple curls was giving the traffic report, lerting the drivers of the Veneto to the potential nconvenience of *traffico intenso* on the A4 and rowning the industrious buzzing of the flies at vork on the old woman's head.

He was accustomed to the sight of death in the ld, but deaths in old age were usually more ecorous than what he saw on the floor beneath im. The old die softly or the old die hard, but ecause death seldom comes as an assault, few esist it with violence. Nor had she.

Whoever had killed her must have taken her ompletely by surprise, for she lay on the floor to he left of an undisturbed table on which stood an mpty cup and the remote control of the television. he flies had decided to divide their attention etween a bowl of fresh figs and Signora attestini's head. Her arms were flung out in front f her, and she lay with her left cheek on the floor. he damage was to the back of her head, which eminded him of a soccer ball his son's dog had nce bitten, deflating it on one side. Unlike her ead, the skin of the soccer ball had remained nooth and intact; nothing had leaked from it.

He stopped at the door, looking around the om, too stunned by the chaos to have a clear lea of what he was looking for. Perhaps he sought ne body of the Romanian; perhaps he feared ne sudden arrival from some other room of the erson who had done this. But the flies told him nat whoever had done this had had more than nough time to flee. He glanced up, his staggered

5

attention caught by the sound of a human voice, but all he learned was that there had been an accident involving a truck on the A3 near Cosenza.

He walked across the room and switched off the television, and silence, neither hushed nor respectful, filled the room. He wondered if he should go into the other rooms and look for the Romanian, perhaps try to help her if they had not succeeded in killing her, too. Instead, he went into the hall and, taking his *telefonino* from his pocket, dialled 113 and reported that there had been a murder in Cannaregio.

The police had little trouble finding the house, for the doctor had explained that the victim's home was at the beginning of the *calle* to the right of the Palazzo del Cammello. The launch glided to a halt on the south side of the Canale della Madonna. Two uniformed officers jumped on to the *riva*, then one of them leaned back into the boat to help the three men from the technical squad unload their equipment.

It was almost one. Sweat dripped from their faces, and their jackets soon began to cling to their bodies. Cursing the heat, wiping vainly at their sweat, four of the five men began to carry the equipment to the entrance to Calle Tintoretto and along to the house, where a tall, thin man waited for them.

'Dottor Carlotti?' the uniformed officer who had not helped in unloading the boat asked.

'Yes.'

'It was you who called?' Both men knew the question was unnecessary.

'Yes.'

'Could you tell me more? Why you were here?'

'I came to visit a patient of mine – I come every ~~w~~eek – Maria Grazia Battestini, and when I went to the apartment, I found her on the floor. She ~~w~~as dead.'

'You have a key?' the policeman asked. Though ~~hi~~s voice was neutral, the question filled the air ~~ar~~ound them with suspicion.

'Yes. I've had one for the last few years. I have ~~th~~e keys to the homes of many of my patients,' ~~C~~arlotti said, then stopped, realizing how strange ~~it~~ must sound, his explaining this to the police, and ~~m~~ade uncomfortable by the realization.

'Would you tell me exactly what you found?' ~~th~~e policeman asked. As the two men spoke, the ~~ot~~hers deposited the equipment inside the front ~~do~~or and went back to the launch for more.

'She's dead. Someone's killed her.'

'Why are you sure someone killed her?'

'Because I've seen her,' Carlotti said and left it at ~~th~~at.

'Have you any idea who might have done it, ~~D~~ottore?'

'No, of course I don't know who he was,' the ~~d~~octor insisted, trying to sound indignant but ~~m~~anaging only to sound nervous.

'He?'

'What?' said Carlotti.

'You said, "he," Dottore. I was curious to know ~~w~~hy you think it was a man.'

Carlotti started to answer, but the neutral words

7

he tried to pronounce slipped out of his contro
and, instead, he said, 'Take a look at her head an
tell me a woman did that.'

His anger surprised him; or rather, the force o
it did. He was angry not with the policeman
questions but at his own craven response to then
He had done nothing wrong, had merely stumble
upon the old woman's body, and yet his unthinkin
response to any brush with authority was fear an
the certainty that it would somehow cause hi
harm. What a race of cowards we've become, h
caught himself thinking, but then the policema
asked, 'Where is she?'

'On the second floor.'

'Is the door open?'

'Yes.'

The policeman stepped into the dim hallwa
where the others had crowded to escape th
sunshine, and made an upward motion with h
chin. Then he said to the doctor, 'I want you t
come upstairs with us.'

Carlotti followed the policemen, resolved to sa
as little as possible and not to display any uneas
or fear. He was accustomed to the sight of death, s
the sight of the woman's body, terrible as it wa
had not affected him as much as had his instinctiv
fear of being involved with the police.

At the top of the stairs, the policemen entere
the apartment without bothering to knock; th
doctor chose to wait outside on the landing. Fc
the first time in fifteen years, he wanted a cigarett
with a need so strong it forced the beat of his hea
into a quicker rhythm.

He listened to them moving around inside the apartment, heard their voices calling to one another, though he made no attempt to listen. The voices grew softer as the policemen moved to the next room, where the body was. He moved over to the windowsill and half sat on it, heedless of the accumulated filth. He wondered why they needed him here, came close to a decision to tell them they could reach him at his surgery if they wanted him. But he remained where he was and did not go into the apartment to speak to them.

After a time, the policeman who had spoken to him came out into the corridor, holding some papers in a plastic-gloved hand. 'Was someone staying here with her?' he asked.

'Yes.'

'Who?'

'I don't know her name, but I think she was a Romanian.'

The policeman held out one of the papers to him. It was a form that had been filled in by hand. At the bottom left was a passport-sized photo of a round-faced woman who could have been the Romanian. 'Is this the woman?' the policeman asked.

'I think so,' Dottor Carlotti answered.

'Florinda Ghiorghiu,' the policeman read, and that brought the name back.

'Yes. Flori,' the doctor said. Then, curious, he asked, 'Is she in there?' hoping the police would not find it strange that he had not looked for her, and hoping they had not found her body.

'Hardly,' the policeman answered with barely

9

disguised impatience. 'There's no sign of her, and the place is a mess. Someone's been through it and taken anything valuable.'

'You think . . .' Carlotti began, but the policeman cut him off.

'Of course,' the officer answered with anger so fierce it surprised the other man. 'She's from the East. They're all like that. Vermin.' Before Carlotti could object, the policeman went on, spitting out the words. 'There's an apron in the kitchen with blood all over it. The Romanian killed her.' And then, speaking the epitaph for Maria Grazia Battestini that Dottor Carlotti would perhaps not have given, the policeman muttered, 'Poor old thing.'